News from the Moon
And Other French Scientific Romances

News from the Moon
And Other French Scientific Romances

translated, annotated and introduced by
Brian Stableford

A Black Coat Press Book

Acknowledgements: "The Future Phenomenon" originally appeared in *The Second Dedalus Book of Decadence* (Black Feast) (Dedalus, 1992). "Martian Mankind" was included in the text of an article published in *The New York Review of Science Fiction 190* (June 2004). "News from the Moon" was included in the text of an article published in *Studies in Fantasy Literature 3* (2005). The other items appear here for the first time. I am indebted to Georges Dodds and George A. Vanderburgh for procuring a photocopy of Albert Robida's *Le roi des singes* for my use, and to Bill Russell for procuring a copy of Eugène Mouton's "L'historioscope." The versions of "L'homme de Mars" and "Le triangle rouge" that I used were both reprinted in the second issue of Philippe Gontier's *Le Boudoir des Gorgones* (February 2002). Thanks to David McDonnell for proofreading the typescript.

ISBN 978-1-932983-89-0. First Printing. February 2007 Published by Black Coat Press, an imprint of Hollywood Comics.com, LLC, P.O. Box 17270, Encino, CA 91416.

Table of Contents

Introduction

There is no equivalent in French of the British term "scientific romance," which evolved in the 1890s as a general term for speculative fiction wholly or partly based in scientific ideas. The corresponding American term, "science fiction," did not come into common usage until the late 1920s, although it was subsequently exported to Britain, France and the rest of the world, becoming the dominant term for all fiction of that kind. This process of coca-colonization had the unfortunate side-effect of establishing the particular nexus of ideas typical of the American subgenre as the tacit core of all speculative fiction, masking the distinctive features and the internal coherency of different native traditions of speculative fiction.

The lack of any distinctive French label has further obscured the fact that, of all the native traditions, the French has the longest history and made the most rapid early progress. This early start was not entirely surprising, given the crucial contribution made by French philosophers to the celebration of the Enlightenment brought about by science–which included the development of the modern idea of progress–and it is a pity that the tradition faltered thereafter, mainly due to the effects of a series of historical interruptions, including various revolutions and wars.

The genrification of French speculative fiction might have been easier to describe if Charles Garnier had only been able to think of a snappier title for a 36-volume series of reprinted texts that he began issuing in 1787, or had the project not been interrupted in 1789 by that year's Revolution.

The collection brought together various *Voyages imaginaires, songes, visions, et romans cabalistiques* [Imaginary Voyages, Dreams, Visions and Cabalistic Novels] with the manifest intention of defining a new genre of imaginative fiction, which introduced a distinctively modern spirit into classical narrative modes such as the fantastic voyage, the Utopian romance, the allegorical vision and the occult romance, renewing all of them with healthy doses of Enlightenment philosophy and wit.

No single text can be extracted from Garnier's collection as a central exemplar around which all the others may be said to orbit, but one of its key inclusions was Voltaire's *Micromégas* (1750), the boldest of his definitive *contes philosophiques*, in which Earth is briefly visited by a giant inhabitant of a planet orbiting the star Sirius, who is equipped with a far more elaborate sensorium–and thus with far greater powers of intelligence–than human beings. While *en route* through the Solar System, the visitor picks up a traveling companion from the planet Saturn, whose size, sensory equipment and intelligence are intermediate between the human and the Sirian. From their hypothetical viewpoint, the pretensions of humankind–especially the kind of faith that insists on pretending to perfect knowledge on the basis of a single ancient text–inevitably seem ridiculous, but the story's moral is less brutal than it seems, for its chief implication is that, although human philosophical and moral progress may have a long way to go, it is a process that might be capable of enabling us to make the journey.

Micromégas was not without precedent in its method or materials; it continued a tradition of scathingly sarcastic satirical writing headed in France by the 16th-century writings of François Rabelais, which employed the hypothetical viewpoints of the giant Gargantua, his son Pantagruel and the latter's priapic companion Panurge. The most significant intermediate item in the tradition, Savinien de Cyrano de Bergerac's *Histoire comique contenant les états et empires de la lune* (1657) and *Fragment d'histoire comique contenant les états et empires du soleil* (1662)–combined in translation as *Other Worlds: The Comic History of the States and Empires of the Moon and Sun*–had been bowdlerized, and some of its text destroyed, because of its religious skepticism, and *Micromégas* itself had initially to be published outside France, bearing a deceptive imprint.

Other writers within the tradition had avoided similar risks by being more earnest and more careful. Gabriel de Foigny's *La terre australe connue* [The Southern Continent Revealed] (1676), had considered the question of whether social equality would only be possible in a society of hermaphrodites with careful diplomacy. Simon Tyssot de Patot's two fantastic voyages, *Voyages et aventures de Jacques Massé* [Voyages and Adventures of Jacques Massé] (1710) and *La vie, les aventures et le voyage de Groenland du Révérend Père Cordelier Pierre de Mésange* [The Life, Adventures and Voyage to Greenland of the Rev. Fr. Pierre de Mésange] (1720), and the Chevalier de Mouhy's *Lamékis* (1737-38), which also featured venturesome speculations in exotic biology and sociology, had been equally careful in muting their satirical components. Even so, speculation based in science was never entirely safe in a Catholic country like France, whose churchmen had been dealing very roughly with perceived heretics for hundreds of years.

Voltaire's *contes philosophiques* are more inventive in terms of their narrative technique than their predecessors, often conserving an appearance of frivolity by borrowing narrative devices from Antoine Galland's translations of Arabic folklore, which had been synthesized into the massive collection known as *Les mille-et-une nuits* (1704-16; tr. as *The Arabian Nights* or *The Thousand-and-One Nights*). The imaginative adventurism and verve of Galland's work had already complemented and fused its influence with a burgeoning literary interest in *contes des fées* prompted by Madame d'Aulnoy, Charles Perrault and others. Borrowings from Galland also infuse another key exemplar in the Garnier collection, the Chevalier de Béthune's *Relation du monde de Mercure* [An

9

Account of the World of Mercury] (1750), in which a "philosophical telescope" permits close observation and evaluation of the lives of the winged inhabitants of the planet Mercury.

Where the Chevalier de Béthune led, others soon followed, including Charles-François Tiphaine de la Roche in the macrocosmic romances *Amilec* (1753) and *Giphantie* (1760; tr. as *Gyphantia*), and Marie-Anne de Roumier (later Madame Robert), whose *Voyages de Milord Céton dans les sept planètes* [Voyages of Lord Seaton to the Seven Planets] (1765-66) describes a tour of the solar system as it was then characterized. Roumier's "seven planets" are the traditional Aristotelian complement (the Sun, the Moon, Mercury, Venus, Mars, Jupiter and Saturn) although the novel's allegorical apparatus is based in a heliocentric cosmology and ideas regarding the plurality of worlds that had been popularized in France–in the context of a long-standing theological dispute– by Pierre Borel's *Discours nouveau prouvant la pluralité des mondes* [A New Discourse Proving the Plurality of Worlds] (1657) and Bernard de Fontenelle's enormously popular *Entretiens sur la pluralité des mondes* (1686; tr. as *Conversations on the Plurality of Worlds*). Roumier was doubly represented in Garnier's collection, her second contribution being a long *conte philosophique* transfiguring mythical imagery, *Les ondines* [The Undines] (1768).

The bestselling work of the latter half of the 18th century in France was Louis Sébastien Mercier's *L'an deux mille quatre cent quarante* [The Year 2440] (1771; rev. 1774; further rev. 1786 and 1799; tr. as *Memoirs of the Year 2500*), which was published anonymously, without the official certification theoretically required to license its publication. This was the first Utopian novel to be set in an actual place in the future, rather than in some remote contemporary geographical location, and it moved Utopian fiction into a "uchronian" mode, defining the ideal state as something attainable within the framework of the existing world order, by means of political action: an object of social progress rather than a comparative exemplar.

Although *L'an deux mille quatre cent quarante* did not foresee a revolution—its Utopian Paris has been created by gradual modifications guided and supervised by an enlightened king—Mercier claimed, once he had owned up to its authorship in 1791, that the book had helped to precipitate the Revolution of 1789. That may have been an exaggeration, but *L'an deux mille quatre cent quarante* did lay the groundwork for a new subgenre of French futuristic fiction. It is extensively discussed as a pivotal text in a long theoretical discussion of the potential scope of futuristic fiction juxtaposed with a further exemplar in Félix Bodin's *Le roman de l'avenir* [The Novel of the Future] (1834). These two examples, in their turn, generated a dialectical counterpart in the form of the skeptical satirical dystopia, Emile Souvestre's *Le monde tel qu'il sera* (1846; tr. as *The World As It Shall Be*), which challenged the supposition that technical progress and social progress would go hand in hand, suggesting instead that technical progress might increase social inequality and injustice.

Although use of the *Memoirs* was proscribed, Garnier did reprint one of Mercier's earlier books—the first of his two collections of fictionalized essays, *Songes et Visions Philosophiques* [Philosophical Dreams and Visions] (1768)—in his collection. One of these tales, a brief sketch of "Nouvelles de la lune" [News from the Moon], proved highly influential. Although it is, in essence, a straightforward theological fantasy regarding the possible nature of the afterlife, it takes care to redesign the afterlife in such a way as to take account of the cosmos revealed by modern science; in effect, it uses the universe of science as an existential framework for paradisal experience, while relegating the inferno to some further and separate dimension. It also takes care to refine its imaginary method of communication with the dead into something resembling a laboratory experiment, employing a beam of coherent light that anticipates the invention of the laser.

The story's republication by Garnier attracted the attention of two writers who were to become important manufacturers of extended *contes philosophiques* that celebrated the

11

philosophy of progress and the discoveries of modern science: Nicolas-Edmé Restif de la Bretonne and Camille Flammarion.

In addition to his famous account of *La découverte Australe par un homme-volant, ou le Dédale Français* [The Discovery of Australia by a Flying Man; or, The French Dedalus] (1878) Restif produced an account of a cosmic voyage that is clearly indebted to Roumier, as well as Mercier, in a section of *Les posthumes* [Posthumous Correspondence] (written 1788-89; published 1802). Flammarion–who launched his literary career with an account of *La pluralité des mondes habités* [The Plurality of Inhabited Worlds] (1862), and made his own attempt to define a new literary genre in his scrupulous comparative account of *Les mondes imaginaires et les mondes réels* [Real and Imaginary Worlds] (1864; exp. 1892)–used it as a model for the longest and most significant of his early fictionalized essays, *Lumen* (1866-69; reprinted in *Récits de l'infini*, 1872; tr. as *Stories of Infinity*). "News from the Moon" thus represents a useful starting-point for this exemplary anthology of "French scientific romances."

The interruption of Garnier's reprint series was one aspect of a significant developmental hiatus in the nascent genre of French speculative fiction. Although it never died away entirely, such fiction did not flourish under the Convention, during the Empire, or in the first phase of the Restoration.

Jean-Baptiste Cousin de Grainville's *Le dernier homme* (1805; tr. as *The Last Man*) formed a bridge of sorts between Mercier and Bodin, but it was a less daring work in ideological terms, which attempted to subsume the idea and imagery of technological progress within religious prophecies of the apocalypse.

Satirical speculative fiction was incorporated into the fiction of the French Romantic Movement by its early leader, Charles Nodier, in a handful of fragmentary Utopian romances, including "Hurlubleu" (1833), but Nodier's enduring preference for the imagery he collated in his influential directory of *Infernaliana* (1822) was reflected in the works of most of his followers. Ventures such as Théophile Gautier's *Les deux étoiles* (1848; tr. as *The Quartette*), which described an unsuccessful attempt to rescue Napoleon from Saint Helena in a submarine, and Victor Hugo's extension of *La légende des siècles* [The Legend of the Centuries] into the future in "Plein ciel" [Open Sky] (1859), were rare.

Bodin and Souvestre published their works between the July Revolution of 1830 and the next attempted Revolution of 1848–a period which also saw the publication of Jacques Boucher de Crèvecoeur de Perthes' lunar romance "Mazular" (1832) and the birth of alternative history fiction in Louis-Napoléon Geoffroy's *Napoléon et la conquête du monde, 1812-1832* [Napoleon and the Conquest of the World] (1836; better known as *Napoléon apocryphe* [An Apocryphal Napoleon]). It was not until Louis-Napoléon's *coup d'état* of 1851 established the Second Empire, though, that speculative fiction resumed the appearance of being about to attain generic status.

Charles Defontenay's magisterial *Star, ou Psi de Cassiopée* (1854; tr. as *Star: Psi Cassiopeae*), which details the history, politics and culture on a complex star-system, remained an isolated tour de force, but the career of Jules Verne, launched in the following decade, provided a vital seed-crystal around which a genre could and did organize itself, with significant assistance from works by Camille Flammarion.

Verne's career as a novelist might have developed differently had he been able to publish an exercise in futuristic fiction written in the early 1860s, but he was persuaded by his publisher, P.-J. Hetzel, to set it aside and it was lost for more than a century before resurfacing as *Paris au XXe siècle* (1994; tr. as *Paris in the 20th Century*). Hetzel persuaded Verne to expand on the kind of adventure fiction he developed in *Cinq semaines en ballon* (1863; tr. as *Five Weeks in a Balloon*), subjecting his speculative imagination to a rigorous discipline that contrasted strongly with the tactics of Voltairean satirists. Verne followed it with a series of classic *voyages extraordinaires*, including *Voyage au center de la terre* (1863; tr. as *Journey to the Center of the Earth*), *De la terre à la lune* (1865; tr. as *From the Earth to the Moon*) and

Vingt mille lieues sous les mers (1870: tr. as *Twenty Thousand Leagues Under the Sea*). Although Verne's first venture into interplanetary fiction was calculatedly restrained in its scope, *De la terre à la lune* did lend momentum to the gradual refinement of the satirical tradition in the direction of greater realism, assisted by such works as Achille Eyraud's *Voyage à Venus* [Voyage to Venus], also issued in 1865.

Verne's contemporaries did not include any other author of similar influence, and other writers of popular fiction interested in speculative material tended to follow the abundant precedents which mingled such imagery with entirely fanciful materials, thus seeming far less significant to modern chroniclers of the evolution of a more restrictive kind of science fiction.

They included Léon Gozlan, whose *Les émotions de Polydore Marasquin* (1856; tr. as *The Emotions of Polydore Marasquin, A Man Among the Monkeys* and *Monkey Island*) brought the satirical tradition of Cyrano de Bergerac into the realm of *feuilleton* fiction, and the equally-prolific Charles Basset, who used the pseudonyms Charles Newill and Adrien Robert to distinguish himself from his similarly-named father, a noted playwright. The Adrien Robert collection *Contes fantasques et fantastiques* (1867) contains an early future war story, "La guerre en 1894," and a tongue-in-cheek account of the legendary inventor of gunpowder, "Berthold Schwartz," as well as the medical fantasy "La main embaumée," translated here as "The Embalmed Hand."

"The Embalmed Hand" is primarily a weird tale, linked in its method and motifs to the contemporary short fiction of Erckmann-Chatrian, and it features a motif that was later to become a staple of horror fiction, employed twice in that fashion by Guy de Maupassant before featuring in numerous 20th-century literary and cinematic shockers. In this version, however, the severed hand does not wreak its revenge by strangling its victim but by writing–specifically, by amending a prescription, making use of its former proprietor's knowledge of chemistry. In this respect, it is a more distinctively modern story than its many successors.

Although the Second Empire came to an ignominious end in the siege of Paris that followed military defeat by the Prussians at Sedan in 1870, Verne's career continued without any significant interruption, including such speculative works as *Autour de la lune* (1870; tr. as *Around the Moon*) and the title novella of the collection *Une fantaisie du Docteur Ox* (1872; tr. as *Dr. Ox's Experiment*). He attracted many imitators once political stability had been restored again in the 1870s, not merely in France but also in Italy, Germany and Britain. His influence even spread to the USA, although most American Vernian fiction was published in the conspicuously lowbrow medium of cheap "dime novels"–a degradation encouraged by the butchery of Verne's works in execrable translations.

French Romanticism continued to flourish in the Second Empire, but as it extended through the 1860s and 1870s, it was gradually invaded by a consciousness of its own decadence, and the fondness for ornate stylistic exercises that many of its key authors exhibited became the hallmark of what Théophile Gautier described as "Decadent" style, appointing Charles Baudelaire as its key exemplar. Alongside Verne's career, therefore, a markedly different kind of fantastic fiction flourished, flatly opposed in its fundamental narrative strategy to the discipline of Vernian fiction.

Stéphane Mallarmé's prose poem "Le phénomène futur" (written c. 1866), translated here as "The Future Phenomenon," illustrates this contrast very well. It offers a prospect of the future whose underlying assumptions are sharply contrasted to that of the philosophers of progress, conceiving it as a process of inevitable degeneration and degradation.

Decadent fiction did, however, retain the fugitive speculative elements that had been featured in Romantic fiction, as displayed in such floridly sarcastic *contes philosophiques* as Jules Richepin's "La machine a métaphysique," from his collection *Morts bizarres* [*Bizarre Deaths*] (1877), which is here translated as "The Metaphysical Machine." Like "News from the Moon," "The Metaphysical Machine" uses an apologetic narrative strategy that was very common in 19th-century fantastic fiction, beginning with a ritual rejection of potential accusations of insanity. In this case, the objective narrative voice that emerges in the story's coda explicitly endorses the concession that is narrator is mad, and licenses the conclusion that his metaphysical speculations ought not to be taken seriously, but the real heart of the story is not the speculations themselves but the methodical way in which the narrator sets up an experiment to prove his hypothesis and gain privileged access to the truth. As an allegory of science and its progress, the story rests on the same bleak assumption as Mallarmé's prose poem–but the situation described is such that the "objective" narrative voice cannot really know what the experimenter actually discovered, and must be regarded as intrinsically unreliable, in exactly the same fashion as the writer of the manuscript.

Many of Verne's imitators clung steadfastly to Hetzel's strategy of producing earnest accounts of exploratory ventures. Several of them, including André Laurie, Georges le Faure, Louis Boussenard and Paul d'Ivoi, produced similarly loosely-knit series of novels. The temptation to reintroduce an element of satire was, however, irresistible to the humorist and illustrator Albert Robida, who began his literary career with a long *feuilleton* serial chronicling the *Voyages très extraordinaires de Saturnin Farandoul dans les 5 ou 6 parties du monde et dans tous les pays connus et même inconnus de M. Jules Verne* [The Very Extraordinary Voyages of Saturnin Farandoul in the World's five or six Continents, and in all the Countries known–and even unknown–to Monsieur Jules Verne] (1879). The first part of the sequence, set *En Océanie* [In Oceania] is "Le roi de singes," here translated as "The Monkey King"–a story that owes as much to lavishly-illustrated versions of Gozlan's *Emotions de Polydore Marasquin* as it does to Verne's *Vingt mille lieues sous les mers* and *L'île mystérieuse* (1874).

16

Robida went on to become a writer of considerably greater imaginative range than Verne, accommodating himself to the tradition of futuristic fiction in such key works as *Le vingtième siècle* (1882; tr. as *The Twentieth Century*) and the pictorial *La guerre au vingtième siècle* (1883; exp. 1887; tr. as *War in the Twentieth Century*), although his light touch and reputation as a caricaturist undermined appreciation of his speculative brilliance.

"The Monkey King" is an unashamed comedy, including several episodes that construe *Vingt mille lieues sous les mers* as a modern version of Galland's account of the adventures of Sindbad, but beneath the comedy, there is a blunt contradiction of the central allegorical affirmation of *Les émotions de Polydore Marasquin*. As an account of the politics of imperialism and European attitudes to other races, its slapstick humor serves to soften some serious criticism, just as the author was later to do in his determinedly pacifist account of *La guerre au vingtième siècle*.

Although Napoléon is never mentioned in the text of "The Monkey King," Saturnin Farandoul's conquest of Australia echoes and parodies aspects of the Emperor's conquests–something that had still to be done with considerable diplomacy, even when Napoléon III had been deposed as the ruler of France for some years. Nowadays, of course, the reader is far more likely to find elaborate parallels between the early phases of Farandoul's life and the career of one of the great heroes of 20th-century popular fiction, Edgar Rice Burroughs' Tarzan of the Apes, although it is unlikely that Burroughs was aware of the precedent.

By the 1880s, speculative fiction had begun to make rapid progress elsewhere in Europe, and influences began to flow into France as well as out, but the diversification of French speculative fiction in that period remained strongly rooted in the native tradition, and its contributors continued to produce a great deal of original and innovative work. The earnest exemplars provided by Flammarion–whose career also continued to flourish after 1870, when he became the most significant popularizer of science in France–also inspired witty responses. The components of *Lumen* provoked three satirical ventures by the humorist Eugène Mouton, included in the collection *Fantaisies* (1883). One of them, "L'historioscope," is translated here as "The Historioscope." The other two were "L'origine de la vie" [The Origin of Life] and "La fin du monde" [The End of the World].

Like "The Monkey King," "The Historioscope" is pure comedy–and goes even further than "News from the Moon" and "The Metaphysical Machine" in its calculated use of a mad narrator–but, as in Robida's novella, the account it offers of the lessons that might be learned by the use of a device that could see through time makes some serious points in a suitably sly fashion. The story's philosophical themes were picked up by numerous 20th-century science fiction stories, including T. L. Sherred's classic black comedy "E for Effort," and were still being revisited at the end of the century in Arthur C. Clarke & Stephen Baxter's *Light of Other Days.*

The expanding genre of French scientific romance began to attract the attention of established writers, many of whom dabbled therein. These included the Belgian writer George Eekhoud, whose collection *Kermesses* (1884) included the remarkable moral fantasy "Le coeur de Tony Wandel," here translated as "Tony Wandel's Heart," in which the progress of medical science is viewed with a scathingly skeptical eye. The socialistically-inclined Eekhoud took leave to wonder whether such potential technologies as heart transplantation might enable to the rich to become vampirically parasitic upon the poor in ways that Karl Marx had not imagined. This story, too, is a comedy, but the tenor of its humor is far darker than that of Robida or Mouton, reverting to the scathing abrasiveness of Voltairean satire

Guy de Maupassant, the foremost French short story writer of his admittedly-brief era, became famous as a naturalist by virtue of pioneering the development of anecdotal slice-of-life stories and calculatedly low-key *contes cruels*, which helped define the narrative method of the modern short story, but the range of his work extended much further. His most famous alliance with speculative motifs was "Le Horla" (1887), an ambiguous story whose distressed narrator becomes convinced that he is being tormented by an invisible creature, which must have come from Brazil on a passing ship, and that its species may be in the process of displacing humankind in the contest for dominion over the Earth. In the same year, he produced "L'Homme de Mars," translated here as "Martian Mankind," which complemented Flammarion's speculations–most elaborately fictionalized in *Uranie* (1889)–regarding the forms that Martian life might have taken in adapting to the physical conditions of the planet's surface.

Although it still retains a plangent echo of the apologetic formula used by Mercier, Richepin and Mouton–which the author had brought to a kind of perfection in "Le Horla"–"Martian Mankind" is a fundamentally earnest story, which is prepared to take its central hypothesis seriously, and the scientific data it quotes were all deemed accurate at the time. Its suggestion that Mars might be a warm world despite its distance from the Sun, by virtue of the influence of the greenhouse effect, proved dead wrong, but its underlying logic deserves some credit. Its account of a brief glimpse of alien life–strikingly similar to modern reports of UFO sightings–strikes a subtle note of exotic poignancy that was to become one of the keynotes of 20th-century science fiction.

The final piece included in translation here, Fernand Noat's "Le triangle rouge" (1902), appeared in the most successful of several magazines of Vernian fiction, the *Journal des Voyages* (1875-1949)–a periodical that had earlier offered useful publishing opportunities to many of the writers who became specialists in that genre, including Boussenard, d'Ivoi, René Thévenin and Jules Lermina.

"The Red Triangle" only retains the faintest hint of the standard apologetic narrative strategy in its narrator's final comment, and its author extrapolates the imaginative ambition that Verne briefly demonstrated in *Voyage au center de la terre*, before he muffled it in order to conform to Hetzel's standards of inventive diplomacy, in order to transpose a Gothic horror story into a modern mode. The story is an unashamed shocker of a sort that was to be elaborately developed in the 20th century, and it provides an early illustration of the inevitable effects of "melodramatic inflation" on a genre dependent on the capacity of its ideas to provoke excitement.

I hope that this anthology will be the first of a series of samplers, whose subsequent volumes will further illustrate the themes and methods typical of French scientific romance, as well as celebrating its distinct attitudes and chronicling its early evolution.

Many of the most significant late 19th- and early 20th-century writers in the genre died in the late 1930s and early 1940s, so the work of such crucial contributors as Maurice Renard, J. H. Rosny aîné, Théo Varlet, Gustave le Rouge, André Couvreur and Edmond Haraucourt will fall into the public domain in the next decade, thus becoming available for translation. Hopefully, therefore, I shall be able to render numerous exemplary novels into English as well as more short stories.

Brian Stableford

Louis-Sébastien Mercier: *News from the Moon*
(1768)

The account I am writing is perfectly true, although the reader might deem me a madman. Believe me if you will; I shall offer no proofs to the incredulous. Let us begin.

I had a friend: a good man whom everyone called inestimable, but with whom very few people were closely acquainted. Friendship is a tree that cannot put down roots in bad ground; it requires everyday virtues to put forth good fruit, and moral defects usually cause it to wither. Two men who do not respect one another rarely come to like one another; in order to be friends they must be able to confide in one another, and they must earn the right to speak frankly to one another by repeatedly proving themselves worthy of trust. Let us return to my friend.

We had become acquainted in middle age; we helped one another through awkward crises more than once. Our characters were not perfectly in tune, but amity and tolerance bridged the gap. Resolved to run a similar course for the rest of our days, we took up residence in the same house. I passed my happiest years in his pleasant company. His death left me alone, prey to regrets which still endure, but I have continued to live under the same roof.

Ordinarily, one does not like one's thoughts to dwell on those whose loss afflicts us, but for me that was my sole consolation. Always alone, revisiting in my thoughts through the places I had discovered with my friend, I recalled our most interesting conversations incessantly. The memories returned so vividly to mind that I was sometimes able to enjoy his imaginary company.

All those who have the habit of reflection know from experience how conducive a fine evening's moonlight is to meditation. Late one night, when the heavenly body in question was full, I was lingering in the garden, thinking continually of the one I had lost, when my sight was suddenly struck by a bright and vivid point of light. It seemed to stay in front of me no matter which way I turned. Eventually I stopped, looked directly at it and examined it more closely. I perceived that the shining point was the tip of a luminous arrow, inscribed on the ground–and that the arrow was an immensely extended ray proceeding directly from the Moon.

Astonished by this phenomenon, I became more attentive. When I approached it, the point of light withdrew, as if to guide me. When I followed it, it stopped on a newly-whitewashed wall, where I saw it trace visible letters, and I read:

It is me! Have no fear! It is your friend. I am living on the star that lights your way. I can see you. I have long sought a means of writing to you, and I have found one. Prepare a set of planks of wood, so that I can more easily trace thereon all that I have to tell you. Come back to the same place tomorrow; it is too late tonight–the star is turning, my line is no longer direct, and it is...

The fiery point abruptly disappeared.

This marvelous apparition threw me into utter confusion. I remained immobile for a long time, my eyes staring by turns at the Moon and the wall. My mind was so agitated that I passed the rest of the night without being able to sleep a wink. The following day I made ready a large number of planks, which I arranged myself in the place where I impatiently awaited the return of night.

Never had the Sun seemed to set so slowly. The Moon displayed its shining disc at last, but so many clouds gathered around it that it was masked by an impenetrable veil. Fatigued by waiting in vain, and not having slept at all the previous night, I could not help falling asleep, much to my regret.

When I woke up, I saw a clear and serene sky, in which the Moon was already close to the horizon. My eyes immediately went to my planks, and I found the following inscribed upon them:

You are asleep, my friend. That is an imposition to which the beings of your world are subject; when you awake, you will see this evidence that I am thinking about you. I want to reveal secrets to you that no other living man has ever penetrated before. Do you remember the moment when I died in your arms? Well, it has not been nearly as painful for me as you have presumed.

No, death is not what one imagines; the living have an idea of it that is false and frightful. Its convulsions, so frightening for the spectator, are a gentle passage into sleep for the dying man. The somber ceremonies with which a corpse is surrounded perpetuate dread and terror, but death is not what is represented by the fearful imagination.

When I felt the beating of my heart stop, I found myself endowed with the faculty of entering into more durable bodies, whose density could not prevent my elevation. All matter appeared to me as porous as a sieve, and my will took control of my ascension. I could transport myself to any place I wished, traversing immense distances without difficulty or dread.

The more I projected myself, the more I felt the flame of life empower and activate me. My understanding, memory and imagination brightened with a new clarity. When I had lifted myself up, I could descend just as rapidly towards any object that I wanted to reach; the wings of a bird are an inadequate analogy for the free movement of which every part of my being was now eminently capable.

What delighted me more than anything else was that a host of ideas that I had never previously entertained became familiar to me. A ready intelligence immediately allowed me to conceive all the marvels of creation–but the one which imported the sweetest rapture into my being was that of rediscovering all those I had loved. Our souls were instantaneously drawn together, and a delicious sentiment bound us together inextricably.

Our bliss comprises an inexhaustible and incessantly-satisfied curiosity. Every day, we apprehend more, and never tire of apprehension. Science, uncertain on Earth, is supported here by the clearest evidence. There is no object that our eyes cannot easily penetrate; we see so profoundly at a distance that I can even read, at this moment, the words that I am writing. I can bend rays of light to my will, making pencils of them that I sharpen according to my taste, and in this manner I can engrave my thoughts in the deepest regions of the sky and touch the boundaries of the universe.

By this means, the Creator has given the eye the privilege of reaching the most distant globe, has deigned to afford to thought the power of manifesting itself in every system populated by sentient reasoning beings. I converse with those whose writings I have admired; distance is no obstacle to the rapid flight of ideas, and print is only the gross simulation of that privileged art by which the inhabitants of the celestial spheres communicate their thought.

I have descended to the Moon in order to select its gentlest ray, for the benefit of your feeble eyelids; your eyes would be dazzled and blinded by a brighter one. I will return tomorrow, if there are no clouds to get in our way, and if I still have permission to reveal to you the strange truths of the sublunary world.

Seeing these last words. I took a piece of chalk in my trembling hand, and I wrote on the plank:

My friend, is it possible that you are on the Moon, and that your sight can penetrate as far as this? Can you read these words?

Yes, perfectly. There is no need to write such large letters. Write quickly and easily, in your own hand.

Oh, how many questions I have to put to you! So, it really is in the radiant spheres I observe in the sky that all the races of humankind who have lived on Earth will be reunited. Tell me, will the wicked and the good be mingled together without distinction? That is the first and most important thing I want to know.

The most secret actions of a past life will be revealed to every gaze; the entire history of our lives is painted on our faces in a manner that is universally intelligible. The wicked are forced to discover their own wickedness; it is by seeing one another, and what they are, that they are themselves horrified. This perpetual display inspires in them a profound repentance, which is their torture, and they try to erase those iniquitous characters that torment them. By performing good deeds they can remove the black imprint that disfigures them; it is necessary that they are without the stain of dishonor in order to communicate with beings who are strangers to all deformity.

If those who are blackened by numerous vices ask questions of those resplendent with light, they obtain no reply; they are punished by disdain, and they feel the distance that separates them from children of divinity. Consternated by their debasement, they seek to escape it, for the record of their sins passes from mouth to mouth and they hear again all the maledictions heaped upon them on the Earth, where their memory excites horror. Whenever they hope to enjoy a few moments of tranquility, the feeble voice that accuses them becomes thunderous, reclaiming their attention, and that accusation is spread throughout the worlds of the cosmos. Crushed beneath the weight of their shame, conscience becomes a dagger that pricks them incessantly: they flee, but they are naked to every gaze; they hide themselves behind uninhabited worlds, in solitude, but the angels of light cry out to them as they pass by: "I see you, and your every iniquity."

As the sentiment of justice ranks above all others among us, our pity must be set aside. We sense in ourselves the necessity of the order that governs us. Everyone expiates his sins by a proportionate shame; no one complains of its magnitude, because it is equitable to endure a just chastisement.

Given the manner in which you speak, and according to what I know about you, it seems to me that you ought not to be too discontented by your lot.

That is true; I have the good fortune not to be among those who suffer the most, even though I have not yet attained the rank of the happiest.

What, then, constitutes your pleasure and your pain?

It is hardly possible for me to make you understand all that. Your joyful emotions are so feeble, and of such short duration, that they cannot be compared to the transports that are excited here by the memory of the good one has done. We also enjoy friendship and love, to a degree which can only increase further and further. Beings of merit are very nearly equal in resemblance, and form a delectable society. Those who are not made to figure in it are excluded.

Must they remain forever in that miserable state, without hope of release?

Nothing in the second world is eternal; everything is temporary, as it is in yours. Those who progress to an advanced age feel a strong desire to elevate themselves towards another sphere; it is a great pleasure to nurture such ideas. Friends and parents understand the sensuality involved in advancing the study of creation, in ascending further, as far as their Author.

Death to you is fearful; here one looks forward to it and celebrates it with glad cries. We are conscious of the glorious destination and future of humanity, the contemplation of all beings who pass and events which occur; for us it is a spectacle, which adds to the sum of our knowledge. In sum, the better one has lived on the Earth, the less one suffers here, and the more pleasure one has in passing further on. Those who retain various hideous stains upon their wings appear to us to lose themselves on a different path, and thus disappear from our view. I cannot tell where these and others like them go.

But you make me envious of the dead–I would like to die now, in order to have the unique pleasure of being with you. Is it permissible to cut short one's term of exile?

No, refrain from suicide; it is an infamous stain that you would be unable to efface for a very long time. One who has lived but little counts for less than one who has borne the bur-

den of life for a long time; those who have sacrificed them-
selves for a genuinely good cause are the only ones granted a
dispensation in the number of their years.

**What becomes of infants then, who often die soon af-
ter birth and pass away without ever knowing anything of
good and evil?**

*They have the opportunity here to make use of their in-
telligence. They attach themselves to their parents, and the
mother rediscovers the son she believed to be lost forever. The
bonds of blood and affection are not broken; souls made for
life draw closely together. In sum, love reigns supreme here,
and reigns without jealousy.*

**Is that because what we have down here is naught but
instinct, whereas love in your world is a sentiment?**

*I have said all that needs to be said in revealing to you
that love has dominion here, in all its strength and all its pu-
rity. It is not necessary to add to these words: all that is loving
is virtuous.*

Adrien Robert: *The Embalmed Hand*

(1867)

I. The Empty Room

There is a large, square room on the ground floor of No. 16 Rapenburgerstraat, in the G3 district of Amsterdam. A bright fire blazing in the hearth lights up the facing sides of various items of furniture: a bookcase of carved oak; a table with spiral legs covered with a red velvet cloth, strewn with books and papers; heavy oaken armchairs rimmed with copper nails; and, between two doors masked by curtains decorated with representations of the story of Samson, a portrait of a man on foot, set in a splendidly carved and gilded frame.

Above the table, which occupies the center of the room, a huge brass chandelier extends its branches, bearing 30 candles of red wax. In a half-shadowed corner, the monotonous ticking of a clock can be heard; its mechanism, tripped at this very moment like the wheel-lock of an *arquebus*,[1] announces the arrival of an hour that remains otherwise unsounded.

The hands stand at midnight.

The flames in the fireplace provide enough light to allow us to make a more detailed inventory of the objects we have mentioned. Let us begin with the portrait.

---

[1] An *arquebus*–sometimes rendered *harquebus* in English–is a primitive portable firearm, invented in the 15th century and rendered obsolete 100 years later by the musket. The name derives from the Dutch *haakbus* ("hook gun"); early versions had heavy barrels that had to be supported by a stand, to which they were attached by a hook.

The person it represents is between 45 and 50 years of age. His features are both forceful and handsome; the straight nose and the jutting chin are indicative of a strong will, while the golden-brown eyes shine with the kind of admirably frank gaze one sees in portraits by Rembrandt. The clean-shaven face and the luminously pale hands stand out very clearly against the black clothing and the somber brown background. The right hand, which is neatly and nobly formed, holds a surgical instrument resembling a scalpel, and bears on its ring-finger a large diamond mounted in a circlet of violet enamel. This portrait, painted by one of the Dutch masters, bears the following dedication beneath its signature: *To my most illustrious friend, Doctor Willem Van Beyren, Amsterdam, 1860.*

The books arranged on the shelves of the bookcase are, for the most part, works on science and medicine. Four volumes on *The Diseases of the Heart* and one *Treatise on Angiology* [2] bear the name of Willem Van Beyren. Another set of shelves, arranged in tiers, throws off metallic reflections of every color. It houses a collection of the most beautiful stuffed birds from the Dutch colonies: miniature parrots from Guyana, hummingbirds from Java and Sumatra, the Celebes and Borneo, flycatchers from the Indonesian archipelago, the Moluccas and Timor. A large Oberhausser microscope, set on its mahogany box, stands on the middle shelf of this unit. The bottom shelf is occupied by surgical instruments, enclosed in morocco leather cases with silver cornerpieces, and several pharmaceutical flasks.

The table is, as we have already noted, heaped with books and papers. Two objects placed at the right and the left, as if they were a pair, invite further attention. One is like a little ebony desk, with a glazed lid, enclosing a large gold medal with four ribbons: the Prussian Order of Merit, the Order of Saints Maurice and Lazare, the Oakleaf-Cluster and the Order of Leopold. The Latin inscription on the medal declares

---

[2] Angiology is the branch of medicine concerned with the blood vessels and lymphatic system.

that it has been awarded to Doctor Van Beyren by the Society Felix Meritis, for the dedication and talent that he has displayed during an epidemic of typhoid fever. The other, enclosed within a dome of glass, is a man's hand: an embalmed hand. It is posed palm-downwards, the long slender fingers slightly arched, set on a red velvet cushion. The sectioned wrist is concealed by a cuff of lace and black silk.

This pink hand, beneath whose skin a lacework of bluish veins is apparent, seems so supple and lifelike in its immobility that one could almost doubt that it is an anatomical specimen, were it not for a slight purple tint at the base of each fingernail, indicative of its morbid condition. Its ring-finger bears an enamel circlet mounted with a diamond: the same ring that is depicted in the portrait. On comparing the hand that rests under the glass dome with the one that seems to emerge from the canvas, one immediately perceives that the former has served as a model for the painter. A singular thing, though: there is more life in the severed hand than in the hand in the portrait, which hangs down inertly, as pale as candle-wax.

Letters and envelopes are scattered upon the tablecloth–envelopes and letters bearing the following address: *Doctor Johan Miereveld, 16 Rapenburgerstraat, G3, Amsterdam*. The red leather blotting-pad and the seal set on the bureau are engraved with the initials *J. M.*

This fine room is the consulting-room of Doctor Johan Miereveld, the son-in-law of the late and much lamented Willem Van Beyren, who has been dead for 18 months.

II. Which brings more of the world on to the stage, and provides a little action.

There are certain ancient prejudices in the world, carved in stone, which time and human reason are impotent to break down. For centuries, one has been used to thinking of the Dutch as the Chinese brought to perfection, spending half their lives dusting their houses from top to bottom and the other half watering their tulip-beds.

Ask a painter to sketch a Dutchman for you; one could safely wager that 80 out of 100 will draw a portly gentleman seated in an armchair, with a long clay pipe in one hand and the other wrapped around a tankard of beer or a bottle of schnapps. If your artist has a sense of humor, he will put a spider's web between the chap's pipe and arm. If it is a writer you approach, for a pen-portrait, he will say: here's a fat man with yellow-tinted hair, a smug and truculent face and a flashy watch in his waistcoat; he is wound up every morning like clockwork; at the final turn of the key, his feet get going and placidly follow their accustomed route to the Stock Exchange, to the tavern, then to his club in the evening, until he senses that his spring has almost wound down again.

It would be vain and pretentious to think that we could challenge this enormous and bruising insult, so we shall not try. Instead, we beg you humbly to allow us to set before you, as two exceptions to the rule, the two central characters of this tale, Doctor Johan Miereveld and his young wife Andrine: two different people in their flesh and bone, but with only a single heart between them—unfortunately.

Two years have now elapsed since Willem Van Beyren had given his daughter to Johan, his student and his friend.

The two young people adored one another, and the good doctor, by conferring on Andrine a dowry of a 100,000 florins and transferring half his patients to his son-in-law's care, thought he had ensured their future happiness. Johan's hot-headed character made him a little uneasy, but he hoped that Andrine's angelic gentleness and calmly reflective temperament would provide a sufficient equilibrating force. Unhappily, this hope was not realized.

By the time he had been married a year, Johan had entered into a society of gamblers and libertines, whose behavior was the scandal of Amsterdam. Nearly always away from home, he lost his patients, and replied roughly to the supplica-

31

tions of his wife and the sage advice of his father-in-law—who understood by then that the fault was incurable.

Andrine had already paid gambling and other debts of more than 30,000 florins, and would have been completely impoverished if Van Beyren, warned by the moneylenders from whom Johan borrowed against his wife's inheritance, had not convinced her that she was making herself an accomplice to her husband's ruination.

Before her marriage, Andrine had sometimes had heart-trouble, but as the affliction was purely nervous, Van Beyren had never worried overmuch about it. Since the marriage, however, the distress that she forced herself to hide had undermined her and renewed the problem; this time, the malady assumed a more alarming character.

Van Beyren's friends, outraged by his son-in-law's conduct, advised him to make his daughter get a divorce, but the doctor shook his head and said: "Only the dead can be forgotten. She still loves him, and still has hope. There's nothing to be done, alas."

One day, Van Beyren left for the Hague, summoned by the greatest family in Holland to perform a difficult operation. He should not have been away more than a week. In the course of his career as a surgeon, he had often left his daughter, called to consultations by his colleagues in Holland and Belgium, but this time, their parting had been stressful. Large tears had streamed from Van Beyren's eyes when he had pressed his lips for the last time upon the blonde head of his child. They had both had a presentiment that they would not see one another again in this world.

On the day after his arrival in the Hague, Van Beyren was seized by a violent bout of fever, and two days later he was on his deathbed.

As the moment of death approached, he said to two of the King's doctors who were seated at his bedside, with a heart-rending smile: "Pernicious fever makes such rapid progress that doctors cannot always keep up with it. I am lost, my friends, and desperate. My daughter no longer has anyone but me to love and console her, but I can still do a little good upon this Earth. God has granted me the time to set my affairs in order, and I am grateful for that... It only remains to do His will.

"Doctor Netscher, I have named you as the executor of my will; as for you, my good friend Dekker, I have a favor of a different kind to ask of you. I want you to cut through my right wrist 24 hours after my death, and embalm my hand, which is to be placed on my work-table in my house in Amsterdam. You must use zinc chloride, rather than any other chemical compound, in the preparation of this anatomical specimen. My diamond ring, a gift from the King, must remain where it is on the finger of my embalmed hand."

In his will, Van Beyren left his son-in-law the sum of 45,000 florins in order to pay his debts, and left the remainder of his fortune to his daughter.

The news of the sudden death of Doctor Willem Van Beyren caused such a profound sadness in Andrine that it seemed for a while that she would not be long delayed in following him to the grave; but Johan, on whom this event had made a deep impression, took very good care of her. In the meantime, he offered her so sincere a repentance of his past conduct that the divine balm of hope was restored to her, little by little.

With the money left to him by his father-in-law, Johan paid his most impatient creditors, and tried to resume work– but there was no longer any widespread confidence in his ability and he only recovered a meager clientele, which could not restore his reputation or his fortunes. Under the evil influence of an old rogue who ran a druggist's shop, and from whom he purchased various empirical remedies, he descended by degrees to the lowest forms of charlatanry. One venture, which earned him 1,000 florins in a few days, encouraged him to follow this course. As the apothecary, Jakob Ruysch, was a very clever man, their commerce in powders, potions and pills brought them considerable benefits.

At about this time, a French singer arrived in Amsterdam to give concerts. She had been christened Mariette Michel–a name of scant poetry, which she had Italianized in order to inspire more confidence among the *dilettanti*. Signora Marietta Michelli was a tall and slender brunette, offering a graceful and rather distinguished appearance. She only had a thin and rather high-pitched voice, but she spoke with such fine aplomb of her triumphs in other countries, and treated the theatre–and concert-directors who had engaged her, having taken her deceptive claims on trust–with such majestic condescension, that she was treated as a star of the first magnitude, until the evening when she murdered a French *romaunt* or one of the maestro Verdi's *canzonettas*.

By virtue of a special dispensation, her failures did not provoke a storm. She presented herself so humbly before the public, offering such a perfect simulation of a sudden malaise, that the least tolerant members of the audiences accepted her excuses. While leaving, they said: "The poor girl is very delicate; fatigue induced by her journey and her many performances had caused her to lose part of her voice." Travel, which educates youth, had educated Signora Marietta Michelli so well that she could have run a school of trickery and made a fair match for Machiavelli's *Principio*.

Summoned to a consultation with this nomadic diva, who had experienced a violent fit of nerves at the end of one musical *soirée* at which the public had shown a little more severity than was usual, Johan Miereveld was abruptly seized by a fervent passion for his new client. For her part, la Michelli took note that her young doctor had big brown eyes full of fire and an admirable head of black hair with a slight bluish glint. However, as these physical assets were only a secondary issue, so far as she was concerned, she immediately commissioned her chambermaid to make inquiries as to the financial circumstances of her new admirer. The detailed report that was delivered to her the following day, as soon as she got up, plunged her into ecstatic contemplation for two hours.

Item number one in the detective's notes revealed that the handsome Johan Miereveld was an incorrigible gambler, capable of ruining himself in a single night, while paragraph 15–a very explicit paragraph–declared that his young wife Andrine was the victim of a serious heart condition, whose afflictions, aggravated by domestic difficulties, grew worse every day. She might die at any moment, struck down by some violent emotion or unforeseen moral distress. Heiress to a considerable fortune, she would leave more than 500,000 florins to her husband. The final item, number 18, affirmed that Johan, who passed himself off as a man with a will of iron, was, to the contrary, an exceedingly weak character. One only had to know how to get the better of him to assume an immediate total control of his mind.

Marietta Michelli had no need to know any more to formulate her plan of campaign. Firmly resolved to offer no compromising favors to Johan for the time being, she nevertheless allowed him to pay his respects to her every day. By means of playing the innocent, she captured his heart and soul so completely within the meshes of her spider's web that she made him into one of those dazed madmen who have but one thought in their heads, and are gradually eaten away by the ruthless vultures of desire and jealousy.

What did she want? What did she expect? He could not understand her, for she was perpetually and flagrantly at odds with herself. Every now and again she would seize his hand passionately, with a warm and welcoming expression; then she pushed it away again as if in disgust, or begged him to return to his wife and let her depart for France. She often spoke of the angelic beauty of Andrine with an angry jealousy that betrayed a love which she was determined to deny–but she had expressly forbidden Johan to reveal the secret of their platonic affection, of which Andrine always remained ignorant.

In the end, light dawned in the shadows of Johan's mind. Marietta loved him, but did not want a love that had to be shared. Andrine, his lawful wife, stood between them like a phantom.

Divorce was unthinkable; it would ruin him. Another thought briefly crossed his feverish mind, but he cast it out with horror.

III. Magical Attraction

Andrine Miereveld was blonde: the clear, silvery blonde of the Netherlands. She had soft, indescribably sweet blue eyes, with long brown lashes that cast a velvet shadow on her soft rosy cheeks. Her oval face, slightly square in the chin, her naturally wavy hair, her slender tapering hands and the calm and tender expression of her features always made artists and tourists who happened to catch sight of her start with surprise. They would say: "We've seen that soft face and those beautiful hands somewhere before"–and after searching their memories, they would discover the secret of the resemblance by which they had been struck: Andrine was the living image of the Virgin Mary in the paintings of Hans Memling.

Now that Johan spent his time in the singer's boudoir, Andrine very rarely went out. Old Jetje, who had brought her up, had to force her to take a walk on the Eastern dyke from time to time. When walking tired her, she sat down near the sluice-gate of the Oosterdoksdijk–and there, with her head in her hands, she breathed the bitter scent of the sea breeze for a long time, watching the yellow waves break upon the quays and cover them with soapy foam. As a child she had often come to this spot to play with her father, and the memory of past laughter momentarily imposed itself on the somber scenery of the present.

Every evening, before retiring to her bedroom, she went to say her prayers in the doctor's consulting room, all of whose interior decorations had been preserved; there, in the midst of all the surrounding objects, she recovered the cherished memory of the one who had loved her so much. As she went out again, she lightly touched her lips to the dome of glass that covered the embalmed hand.

She was entirely ignorant of Johan's love for the singer, and believed that he had forsaken her only because his terrible passion for gambling had absorbed him entirely.

Now, on the night when the fire burning in the grate allowed us to take an inventory of the furniture, Johan came home at about two o'clock, his features pale and drawn. After placing a little lamp on his bureau, he rummaged hastily in the drawers of an oak cupboard and took out a number of *rijksdaalers*,[3] which he brought into the lamplight in order to count them. The whole lot added up to no more than 60-some francs. In a fit of mute anger, he threw the coins on the table, and let himself fall, panting and shivering, into an armchair. The *rijksdaalers* rebounded, scattering themselves upon the tablecloth–but one of them had broken the glass dome that covered the embalmed hand.

Immediately, a spark brighter than the brightest star of that cold November night, sprung out of the shadows. Johan raised his head, supporting himself on the arms of the chair, and a dull exclamation escaped his pallid lips.

It was Doctor Van Beyren's diamond that had thrown forth that red and green ray: the ring on the finger of the embalmed hand. Johan threw himself backwards, resting his head on the back of the armchair, and closed his eyes in order to avoid the sight of that flame, which drew him irresistibly–but the intoxication of the gambler took even firmer possession of him when he only beheld it with his mind's eye.

The magical spark passed like a ray of gold through his closed eyelids, and he saw the players of the *Cercle d'Argine*[4]

---

[3] Robert adds a footnote here giving the value of the *rijksdaaler* as 5 francs 28 centimes.

[4] The *Cercle d'Argine* is obviously a gambling-den. The significance of the name derives from the fact that the court cards in 19th-century French packs often bore individual names, Argine being the Queen of Clubs; the word is an anagram of *regina*.

pile up a heap of beautiful golden ten-florin coins in front of him, and he heard the nasal voice of Jakob Ruysch murmuring in his ear: "Go make a vortune, Johan, my boy, a big vat vortune!"

The attraction was irresistible. He pounced like a predatory beast upon that inert hand, which had been so often extended towards him in friendship, and tore off the ring, like one of those pillagers of battlefields who come by night, turning up the faces of the dead in order to steal their shirts. In committing this profanity, he experienced a thrill of horror. The hand that he gripped was as warm and supple as the hand of a living man.

The hands of the big clock stood at 2:30 when Johan got up into the *vigilante* [5] that awaited him at the street door.

IV. Which proves that one can have a generous inspiration when leaving a gambling-den

On the following day, which was Sunday, while Andrine was going to mass with Jetje, a young man dressed like a ship's master, who was standing at the corner of the Portuguese synagogue, approached her.

After greeting her very respectfully, the man said: "Madame, it is thanks to the good Doctor Van Beyren, who once worked a miracle on my behalf, that I am still in command of the *Ruyter*. Last night, I went into a gaming-house to look for the son of my ship's owner, who is on the road of ruin and dishonor. He had been lucky at *lansquenet*, [6] so I was able to

[5] This reference is presumably to a cab available for hire at night.

[6] *Lansquenet* is a card game ancestral to such modern games as blackjack, in which each player in turn decides his stake according to the level of his confidence that his card will turn out to have a higher denomination than the one held by the banker. It was said to have been devised by German foot-

38

buy back from him an item whose memory has always been precious to me, and which would be far better placed in your jewelry-box than in the drawer of one of the pawnbrokers of Zuanenburgerstraat."

And the young seaman returned to her the diamond stolen from the embalmed hand.

Andrine lifted her beautiful pale blue eyes to his, expressing a sentiment of profound thanks, but her voice broke into sobs as she tried to speak.

"We have no time now to settle this little account," the young man said, "because I have to put to sea for Sumatra in two hours, but I shall return in six or eight months, and I will come to you then to get my money back. Good luck and farewell, Madame. My name is Captain Adriaan Wildt."

V. In which the ethereal prose of Signora Marietta Michelli
appears and disappears like an imp in fairyland

This meeting provoked such a violent emotion in Andrine that she was obliged to take a cab to return home. It seemed to her that a knife-point was pricking her heart again and again. At the doorway of her room, she lost consciousness and remained still and cold for more than two hours. Johan was out all day; it was the loyal Jetje who brought her round and put her tenderly to bed.

That evening, shortly before the hour when Andrine always came down to say her prayers in her husband's consulting-room, Signora Michelli's chambermaid rang the doctor's doorbell and asked if she might leave a written message for him. While the manservant who admitted her went in search of a pen and ink, she slid surreptitiously into Johan's study, deposited a letter on the table, and quickly slipped away. When

---

soldiers and introduced by them to other European nations–the name is a gallicization of the German *landsknecht.*

the manservant returned, at the measured pace typical of Dutch domestics, he found that there was no longer anyone there, and thought that someone had played a trick on him.

Like those letters impregnated with subtle poison, which strike down those who open them, the letter deposited by la Michelli's chambermaid contained within its perfumed folds a mortal blow for Andrine.

One evening, Johan had explained to the singer the shattering effect that moral commotions might have on individuals afflicted with weak hearts. Signora Michelli knew that the unhappy child's crises were now becoming more frequent and more violent, and she intended to fell her with a single stroke, after the fashion of those Florentine *bravi* [7] who know exactly how to make a fatal strike in such a way that no wound will ever be found on the corpse.

It was to ensure the success of this cowardly ambush that she had insisted that Johan keep their liaison well hidden from his wife. In view of his own disorderliness, Johan had asked Andrine to open his mail, and to make a list of the patients whom he had to visit the next day; this detail had engraved itself upon the memory of the singer.

This is what she had written to Johan–or, to be strictly accurate, to Andrine:

Johan, my beloved Johan,

Forgive me for the great distress I must cause you, but my strength and courage are exhausted. As God is my witness, I love you with all my heart, and you fill my soul completely. I have struggled as long as I could. I have done everything to put out of my mind the dreadful thought that you belong to another; another who has the right to love you and to speak to you; another to whom you are bound until death

I sense that I will weaken if I see you crying and begging at my feet one more time, and I do not want to become your mistress. Poor Johan! You told me yesterday that I have made

---

[7] *Bravi* were hired assassins, who acquired legendary status in several Italian city-states.

you suffer all the tortures of the damned. Oh, how you would have pitied me if you had known how agonized and heartbroken I was at that very moment! Tomorrow I shall leave the city, where I have been so happy and so miserable at one and the same time. I shall go wherever it pleases God to take me– far away, I hope

Johan, have pity on me; do not try to see me again, I beg of you. There is a wall of ice between us. Oh, when I think of her I tell myself how very fortunate it is that I have not taken pity on you during these moments of fever and delirium... I would only have felt hatred and disgust for you afterwards. Goodbye, Johan, forever! You must forget me. For myself, I will try not to see you through my tears!

Your dearest friend,
Marietta Michelli

The study windows were firmly shut, and no one else went into the room after the chambermaid had slipped in. Even so, when the pale and tremulous Andrine came in that evening, supported on Jetje's arm, to accomplish her daily mission, the singer's letter was no longer on the table.

VI. A prescription, reviewed, corrected and considerably augmented

That same night, shortly before ten o'clock, a thin ray of moonlight that filtered through the closely-drawn curtains fell obliquely upon the doctor's table, and threw a greenish light upon an object of indeterminate shape, which was moving on the velvet cloth and making a peculiar noise. One might have taken it for a rat playing with a ball of paper.

It lasted for no more than a moment, before everything fell back into silence and immobility.

The first thing that caught Johan's eye when he returned home was la Michelli's letter. Placed close to its open envelope, the page had been turned to the reverse side, where the

41

signature was. He read it with a kind of numbness, like a drunken man who does not know what he is looking at. Then he let the paper fall back upon the table, and put his clenched fists over his eyes.

A groan resembling a death-rattle rose from his breast. His moral anguish was redoubled at that moment by an even sharper physical pain. The last few nights passed in the delirium of gaming had set his head on fire, and his features, convulsed by neuralgia, displayed the anguish he had experienced.

He was still immobile, as if stupefied by pain, when Jetje came to warn him that Andrine, who had been suffering considerably all day, was still afflicted while she slept, and that her respiration was becoming more and more labored.

Johan made the effort to get up and followed the old housekeeper into the sick woman's bedroom. He thought that Andrine must have read the singer's letter, and that she also knew about the theft of the diamond: two thunderbolts!

Andrine made only a slight movement when her husband placed his ear over her heart to examine its beat. Johan looked at her silently for a moment, then he withdrew slowly, signaling to Jetje not to wake her.

Having returned downstairs, he told the manservant that he would need him to take a prescription to Jakob Ruysch. His hand was seized by a convulsive shudder when he dipped a pen into the inkwell in order to write the following prescription on a rectangular sheet of paper bearing the heading:

Dr JOHAN MIEREVELD,
Rapenburgerstraat no. 16, G3:

POTIO

R. Aqua distillata tiliae flor.................................... tres unc.
Pulvis gummae,..una drachm.
Sublimat,...una drachm.
Sirup. flor. Auranth...una uncia.
M.S.A.

POTIO

R. Solutum gummi,..tres unciae.
Oxyd. Antimon.,..una drachm.
Sirups altheae,...una uncia.
M.S.A.

The first of these potions, intended for Andrine, contained a lethal poison that would kill her in a matter of hours. The second prescription was for himself; it was composed of soothing substances of an altogether innocuous nature.

As Johan came to write the final lines of this double prescription, a stabbing pain shot through his temples and made him dizzy. The pen slid from his fingers, his eyes closed and his head, seized from behind by a nervous convulsion, struck the back of the armchair and remained there, as if nailed to it by some mysterious power.

Then something frightful and horrible occurred. The embalmed hand stirred on its velvet cushion, amid the fragments of broken glass.

First, the fingers extended themselves, making the joints crack audibly as they relaxed; then they moved like the feet of a scarab beetle, and the hand drew itself slowly towards the center of the table. Its determined and eccentric gait, reminiscent of one of the pinkish-yellow crabs of the Indonesian islands, was hideous.

Arriving at the prescription, it came to an abrupt halt; then the index-finger passed over each line in turn, reading it by touch.

When the finger had skimmed the last line, a tremor passed through all the muscles of the hand, which immediately resumed its march; hurriedly, it took up a pen, dipped it in the ink–an exertion that was both grotesque and sinister–and returned to the prescription.

It added the word *Camphora* before the word *Sublimat*,[8] then went down several lines, to the prescription that Johan had written for himself, and traced the five letters *T-a-r-t-r* before the words *Oxyd. Antimon.*[9]

---

[8] Sublimation is a chemical process by which compounds pass from a solid state to a gaseous one, and vice versa, without passing through a liquid phase. The unmodified term *Sublimat.* would be taken to refer to *corrosive sublimate*: mercuric chloride derived by subliming mercuric sulphate with common salt; although it is a virulent poison, it was widely used at the time the story was written as an antiseptic, particularly in the treatment of syphilis. Adding *Camphora* to the formula would change its significance completely, to *Japan camphor* obtained by sublimation from the bark of the camphor tree, which was used in 19th century medicine both as a stimulant and–as the narrator states–as a sedative. It is interesting to note that Johan's subsequent warning to Andrine–that the potion would make her symptoms worse before bringing any relief– might have been accurate despite the substitution.

[9] *Oxyd. Antimon.* might refer to any of the oxides of antimony, most likely to antimony trioxide, but that compound was not widely used as a "soothing substance" and is not innocuous. Although antimony compounds were popular in primitive medical treatments–especially those influenced by alchemical ideas, which extend into modern times in such schools of "alternative medicine" as "spagyrics"–their toxicity probably ensured that they did more harm than good. Adding *Tartr.* to the formula would, however, change its significance to potassium antimonyl tartrate, or *tartar emetic*, a poisonous salt used in dyeing as a mordant and in medicine as a powerful emetic (inducing vomiting) and diaphoretic (inducing sweating). The substituted compound would undoubtedly have been considered more dangerous than the original at the time when the story was written, although it is unlikely that the substitution would actually accomplish quite such a dramatic reversal of effect as the one promised by the narrator.

Two words! Only two words!

But those two words saved Andrine's life, and killed the poisoner.

That infernal mercuric drug, whose effect on the unhappy child would have been fatal, had been converted by the dead hand into a powerful sedative. As for the other, it was a sentence of death: death with all the symptoms of cholera; death almost akin to a thunderbolt.

An hour went by before Johan emerged from his lethargic stupor; he looked around in astonishment and saw two small pharmaceutical phials on the table in front of him. While he was asleep, the manservant had come in and, finding the prescription written, had taken himself off to Jakob Ruysch's shop. Johan read the labels on the two phials very attentively, then he put one into his pocket, took the other in his hand, and went up to his wife's bedroom.

Andrine was awake.

At the sight of Johan, a sad smile passed over her lips and, from a distance, she held out her hand to him. He pretended not to have noticed the gesture, uncorked the phial, and emptied the entire contents into a cup. His hand did not tremble as he brought the poison to his wife's lips, and his voice was soft and gentle as he said; "Don't worry if this potion seems at first to aggravate your symptoms. I have to initiate an attack in order to bring about a forceful reaction."

She swallowed meekly, thanked him with a little nod of the head, and sank back upon her pillow.

Johan observed her for a few moments. Taking advantage of the absence of Jetje, who was making up a bed in the next room, he carefully rinsed out the cup.

His work completed, he went downstairs again and threw the empty phial into the fireplace. Avidly, he drank half the potion prepared for him directly from the bottle. That done, he took his coat and his hat, gathered up la Michelli's letter, which had fallen on to the carpet, and ran out of the house like a madman.

Stéphane Mallarmé: *The Future Phenomenon*

A pale sky above the world at the end of its decrepitude
might disappear within the clouds: the threadbare purple tat-
ters of sunsets fade into the dormant river at the horizon,
drowned by rays of light and water. The trees languish in en-
nui, and beneath their blanched foliage (blanched by the dust
of the ages rather than that of the roads) the Showman of Past
Things has erected his tent. Many street lamps await the dusk,
retouching the faces of a miserable crowd of men, conquered
by the undying malady and sin of centuries, beside their puny
accomplices pregnant with the wretched fruits by which the
Earth shall perish.

The showman's patter spills into the unquiet silence of
all those eyes, imploring with a despairing cry the descending
Sun that slides into the water. "The spectacle inside has no
signboard to advertise it, for there is nowadays no painter capable of displaying a pale shadow of it. I bring with me, alive–
preserved over the years by superscientific means–a Woman
of the olden days. Some novel and naïve madness, an ecstasy
of gold or I know not what, which she called her hair, is
draped with silken grace about a face illuminated by the
blood-tinted bareness of her lips. Instead of the conceit of
clothing, she has a body; and even her eyes, which have the
semblance of exotic stones, cannot surpass the glare emitted
by her blissful flesh: from the breasts uplifted as though they
were replete with eternal milk, nipples towards the sky, to the
lithe legs which guard the salinity of the primal sea."

Mindful of their paltry spouses–bald, ghastly and full of
horror–the husbands press forward. Their wives, too, moved
by melancholy curiosity, desire to see.

When all have contemplated the noble creature, a relic
of some earlier accursed age–some indifferently, for they will

not have the power of understanding, but others heart-broken, their eyelids moist with tears of resignation–they will look at one another. Then the poets of those times, sensible of the rekindling of their extinguished eyes, will make their way towards their light-source, their brains intoxicated for a moment by an ambiguous glory, haunted by Rhythm, forgetful of the fact that they exist in an era that has outlived beauty.

Jean Richepin: *The Metaphysical Machine*

Why do they say that I am insane?

Just because I am not like absolutely everyone else, just because I do not play my role like one of Panurge's sheep,[10] just because I remain indoors for weeks and months at a time–is that any reason to call me insane? On the contrary, I believe that, thanks to the life I have led–above all to the great idea which that life has revealed to me–I am a sage. I was certainly not in the least insane when I first conceived that idea.

I had read a great deal, studied a great deal. I was particularly attracted to works of philosophy–but I do not like the philosophers of our own day, because they do not know how true philosophers must live. In order to conceive a philosophical system, it is necessary to follow a contemplative lifestyle, solitary and absorbed. Now, how can you find such studious conditions in our hectic world, whose distractions seep into a man's every pore? I therefore confined my studies to the pleasurable company of the ancient philosophers. I sought out those whose mutilated works are only known to us through fragments or translations: Leucippus, Democritus, Empedocles, Heraclitus, Parmenides. I felt a singular joy in reconstructing old systems of thought with the aid of their remaining debris, much as Cuvier has reconstructed antediluvian species from a few bones. Men who occupy themselves with decaying things are the only ones who will comprehend the happiness that I obtained by thus rediscovering the homoeomeric theory of Anaxagoras and a few others.[11] Along-

---

[10] In Rabelais' *Pantagruel* (1533).

[11] Anaxagoras of Clazomenae (c. 500 BC-c. 428 BC); *homoeomery* was a subspecies of Greek atomic theory whose

side these fragments, I also cherished the complete but obscure systems of mystics and theologians: subtle depths into
whose metaphysical exercises a wounded spirit plunges with
delight. The Alexandrines, Plotinus, Porphyry and Iamblichus
have enraptured me, and I have tasted ineffable sensuality
with St. Anselm and St. Thomas Aquinas.

I do not offer this reading-list, any part of which would
suffice to prove that I am a savant, out of vanity; I offer it
partly to demonstrate that I have merely been a scholar, not a
madman, and–more importantly–to explain how the great idea
of which I spoke before first came to me.

This is it!

In the course of all this reading I was struck by one thing,
which became the point of departure for my own system: the
knowledge that in the midst of cosmogonic and theological
hypotheses, the human spirit locates itself less by reasoning
than by intuition. This is not a matter of logical deduction,
since one does not move from "the assertion of what is
known" to "the contents of the unknown." It is a matter of
positing the "contents of the unknown" directly–which is to
say, in other words, of seeing the absolute. Proof is not a issue;
the absolute must be seen. One sees, or one does not see. I
might experience it myself at any moment.

Such an enlightenment, of which I had not previously
been able to obtain any sensation, came to me suddenly after a
long meditation. The absurd became an evident truth. I felt
like a blind man, who had had the concept of color explained
to him at length without having any ability to understand it,
whose eyes were suddenly opened to sensation.

If this process allowed me to understand the truths of
metaphysics, it followed that they had also been discovered by
this procedure: such was my first step. I inferred that the absolute was, for us, not a conclusion but an apparition. A fact
which seemed at first to be bizarre and unreasonable was soon

---

central postulate was that the ultimate particles must be of the
same kind (*homo* = like, *meros* = part).

proven by me, by means of a superhuman sense which some-times seizes words.

A word, or an assemblage of words–a phrase–is there before me; it becomes an absurdity, as if inscribed in hiero-glyphics. I repeat the word–the phrase–without any longer being able to attach any meaning to it; somehow, I fix my spirit to the material form of the word, to the image of the alphabetical signs, to the sound of the syllables. For a week, a month, many months afterwards, I have arranged matters so that I am voluntarily haunted by an incomprehensible absurdity. Then, one fine day, the human sense of that absurdity obliterates itself, the form and the sound of the word become symbols, and I comprehend the incomprehensible.

I had found the key to metaphysics.

I shall not tell you how the idea was refined, little by little, to the point at which it condensed into a theory. That would take too long. The slow and shadowy transformations of an idea are a labyrinth of reflections, whose thread is lost even while one is extending it. Having shown how I arrived at the portal of the labyrinth, I will simply tell you what I sought to draw out of it: my system of perceptible metaphysics.

Until now, only three aspects of human inner life have been considered: sensation, consciousness and reason. To make the next part of my discourse clearer, I will call the senses by the correct term "external senses," inasmuch as they apply themselves to external objects; and I will reunite consciousness and reason under the term "internal senses," inasmuch as they both apply themselves to my interior self and its modifications.

The metaphysical error which still weighs us down thus becomes palpable: the materialists apply the external senses, and the spiritualists the internal senses, to the absolute–-but the absolute is neither in me not in the objects exterior to me. There is the reason for the impotence of human research into the absolute–an impotence that has remained constant throughout the ages. The skeptics have set metaphysical questions aside. Sincere searchers have tried to escape the error, the mystics by means of ecstasy and the theologians by means of faith; they were in the right in searching for a new means, but both fell back into error by subjecting ecstasy and faith to the procedures of reason.

Only one man, prior to myself, has glimpsed the infallible procedure which leads to the Absolute. That was the theologian Thomassin,[12] who wrote these words:

Mens, sola sibi reddita, naturae suae ingenium et praestantiam totam obtinens, naturaliter ominatur SENSIT que summum aliquid et INEXCOGITABILE principium.

Which means:

The soul, reduced to itself alone, in possession of all its being and all its power, perceives naturally and SENSES that something, that sovereign principle, which is INACCESSIBLE TO REASON.

The words are clear, and I think that even the most vulgar intelligence can understand them. This quotation renders in simple terms all that remains for me to say in completing my theory, which can now be summarized in a single affirmation:

Besides the external senses and the internal senses, there is another sense, internal and external at the same time, knowing its object as the external senses do, immaterial as the internal senses are, but having absolutely nothing in common with either of them–and that is the SENSE OF THE ABSOLUTE.

But what am I saying? What have I written there? To tell the truth, I am afraid. I have kept my mind as calm as I could in order to explain my discovery in simple terms. Now that task is complete, I am terrified. Have I read the meaning of what I have written? It is as if I have written that human beings have a third eye! Worse than that–I have written that human beings have a new sense. A monstrosity!

---

[12] Louis Thomassin (1619-1695), best-known for his treatise on the incarnation.

It seems to me that I can hear laughter all around me, and voices saying: mad, mad, mad! I am, however, perfectly lucid. My intellect is sound–I am certain of it. No, I am not mad; that is not true. I can see–I tell you. I can see. But they will not believe that I can see, because they are blind. How unfortunate! Who, then, will hear me without laughing? How can I show that?

That is nothing in itself. The eyes cannot see it; the ears cannot hear it; the fingers cannot touch it; consciousness cannot speak of it. What horror! Reason itself cannot comprehend it. Ah! You see, you admit that you are beyond reason–you must be mad! No, no, a thousand times no. Who calls me mad, then? You lie! The whole world is laughing, isn't it? Oh well– if I am mad, I might as well go all the way; I'll die of it if I have to–but that which I see, you will see too.

My sense of the absolute is real; it exists; it is. I shall exercise this new sense; I shall sacrifice everything in its cause; I shall write down the things that it has revealed to me, and those things will be so prodigious, so resplendent, so true, that the world will be dazzled by them. They will have to listen to me when they hear about the manifest Apocalypse!

An analogy immediately suggested a means by which I might exercise this new sense vigorously. I observed that blind men have an extremely delicate sense of touch, and that men who become deaf are recompensed by tracking the movements of the lips with their eyes, thus coming to understand the words which they do not hear. It is easy enough to conclude that the atrophy of one sense makes the others sharper.

I understood, then, why the priests of Buddha are compelled to seek solitary and silent immobility, and I no longer found the situation of those seers who absorbed in contemplation of their navels ridiculous. They seek in contemplative ecstasy to forget the sensible world. Unfortunately, ecstasy does not last; and in spite of their heroism, these immobile ones experience sensations between their cataleptic fits. Nor are they limited to indistinct and confused sensations; they are eternally confined within the workings of Consciousness and

Reason, so they are perpetually distracted, if not by the external senses, at least by the internal ones.

It was necessary, therefore, to find a state in which the mind was unoccupied either by sensations or by thoughts.

Was that possible?

As for sensations, yes. Nothing is easier, given a firm and resolute will, than to render oneself blind, deaf and dumb. It is a matter of paralyzing the nerves, nothing more. When the day came, I could deprive myself of my senses, conserving only touch, so that I would be able to write down my visions in the dark. Eventually, I would arrive at the point of having no more memories of sensations–they would be effaced, little by little, from a mind that was no longer cultivated in that manner.

As for thoughts, that was not so easy. If one ceases to think, does one not cease to be? Yes, in the everyday sense of the word–but not in mine. What need had I of the modes of thought in common usage? What did reasoning matter to me, in all its forms? So, it was necessary to cease to think, or at least to think as little as possible. To cure me of that particular malady, I had a remedy already: obsession. Obsession atrophies all other ideas, leaving one and one only in possession of the mind. That would complement the atrophy of the senses within my mental regime.

That regime, which would soon be mine, was therefore reduced to this: to annihilate, as far as was possible, all my internal and external senses, in order to allow free play and give an exceeding acuity to the sense of the absolute.

It remained, before undertaking the great work, to identify the precise circumstances in which that sense is at its most vigorous, and in which it could be most comfortably exerted. My reflections and researches on this point were lengthy. A memory of my youth put me on the track of that which I was trying to find. Delicate as the subject of this memory is, I must insist on its introduction here, in the interests of science and better to understand the means that I believed I had to employ.

Everyone knows that in the course of pleasurable excitation [13] there is a brief–and, in consequence, very little studied–moment, during which one's entire being melts, like a filament of metal in an electric current. It is like a flash of lightning in which a human being is engulfed in a substance, of which it is at that moment a sort of conductor. All of creation is alive in that flash; it is, if I might express it in such terms, the microcosm of the absolute. I discovered this subtle explication while recalling to mind the sensation itself.

On the other hand, I had to consider that the moment in question is, as I have said, a mere flash. There is no way of making that kind of flash last indefinitely–but I took note of the fact that this pleasurable excitation possesses its strange property, not because it is pleasurable, but because it is an excitation. The Orientals have prolonged it by introducing pain into the ecstasy. By the excitation of pain, in effect, the flash becomes less vivid but more durable. One can produce by this means an agitation in which everything is annihilated, a kind of current that melts humanity. This, then, is the exact state in which the startled mind can attain the absolute.

I had only to imagine a kind of continuous pain, powerful enough to throw me into that state, and an apparatus that, while making it utterly impossible for me to escape the pain in question, would permit me to write down my visions. The kind of pain that I eventually settled on was the prolonged irritation of the dental nerves, and the choice inspired me in no time at all to devise the ingenious apparatus within which I was soon seated.

So, this is what is firmly decided at the present moment: I shall deliver myself to the absolute. After 15 years spent working on my system and putting my regime into effect, I believe that I have finally brought about the conditions necessary for an attempt of the last and greatest experiences of all. I

---

[13] The French *jouissance nerveuse* is difficult to translate; *jouissance* can signify both enjoyment and possession; the phrase is obviously a euphemism for orgasm.

have subjected myself to all the necessary mutilations. I am blind and deaf. I have not spoken a single word for 15 years. I have renounced the use of gross and imperfect senses, including Consciousness and Reason, which might constrain my new sense. I have kept nothing of the old humanity but attention and will. I know how to write in the dark; the words I shall write will provide illumination!

My first experience will last about an hour. It is now seven o'clock in the morning. My old manservant will come to my room at eight. There, he will find my written instructions, as he is accustomed to do every day. In these instructions, I tell him to descend to the basement of my house, which he has never entered, and I explain how he can let me out of the apparatus if he finds me unconscious. I write all these details so as to establish firmly that I act entirely freely and knowing perfectly well what I am doing.

As I could die during the experience, I have also taken the opportunity to record the history of my theory briefly and clearly. For the same reason, desirous of leaving no mystery behind me, I shall now describe my metaphysical apparatus.

It is a mechanical chair, all of whose parts I have made and assembled myself. My legs will be immobilized by a sheath into which I will introduce them as I sit down. Once seated, I shall place my left arm on the arm of the chair, and my head upon an earflap to the right. In this position, I shall open my mouth, which will be kept open by a solid leather plug covered in India-rubber, which I can bite without breaking my jaws. Beside the earflap, in the gap made by my open mouth, I shall place the little mechanism which will produce the pain, which comprises a drill-bit that moves back and forth rapidly and continuously.[14]

---

[14] Primitive dental drills were in use when this story was written in the 1880s but they were not automated; most were foot-powered by a mechanism similar in design to a treadle-driven sewing machine. Electrical drills powered by storage batteries were invented in 1868 but never caught on; it was not until

This drill will plunge into a hollow tooth, progressing automatically to a depth of half a centimeter in the course of an hour. Another mechanism will gradually unwind a scroll of parchment under my right hand, on which I shall record continuously whatever I see.

To avoid the natural laxity of humanity, which might incite me to stop the drilling-mechanism, I have arranged the whole machine in the following manner: one button is situated within range of my left hand; to the first pressure I exert the machine will respond and I shall immediately be secured to the chair by shackles of iron which will encircle my arms and fix my head. At the same time, the two mechanisms will begin to operate; once started, it will be impossible for me to stop them.

The clockwork movement is set for one hour.

I am here–everything is going well...

I am writing this on the scroll, as a trial...

atrocious pain–good–the beginning...

I'm waiting...

joy–horror–absolute–absolute–words?–I can see at last–inexcogitabile–mad–mad–mad–joy–joy... [15]

words to express?–obvious–of course–yes...

enough–triangle–enough...

absolute–here it is–at last–here it is–here it is...

---

mains electricity first became available in the USA in the late 1890s that the modern dentist's drill was pioneered by prolific inventor and dental practitioner C. Edmund Kells.

[15] The Latin word *inexcogitabile*, which occurs in the quotation from Thomassin, is reproduced at this point in the story; it was earlier translated into French by Richepin as *inaccessible à la raison*–which I rendered into English as "inaccessible to reason." There is, however, an English word inexcogitable, whose meaning is closer to "unthinkable" or "inexpressible in thought," which I have retained here.

At eight o'clock, the old manservant went into his master's room, found the written instructions and went down into the basement.

The madman was in his chair. He was dead.

The convulsions of his legs had twisted the sheath without being able to get out. The wrist of his left hand was badly torn by the iron bracelet, against which it had strained in vain. Flayed tendons were visible, taut as violin strings. The right arm was restrained between the shoulder to the elbow but free from the elbow to the wrist. The hand, unable to reach as far as the head, was stuck to the breast, which it had clawed repeatedly with its fingernails. Two of the fingers were embedded to the depth of the first knuckle. The head, half-turned around but maintained in its position by the earflap, displayed a hideous grimace. Bloody froth oozed from the gums. The teeth had cut through the rubber and had broken in their anguished mastication of the plug within.

The roller was still advancing the parchment, and the drill was still boring implacably into a molar, making an almost imperceptible grinding sound: *bzi, bzi, bzi.*

It was the laughter of the absolute.

Albert Robida: *The Monkey King*

I. How Saturnin Farandoul,
aged four months and seven days,
embarked upon a career of adventure.
His adoptive family take him for an incompetent monkey.

In the mid-Pacific region of the 10th north parallel and 150 degrees of western longitude–which is almost the same as that of the Polynesian isles of Pomotou [16] –the great Ocean, so fecund and so tempestuous, belied its name even more than usual on that day. In the utterly disordered sky, masses of purplish-black cloud streamed from the distant horizon at an incalculably rapid rate of knots. The waves climbed to heights unknown in our paltry European seas. Howling and roaring, they hurled themselves one after another and one upon another, as if the furious sea were mounting an attack, which burst forth in frightful waterspouts, under whose weight the highest waves loudly collapsed in whirlwinds of foam.

A few fragments of the masts and timbers of ships and barrels, floating here and there, indicated that the god of storms would not be returning to his deep caverns with an empty bag, alas. Amid the debris, however, one peculiar item of wreckage was discernible, sometimes thrust up to the crests

---

[16] Pomotou is an alternative name for the Tuamotu Archipelago, a group of islands south of the Marquesas which became a French Protectorate. Their longitude extends from about 140 degrees west to 150 degrees west (Robida was presumably using Paris as a baseline rather than Greenwich, but it makes little difference). Tuamotu lies about 15 degrees south of the equator; 10 degrees north, where Robida locates his castaway, is in the middle of a vast tract of open sea.

of the waves and sometimes disappearing in the hollow valleys between the monstrous billows.

This wreck was a cradle, and the cradle in question contained an infant, well-swathed and well-secured. The child was sleeping like a log, apparently finding no difference between the rocking effect of the Ocean and that employed by his nurse.

Hours had passed. Miraculously, the cradle had not sunk; the ocean continued to swing it to and fro. The storm had calmed down; the sky, clearing little by little, allowed a long line of rocks to become visible upon the horizon. The frail craft, evidently carried by a current, was steering towards an unexpected port!

Little by little, the coast became more visible, its sheltering cliffs cut through by little creeks calmly stirred by the waves. In order to get that far, though, it was necessary to pass through a chain of coral reefs, on which the waves broke into cascades of foam, without the little vessel breaking up.

In the end, the cradle came through and ran aground, still accompanied by fragments of mast. One last roller carried it up the beach and left it behind on the dry sand–and the brat, abruptly awoken by the cessation of movement, cried out for the first time with all his might.

It was evening. The Sun, which had not appeared all day, finally showed through, and, having arrived at the end of its course, proceeded to extinguish its last fierce orange rays in the waves of the open sea. To take advantage of this hour of delicious calm after a stormy day, and also to take a little exercise after the evening meal, an honorable family of monkeys was taking a walk on the damp beach, admiring the splendors of the setting Sun. [17]

---

[17] Robida's illustrations depict these creatures with the long prehensile tails typical of New World monkeys, and it soon transpires within the text that their possession of such tails is crucial to the development of the story. I have therefore

The entire natural world seemed to be their personal domain. They were enjoying an admirable view with a tranquil proprietary right that no anxiety could trouble. All the beauties of the tropics were displayed there, as if in a magical frame: all the glorious flowers that the equatorial Sun could bring into bloom, marvelous plants, giant trees and interlacing lianas by the thousand.

---

thought it appropriate to translate *singes* as "monkeys" rather than "apes." Robida's knowledge of primate taxonomy is, however, understandably primitive; a subsequent passage is insistent that the reader is being introduced to "a family of orang-outangs," and another declares that their species is intermediate between orang-utans and chimpanzees. I have retained these terms within my translation even though they make no sense in the context of modern primatology (neither of the species cited is equipped with a tail).

At the time the story was written, the orang-utan was still a semi-legendary creature in Europe, whose reputation was partly based on unreliable traveler's tales and partly on the equally-unreliable ruminations of early evolutionist anthropologists, who had not yet reached agreement as to how many species of human beings there were, or how the concept of species related to that of race, or whether–and, if so, where– orang-utans and other great apes ought to figure in this classification. Such issues had been even less clear at the time when Léon Gozlan wrote *Les émotions de Polydore Marasquin*, which is obviously one of the key sources of Robida's inspiration. In that novel, Gozlan deliberately confuses distinctions between men and monkeys, which had already been considerably declarified by the advent of evolutionary theory, for satirical purposes.

As a postscript to this point, I have translated *guenon* as "she-monkey" because that is clearly what Robida means by it; he is not implying that Farandoul's adoptive parents belong to one of the species that the English language now terms *guenons*.

Four little monkeys of various heights gamboled on the grass, swinging from descending lianas as they went past, and chasing one another around the coconut palms under the protective eyes of their father and mother. The latter were more serious individuals, content to mark their joy at the good weather's return by quietly shaking their hindquarters with perfect panache. The mother, a lovely she-monkey with an elegant figure and a graceful demeanor, carried in her arms a fifth offspring, which she suckled as she walked, with a candor and a dignified serenity that would have tempted the chisel of a Praxiteles.[18]

Suddenly, their tranquillity was disturbed. The father, at the sight of an object extended on the beach, turned two or three somersaults–a gesture which, among the monkeys, signifies the most colossal astonishment. Without ceasing to nurse her infant, the mother and the four little monkeys likewise turned half a dozen simultaneous somersaults before coming to rest on all fours. The reason for their alarm was that the object perceived by the monkeys was stirring and struggling, desperately twirling its arms and legs, as a crab does when one plays the practical joke of setting it down on its back.

It was our recent acquaintance, the young and charming castaway who, having been awakened by the landing, was giving vent to unfathomable feelings. Papa Orang-utan–for it is a family of orang-utans that we are introducing to our readers–made a cautious tour of the disquieting object before allowing his family to approach it. Having judged it unlikely to be dangerous, he signaled to the mother with a reassuring gesture and showed her the cradle, scratching his nose in a puzzled manner.

What could the unknown animal be which the sea had brought and cast up on the beach? That was what the reunited

---

[18] Praxiteles, a famous Athenian sculptor active in the 4th century B.C., was reputedly responsible for several fine statues held in the Louvre and familiar to all cultured Parisians.

family were asking themselves as they encircled the cradle to discuss the matter. The little ones, full of surprise, had no idea at all, but sought to read the results of their parents' reflections in their faces.

Eventually, the father, taking every possible precaution to avoid being bitten, delicately picked up the little castaway, who was still gesticulating wildly. He plucked the child out of the cradle by one leg and passed him to the she-monkey–who looked at him for a long time, placing him beside her last-born for comparison, reflected carefully, and showed by a few significant shakes of the head that she considered this new species of monkey greatly inferior in physical beauty to the family of orangs.

The little castaway continued crying, despite the antics of the young monkeys, who were fully reassured by now and wanted to welcome this new comrade into their company. The she-monkey understood the reason for these cries. Passing her nursling to the father, she took hold of the infant's head and generously offered her maternal bounty to the child.

What joy for the little castaway! For many hours he had wandered without nourishment on the crests of the waves, tormented by a hunger he could at last appease! He drank so much that, having suddenly become comfortable again, he ended up falling asleep on the breast of his exotic nurse.

Meanwhile, the little monkeys had been rummaging around in the cradle, to make sure that it did not contain a second example of this peculiar species. They had found nothing there but a kind of bag sealed by a leather thong. This bag intrigued them enormously at first sight, but their perplexity was even further increased by the sight of the piece of paper that the eldest of the little monkeys took from it. They turned it over and over without result, then passed it to their father in the hope that he might explain it. After examining it for a quarter of an hour, he too could make nothing of the bizarre symbols with which it was covered.

The thing was very simple, though; let us admit right away that the bag found in the cradle was a tobacco-pouch–probably the paternal tobacco-pouch, which the unhappy

obably the paternal tobacco-pouch, which the unhappy parents had confided to the hazards of the tempest along with their child, at the moment when their ship sank. As for the paper covered with hieroglyphs that had so intrigued the naïve orangs, it will clarify for us the status of the young castaway, for it was nothing other than his duly-registered birth certificate.

The infant's name was Fortuné-Gracieux-Saturnin Farandoul.[19] The names of the parents and witnesses are ir-

---

[19] Many of the names improvised by Robida for French characters involve humorous misappropriations of common French words, most of which are too obvious, even to an English reader, to require annotation. The hero's name is more complex. *Farandoula* is an Occitan word (Occitan being the ancient language of Provence–the *Langue d'Oc*) referring to a lively kind of dance, known in both French and English as a *farandole*. The first two elements of the Christian name, which declare him to be fortunate and gracious, are unsurprising, but coupling them with Saturnin sets a puzzle before the reader.

The French adjective *saturnien*, derived from the planet, has the same metaphorical meaning (gloomy) as the English saturnine, but Saturnin Farandoul is by no means gloomy, and *saturnin* has a different meaning: pertaining to [the metal] lead. It is not impossible that Robida had the geological *Période Saturnienne* in mind when he coined his globe-trotting hero's name, that being the era in which the continents acquired their modern form. It is far more probable, however, that he really does mean to imply "pertaining to lead," lead being the material from which bullets are made. Robida–whose *La guerre au Vingtième Siècle* consists of a spectacular series of illustrations representing the technological transformation of warfare as a gaudily sarcastic black comedy–was a pacifist darkly fascinated by the mechanization of mass murder, and was thus obliged to regard Saturnin Farandoul's eventual influence on the population of the idyllic Isle of Monkeys (which, as the text observes, is still in its Golden Age at this point in the story) as problematic, if not actively

relevant to our story, so we shall pass over them in silence, but we must cite two further items of information revealed by this document: firstly, that Saturnin Farandoul was a French citizen; and secondly, that he was aged only four months and seven days. Thus did the youngster make his debut in his career as a castaway.

After mature reflection, Papa Orang-utan evidently came to a decision in the matter of the newly-discovered infant. He made a gesture signifying that five might just as well be six, and got up. The child was adopted; the family, thus augmented, ambled back along the path to their abode. It was a good night for all concerned. The Moon illuminated the tranquil sleep of our hero in the bosom of his adopted family, in the deep forest. The Sun rose to find Farandoul perfectly comfortable in his new social estate, and his adoptive parents quite content with their lucky find.

In her hut, made of branches covered with large banana leaves, the good she-monkey studied her nursling while he feasted greedily upon the banquet offered to his lips by beneficent Nature. In addition to the little monkeys, fascinated by the appearance of their new companion, there was a large crowd in the hut, dominated by she-monkeys.

What astonishment there was on every face! With what curiosity they followed the least movement of little Farandoul!

---

evil. Farandoul's conversion of the peaceful monkeys into an army of conquest surely qualifies as a metaphorical *malaise saturnin* (lead poisoning).

Despite his frivolous tone, Robida clearly intends to imply that Saturnin Farandoul is somewhat symbolic of his entire race, whose pretension to be humane rather than merely human is not to be taken too seriously. The implication of the story, although the author refrains from spelling it out as an explicit moral, is, in effect, that man is merely a "monkey king," so corrupted and perverted by civilization that he has contrived to forget that at bottom (so to speak) he is merely an incompetent example of primatekind.

At first, the young she-monkeys could not suppress a thrill of fear when the nursing mother jokingly extended the infant towards them, but the gentleness of Farandoul won every one of their hearts, and the entire audience was soon competing for the privilege of petting him. The hut never emptied; male and female monkeys came from the neighboring forests carrying gifts of fruit and coconuts, which Farandoul pushed away with his hands and feet in order to thrust himself back upon the quasi-maternal breast.

Outside, Farandoul's foster-father, surrounded by old white-bearded orangs, seemed to be telling the story of his discovery. Perhaps he was giving his report to the authorities; in any case, he saw by their benevolent gestures that the elders approved of his conduct and appeared well pleased with him. Little by little, the fuss caused by the new arrival died down, and life resumed its ordinary course.

If Farandoul had been older, he would have been able to marvel at the patriarchal existence led by the monkeys. Indeed, the happy population of that fortunate isle, lost in the vastness of the Pacific far distant from the customary shipping routes, was still in the Golden Age! The island was extraordinarily fertile. All the fruits of the Earth grew in abundance, lavishly distributed without the least requirement for cultivation. No fearsome wild beasts infested the forests, where even the most inoffensive creatures lived in total security.

The simian race was the summit of the evolutionary scale, dominating by its intelligence the entire natural order of the island. Man was unknown there, never having repressed it with his barbarity or perverted it with his example—as he has those fallen races of monkeys, condemned to ignominy, which will vegetate forever in the lands inhabited by humans, unless some monkey of genius arrives one day to effect their return to the purer life of ancient times, in some wilderness inaccessible to humankind.

These monkeys belonged to a race intermediate between the Orang-utans and Chimpanzees. Aggregated in tribes, whose villages were composed of about 50 huts made of small

65

branches, they lived quite happily. Each family enjoyed the most complete individual liberty, and where matters of communal interest were concerned they looked to the elders, who often came together in council at the foot of a giant eucalyptus, in the branches of which the young ones frolicked without taking part in the discussions.

It must be said that everyone was full of respect for these worthy ancients, and that the smart young monkeys would never allow themselves to jump on their backs or to grab their tails in passing, without previous authorization.

Farandoul spent a year with the family. He rolled in the grass with his foster-brothers; he played all the exciting games with them that young monkeys play. To the great astonishment of his parents, however, he remained remarkably inept in leaping about, and adamantly refused to climb coconut palms.

Such timidity in a healthy youth of 18 months worried the gallant monkeys exceedingly. Although his brothers set him an excellent example by means of the most audacious ascensions and aerial somersaults, Farandoul never got the hang of gymnastics. As he grew apace into a sturdy little chap, the anxiety of his parents increased. It became a veritable anguish as they saw that he was quite incapable of following them when the family went off on expeditions in search of amusement, hurling themselves about in the crowns of tall trees and forming troupes of acrobats to swing on the natural see-saws generously provided by the coconut palms. Farandoul's brothers made as many footholds as possible for him and ran away into the trees in order to invite him to climb after them, but he stayed on his feet, astonished and angry because he was unable to do as they did.

Farandoul's foster-mother, who loved him at least as much as her other children, and perhaps a little more–for he was undoubtedly the weakest–did not know what to do to develop the gymnastic talent that must, she believed, exist in him as in every other monkey. Sometimes, while suspended by the tail from the lower branches of a trees, she would throw herself into space and swing there, calling to Saturnin with little reproachful cries; on other occasions, she turned a thousand somersaults, walked on her hands, made him climb up on her back, and clambered up into the branches with him–but in the former instances, Saturnin Farandoul stayed down below, deaf to her appeals, and in the latter, he clung fearfully to his mother's fur, refusing to let go. What a torment he was to those brave orangs!

Soon, this preoccupation became perpetual, a constant worry. Farandoul continued to grow without becoming any more agile. His foster-father–who, since his lucky find, had become one of the most respected monkeys on the island–held frequent consultations with the elders: the venerable monkeys who, as we have said, held their assemblies under the largest eucalyptus in the village. It was obvious that Saturnin Farandoul was the subject of these conversations. These monkeys occasionally summoned him, placed his hand on his head, looked at him intently, made him walk and run, consulted one another, scratched themselves, shook their heads, and finally confessed that they did not understand it at all.

One day, the astonished Farandoul saw his father come back from a longer-than-usual trip with a very old monkey whom he did not recognize. He was wrinkled and bent over, with a great white beard framing his majestic face and bald patches in his coat of long white hair. This ancient, who might easily have been a hundred years old, came from a distant part of the island to which Farandoul's foster-father had gone in order to consult him. He obviously enjoyed a great reputation for wisdom, because all the monkeys in the vicinity hurried forth in a crowd, with lavish gestures of respect, eager to assist him in his tottering walk, while the she-monkeys showed him off to their children from a distance.

Having been greeted by the elders at the entrance to the village, the old monkey sat down at the foot of the eucalyptus, in the middle of the greatest gathering of monkeys that Farandoul had ever seen. Saturnin Farandoul seemed, along with the old monkey, to be the object of everyone's attention. His foster-father came to look for him among the urchins with whom he was rolling in the grass, in order to bring him to the ancient, who considered him carefully from every angle.

The old monkey sat the child on his knee, then stood him up again and flexed all the joints of his arms and legs. All of them were working perfectly, which seemed to amaze the old fellow. He began again, with the same result; seeing this, he plunged into a long meditation from which he roused himself only to recommence his examination. Then he struck his forehead, as if he were proclaiming to himself some triumphant Eureka, and called for one of Farandoul's young brothers. He placed the two of them side by side, with their backs to the crowd. By this means, he showed that the hindquarters of the little monkey were equipped with a magnificent caudal appendage: a flamboyant device, perfectly designed for aerial gymnastics—a fifth hand which wonderful Nature had generously granted to the species—of which poor Farandoul could not display the slightest indication.

They all lifted their hands to the heavens then. The most distant, who were unable to see anything, drew closer, clamoring to know the reason for this exclamatory gesture. The tribal elders restored order, debating with the most astounded by means of grandiose gestures. In the end, all the monkeys formed a procession to file past little Farandoul—or, rather, behind him—pausing one by one to examine him and to take stock of Nature's fatal forgetfulness.

A few passed comment, seemingly inquiring as to whether the condition was incurable. The old white monkey's response was to make them see that that one could not reasonably found the least hope on the slightest of appearances. However, at an order which he gave after further reflection, several monkeys took themselves off into the rocks while the assembly waited anxiously.

After a few minutes, they came back bearing bundles of herbs, which were heaped up between two stones, along with large slugs and snails. An uncommonly dexterous she-monkey made a compress out of it, and pressed it forcefully upon the deficient part of the stupefied Farandoul's body. Despite his cries of rage, the compress was so firmly attached that the poor little chap, so cruelly afflicted, was no longer able to lie down in comfort.

A light snack was prepared for the venerable monkey, who took nothing but half a dozen coconuts. After an hour's rest in the shade of the eucalyptus, during which he offered a few more items of advice on the teething troubles of little monkeys, the old fellow went back with Farandoul's foster-father to the path that led to his hermitage. They separated there and returned to their usual dwellings.

For the first time, Farandoul went in search of solitude, walking alone on the beach, still wearing his compress, which continued to cause him considerable distress.

The medication having brought about no alteration in the state of things, the compress was not renewed after eight hours. The poor she-monkey who was Saturnin Farandoul's adoptive mother tried again, in secret, to rub him with an unguent given to her by some of her cronies, but that remedy worked no better.

The months and the seasons flew past, and the inferiority of Saturnin Farandoul was further accentuated. He was a tall, strong and well-set lad, lithe and agile, skilful in all his bodily exercises, who could easily have got the better of four boys of his own age–but by comparison with his foster-brothers, these advantages amounted to nothing. Farandoul had to admit that he was beaten.

Sometimes, his brothers would lie in wait for him while he walked, hidden in the trees. At the moment when poor Saturnin Farandoul passed by, sucking on a sugar cane without an evil thought in his head, the playful band would form a chain, the strongest of them suspended by the tail from some high branch and the others clinging to one another, as the last in line seized Farandoul under the arms without warning and drew him upwards. They would swing him in the air then, without a care for the kicks that he distributed so liberally, until the entire troop allowed themselves to fall upon the grass.

Little by little, though, these games petered out. In growing older, his brothers came to understand that it was unkind to abuse their physical advantages and to remind their young brother continually of his inferiority. To the contrary, they took it upon themselves to help him forget, taking every precaution, and by means of conventional fraternal attentions. It was too late, though! Farandoul's intelligence understood the reason for this consideration, and it served only to increase his humiliation. Besides, as he saw very clearly, the entire tribe regarded him with an offensive attitude of commiseration. Pity was all too evident in every eye.

The good she-monkey who was his adoptive mother loved him even more tenderly, because she believed that he was destined for an unhappy and probably solitary life. With the future in mind, she began to worry a great deal about her son's prospects. Would he ever find a mate? How would he be received by the young she-monkeys of the village, when he began to think about them? And if his heart spoke, how painful it would be for him if his beloved refused his hand, and if he subsequently saw her in another's arms! What misery awaited him! What dramas, perhaps...

All these considerations saddened the hearts of Saturnin Farandoul's parents. Nor were the brains of the brave monkeys the only ones haunted by such anxieties; Farandoul was troubled too. Indeed, Farandoul had seen how different he was from his brothers and the other young monkeys of the tribe. He had given himself a crick in the neck staring at his reflection in the clear water of a spring, but he had seen nothing to authorize the least hope that he might one day possess the same triumphant appendage as those he truly believed to be his blood-brothers.

Poor Saturnin Farandoul believed himself irredeemably deformed. From the day of that discovery he dreamed of running away, exiling himself far from those he loved, in order to hide his sorrow and humiliation. For weeks and months he wandered the island's beaches in the vague hope of finding some means of putting this plan into operation.

Eventually, on the day after a tropical storm, he found a huge coconut-palm uprooted, lying on the shore–the means was found! Early the following day, having embraced the good monkey and the gentle she-monkey who had treated him with such affection for years, Saturnin Farandoul went with his five brothers to the beach where the coconut-palm rested. As if it were a game, he bid them push the tree-trunk to the water.

When the moment of embarkation drew near, the resolute Farandoul embraced his brothers tenderly but rapidly, and leapt on to the coconut palm as it floated parallel to the shore. The five brothers let loose five cries of horror, and lifted five pairs of arms despairingly into the air. The poor monkeys understood that he was already too far away to be recaptured. While they ran like maniacs along the shore, other monkeys hurried in response to their cries.

Farandoul, profoundly moved by their distress, recognized his parents, but turned his head and his weeping eyes towards the open sea. He used a branch to steer the coconut-palm adroitly through the reefs, and passed through the barrier without capsizing. The cries of the poor monkeys had scarcely faded away when the leaves of the palm tree caught the strengthening breeze and it was carried out to sea.

Some hours later, the isle of monkeys had disappeared and the coconut-palm was cruising the Pacific Ocean. Saturnin Farandoul, tranquilly seated at the junction of two branches, felt an excitement growing within him as the instincts of a navigator awoke.

His resources consisted of several scores of coconuts still suspended from the tree. The Sun directed its rays upon his naked body.

Having always lived among monkeys, believing himself to be a monkey, he had no knowledge whatsoever of clothing. Ever since his arrival on the isle, however, he had worn the tobacco-pouch containing his birth certificate around his neck; his adoptive parents had attached it there without really knowing why, and Farandoul had become accustomed to wearing it.

II. In which we are introduced to La Belle Léocadie.
*The Bora-Bora Company
for the Skimming of the Sunda Islands.
The boar filled with grape-shot.*

"Captain Lastic–look there, out to the south-south-east!"

"*Tonnerre d'Honfleur*,[20] Lieutenant Mandibul, I've been watching it for the last half-hour through my telescope!"

"Well, what do you think, Captain Lastic?"

"*Tonnerre d'Honfleur* may have my tongue, Lieutenant Mandibul, if it isn't a castaway!"

"And it's moving, Captain Lastic!"

"*Tonnerre d'Honfleur*, it's a tree, Lieutenant Mandibul, and there's someone on it."

This curt dialogue took place on the quarter-deck of *La Belle Léocadie*,[21] a fine three-master out of Le Havre, between the vessel's captain and first lieutenant. Having carried a cargo of pianos, dresses and confections for the young women of the town of Auckland, *La Belle Léocadie* was now hastening back to her port of origin with a cargo of hides.

---

[20] Honfleur is a port on the estuary of the Seine, opposite Le Havre. It was the focus of frequent heavy fighting during the Hundred Years' War, when it was captured and recaptured several times over. I have left *Tonnerre d'Honfleur!* ("Honfleur's thunder!") untranslated as a matter of policy, continued in respect of the oaths featured in the next chapter.

[21] *La Belle Léocadie* means "the beautiful Leocadia," The name Léocadie was not uncommon in the 19th century, especially for girls born on the feast-day of Saint Leocadia of Toledo, one of the virgin martyrs that the early Church's legend-mongers manufactured in such awesome profusion.

Captain Lastic was a man of prompt resolution; two minutes after having given his telescope to Lieutenant Mandibul, he had given the command to heave to, and oarsmen were steering a long-boat towards our hero's coconut-palm.

Saturnin Farandoul opened his eyes very wide at the sight of the distant vessel, which he took for a terrible monster. Even so, he did not attempt to flee and awaited developments.

The long-boat took no more than half an hour to reach him; the appearance of the men who were aboard it plunged Saturnin into a stupor. They bore no more than the remotest resemblance to the monkeys of his island and their faces did not seem to him to be imprinted with the least moral quality. Saturnin was by no means calm, but he stoically presented a smiling face to these unfamiliar monkeys.

"*Tonnerre d'Honfleur*, what are you doing there?" said Lieutenant Mandibul, who was in command of the long-boat and judged it necessary to his dignity to employ his Captain's oaths while standing in for him.

Saturnin had never heard a human voice; he did not understand this greeting at all, and it seemed to him less harmonious than the little monkey cries of his family.

"Are you deaf?" the Lieutenant demanded.

Saturnin made no more response to this speech than the other, but took it for an invitation and leapt aboard the long-boat, in a fashion that astonished the sailors.

The long-boat turned aside and set a course for the ship. The Lieutenant addressed no further questions to young Saturnin; that was, after all, the Captain's business. Aboard *La Belle Léocadie*, every eye was fixed on the long-boat. Captain Lastic did not lower his telescope until it was no more than a few cables distant.

Saturnin was the first to clamber up on to the bridge, in response to a gesture from the Lieutenant. He did so with a single motion that nearly caused the Captain–who had never witnessed such agility–to fall over.

"*Tonnerre d'Honfleur*, little porpoise, don't you have any manners? I'm Captain Lastic!"

The child's only response was a smile. All the sailors surrounded him, and Lieutenant Mandibul admitted that he had not been able to get a word out of the castaway. Saturnin stared raptly, still plunged in the most profound stupefaction. Suddenly, he walked around the Captain, then around the Lieutenant, then around each of the crewmen. One of the men was up on the mizzen-mast; Saturnin grabbed a rope without hesitation and was level with the topsail within an eyeblink.

The seaman had seen him coming, but could not understand why the naked castaway was suddenly climbing up towards him. Saturnin went around him just as he had gone around the others, then let loose a loud cry and slid back down to the bridge. *O joy! O happiness!* he thought. This new species of monkey was conformed almost like himself. No more humiliation! No more shame! In an eruption of delirious joy, Saturnin made several circuits of the ship, turning head over heels. With one last bound he jumped over the flabbergasted sailors and landed on his feet in front of the Captain, around whom he walked once more, just to be sure.

"What's all this, *Tonnerre d'Honfl...*?" cried the Captain, in alarm.

The ecstatic Saturnin naturally made no reply.

"Well then, *Tonnerre d'Honfleur*," the Captain continued, "tell us who you are!"

"Perhaps the porpoise doesn't understand French," suggested the Lieutenant.

"Let's try English, then," said the Captain, taking Saturnin by the arms. "What is your name?" he asked, in that language.

No response.

"*Was ist ihre name? Siete Italiano? Habla usted española?* Away with you, then, *Tonnerre d'Honfleur*," the Captain expostulated, having exhausted his linguistic resources. "Have you fallen from the Moon?"

Saturnin Farandoul tried to make sense of all these novel sounds. As far as he could recall, no human voice had ever struck his ear; the language of monkeys was the only one he understood.

"Look in that tobacco pouch around his neck," the Lieutenant suggested.

The Captain, who had not previously noticed it, took the pouch. "He has papers on him," he said. "Let's see... ah! He's French, born in Bordeaux..." The Captain stopped short. "A thousand million *Tonnerres d'Honfleur*!" he cried, seizing the child by the arms. "Your name is Saturnin Farandoul, my lad, and you're the son of poor Barnabé Farandoul, a Captain like me, who was lost at sea at least ten years ago!"

"Impossible!" said Lieutenant Mandibul.

"See for yourself, Lieutenant—here's his birth certificate. He's now 11 and a half years old."

"I'd have said at least 15, Captain."

"Me too—the porpoise hasn't suffered for lack of a nurse, *Tonnerre d'Honfleur*! What a seaman he'd make! I'll adopt you, my boy!"

And Saturnin Farandoul, whose exact age we now know, entered into a new phase of his life. How he succeeded, by means of vivid and animated pantomime, in communicating his history to Captain Lastic, we cannot hope to explain. Even so, the Captain was soon acquainted with the most trivial details of that existence, troubled—from poor Farandoul's viewpoint—only by a humiliating infirmity of constitution.

There were a few books aboard *La Belle Léocadie*. Some engravings of monkeys in an account of ocean voyages were shown to Farandoul, who covered them with tender kisses.

"Let's make shift to be a man, my son—there'll be time to later to bid them good-day, *Tonnerre d'Honfleur*!" So saying, the good Captain cut out the monkeys and pasted them to the wall of the little cabin he had given to Farandoul, not far from his own. Our hero was thus able to have the image of his parents on their beach constantly before his eyes, knowing that they might perhaps still be weeping, mourning their poor exile.

Farandoul had a good deal of trouble getting used to the clothes worn by civilized men. He was by no means elegantly turned out during the early days, when he wore his jacket in place of his trousers and his trousers in place of his jacket; as he wished to make himself agreeable to Captain Lastic, though, he soon managed to make himself presentable.

In addition, he made rapid progress in the study of languages. With sailors of every nationality around him, Farandoul learned French, English, Spanish, Malay, Chinese and Breton all at the same time.

Captain Lastic never left off telling Lieutenant Mandibul how pleased he was. "*Tonnerre d'Honfleur*, Lieutenant Mandibul, what a seaman! This porpoise is a charming young man. He slides down a rope in two ticks, from the royal to the topgallant–he could give pointers to the finest seaman in the merchant marine. That boy will do me great honor, Lieutenant Mandibul!"

Indeed, although Farandoul had been obliged to lower the flag before the agility of his foster-brothers on the isle of monkeys, his superiority to the sailors aboard *La Belle Léocadie* was obvious. None could compare with him in the feats of wild gymnastics that he performed on the topmasts. The masts reminded him of the coconut-palms to which he had been born–very nearly–and his greatest pleasure was to swing in the breeze from the crow's nest on the highest mast.

No one who caught sight of Saturnin Farandoul five years after these events would have been able to recognize the monkeys' foundling in the young man with the thin moustache, the intelligent face and the forceful gestures walking on the poop-deck of *La Belle Léocadie*, in the company of Captain Lastic and Lieutenant Mandibul–both of whom had aged a little. The benefits of education and civilization had converted the unsuccessful ape of other days into a superior human being!

From time to time, Saturnin still thought of his adoptive parents with a certain tenderness, but his mind was fully engaged at present with navigation and commerce.

For five years, he had sailed with *La Belle Léocadie*, carrying clocks, leather gloves and crinolines to the Sandwich Islands, champagne and parasols to the Indies, footwear, haberdashery and perfumery to Chile, returning with cargoes of logwood for the wine-merchants of Bordeaux–teak, rosewood, ebony and so on. Having believed during his early youth that the world was bounded by the horizons of his island, with monkeys for all humanity, he now found the entire universe quite small. He had already sailed the seas of every quarter of the globe, set foot on every continent, relaxed on many an isle.

Captain Lastic had nothing but praise for his adoptive son; Farandoul had never caused him the slightest trouble. He had been obliged on one occasion to bail him out of Liverpool jail, where he had been committed after an instant's forgetfulness, but that peccadillo had only warmed the Captain's heart. The incident had taken place at the Liverpool Museum of Natural History, where Saturnin Farandoul, at the sight of a stuffed monkey, had been unable to restrain his sorrow and anger. He had thrown himself upon the terrified curators with such fury that they had only been torn from his hands in a considerably damaged state.

At present, *La Belle Léocadie*, out of Saigon bound for New South Wales, was passing through the Sulu Isles, about to enter the Celebes Sea. Captain Lastic was untroubled. There was nothing to fear on the part of the elements; the sea and sky were calm and everything was set fair for a pleasant voyage. These latitudes were said to be infested with pirates, but Captain Lastic–who had never encountered any–did not believe a word of any tale of sea-raiders.

"Pirates! *Tonnerre d'Honfleur*, Lieutenant Mandibul!" Captain Lastic often said. "It's 50 years since the last one was hanged. Then again, if there were any left, I wouldn't be sorry to see a few!"

Alas, this wish was to be granted much sooner than the poor Captain imagined! That same night, profiting from a moonless sky, Malay canoes came alongside without the slightest noise or splashing sound alerting the sailors on *La Belle Léocadie*. Were the men on watch asleep, or lost in seductive memories of their recent voyage to Tahiti? At any rate, they did not wake up again once the Malays' daggers had done their work.

Still without making the slightest noise, the pirates overran the ship. Captain Lastic woke up, but only to find himself in the hands of the Malays, trussed up so tightly that he was unable to lift a finger. Lieutenant Mandibul, Saturnin Farandoul and the remainder of the 15-man crew were also tied up like parcels.

It was a sad moment.

The pirates came and went on the bridge. In the Captain's cabin, two or three chiefs with atrociously grim faces discussed what had to be done. Poor Captain Lastic, who had some slight acquaintance with the Malay language, was anxious to know whether the crew would be massacred immediately or on the following day, when the ship was brought to land. He understood enough to know that the Malays were steering the ship towards Bassilan, one of the Sulu Islands, which was only a few leagues distant.

At dawn, Bassilan came within view. The pirates, who were passable seamen, dropped anchor on a sandy sea-bed a few cables from a hazardous rocky coast. A colossal racket then rose up on the ship as 50 or so sinister-looking villains occupied themselves with unloading *La Belle Léocadie* and transferring their booty to the island.

The island's interior, thickly wooded and teeming with life, seemed very pleasant. Even so, Saturnin had no intention whatsoever of admiring the scenery; the pirates had deposited their prisoners on a tall rock, from which they could follow the plundering of the ship.

The Sun, rising above the horizon, reminded the corsairs that it was nearly time for breakfast. The fine wines of Captain

Lastic's store-room had already furnished the occasion with frequent libations; on their final trip, each pirate carried the greatest possible number of bottles, and the orgy began–much to Captain Lastic's distress.

"Let it go," said Saturnin Farandoul. "Perhaps it will be our salvation."

"*Tonnerre d'Honfleur*! It breaks my heart, all the same! Such excellent cognac!"

What rogues these pirates were! Beards of every color, eyebrows and noses of every possible shape! Frightful bandit faces tanned by the tropical Sun! And what walking arsenals! Pistols of every caliber and every kind in their belts–operated by flintlocks, matchlocks, firing-pins–and daggers of every dimension in their packs, some of them straight-bladed, others twisted like flames, some toothed like saws and nearly all of them poisoned. As they walked, these sea-rovers made a clanking noise that was exceedingly satisfying to their ears.

The three chiefs, naturally, possessed the most complicated and the most tortuous arsenals of all, and therefore cut the most rascally dash. By the same token, they had the right to the finest liqueurs of all, and did not stint themselves in the least.

It must be said that these sinister corsairs were known and famed throughout the Sunda Islands.[22] The first, the celebrated Bora-Bora, had exploited the troubled seas for many long years, ravaging the archipelagoes, seizing ships, massacring their crews and–the last and most important part of the operation–finding advantageous means of selling the produce of what he called his business, in Java, Borneo and Sumatra. The other two, Sibocco and Bumbaya, were his lieutenants; they had learned their trade in his school and knew no better way to balance their mercantile accounts than by cutting off the heads of tradesmen.

---

[22] The Sunda Islands–*Les îles de la Sonde* in French–constitute the archipelago whose largest elements are Sumatra and Java, now part of Indonesia.

79

Thirst satisfied gives rise to thoughts of food; soon Bora-Bora was hungry. The individual who seemed to be the robber-band's chief cook was given orders to prepare a meal. By way of hors-d'oeuvres, they began to make free with the provisions of *La Belle Léocadie*, while the cook busied himself with putting an enormous wild boar, killed that same morning by one of the Malays, on a roasting-spit.

The cook devoted five relatively tranquil minutes to this serious occupation, but became distracted thereafter, directing envious looks towards his 50 comrades–who, forming a great circle around the fire over which the boar was cooking, were avidly emptying Captain Lastic's beloved bottles. An idea sprang up in that cranium bronzed by the Pacific Sun; in order to have his share of the liquid nourishment, it was only necessary that he should be replaced in his kitchen by one of the prisoners. Taking up an immense cutlass, the cook made his way towards the mariners–who thought, seeing him approach, that their sacrificial hour had come.

With mighty kicks, the cook knocked several sailors aside in order to get to Saturnin Farandoul, whose bonds he cut before telling him what was required of him.

"By all means, with pleasure!" said our smiling hero–and the two men made their way back to the feast.

Everything was going well. The gaiety of the honorable assembly had reached its highest pitch. Two or three pirates had already been moved by the heat of debate inadvertently to bury their well-sharpened daggers in the bellies of their neighbors. Paying no heed to such mere bagatelles, the cook threw himself upon the bottles of spirits, determined to catch up with his fellows.

Standing before the fire, Farandoul took stock of the situation. The pirates had deposited their more cumbersome weapons–rifles, pistols and yataghans–some 20 meters away, along with numerous cartridge-pouches, powder-horns and boxes of bullets. That was all Farandoul required; he had his plan. He turned the boar on its spit, and then–pretending to need firewood–left the circle and made his way towards the pirates' weapons.

His companions followed his every move from a distance, believing that he had gone to seize as many sabers as he could and would make haste to cut their bonds.

Not at all: Saturnin Farandoul gathered wood and foliage, dexterously hid some cartridge-pouches and boxes of bullets among the leaves, and returned to the boar.

Not a single pirate had deigned to stir.

Saturnin had plenty of time to make the boar's guts into a magnificent infernal machine: the powder on a bed of dry leaves underneath, the bags of bullets on top, augmented by pebbles gathered from around the fire. A fuse taken from a firearm completed the equipment of the bomb.[23]

When everything was ready, Saturnin let the end of the fuse fall into the fire, blew on it to enliven the flame, and moved away from the group unhurriedly.

There was not long to wait.

The cook, realizing that his replacement was no longer to be seen, got up and brandished his *kris* at the boar; he was just

---

[23] The original *machine infernale* was a nail-bomb mounted on a cart, which was supposed to explode as a carriage carrying Napoléon Bonaparte (who was then the First Consul) passed by on the way to the Opera; the timing being slightly amiss, it only killed a number of innocent bystanders. The term "infernal machine" was applied thereafter to all kinds of life-threatening booby-trap, especially those involving explosives. The references to Farandoul's fashioning of the boar into a bomb-distributing *mitraille* (grape-shot) would also have reminded Robida's readers of Napoleon, whose rise to fame began when he dispersed a Parisian mob with a celebrated "whiff of grape-shot." As observed in the introduction, Robida never mentions Napoléon's name in the course of the narrative, but comparisons become irresistible when Farandoul eventually becomes a General and an Emperor.

bending over to ascertain the progress of the roast when a jet of flame shot out of the animal.

A frightful detonation rang out. The infernal machine had exploded.

No more boar, no more cook! The first was in shreds, the second had had his head blown off. Twenty pirates were writhing on the ground. The bullets and pebbles with which Farandoul had charged his Saint Barbara boar [24] had struck to the right and the left, as if they were a blast of grape-shot, smashing arms and legs, drilling holes in chests and bursting eyeballs in their sockets.

With lightning rapidity, Farandoul threw himself towards his companions, gathering up an armful of weapons as he went. With 15 thrusts of a dagger, he freed them from their bonds. In no time at all, they were armed and, under Farandoul's direction, they fell upon the terrified pirates before the brigands were able to collect themselves.

What a fine spectacle it was! Those who had been spared by the grape-shot, or who only had small pebbles embedded in their bodies, snatched up their famous blades and defended themselves like demons! But how could they resist brave mariners who had their revenge to take?

Within two minutes, 25 pirates were strewn about the sand, and the rest were fleeing into the island's interior like vultures scattered from their prey. Some 40 or 45 Malays were out of the fight, but the crew of *La Belle Léocadie* had, alas, to mourn the loss of their chief. The bold Captain Lastic, after

---

[24] The (fictitious) story of Saint Barbara–Sainte-Barbe in French–as preserved for the delectation of pious Frenchmen in Voragine's classic *Golden Legend*, claims that her father imprisoned her in a tower to preserve her virginity and then had her condemned to death when she became a Christian. He was subsequently struck by lightning, for which reason his daughter became the patron saint of those in danger of being abruptly struck dead, including miners and victims of artillery fire.

having personally brought down two Malays, had been run through by the pirate Bumbaya's poisoned kris! Captain Lastic managed one last "*Tonnerre d'Honfleur!*" as he gave up the ghost, while Saturnin perforated the hideous Bumbaya in his turn.

There was no time for Saturnin to give vent to his anguish; he had heard the pirate chief Bora-Bora complain about the lateness of a company of his followers, whose return he was expecting at any moment. About 15 corsairs had fled, Bora-Bora himself among them; they would be able to return in force to crush the mariners. Saturnin therefore made haste to re-embark in order to get away from the fatal island. All the weapons were gathered up; Captain Lastic's body was taken aboard the three-master, and the anchor was raised as soon as the pirates' boat had been scuttled.

Just in time! Hundreds of men were descending upon the beach, frantically hurling spears and firing rifles.

La Belle Léocadie sent forth a blast of grape-shot from its only cannon before her final departure.

As soon as they were at sea, the mariners rendered their final duty to poor Captain Lastic. His command should rightfully have reverted to Lieutenant Mandibul but the Lieutenant, overcome by emotion, declared that Saturnin Farandoul had displayed the very finest qualities during the affair and had saved all their lives. He thought that they could do no better than to appoint him their Captain—as for himself, he intended to continue as second-in-command, under the heroic Farandoul.

The crew applauded.

Farandoul was now Captain of *La Belle Léocadie*. Moreover, Captain Lastic, the three-master's owner, had made him his heir. Everything, therefore, worked out for the best; in honor of poor Lastic, a number of pirates who were found dead drunk in the steward's room were hanged.

The sea was calm; this time, the crew exercised the most extreme vigilance.

Still weeping for the poor Captain, Saturnin Farandoul remembered that at the end of the battle, he had seized the pirate chief Bora-Bora by the belt, and had been about to cleave his skull when the belt had broken, remaining in his hand while Bora-Bora fled. He had kept the belt without bothering to examine it, but he was now curious to do so, in company with Lieutenant Mandibul.

The pockets sewn into the belt's inner surface were stuffed with papers. Some seemed to be business documents covered with figures, statements of account and contracts; others seemed even more interesting to Captain Saturnin Farandoul. He studied them carefully and, thanks to his knowledge of the Malay language, he eventually understood that he had between his hands a genuine deed of incorporation, which established–under the trade name Bora-Bora & Co–a Company for the Skimming of the Sunda Islands. This company was financed by the Malay merchants of Borneo, charged with the disposal of goods and the investment of profits. All the documents were in order; Bora-Bora had a warrant. Saturnin Farandoul could read the details of operations recorded on a day-to-day basis, but the document which made him leap to his feet was a sort of current account containing a list of the receipts and savings of Bora-Bora & Co.

The total shown was 54 million "coins"–without specifying whether these were gold, silver or copper–and these savings were deposited in a bank in Borneo.

Farandoul assembled the crew of *La Belle Léocadie* and told them what the documents were. They all cheered enthusiastically. "Friends," he said, "these riches are ours, by right of conquest! Everyone shall have a share in the prize. Set sail for Borneo! But we'll have to keep a weather-eye open; Bora-Bora isn't dead, and he'll be looking to overtake us!"

III. Siege and blockade.
The heroic conduct of the tortoises of the Mysterious Island.
A terrible stew!

Sailing towards Borneo, *La Belle Léocadie* had no unfortunate encounters. She gave a wide berth to all the islands
and guarded against the approach of Malay canoes which appeared to be standing off from her in the channel between the
Bonggi islands and the north tip of Borneo.

As soon as the ship lay at anchor, Farandoul went ashore
with Lieutenant Mandibul, both of them heavily armed, and
made for the pirates' bank. Without offering any explanations,
Farandoul laid before the eyes of the crooked banker–a shifty-
looking individual–the deed of incorporation of Bora-Bora &
Co and the pass-book for the current account.

The banker went slightly pale, but did not manifest any
surprise.

"Have you the funds?" Farandoul demanded.

"No bank, however well fortified, ever has 54 million
coins in its coffers," the banker replied, evasively.

"I'll give you until tomorrow," Farandoul said.

"Impossible, sir! Besides, we must have the signature of
my friend Bora-Bora, the company's chief executive. He
should have told you that when he sent you to collect..."

"He didn't send us. We're the ones in control of the
business..."

"*Ventre de phoque*,[25] you'll settle up, you old villain!"
cried the conciliatory Mandibul.

"No signature, no money," declared the banker, flatly.

"In that case, we'll take it to court," Farandoul calmly
replied. And that same day, the suit was launched, under the

---

[25] *Ventre* is translatable as belly or (as in the previous chapter)
guts, but the literal meaning of *phoque* (seal) is irrelevant in
this particular phrase, where the word is employed purely for
its euphemistic phonetic implication. To translate the phrase
would, in consequence, obliterate its intended effect.

auspices of the Bornean authorities. Farandoul was worried. Evidently, Bora-Bora had warned the banker; perhaps he was in Borneo himself, lying in wait for an opportunity to get his hands on *La Belle Léocadie* again. They had to keep their eyes open, as Mandibul put it.

The *Léocadie*'s sailors, knowing that they had to watch over their fortune, were on their guard–but what could they do if they were attacked some day and overwhelmed by superior forces?

Farandoul understood that the case might drag on for a long time. Justice in the Sultanate of Borneo might perhaps be corrupted, the pirates having friends and accomplices–and who could tell whether the Sultan might not be glad to appropriate the cash-box himself, in order to settle the case?

He judged it politic to recruit to his interests a man who was all-powerful in the sultan's court. This person, for a modest commission of 20%, committed himself to watch over the case and to do everything that circumstances permitted to favor the interests of *La Belle Léocadie*. He made no secret of the fact that the thing might be long-drawn-out, and ended up by advising Farandoul to make himself scarce during the negotiations. Farandoul appreciated the soundness of this advice; after having given power of attorney to his agent, he set sail on the next clear night.

"Friends," Captain Farandoul said to his sailors, "we're taking a holiday; we'll come back again when the case has reached a successful conclusion."

Everyone applauded.

Captain Farandoul's intention was to leave those hostile latitudes and to sail via the sea of Java, the Banda Sea and the Torres Strait towards the isles of Polynesia. He thought of the isle where he had spent his infancy, and said to himself that since Providence had given him the leisure-time, he could not employ it better than by searching for his adoptive family.

The late lamented Captain Lastic had often told him that he had picked him up not far from the Tongan archipelago, and it was to that region that Farandoul intended to direct his research. He told himself that it was impossible that he would be unable to rediscover his island–in the absence of any other indicator his heart would serve as his compass.

In the meantime, a vigilant watch was kept–but there was no trace of pirates on the horizon.

When *La Belle Léocadie* had passed between the New Hebrides and the Solomon islands, and set a new heading due east, Farandoul, thinking that there was nothing more to fear, gave himself over entirely to his search. A course was set for every island sighted by the lookout, at least until it was found to be inhabited. Thus it was that, one day, *La Belle Léocadie* arrived at an island that was absolutely deserted, and not marked on the map. As with the Isle of Monkeys, its shores were defended by a barrier reef, but when that barrier was crossed the sea was absolutely calm, permitting the anchor to be lowered in perfect safety.

The rocky cliffs of the coastline were interrupted by beaches where the coconut-palms descended as far as the sands. Beyond the palms were fleecy hills covered with the most luxurious vegetation. An immense virginal forest covered the island as far as the eye could see, save for the upper slopes of a volcanic peak, which projected 250 meters above sea-level. A narrow river snaked through the woods, its limpid and murmurous waters gushing out into the ocean, across a beach of the finest sand. All around the island, within a few meters of the shore, the terrain became precipitate, as if the isle itself were merely the summit of a mountain emerging from the waves.

The steepness of the sea-bed allowed *La Belle Léocadie* to drop anchor very close to shore. It also gave Farandoul the idea of profiting from the tranquil harbor and the resources that the hospitable coast was sure to furnish in order to make a few necessary repairs to the three-master.

The ship was solidly established on the beach, and the caulkers and carpenters set to work under the direction of Lieutenant Mandibul. Saturnin Farandoul and the rest of the crew devoted themselves to the exploration of the island. Although Saturnin had observed that its flora was very similar to that of the Isle of Monkeys, he had quickly recognized that it could not be the place where he had spent his infancy. Although there were certain points of resemblance in its general configuration, as seen from a distance, the vague similarities disappeared as soon as they passed through the rocks.

The island seemed to be uninhabited; no tribes of monkeys haunted the forest. Other animals–including kangaroos and opossums–hopped away into the undergrowth, and innumerable tortoises of giant proportions were walking slowly along the river banks. These tortoises had, over time, hollowed out veritable pathways between the mountain and the coast.

While Farandoul was pleased to devote himself to the business of exploration, the sailors amused themselves by playing every possible trick on the poor tortoises, except for that of making a succulent daily soup. When they surprised the tortoises on the bank, the sailors, passing sticks under their bellies, turned them on their backs and left them there in distress, kicking their legs in a comical fashion.

This pleasantry had the result of reducing the entire crew to tears of laughter. Able-Seaman Kirkson, a pure-blooded Englishman with a passion for racing, who did not often have the chance to indulge his passion while on ocean voyages, took the opportunity to improvise tortoise races. He required no more, in order to organize derbies of this new kind, than to happen upon a few tortoises travelling together. The chelonians were brought into line by force of arms, sailors leapt upon their carapaces at a prearranged signal, and the race was on. Equilibrium was difficult to maintain; some of the makeshift jockeys fell off, while others collapsed into a sitting position on animals which retracted their heads in fear. The man who remained standing longest won, and pocketed the bets.

On the slope of the mountain, Captain Farandoul had discovered the entrance to a spacious grotto, whose tunnels and ramifications could only be explored with torches. On that side, the mountain was quite steep. The cave's broad mouth, overlooking the blue of the sea, opened on to a sort of platform at the summit of a crag looming over a damp ravine, where hundreds of tortoises were constantly crowding.

We shall see how useful this discovery was to the brave mariners in the midst of the complications in which they were soon to be embroiled!

The repairs to *La Belle Léocadie* had been effectively carried out, and the handsome three-master was as good as new, ready to put out to sea again. The sailors, after a final stroll in the forest, were relaxing on the grassy slopes of a hillock in the lowest foothills of the central peak, some distance away from the beach where *La Belle Léocadie* still rested on her keel.

Captain Farandoul, lost in thought, had wandered up to the crest of the hill, from which the entire outline of the coast, with its sharp promontories and deep creeks, could be seen. He had been standing at the summit for several minutes staring into space when he suddenly lowered his gaze towards the coast.

Farandoul went pale. He thought he was dreaming–but no! He rubbed his eyes and let out an exclamation. A veritable tide of Malay canoes was strewn upon the sea, as rapid and as sinister as a flock of vultures. More were appearing by the minute, doubling one of the island's capes some 1500 meters from the hill on which Farandoul stood.

In response to the Captain's cry, the sailors had hastened to their feet and were looking at the innumerable canoes with stupefaction. The vessels were becoming more numerous with every passing moment, seemingly following the strategy of hugging the coast, so that they would have the least possible exposure to the open sea.

"It's Bora-Bora, beyond the shadow of a doubt!" Farandoul said, in the end. Turning to his sailors, he cried: "Forward! To *La Belle Léocadie*! We must warn our friends!"

The entire company filed into the forest in the direction of the ship. Thoughts crowded hurriedly into Farandoul's mind. The impossibility of saving *La Belle Léocadie* seemed obvious. At sea, it would have been possible to make a fight of it; run aground as she was, though, she could not even serve as a citadel for the mariners.

"The cave will be our salvation!" Farandoul said, as he ran. "We'll take all the weapons from *La Belle Léocadie* and take refuge there."

Breathlessly, they came in sight of the ship. Lieutenant Mandibul and his men were asleep in the shade, but they leapt to their feet when they heard their companions running towards them.

"To arms!" said Farandoul. "We're under attack–the pirates are here! Grab everything you can carry and climb up to the cave."

"*Ventre de phoque*! But can't we fight here?"

"Impossible, Lieutenant. There are at least 600 of them! They'll be here within the hour–we haven't time..."

Everyone went to work without further explanation. Everything that it was possible to carry–weapons, powder, camping equipment–was taken up. The first canoes were rounding the point of the little bay when Farandoul left the ship. The pirates shouted excitedly at the sight of the three-master, and hastened their progress.

"Quickly!" said Farandoul. "Let's get ready for them."

The sailors hurriedly deposited everything that they had saved within the cave. Standing on the little platform, they shook their fists at the pirates who were visible on the shore, swarming like ants around *La Belle Léocadie*.

"No time to lose, lads," Farandoul shouted. "Let's prepare our defenses."

We have observed that the grotto pierced the mountain above a rather steep ravine. Scaling the slope would be difficult, in the face of several carefully disposed carbines, but to repel the assailants it was necessary to establish some cover on the platform–the weak point of their fortress. Farandoul looked around urgently, and immediately caught sight of a few blocks of stone which might be used to form a parapet. Alas, he was soon convinced of the impossibility of extracting the smallest of them without long hard labor, which would not want for interruption by the corsairs.

What was he to do? Farandoul, leaning over the ravine full of tortoises, had a flash of inspiration. The tortoises could be used as a means of fortification.

Two men descended into the ravine. As they approached, the tortoises retreated into their shells and did not budge. The two mariners rapidly passed ropes, which had been thrown down from above, beneath the bellies of the largest tortoise, making a seaman's knot to prevent the rope from slipping.

"Pull!"

In response to this signal, vigorous arms lifted up the poor tortoise, which was terrified to find itself borne aloft. Once arrived at the top, it was laid on its back, and the rope was thrown back down to the men in the ravine.

Thirty tortoises were sent up in succession and laid on their backs, placed one atop another with an artistry proving that Farandoul possessed a genius for fortification. To prevent the rampart from collapsing, a number of sturdy stakes were wedged into the rock, to which ropes were attached before being tightly knotted around each carapace.

The two men in the ravine had scarcely climbed up again when the pirates made their move. A hundred men set off together to climb the mountain.

"Let them get as far as the ravine," Farandoul said, "and don't fire unless you're sure of your shot."

The gaps between the tortoises formed natural loopholes, through which the men of *La Belle Léocadie*, with rifles in hand, watched the pirates advancing.

"*Bigre de bagasse!*" [26] murmured the southerner Tournesol, a seaman first-class. "There's every possible color there."

---

[26] *Bigre* has no literal meaning, being everywhere employed in exactly the same spirit as the final term in *Ventre de phoque!* *Bagasse* is a colloquial term for a sugar cane, here employed for its phallic symbolism. When modern English speakers who utter obscenities in inappropriate circumstances excuse them-

Indeed, yellow men from Formosa were discernible among the copper-colored Malays, along with black dayaks from Borneo and various half-breeds without any distinguishable nationality. Their armaments were just as varied; there were long Muslim rifles, Portuguese blunderbusses, spears, bows and pistols in addition to the familiar arsenal of daggers and Malay *krises*.

Lieutenant Mandibul nudged Farandoul's elbow. "Look, Captain! There's that beggar Bora-Bora. I recognize his big red turban."

"It's him all right," Farandoul replied. "The brigand's keeping out of the way, directing the attack without exposing himself."

After a pause of several minutes, Farandoul called his men to attention. "Here they come!"

The pirates had climbed to within 30 meters, quite bemused not to have been greeted with rifle-fire. Thinking, in consequence, that the mariners had not been able to carry their weapons with them, they were grouping to mount an assault, howling horribly.

"Fire!" cried Farandoul.

Fifteen rifle-shots were discharged. It was like a broadside; a terrible collapsed mass rolled down the mountainside, the dead and the wounded carrying those who had not been

---

selves by saying "Pardon my French!" they usually have no idea how the convention originated, but anyone with a little imagination can see how the two most common English obscenities might be regarded, mischievously, as mispronunciations of *phoque* and *bigre*–and the third as a mispronunciation of *conte* (tale)–each of them substituting a guttural Anglo-Saxon version of the vowel "u" for more refined French vowel sounds. (Ever since the Norman conquest of 1066, Englishmen descended from Anglo-Saxon stock have regarded French, somewhat resentfully, as an essentially aristocratic language.)

wounded along with them. The howling redoubled, this time caused by pain and fear.

Bora-Bora, leaping about like a demon, rallied his men behind a clump of trees.

"While we have a moment's respite," Farandoul said, "we have to think about food. We can't eat our rampart, so we must have more tortoises for our larder, and sufficient quantities of grass to nourish them. Someone has to go back down into the ravine to get tortoises and hoist them up at the least exposed spot, while four of our best shots provide them with covering fire."

The pirates perceived this maneuver from a distance, and a few moved to prevent it. A few well-directed bullets caused them to make their way back to those who had not been felled.

The tortoise-hoisting operation worked out marvelously. Some 30 tortoises were stacked up in the cave in less than an hour, and the men climbed back up without any accident befalling them.

Meanwhile, the pirates, huddling in the shelter of a clump of trees, seemed to be preparing themselves for a new and more vigorous attack. In the distance, more could be seen dragging their canoes aground to either side of *La Belle Léocadie*. Sturdier Malay boats were mingled with them closer to the shore–and all the crews, as soon as they were disembarked, came to swell the ranks of Bora-Bora's army, brandishing their weapons.

It was indeed a veritable army, which Farandoul estimated at 700 or 800 men. Bora-Bora seemed determined to capture the sailors' citadel no matter what the cost. While he formed his best men–the Malays–into an assault column, he posted others as snipers to harass the besieged men from every side. The Dayaks, armed with ironwood bows, were creeping among the rocks in search of advantageous positions, while other pirates, the Formosans, were opening fire from such a long range that the mariners judged it useless to respond.

The whistling bullets struck the carapaces with dry clicks, at which the armored heads of the tortoises emerged momentarily before immediately withdrawing–especially when a mariner, lurking behind his loophole, found a good opportunity to direct a bullet at some overly audacious Dayak. The poor tortoises, terrified by these flashes of fire and thunderous detonations, attempted to turn somersaults, which made the rampart ripple with movement.

Farandoul told his men to concentrate their fire on those Dayaks whose upward-directed arrows might fall within the citadel; not one of these savages came close enough to the cave to reach its defenders.

Suddenly, a howl let loose by 600 voices burst forth at the foot of the mountain. Bora-Bora was launching the bulk of his forces upon the blockade.

Six hundred demons climbed the escarpment with a resolution that testified to their determination to crush and finish off the 15 besieged men by sheer weight of numbers.

"Save your ammunition, and don't fire unless the shot's certain," said Farandoul, mopping sweat from his brow.

More than 50 Malays had already rolled to the bottom of the slope, the dead and wounded making a ladder of sorts for the others. The besieged men soon saw them a few meters from the platform: hideous, covered in blood, with rifles in their hands and daggers in their teeth.

"*Bigre de bagasse*, this is getting worse!" cried Tournesol, "Step on up, though–we'll lay a few more carcasses down before they get past!"

"*Ventre de phoque!*" Mandibul added. "I won't go to pieces before that beggar Bora-Bora!"

The howls of the corsairs were redoubled. They believed that their victory was certain. The citadel was, in fact, in serious danger–a few more minutes, and they would reach the platform. Excited by the hope of carnage, they pressed forward in ever greater numbers.

"Keep firing! Watch out!" Farandoul commanded, having observed the progress of the attackers for some minutes without shooting. Then, taking his knife, he quickly cut through several ropes.

"Do as I do, shipmates! All together... push hard!" Matching actions to his words, he set his rifle down and threw himself against the rank of tortoises that formed the crown of the rampart. All those comprising it were dislodged.

The entire tier collapsed; ten tortoises, each weighing at least a hundred kilograms, rolled down on to the pirates, breaking heads and ribs and scouring the wall of the crag within the blink of an eye.

Before those who had not been overtaken had time to get out of the way, the tortoises comprising the second tier descended upon them like an avalanche, pulverizing everything in their path and rebounding from the rocks to shatter in the midst of the panic-stricken throng.

The citadel had been saved once again. The pirates were fleeing from the accursed mountain, paying no heed to the exhortations of a few chiefs who were trying to rally them.

Losing no time, Farandoul had the rampart rebuilt, using the tortoises placed in reserve.

A number of men went back down into the ravine, some to recover as many munitions as possible from dead pirates and others to capture more tortoises. Those pirates who had remained in the ravine, understanding that the place was not safe, had run away as quickly as they could, far from the scene of carnage. There was only time for a handful to return to hinder the operation.

"Now, shipmates, there's only one thing I'm afraid of," Farandoul said to his men, "and that's Bora-Bora turning the siege into a blockade."

"The brigand kept out of range," Mandibul complained. "I would have been so glad to avenge poor Captain Lastic! Yes, the scoundrel stayed back; a man who has come to possess 54 million gold, silver or copper coins looks after his skin! And that makes 54 million reasons why he's determined to have ours, whatever the cost. I don't believe our troubles are over yet."

"In the meantime, it's nearly supper-time," Farandoul replied. "It's time to sacrifice one of our tortoises–we've certainly earned some turtle soup."

The evening and the night passed without incident. Farandoul lay awake for half an hour, his insomnia caused by disquiet.

He told himself that a blockade could have the most disastrous consequences for *La Belle Léocadie*, which he deemed to be very nearly lost, and particularly for her crew. The pirates would be able to find abundant food on the island, while his own men would be dependent on the meager provisions brought from the ship and the tortoises in the rampart.

"It's very hard," said Lieutenant Mandibul, who was also troubled. "It's very hard for besieged men to have to eat their fortifications!"

On the following day, the Malays could be seen making an encampment on the beach. This testified clearly to fact that they had no thought of leaving. In the afternoon, a band of fifty men left the camp and established themselves in the woods from which the attack columns had been sent.

A blockade was being organized.

Nothing changed on either side for several days. A stream of water, which ran through the grotto and exited into a fissure leading down to the tortoises' ravine, was adequate to the needs of the besieged men, but they took care every morning to bring some grass to the tortoises of the rampart, to keep them alive and in good health.

Farandoul began to find the time weighing heavily and searched for a means of hurrying matters along. In the hope of making some advantageous discovery, he and Lieutenant Mandibul followed each of the tunnels leading from the cave to its very end.

These ramifications extended deep into the mountain, but the corridors usually ended abruptly in solid walls. One of the narrow fissures, however, took them a long way away from their companions.

"*Ventre de phoque*, what can we do?" said Mandibul.

"Ah, if I had my monkeys, the pirates wouldn't hold on for long!" Farandoul replied.

"I can save you," said a firm voice, which suddenly emerged from the depths of the tunnel.

Farandoul and Mandibul drew their revolvers.

"Fear not, I'm a friend," the voice added. To the great astonishment of the two mariners, an unknown man came towards them. "Don't be astonished, and don't ask me any questions–just listen to me," he said. "I'm a European like you, and I'll save you."

The three men squatted down on the rocks. The conversation lasted a long time. Since it was agreed between them that the identity of the unknown man would not be revealed to the sailors of *La Belle Léocadie* as yet, we shall keep the secret from our readers until the next chapter.

Mandibul returned from the cave alone. He contented himself with saying that the Captain had found a means of saving everyone, that he had gone to put his plan into action, and that all he had asked of the sailors was to wait patiently without risking any useless combat. Any attack that occurred would have to be forcefully repulsed; the pirates must be kept back at all costs.

Farandoul was absent for two weeks–two weeks during which the corsairs, without renewing their assault, sought to inconvenience the crew of *La Belle Léocadie* by every available means. Lieutenant Mandibul never stopped fuming with rage throughout the fortnight; as for the sailors, they dreamed of nothing but sorties and hand-to-hand combat.

Soon, the situation, already critical, became terrible. The infernal Bora-Bora had a plan of his own, and we shall see how it put the mariners into a lamentable position.

One morning, 200 pirates scaled the far side of the mountain, and established themselves directly above the platform, at the point of origin of the stream that descended into the cave via fissures in the rock. The wretches had brought their cooking-pots and abundant supplies of dry wood. Twelve

97

fires were lit, on which 12 large cooking-pots were set, filled to the brim with water from the spring.

"*Ventre de phoque*, what diabolical cookery are these brigands up to?" grumbled Lieutenant Mandibul.

The answer was not long in coming

Suddenly, a flood of boiling water fell upon the unhappy tortoises in the rampart, and clouds of hot vapor invaded the grotto. The wretches, being unable to bring active force to bear on the bastion of tortoises, sought to defeat it by slow cooking! All through the day, the cooking-pots were continuously at work; the poor tortoises expired in the terrible boiling flood [27] that fell incessantly upon their backs. Mandibul was seething!

There was nothing to be done! That evening, six tortoises having been cooked, the mariners cut their losses by eating them for supper; six replacements were installed under cover of darkness. It was scarcely worth the trouble. Eight more death certificates were issued the following day: eight boiled tortoises to be put on the menu.

The bastion lasted eight days, after which it was comprised of nothing but empty and broken carapaces.

The crewmen of *La Belle Léocadie* were visibly fatter, but thirst began to make itself felt, for the pirates had found a

---

[27] The word I have translated here as "boiling flood" is *bouillon*, which I translated as "stew" in the chapter heading. The word has several other meanings, including–in such phrases as *avaler un bouillon* and *boire un bouillon*–one very similar to that signified by the English expression "to land in the soup," i.e., to come to grief. The puns continue to pile up as Mandibul "seethes" and the crew find themselves "in hot water." Taken in association with earlier references to "turtle soup" (a phrase rendered, as is customary in France, in mock-English), there is a curiously convoluted irony in the sad fate of the "heroic tortoises," which is itself part of a flamboyantly absurd pattern in Farandoul's exploitative relationship with the animal world.

means to heat the spring itself, so the mariners were really in hot water. This was the state of things when, one night, Lieutenant Mandibul, returned from the depths of the tunnel within the cave, gathered his men together and told them to make ready for a sortie the following day.

"Is there news then, Lieutenant?" asked Seaman Tournesol.

"Goodbye hot water–the Captain's back," Mandibul replied. "*Ventre de phoque*, we're going to fight! Tomorrow, when the first rifle-shot sounds on the beach, we'll fall upon the beggars down below!"

The night seemed endless to the bold sailors, weary of the vast soup of tortoises which Bora-Bora–in return for the grapeshot-filled boar of Bassilon–had been serving them for more than a week. At dawn, though, Mandibul ordered them to go down into the ravine–where they all waited for his signal, rifles in hand.

IV. Captain Nemo's divers.
Lieutenant Mandibul is swallowed by an oyster.
Love in a diving-suit.

Let us take ourselves off to the pirates' camp, where the last vicissitudes of the drama will unfold. The wretches are grouped on the beach, around the handful of tents reserved for the principal chiefs. Some are asleep on the grass, wrapped in blankets, others around a few fires–whose last logs, almost burned-out, occasionally hurl a few sparks and spirals of blue smoke into the still-starry sky.

Overturned canoes and felled trees form the camp's only entrenchments.

Bora-Bora wakes up and shakes his fist at the mountain.

"If they haven't finished eating their tortoises," he says to himself, "we can't risk an attack. I'll send a few scouts their way." And Bora-Bora, prodding a few of his snoring companions with his foot, thrusts his arsenal into his belt.

He has scarcely finished when a rifle shot rings out, no more than 20 paces distant! Savage cries burst forth, and before the bewildered pirates have had time to leap upon their weapons, a hundred black shadows have jumped over the feeble ramparts of the camp and are flinging themselves upon them!

The tents are beaten down beneath the feet of combatants as a frightful confusion breaks out in the half-light of dawn. The attackers have the advantage, and pirate corpses are soon strewn across the ground. It is as if some infernal vortex were whirling around, crushing everything in its path...

Bora-Bora has drawn his pistols, but he does not know which way to shoot. Suddenly, he starts in alarm. These new enemies, worse than men, are sturdy monkeys armed with stout clubs!

The whirlwind of four-armed creatures has already pulverized half the pirate band; the remainder are trying to flee, rolling with the blows of the terrible clubs.

A strange thing! A man–is it really a man?–is directing this troop of monkeys; he mingles human words of command with guttural cries that make the monkeys jump.

Bora-Bora thinks he must be dreaming, but by the flash of two pistol-shots, he recognizes Saturnin Farandoul! After that, he has but one thought–to rally his men and re-embark.

A fierce fusillade erupts from the side of the mountain now, and the pirates who were blockading the mariners beat their own retreat towards the sea. Bora-Bora and 30 of his men who have escaped the carnage make for the boats; 50 more are there, making haste to put the boats into the water.

Daylight has come. The Sun illuminates the beach, where Bora-Bora's adversaries are now clearly visible. The pirates watch in terror as the mariners of La Belle Léocadie and Farandoul's terrible monkeys hurtle upon them.

"Put to sea!" cries Bora-Bora.

A new prodigy, even more inexplicable! Fifteen fantastic creatures suddenly emerge from the bosom of the sea! The pirates' eyes grow wide in horror. Each of these bipeds, clad

in a thick pelt, has an absolutely spherical iron head with neither mouth nor nose, within whose face a single vast yellow
eye is staring! A sort of pipe emerges from the head, connected to a sack attached to the back.

What can these creatures emerging from the waves possibly be? Bora-Bora has no time to ask himself; these fish-men
have iron hatchets fixed at the ends of their solid arms, and
they are falling upon the pirates, who are still harassed from
behind by the monkeys.

"Onwards, *La Belle Léocadie*! Onwards, monkeys!"
cries Farandoul–and, with one blow of a club that he wields
with the same dexterity as the monkeys, he lays Bora-Bora flat
out beside his canoe.

The fight did not last long.

Those whom the monkeys' clubs or the mariners' carbines had been unable to reach fell beneath the hatchets of the
fantastic creatures who had emerged from the bosom of the
sea, as if born therefrom.

We shall make haste to explain these facts to the reader.

The man who popped up providentially in the grotto was none other than the celebrated Captain Nemo, who is so well-known to the readers of Jules Verne–which is to say, everyone in the world–that we can dispense with his description. The island where *La Belle Léocadie* had put in for repairs was none other than the Mysterious Island, and it was in the bowels of its mountain-citadel that the secret port of Captain Nemo's magnificent submarine the *Nautilus* was hidden.

Captain Nemo, having heard Farandoul speak of the Isle of Monkeys, had revealed to him that there was an island 150 leagues to the east inhabited solely by numerous tribes of these animals. The description of the island that he gave to Farandoul settled all further doubts. "Let's go there in my *Nautilus*," Captain Nemo had added. "If you are recognized, and can convince a troop of your old friends to come to the aid of *La Belle Léocadie*, it will be possible to do battle."

It had all worked out very well. Farandoul had found his family again, his foster-brothers having grown up into magnificently sturdy lads. He had had no trouble recruiting 100 of his old comrades of the forest, and we have seen how enthusiastically they fell upon the pirates.

As for the fantastic creatures with iron heads, that was a company of divers provided by the crew of the *Nautilus*. The divers too had done marvelously well!

The different units of the little army, having come together on the beach, were introduced to one another, that formality having been impracticable during the heat of battle.

The sailors and the monkeys looked at one another with mutual astonishment, but what intrigued the brave monkeys most of all was the men with iron heads: the divers from the *Nautilus*. Where could these bizarre creatures with round heads, and tails attached thereto, possibly have come from? Were they another new race of men? It overturned all their notions of natural history, which had already been disturbed by the reappearance on their isle of their friend Farandoul, accompanied by beings of a similar kind.

Farandoul was surrounded by his family, his foster-father and his five brothers enfolding him in their arms. What joy! What a picture! The other monkeys crowded around them, happy to stare at the little handicapped monkey with whom they had all played when they were young! It was evident that they no longer considered him as having a deplorable infirmity, having seen, by courtesy of he mariners of the *Nautilus*, that all the members of his race were in the same condition.

Farandoul and Captain Nemo wanted to celebrate their victory with a huge banquet. As soon as the beach had been cleared, the feast was organized. Forty monkeys went forth in search of coconuts, bananas and other vegetables. The cooks from the *Nautilus* and *La Belle Léocadie* roasted some opossums, prepared numerous tortoises–less heroic than those of the rampart but just as succulent–with various sauces, and the tablecloths were soon set out on planks extended on the grass.

Farandoul, his brothers and his foster-father took their places at the head table, along with Captain Nemo, Lieutenant Mandibul and the leader of the divers. The monkeys and the mariners were grouped around the other tables. It was noticeable that every movement of the divers was observed with trepidation by the monkeys, who asked themselves how these creatures with iron heads devoid of any opening were able to eat. When they saw the divers divest themselves of their apparatus, they burst out laughing. The problem was solved—these unknown bipeds were part of the Farandoulian race!

The meal was most enjoyable. The monkeys, of course, did not want to partake of anything but fruit, but they consented to empty a few bottles of champagne furnished by the excellent Captain Nemo. A few, as might be expected, became a little light-headed—but on such a great day, who could blame them?

A big conference was held afterwards, in which a solemn vote of thanks was addressed to Captain Nemo. Then it was agreed that the pirates' canoes and boats should be carefully hidden in a creek identified by the good Captain. He advised that they should await the result of their legal action before showing themselves in Borneo.

Farandoul, always eager for action, resolved to depart no later than the following day in *La Belle Léocadie*, along with the biggest of the Malay boats, in order to take the monkeys home.

As the Sun rose the next day, the two ships made ready to sail. The moment of farewell drew near. Captain Nemo, who held Farandoul in singularly high esteem, came to shake him by the hand one last time, and Farandoul was obliged to accept six superb Denayrousse diving-suits as a souvenir.[28]

---

[28] Auguste Denayrousse was an associate of the French pioneer of diving-suit design Benoit Rouquayrol; their work attracted little attention until Jules Verne popularized it in *Vingt mille lieues sous les mers*, where Robida undoubtedly found the name.

They promised to meet up again as often as possible, then went their separate ways, after a dozen muskets had fired a salvo in honor of the generous Captain Nemo.

The voyage was a happy one. The three-master sailed in convoy with the pirates' boat, crewed by two men from *La Belle Léocadie* and 30 monkeys, who showed every indication of becoming excellent mariners. They reached the Isle of Monkeys in six days, where their arrival–signalled in advance by lookouts–caused such a commotion that the entire population, save for the sick, thronged the shore while the long-boats came ashore with the monkeys, proud of their campaign.

We shall not undertake to recount every detail of the warm reception given to *La Belle Léocadie*, nor of the celebrations that followed. At any rate, Farandoul, possessed by an all-consuming restlessness, soon announced his intention to return to sea. The pirates' boat was left to the monkeys, with two men to complete their naval education, and *La Belle Léocadie* resumed its course through the archipelagoes.

Farandoul was avid to devote himself to serious submarine exploration, in order to profit from the diving-suits so generously donated by Captain Nemo. He, Lieutenant Mandibul and four sailors soon became used to living and moving in the great depths, in the world of gigantic submarine forests inhabited by oceanic monsters. It was there that Saturnin Farandoul developed the instincts of a hunter, which he had not previously had time to cultivate.

Armed to the teeth, with hatchets in hand and two pistols operated by compressed air in their belts, along with sharp knives, the mariners threw themselves upon the slimy rocks and ventured into caverns inhabited by monsters unknown to man, which only the most deranged imagination could have dreamed up: six-meter-long lobsters, sea-crocodiles, torpedo-squids, crabs with a thousand feet, sea serpents, finned elephants, giant oysters and so on.

They had some terrible fights with these hideous animals. One such encounter was nearly fatal to Lieutenant Mandibul. The mariners were about to put to death a 15-meter serpent, which they had taken by surprise while it was eating a sea-crocodile–whose tail still protruded from its mouth–but which was still able to defend itself. Their attention was suddenly caught by the entry on to the scene of a strange creature. It was a gigantic oyster three meters in diameter, hugely rounded, running at a trot on six slender feet. Its half-open shell allowed two round, staring eyes to be seen, in which the greatest ferocity could be read.

"*Ventre de phoque!*" murmured Lieutenant Mandibul. "If there's a pearl in that oyster, my fortune's made!" After marching up to the oyster, he seized it by the upper shell and plunged his arm into the slit, with a dagger in his hand.

Horror! The oyster opened much wider, and swallowed Lieutenant Mandibul in a single gulp.

Fortunately, Saturnin Farandoul had seen everything. With the four sailors he ran towards the oyster, which had paused and seemed to be savoring poor Mandibul voluptuously. A sort of internal hullabaloo was, however, audible when they put their ears to the shell.

"He's still alive!" Farandoul cried. "To work, my friends!"

Hatchet-blows rained like hailstones upon the shell of the oyster, which defended itself feebly with its feet. The monster soon had to open up slightly, in order to breathe, and a few stifled words emerged from its interior. It was Mandibul, shouting: "Help me! I've got the pearl!"

Farandoul attacked the oyster at the hinge, causing the upper shell to jerk spasmodically. They forced it open with their arms, and the interior of the ferocious animal appeared at last. Lieutenant Mandibul, who was in a sorry state, was quickly lifted clear, while the oyster was finished off with pistol-shots.

Lieutenant Mandibul had secured a pearl as big as his head! In the aftermath of this adventure, though, he had to take to his bed for several days–which annoyed him greatly.

La Belle Léocadie returned through the Torres Strait and found herself once again approaching the Sunda islands.

"*Ventre de phoque!*" Lieutenant Mandibul grumbled from his sick-bed, "I once dropped a cherished pipe into the water in these parts–perhaps I can retrieve it by means of our diving-suits!"

The three-master made its way through the shallow waters around the Sunda Islands, not far from the island of Timor. Saturnin, who had suddenly become fond of solitary submarine excursions, would not consent to leave this dangerous region.

According to the maps, half of the island of Timor belonged to the Dutch, the masters of the archipelago, and the other half to the Portuguese–which is to say that both nations had a few trading-posts on its shores. In reality, the whole island, land and population alike, belonged to the Rajah, the aged and ferocious Ra-Tafia: an excessively absolute monarch who, in return for a few concessions, permitted the Dutch and the Portuguese to undertake commerce at various points on the coast.

Ra-Tafia, an old white-beard Malay, who had been a great lover of piracy in his youth, now spent his life secluded in his palace with his wives and his bottles of liqueur. His people accused him of favoring the Dutch at the expense of the Portuguese, in recognition of the tribute of curaçao paid by the Batavian government. We shall not allow ourselves to indulge in political criticism; after all, a monarch may have his preferences, and his tastes are not under his command.

The old Rajah Ra-Tafia had but one daughter, the young and beautiful Mysora, a dove hatched in a vulture's nest. Mysora was the daughter of a Frenchwoman carried off by Ra-Tafia during one of his expeditions to the Indian Ocean. Ra-Tafia had still had a heart in those days, and, that heart having quickened its beat, the poor little Frenchwoman had been spared. The slave soon became the Queen of Timor.

If we want to meet the Rajah's daughter, Mysora, we have only to go down one of the dark footpaths that lead from his palace to the sea-shore; we must, however, beware of letting ourselves be seen by the ferocious Malays who watch over every pathway with spears in their hands. These sentries protect the part of the shore where Mysora and her maids of honor take their daily bath from all indiscreet eyes. Sheer rocks covered with lianas shelter a tranquil little bay, where the young girls frolic on the sand. Such merry games in the clear water! Such bursts of laughter! Such joyful swimming-parties! Mysora is distinguished from the young Malays by the paleness of her skin, the long black hair cascading to her shoulders and her modest dress.

All of a sudden, a sharp cry raised by the 15 young girls causes Mysora to lift her head. A fantastic apparition in thrusting up from the foam of the sea: a man-fish with an iron head, who tries to reassure the bathers with benevolent gestures. To no avail–they all hasten out of the water with cries of terror. They flee into the rocks without even gathering up their clothes. Mysora alone, sitting on a spur of rock that forms a sort of islet, has been unable to flee.

The apparition came closer.

"Fear not, O Queen of Timor!" said a voice that we would have recognized as that of our friend Farandoul.

"Who are you?" stammered the beautiful Mysora.

"O Mysora," Farandoul replied, "I am he who burns for you with a love that all the waters of the Ocean are insufficient to extinguish!"

The confused young woman covered her face with her hands.

"O flower of the tropics," Farandoul went on, "I have known you for a week, I see you every day like a Malay siren, playing among the foamy waves of the fortunate Ocean!"

"O Monsieur!" said Mysora, becoming even more confused.

"Be reassured, queen of my soul–it was only from a distance, while hiding myself beneath the waves, that I dared to lift my eyes towards you! Today, for the first time, I have passed through the girdle of reefs that protect this inlet. O Mysora! I am the Captain of that three-master which you saw eight hours ago cruising off Timor. For eight hours, my heart has plunged fully-clad into the waters of passion–and that heart, which has never quickened its beat for any other, is ready to lower its colors before you!"

As he spoke these words, Farandoul knelt down and lowered the head of his diving-suit towards her hand, which Mysora allowed him to take. The poor girl understood that her own young heart, full of emotion, had begun to beat in a different way.

"O Captain," she said, finally, "make haste to depart; my followers, by fleeing, must have raised the alarm among the servants of my father, the terrible Ra-Tafia, Rajah of Timor! He will come to kill you before my very eyes."

"So be it! Death will be sweet if the heart of Mysora is averse to me! If I must never see you again, they shall kill me!"

"Don't say that, Captain! See how troubled I am by emotion, and take pity on me! Go... and come back when night falls on the shore..."

Shouting could be heard in the rocks; the Malays were coming at a run.

Farandoul lifted Mysora's hand passionately to his iron lips, and vanished beneath the waves.

The appearance of a sea-monster totally unknown in the archipelago caused a good deal of talk in Timor; the Malays did not dare to venture out to sea for a fortnight. Many would not even go down to the shore, and Mysora's followers gave up their sea-bathing.

That same evening, however, Mysora was running over the deserted beach; she had seen such determination in the Captain that she feared some imprudence on his part.

Farandoul was there. He had brought a second diving-suit, which Mysora put on, in order to follow the adventurous Farandoul into regions where they would be in no danger of any surprise.

Mysora felt herself subjugated, little by little. The poor girl's heartbeat quickened until it was overwhelmed by an immense and profound invasion of love.

What delectable moments! The hours fled by during this submarine conversation, whose purest poetry refreshed them both. The two young people, sitting one beside the other hand-in-hand, seemed lost in the azure realms of a dream. Time no longer existed while their two souls melted in the ardent light of love. Farandoul had taken the precaution of bringing a pocket telephone so that their conversation, conducted at a depth of seven or eight meters, would not require excessive vocal effort.[29]

In the end, it was necessary for them to separate. Mysora left her diving-suit in a hollow, hidden beneath the hectic vegetation hanging down the cliff. She promised to return in daylight on the following day, and to descend in her diving-suit to the bottom of the bay.

Farandoul had proposed to Mysora that he should ask her father for her hand in marriage. He spoke of arriving in great pomp, at the head of his crew, to present his request to Ra-Tafia, but Mysora had put him off the plan. Knowing her father well, she thought that the old Rajah, infatuated with the nobility and antiquity of his race–whose tradition of piracy had been handed down from father to son for 15 centuries–would never consent to give his daughter to a simple merchant

---

[29] The device that Robida intends to indicate by the phrase *téléphone de poche*–which I have translated literally as "pocket telephone"–is probably a mechanical one, not much more sophisticated than a children's toy linking two tin cans by means of a cord. The first telephone had been patented in 1876, three years before the publication of Robida's novel, but it had not yet been adapted for mobile use, and wireless telegraphy had still to be invented. Captain Nemo was, however, way ahead of his time, and may have developed methods of communicating with his divers that did not require cumbersome cables, so it is conceivable that this passage really is as prophetic as it seems.

uld never consent to give his daughter to a simple merchant Captain. At the mere mention of such a misalliance, she knew that Ra-Tafia would leap up from his throne and strike Farandoul's head from his shoulders. It was therefore necessary, until circumstances were altered, to keep their love secret. As it was impossible for them to see one another on land, they would meet each day to spend long hours in the oceanic depths, far from all terrestrial noise, and anything else that might trouble their poetic chat.

No, we shall not attempt to report everything that they said during those divine hours, when their two hearts beat as one as the lovers flew away to the ethereal realms! That would be the work of a poet–a poet born and bred to describe, in emotion-laden verse, the sublime modulations of their submarine duet. Only a poet could do justice to the two motionless creatures, so young and so beautiful, quartered on a rock beneath the floating reflections of a vague and indecisive light, in the tremulous green water. Never could the eye of a painter–if painters had frequented those depths–have found a more seductive subject! O diver Romeo, O submarine Juliet!

Farandoul's tall frame gained even more stature in the liquid element, and no suited diver had ever displayed more charming contours or a more graciously undulant figure than Mysora's. Schools of fish halted in stupefaction before the pair. Enormous tuna and indiscreet rays made circuits of the two young people without distracting them from their ecstasy, even when the dazed fish bumped into the floating tubes which conveyed breathable air to them. Sometimes, whole assemblies would gather round. Farandoul took no precautions against them; knowing from experience that submarine monsters only showed themselves in the greatest depths, he had no fear of encountering one a mere eight meters below the surface.

One day, though, Mysora wanted to take an excursion in his arms, into the submarine valleys that he traversed every day in order to come to her–and Farandoul did not have the heart to refuse to satisfy her whim, even though he was fully conscious of the risk.

The two young people had moved without any hindrance to a certain distance from the coast. Farandoul, by means of a little pocket pressure-gauge, had established that they had attained a depth of 150 meters, when an unexpected spectacle suddenly presented itself to them.

A terrible battle was raging, a short distance away, between a small whale and a sea-serpent more than 100 meters in length. The poor whale had been attacked from behind by the horrible constrictor, whose immense mouth had snatched it by the tail and was striving to swallow it, despite its desperate resistance. The whale's head and a part of its body were still protruding from that mouth, further ingestion having been halted by the fins. The constrictor, in order to finish the job, was twisting its body in terrible effort while its convulsively-rolling coils were striking the sea-bed with a frightful noise.

It was obvious that the whale must succumb. Mysora, seized by pity, begged Farandoul to hurry to its aid.

"Take your hatchet, my handsome Farandoul," she said, "and slay the monster." And when Farandoul hesitated, she added: "Don't worry about me–save the whale!"

Farandoul leapt forward. His hatchet in his hand, he fell upon the serpent as if he were on horseback. Despite the reptile's sliminess, he pulled his way to the head, which he struck furiously. The serpent, which had paid no attention to this new adversary until that moment, thrashed about in a terrifying manner.

Without allowing himself to be unseated, Farandoul redoubled his hatchet-blows, so effectively that the monster's skull finally burst asunder with a great crack! The two jaws opened as wide as possible, while the reptile shuddered convulsively, and the whale freed itself with a sudden effort.

At the same moment–to Farandoul's great horror, and before he could throw himself forward to prevent it–the whale advanced with two thrusts of its right fin upon Mysora, who was following the vicissitudes of the combat with interest.

Within a second, its immense maw had engulfed the unfortunate young woman.

An appalling darkness of the soul! The monstrous cetacean could offer no better acknowledgement of the sweet girl who had saved it than to swallow its benefactress whole!

The monster, doubly delighted to have escaped the serpent at the same time as it had snapped up a fine windfall, hurled itself towards the light in order to enjoy its good fortune in peace. As it passed him by, the maddened Farandoul grabbed hold of a cord that was still dangling from its mouth, and arrived at the wave-tossed surface at exactly the same time.

What Farandoul had seized was the floating tube which conveyed breathable air to Mysora's diving-suit. His only hope was that it was still attached; he did not want to let go of the last thread upon which Mysora's life might possibly depend.

By an extraordinary stroke of luck, on arriving in daylight, Farandoul perceived his ship only a few cables distant. A certain tumult was evident on board, the crew having caught sight of the monster and decided to attack it, by way of passing the time. Farandoul waved his arms above his head, and a general cry went up in response–and, in less time than it takes to say so, the long-boat had put to sea.

Lieutenant Mandibul, harpoon in hand, gestured to the men, urging them to row vigorously. Two minutes later, the long-boat had reached Farandoul–who seized the harpoon and, throwing with a sure hand, hit the monster's flank. Lieutenant Mandibul had once been a whaler. He noticed that, contrary to the habit of whales–which usually dived with vertiginous speed and threaded their way into the depths as soon as they were hit–this one was only moving feebly. Evidently, it sensed that it had fallen prey to some profound difficulty.

No crime ever goes unpunished, and Providence the Avenger would doubtless have struck it fatally soon enough, but the whale's hour of punishment had sounded and the crime that could not weigh upon its non-existent conscience was weighing upon its stomach!

In the first moments after swallowing its prey without examination, the whale had perceived its roughness. Trusting to the strength of its constitution, however, it had expected to be quickly rid of the extraordinarily lumpy morsel–but within its inner tribunal,[30] it now began to regret its gourmandizing, its stomach being over-full. Moreover, the creature that it had swallowed was flinging itself recklessly about–and here, adding to its misfortunes, were yet more enemies attacking it, as if it did not have enough to do to counter the enemy within!

Farandoul made a sign, which Mandibul understood; another harpoon was thrown, and before the whale could make up its mind, the two cables were made fast to the bow of *La Belle Léocadie*. Farandoul had leapt upon the monster; he strove with all his might to hack through its outer tegument with hatchet-blows, in the hope of making a hole by means of which he could go into its body and save Mysora. Meanwhile, the final preparations were made to haul the whale aboard the ship.

Suddenly, the whale recovered its strength. With a single blow of its tail, it up-ended the long-boat, which nearly turned turtle, and darted southwards like an arrow. *La Belle Léocadie*, in tow to the monster, took the same course.

The desperate Farandoul was taken aboard with the sailors from the long-boat. It was all over! Mysora seemed to him to be lost forever; even though the air-hose was still afloat, it seemed impossible to him that she could stay alive until *La Belle Léocadie* caught up with the dying whale.

At any rate, he was determined at least to kill the monster. To do that, it was necessary to follow it until its strength

---

[30] *Le for intérieur*, here translated literally as "inner tribunal," is commonly employed in French as a metaphorical synonym for conscience, but the text has already established that the whale is devoid of conscience, and that its internal trial is essentially dyspeptic.

was exhausted. The harpoon-cables were firmly-attached and would not break, all the sails were furled–and *La Belle Léocadie*, her canvas dry, flew like lightning in the monster's wake.

V. How poor Mysora ended up in the aquarium
of Valentin Croknuff, an aged but very ardent man of science.
Saturnin Farandoul declares war on England.

Sibilantly skimming the crests of the waves, *La Belle Léocadie* was drawn along at a prodigious velocity. The whale that was towing her was traveling at an incalculable pace, and it was only very approximately that Farandoul estimated her speed at 40 leagues an hour.[31] The sailors were scarcely able to move without falling violently on their behinds, unless they lashed themselves to the stays. They were quite out of breath.

How would the mad dash end?

The ships that they encountered put on full steam in order to escape the path of the infernal ship, which they took for the Flying Dutchman. A big steamship going from Liverpool to Melbourne, full of terrified passengers, was struck amidships and cut in two following an unwise maneuver.

At 15:00, Farandoul saw land on the port bow, which he judged to be the coast of Western Australia, near Perth. If the whale did not change direction within a quarter of an hour, they would be at the south magnetic pole,[32] bound to be bro-

---

[31] A French league is four kilometers, so 40 leagues an hour is exactly 100 miles an hour–an incredible velocity for a swimming whale, especially with a three-master in tow.

[32] The text has *au pôle sud*, but it must mean the magnetic pole, which is located in the sea off the Adélie coast; there is now a French base on that coast, named after the Antarctic explorer Jules Dumont-d'Urville (1790-1842) who first touched upon it.

ken on the polar icebergs or the desolate cliffs of the Antarctic continent.

And Mysora, alas! Could any hope still remain?

The whale suddenly veered eastwards. Cape Leeuwin and King George Point were doubled; the whale's speed seemed to be increasing even more. It soon began to make such violent leaps and jerks that Farandoul feared the cables would snap. Soon afterwards, a violent tempest was added to the perils of the situation; it seemed that the Heavens were taking the side of the monster against the defenders of the beautiful Mysora. In the midst of the unleashed elements, the whale's convulsions became even more violent. The monster was blowing hard and suffering.[33] For a moment or two, the Australian coast became clearly visible to port; then everything was swallowed up by the blackness of the tempest.

The chase had lasted 23 hours when, at the height of the storm, both cables suddenly broke simultaneously. The whale, abruptly set free, redoubled its velocity and its convulsions, leaving *La Belle Léocadie* dancing angrily on the waves as the creature was lost to view.

For a further hour, the breathless monster ate up the distance. Whirlpools of foam traced a long wake behind it and every time it vented air from its blowhole immense cascades of water fell upon its head. Every time that huge head emerged from the waves, a sort of bellowing sound was audible. The monster was moaning!

A fisherman named John Bird, who lived in a little maritime cottage in Port Philip, a few leagues from Melbourne, made a fortunate discovery that day. Having not put out to sea because of the storm, he was walking on the beach, taking long puffs on his pipe by way of consolation, when–to his great surprise–he saw a gigantic fish coming straight towards him. He had no time to get out of the way. The whale, at the limit of its strength, ran blindly aground upon the rocks, hur-

---

[33] The assonant pairing of *soufflant* et *souffrant* cannot be reproduced in English.

tling at such a speed that it smashed to Earth 50 meters from the waves. Then, lying on its side, exhausted and motionless, it seemed ready to expire at the feet of the stupefied John Bird.

A third individual now appeared on the scene. A tall, gaunt and ungainly man, bald and bespectacled, strode up rapidly, waving his arms and an oversized umbrella. A long yellow overcoat floated behind him. The newcomer, careless of his unprotected shoes, bounded through the puddles, splashing himself from top to toe.

Thus we introduce to our readers, with their permission, the celebrated scientist Valentin Croknuff,[34] founder and Director of the Great Melbourne Aquarium, an establishment almost without rival, where all known species of fish swim back and forth in continuously-recycled sea-water. Mr. Croknuff's Aquarium lacked nothing but a whale, so his joy may be imagined when, at the very moment he was turning for home, he observed from a distance the monster stranded on the sand.

John Bird was just about to finish the creature off, brandishing a harpoon that he had recovered from its flesh, when a violent blow from an umbrella fell upon his head. His pipe fell out of his mouth and broke. The furious John Bird rounded on his opponent to deliver his riposte.

"I'll buy your whale–don't touch it, you imbecile!" cried Mr. Croknuff, the man with the umbrella.

John Bird lowered his fist. "How much?"

"Fifty pounds!"

"Pay up!"

---

[34] I have resisted the temptation to further Anglicize this name by amending its spelling to "Valentine Crocknough." I have retained the appellation "Mr. Croknuff" where Robida has "M. (for Monsieur) Croknuff," although it seems slightly awkward, because the occasions when Robida elects to abandon the honorific have a certain narrative significance, implying that the name is being used contemptuously.

Having received his money, John Bird turned on his heel, saying: "Now take your whale away, if you can!"

That was the difficult part, but Mr. Croknuff got it done regardless. That same evening, all Melbourne was informed, by means of huge posters, that the scientist Mr. Croknuff had finally acquired for his Great Aquarium the whale of his dreams.

Valentin Croknuff spent the whole night lavishing much-needed care upon his cherished whale. The unfortunate creature was in a sad state, flapping its fins lamentably.

Mr. Croknuff's Great Aquarium was situated in a nice part of Melbourne, on a grand avenue called Aquarium Road. A beautiful garden was laid out in front of the building, in whose shade passers-by could often observe the worthy Mr. Croknuff walking for hours with a sick baby seal in his arms, or a sea-lion overtaken by nostalgia.

The Aquarium was octagonal in shape, comprising eight immense tanks surrounding a central room–which Mr. Croknuff, in order to be always in the midst of his pupils, had made into his workroom and his bedroom. In a way, he actually lived in a submarine world, and could watch over the health of his stock as easily by night as in the daytime. He was, in consequence, familiar with all their little habits. He had studied their characteristics and had made himself master of them all, a good father to his family. He made them change tanks when they became bored, and alleviated the tedium of long summer evenings by charming them with symphonies played on the piano, performed with the most marvelous verve.

It ought to be said that it was entirely for the benefit of his inmates that Mr. Croknuff had acquired the piano. Mr. Croknuff, like all sensible men, detested music, particularly piano music–but he told himself that even though music was a prehistoric invention, a last relic of barbarism which civilization would one day sweep away, the savage art might perhaps still be agreeable to the scarcely-elevated natures of his boarders.

That night, Mr. Croknuff was entirely devoted to his whale; the other fish, glued to the glass, waited in vain for the concert that sent them to sleep every evening. The whale wheeled around and around in its aquarium like a mad thing. Mr. Croknuff was desperate to do something to ease its distress. He had scratched away distractedly at his denuded skull for hours, without seeing any means of putting an end to its suffering.

Suddenly, the whale made a convulsive movement. Its jaws opened very wide, and its eyes closed. Mr. Croknuff, believing that it was about to give up the ghost, pounced on his piano–on which, in order to soothe the poor whale's last moments, he plucked out the despairing chords of Mozart's Requiem, while watering the keys with his tears. When he lifted his head again, however, the whale was not dead–and it was no longer alone. A bizarre creature was standing by its side!

Mr. Croknuff, rubbing his eyes, realized that the trespasser was a diver dressed in a suit!

Leaping briskly on to the aquarium's platform, Mr. Croknuff slid a ladder into the tank and, without saying a word, signaled to the diver to climb up. Our readers will recognize Mysora, who had survived being swallowed by the gluttonous monster, thanks to her extra-strong costume.

Mr. Croknuff and Mysora climbed down into the scientist's bedroom. Mr. Croknuff seemed to be furious. Standing before Mysora with his arms folded he began cursing explosively. "Ah! ah! ah! Wretch! So it's you who've been hurting my whale! Do you know, infamous torturer, that I can have you up in court–you've no right to damage my property!"

Mysora, who did not speak a word of English, understood nothing of this discourse. In any case, the poor girl was at the end of her tether. Without making any response, she fainted, letting herself fall into an armchair.

"Here we go!" Croknuff grumbled. "Look who's ill now! There's a chap who doesn't stand on ceremony! As if I had time to attend to him, when the poor whale he's hurt is suffering so! Let's see now–come round, my friend. Hang on–drink this. It's a bottle of sugared water I prepared for a baby seal with the measles... drink up! Quickly! I've got to get back to my whale!" And Mr. Croknuff, his head turned towards his whale, rapped on Mysora's iron helmet with the bottle of sugared water. "Well, drink it, then!" he went on. "Ah, I get it! It's his diving-suit getting in the way!" Replacing the bottle on his desk, Mr. Croknuff set about unfastening Mysora's diving-suit.

Suddenly, he cried out and let the helmet fall to the ground. Mysora's pretty head had appeared before his eyes, pallid with the emotion of those 30 terrible hours. Her long hair had come undone, and made a magnificent ebony frame for the bleached canvas of her face. Life seemed to be returning; her large eyes opened wide with effort as she tried to get her bearings.

Her gaze fell first upon the glass partition of the huge tank where the whale, finally restored to normality, was swimming quite calmly back and forth. Mysora let out a feeble scream at the sight of the monster–which, bumping its nose against the wall of its prison, fixed its little round eyes upon her. She fainted again.

No scientist had ever experienced an emotion as great as Mr. Croknuff's. His heart beat faster and his spectacles jumped on his nose as his eyes flickered back and forth between the whale and the girl. What blows he rained upon his forehead with his fist! Eventually, having moved an atlas and a stuffed tuna out of the way, he sat down on a low chair beside the young woman and began slapping her gently with both hands to bring her round.

A few feeble sighs were the only response. Mr. Croknuff jumped up, satisfied, threw himself upon the bottle of sugared water and tried to force a few drops between the young woman's lips.

"How beautiful she is! How beautiful!" murmured Mr. Croknuff, his attentions becoming more profuse. "What long hair! What little hands! And the nose–what lovely curvature!

What eyes! What eyebrows! What teeth! How beautiful she is! How beautiful! Drink this for me, my girl. Oof! What a woman! There's an adventure–walking on the sea-bed in a diving-suit, being swallowed by a whale! She loves fish! How beautiful she is! How beautiful! I love them too, and I've always dreamed of a Mrs. Croknuff who would love fish... but I've never found one, and have remained a bachelor. Yes, my girl! That's what you see–a bachelor! Drink this for me, my girl. I made it for my baby seal; it's very good. How beautiful she is! How beautiful!!!"

Mr. Croknuff was beside himself. None of his friends would have recognized the illustrious scientist–author of eight conscientious volumes on the morals of the lobster before dressing, and lengthy patient studies of the habits of reef-building polyps–as he knelt beside Mysora, sighing frantically and bathing the hands of the girl abandoned to his care with tender tears.

It must be acknowledged that although Mr. Croknuff no longer had any hair or teeth, he still had a heart–and that heart had quickened its beat for the very first time! Mr. Croknuff firmly believed that he had committed himself entirely to pisciculture, but here was his heart in sudden rebellion, up-ending everything in its way, laying down the law to its former master, Mr. Croknuff's brain.

It was all over! Mr. Croknuff could no longer contain himself.

"Angel!" he said to Mysora–for he was already thinking of her as an angel, and addressed her thus. "Angel! I love you, and I offer you my hand and my Aquarium! Accept them! You love fish; I love them too! I love you; you shall love me; we shall love one another, here! Give me your answer, angel!"

Mysora, coming round, had opened her eyes. At first, she understood nothing of what Mr. Croknuff said, taking him for an aged doctor–then, confronted by the scientist's fervent pantomime, she began to wonder whether she had miraculously escaped one great peril only to fall into another, no less terrible.

Poor Mysora pushed Mr. Croknuff away and stood up, her face pale, her hair in disarray and her expression distraught.

"What do you want from me?" she cried, in Malay. "Do you know that I'm the daughter of the Rajah of Timor, and the bride-to-be of Saturnin Farandoul, Captain of *La Belle Léocadie*. Beware the vengeance of my father, or that–more terrible still–of my beloved Farandoul!"

Mr. Croknuff had grasped nothing from this speech except for one thing: Mysora was angry. Mr. Croknuff's rejuvenated heart ached at that sad thought, and its proprietor groveled desperately at the feet of the incensed young woman.

"Pardon me, sweet dove! I would give my whale, and my Aquarium with it, not to have offended you! You don't understand–I love you! It's my heart, my hand, my Aquarium, that I offer you! Permit me to speak to you of love; listen to me! Your arrival has turned my life upside-down, and thanks to you I have experienced what experts in these matters call love at first sight! I have not studied the physiology of the passions; like a madman, I denied love, but a single instant has revealed it to me. Angel, I love you!" And Mr. Croknuff, still on his knees, extended his arms towards Mysora.

Mysora leapt backwards, abruptly took up her helmet, refastened her diving-suit, and leapt on to the platform of the aquarium as rapidly as a flash of lightning.

"Greybeard," she cried, "you have shown me that there are monsters more dreadful to young women than those one meets at the bottom of the sea! Since you force it upon me, I shall return to the whale–but tremble, for my Farandoul will come to save me!"

Saying these words, the heroic young woman slid into the aquarium. The whale, which had not been paying attention, started with fright and retreated to the most distant extremity of the tank.

Mysora had not been unaware of the dangers that she might run in cetacean society, but she had decided to brave them in order to keep herself pure for her beloved. She was delighted to see, however, that it was she who frightened the whale. The voracious cetacean was conscious of the torment it had suffered as a result of taking such an indigestible creature into its gut, and was now disposed to keep well clear of Mysora.

Mr. Croknuff, on the other hand, stood on the platform wringing his hands, at the risk of tearing out the last of his hair in his anguish.

At one point, he seemed to be on the point of throwing himself head-first into the aquarium to end his life, but then he tried to move Mysora to pity. The young woman obdurately refused to leave her protective shelter.

At sunrise, Mr. Croknuff went away. The doors of the establishment were soon opened to the waiting crowd, whose members had come from all over Melbourne to see his whale.

The general astonishment was immense when they saw that, in addition to the whale, the central tank contained a creature clad in a diving-suit, which seemed to be living on amicable terms with the enormous cetacean. Mr. Croknuff was there, in the process of receiving the congratulations of the Scientific Societies of Melbourne; pressed by questions, he tried to keep his explanations vague, but only succeeded in further exciting their curiosity. Some of his employees, cunningly interrogated, were less discreet; several rumors began to circulate within the crowd.

Soon, all Melbourne knew that Mr. Croknuff had a live siren in his Aquarium, so accomplished and so marvelously beautiful that he had been obliged to take it upon himself to dress her in a diving-suit, in order to spare her the fervent curiosity of the public.

Poor Mysora, finding herself the object of every gaze, sought to hide herself as completely as possible behind boulders covered with algae and marine plants; but there, on the opposite face of the aquarium–which, as we have observed, looked out into Mr. Croknuff's office–she found her odious persecutor plastered against the glass, blowing her the most tender kisses. The poor girl quickly took herself off to the other side, where numerous hurrahs greeted her return. It was the same all day. As evening approached, she contrived to make herself a refuge within the boulders–a sort of cave where, exhausted by fatigue, she went calmly to sleep, after having first partaken of a light supper dispensed by Mr. Croknuff from the platform of the aquarium.

Mr. Croknuff gave himself up completely to the most brilliant improvisations on the piano, but Mysora refused to pay the least attention to the waves of harmony that rolled through the aquarium, to the great delight of the other inmates. That night, not a single resident fish went to sleep; Mysora alone found forgetfulness of her troubles in slumber–and traveled the empire of dreams in company with her beloved Farandoul.

What was our hero doing in the meantime? Had *La Belle Léocadie* perished when the tempest took hold of her, after the cables attaching her to the whale had ruptured?

Not at all. Farandoul was an excellent mariner; mastering his grief, he thought only of saving his crew, and *La Belle Léocadie* had, fortunately, extracted herself from all danger.

Two days after the storm, the three-master had come into Sandridge, Melbourne's port, situated a few kilometers away from the town. Farandoul hoped to pick up the track of the whale there, as the monster had been racing towards Port Philip when it had given him the slip. He had soon discovered John Bird, and had obtained from him, by courtesy of a few well-placed guineas, every detail of the purchase and removal of the whale by the scientist Mr. Croknuff.

Farandoul went forthwith to Melbourne's Great Aquarium, and entered the establishment at the moment when the greatest influx of curiosity-seekers was crowding into it.

Scientists, naturalists, academicians, journalists and tradesmen were overrunning the Aquarium. Mr. Croknuff found himself pulled in every direction, by the members of a special commission sent by the Melbourne Institute, by doctors desirous of dissecting the so-called siren, by photographers and reporters from every newspaper in the state of Victoria–and so on, and so on.

Farandoul elbowed his way through the crowd.

"Where is she? Where is she?" he cried, shoving the scientists out of the way.

"Who do you mean?"

"My whale–let me see my whale!" He had arrived in front of the largest tank in the Aquarium despite the efforts Mr. Croknuff made to repel him.

One glance was sufficient. The whale was there–and, alive within the aquarium, separated from him by a mere pane of glass, Mysora put out her arms to him.

What luck! Farandoul wanted to embrace Mr. Croknuff–but Croknuff, having inferred that he was an enemy, thrust him away acrimoniously. "Who are you, sir? What do you want?"

"I am her husband-to-be, worthy scientist, and I have come to find her!" Farandoul replied, at the summit of happiness, "I believed her dead, my dear Mysora–imagine my joy on seeing her again... on...."

"My dear sir," Mr. Croknuff interrupted him. "I've bought the whale. I've paid for it, so it belongs to me..."

"I'm not laying claim to the whale, but..."

"But the creature that you see there was inside the whale at the time of the transaction, and was included in the price! I'm holding on to it–holding hard, Devil take you! You don't think that I'll generously make you a gift of it, now that it's the most important inmate of my Aquarium, do you? I've got it, and I'm keeping it!"

Farandoul had gone from joy to surprise, and from surprise to anger. He seized Mr. Croknuff by the throat, and was preparing to throw him through the glass of the aquarium in which the trembling Mysora was imploring his help when hastily-summoned policemen restrained him.

"I place my property under the safeguard of the authorities!" Mr. Croknuff shouted, as Farandoul held on to him.

"I'm an Australian citizen. I've a right to the protection of the law, for myself and my goods!"

How can we describe Farandoul's rage? How can we speak of the plans for massacre that bubbled up in his head? As soon as he was out of the hands of the police, he hurled himself towards *La Belle Léocadie*'s mooring. He assembled his men on the bridge and told them what had happened. A unanimous demand for revenge went up from every mouth. The sailors immediately armed themselves with revolvers and boarding-hatchets. Leaving two men to guard the ship, they set off for Melbourne.

Farandoul wanted to wait for nightfall before attacking the Aquarium, for fear of raising too great a commotion in Melbourne. This delay proved fatal! The wily Croknuff had had him followed to his ship by one of the Aquarium's keepers. This man, having seen the sailors disembark with obvious hostile intent, had retraced his steps in a hurry in order to warn his master.

Croknuff had lost no time. The Aquarium had been rapidly prepared for its defense. The authorities, forewarned, had sent a battalion of provincial militia to its aid, with two cannons and 40 mounted policemen.

When the shadows of night extended themselves over the city, Farandoul and his little troop marched on the Aquarium. When they arrived, the mariners ran into an armed camp. Farandoul went pale at the sight of the bivouac fires. Nevertheless, he advanced boldly as far as the first guard-post.

"Halt! Who goes there?" shouted the sentries–and, as the mariners continued to advance, a shot was fired in the air.

An officer and several horsemen hastened forward. Farandoul began to negotiate with the officer, and obtained consent to go alone to the threshold of the Aquarium. There he tried to obtain by eloquence what he could not take by force.

It was utterly useless.

"I'm personally very sorry for you, sir," the Colonel said to him, in conclusion, "but I can't grant your desire. I entirely understand that your motives may be respectable, but the law is the law and the property of every Englishman is sacred. As a militiaman, I must protect public safety, and it's my duty to force you to re-embark. at least until you consent to abandon all hostile plans."

"Never! I shall have Mysora, by agreement or by force."

"Then it's war, sir. If you dare to attack, you will find yourself facing all the combined forces of the state of Victoria, Australia and old England!"

"As you say, it's war," Farandoul replied, with grim resolution. "And if I don't attack today, know that you'll lose nothing by waiting. Ah, perfidious Albion, you're protecting a crime, sustaining the oppressors of innocence. The day of vengeance will come, and you shall know the weight of arms borne in a just course! I, Saturnin Farandoul, Captain of *La Belle Léocadie*, declare war on the State of Melbourne–and on Australia and England too, if they so wish! Hear me, soldiers! I tell you that this will soon be a battlefield!"

Saturnin Farandoul and his little troop retraced their steps to the ship. Farandoul, mulling over terrible plans, said not a word on the way.

La Belle Léocadie put on sail the following morning. At the same hour, huge posters were affixed to every wall in Melbourne, bearing the simple words:

WAR TO THE DEATH AGAINST AUSTRALIA.
SATURNIN FARANDOUL.
SEE YOU SOON!

VI. The Conquest of Australia.
Telegrams and Correspondence in the Melbourne Herald.
The great Melbourne Aquarium will not capitulate!

Three months have gone by since the fatal events that we have related. Sir James Collingham, Her Majesty's Governor of the State of Victoria, is surveying his office in an indescribable state of agitation. Sir James appears distraught; his uniform is unbuttoned, his face has taken on the hue of a cooked lobster and he seems close to collapse. He reads and re-reads dispatches brought in one after another by men as agitated as their commander.

This is what these dispatches say:

Geelong, May 16th, 5:45 a.m.

Rumor has it that hordes of armed brigands disembarked last night four miles from here. Have sent for confirmation.

Geelong, May 16th, 10:50 a.m.

Fugitives bring news. The disembarkation continues. Brigands marching on Geelong. Militia summoned. Scouts have not returned. Request help.

Geelong, May 16th, 11:30 a.m.

Messenger arrived under flag of truce. Sent by Saturnin Farandoul, General-in-Chief of the Oceanian army, who sent declaration of war three months ago. Says he will attack in two hours if we do not surrender. Request help. Urgent.

Geelong, May 16th, 2 p.m.
Attack has begun. Militia falling back to town. Help!

Geelong, May 16th, 3:15 p.m.

Town taken by Farandoulian troops. Station under attack. We are retreating.

Geelong, May 16th, 4:50 p.m.
Colonel Campbell to Governor:

Arrived too late. Geelong taken by Farandoulian troops; we are covering the retreat. The enemy is coming. Hurrah for old England!

Geelong, May 16th, 4:58 p.m.

Attack begun. Our advance-guard is retreating. Strange! The Farandoulian troops are hairy. Beating a retreat so as not to be cut off by an enemy flanking movement. Losses considerable. Send help.

Melbourne, May 16th, 5 p.m.

Croknuff, Director of the Great Aquarium, to the Governor.

Request permission to establish a battery of torpedoes for the protection of the Aquarium against Farandoulian attack.[35]

Sir James, to avoid suffocation, decides to take off his uniform. Officers press in upon him from every side, some bringing news, others coming in search of orders, all shouting and jostling. Troops are massing in front of the Governor's mansion; dispatch-riders clatter across the pavement; drums beat; clarion calls reverberate.

Heavy artillery-pieces are arriving at the gallop with a terrible racket of bronze and old iron. The lugubrious strokes of the tocsin, sounding in every edifice, can be heard over the uproar, completing the sinister symphony.

The Assembly (the upper chamber) and the Council (the lower chamber) have been urgently summoned to vote through all the defensive measures proposed by the Governor.

The attack has been so sudden that it has thrown everything into disarray. No one has any but the vaguest information about the enemy; nothing is known of its strength or its

---

[35] The word "torpedo" originally signified a kind of mine. In 1797, Robert Fulton, an American living in Paris, had volunteered to build a submarine vessel for the French to use against the English; he constructed a vessel called the *Nautilus* in 1800, inventing a "torpedo" for use therewith that consisted of a mine that the vessel was supposed to tow into position (it was never successfully used). The name was subsequently borrowed by Robert Whitehead for a self-propelled mine that he called an "automobile torpedo," and it was that application of the word that eventually became associated with the principal assault weapon employed by actual submarines in the early 20th century.

intentions, for the successive telegrams shed no light on the situation and officers sent out on reconnaissance do not come back.

The Geelong railway has been requisitioned to carry battalions of militia rapidly to the aid of Colonel Campbell, but it is feared that they never arrived, the line having been cut by the enemy in advance of that officer's position.

In the middle of this military tohu-bohu, a carriage arrives at the Governor's mansion. A man gets out and hurries up the grand staircase. It is the editor of the *Melbourne Herald*, the most important newspaper in the state of Victoria. "Where's the Governor?" he shouts, brandishing a piece of paper. "Here's news from Dick Broken, the reporter I sent to Geelong this morning! Do you want the details?"

A group of officers form a circle around the editor of the *Melbourne Herald*; the Governor gives him permission to speak.

"This is the letter from my reporter–listen!

"*Cheep Hill, 5:15 p.m.*

"*Sick at heart, I write to you from the depths of the profoundest astonishment. The sinister rumors that reached Melbourne this morning are not unfounded; the enemy has disembarked during the night near Geelong and has seized the town.*

"*Despite my best efforts, I cannot get into Geelong, which is occupied by Farandoulian troops. The rout of the defenders of that unhappy town has caught me up and carried me several miles back like a torrent. The enemy has lost no time in catching up with us and, as you can imagine, I have made every effort to place myself in the front rank.*

"*Having forced my horse through the crowd, I soon found myself at the battle-front. The enemy fire was intermittent, sometimes dying away entirely and sometimes sweeping across certain targets with an extraordinary regularity that astonished our old warriors. There was something mechanical about it, something like the rotation, so to speak, of a sewing-machine. I could not make out anything on the enemy side*

130

except for the smoke of their guns, and great black masses moving in the distance.

"At four o'clock, Colonel Campbell's reinforcements arrived; that veteran of the Indian wars, full of confidence, immediately resolved to charge the enemy to resume combat; it goes without saying that I took my place in the attack column.

"I cannot describe the hurricane of fire and steel that was unleashed around us as we formed up; we were advancing regardless, when a wood situated to our left disgorged upon our staggering column an avalanche of warriors protected by huge shields and armed with clubs. Thus we came to see the Farandoulian troops at close range! These warriors were bounding with superhuman vigor, so rapidly that they were on us before we could square up to them. Hardly anyone fired a shot before we had to defend ourselves with bayonets against the demons.

"War cries also sounded to our right, and we soon saw new enemies leaping with extraordinary agility over the closely-pressed ranks of militiamen. It was then, for the first time, that I saw something that terrified me! I rubbed my eyes, but a great cry let loose by the staff officer made me understand that my sight was not at fault! At the same moment, the column fell into total disarray, and the retreat began.

"How can I tell you what we had seen? Expect the most thunderous surprise, the strangest and most frightful revelation! Know, then, that we were beating a retreat before an army of fearsome monkeys! Yes–all those who survive will be able to swear to it–our enemies are monkeys, armed, trained and commanded by regular troops!

"Their leader, of whom I caught a glimpse during the heat of the battle, is none other than the audacious mariner who threatened Melbourne three months ago! My horse having been killed, I had to follow the retreat sitting on a cannon. We have arrived at Cheep Hill, which Colonel Campbell believes he can hold. I shall send news!

"Dick Broken."

131

Everyone was stunned by this recital. A few officers having expressed doubts, the editor of the *Melbourne Herald* defended his reporter animatedly, while a new dispatch arrived to put paid to the last uncertainties.

It consisted of the following:

Cheep Hill, May 16th, 7 p.m.
The monkeys are mounting a flanking movement. We are surrounded. Troops demoralized. Awaiting assault.
Colonel Campbell.

A council of war was immediately assembled. Melbourne was put under martial law; detachments were sent out to scour the country along the Geelong road. Soon, an entire army, comprising militia and volunteers, took up positions in that direction to defend the city.

The night passed without any further news from Cheep Hill. Colonel Campbell's silence caused the Governor tremendous disquiet and foreboding. At 5 a.m., however, the *Melbourne Herald* received a second letter from its reporter.

Cheep Hill, May 16th, 10 p.m.
The dark specter of defeat hovers relentlessly overhead. Cheep Hill is taken; Colonel Campbell has been obliged to surrender.
I am a prisoner of the Farandoulian monkeys. Nevertheless, I will do everything I can to get this letter to you. I told you that Colonel Campbell believed that he could hold his position and keep the monkeys in check long enough to allow the defense of Melbourne to be organized. Our troops, harassed and demoralized, camped on the hill while the Colonel established his general quarters in the buildings of Cheep Hill Farm. Large woods enveloped the hill to our rear and Colonel Campbell counted on taking refuge there in case of a reverse.
Unfortunately, the darkness of these woods also served to hide a flanking movement which the left wing of the monkeys' army carried out–with a rapidity that no longer aston-

ishes us now that we know our enemy–while our troops were drawing breath. The battle recommenced at the center of the position at about seven o'clock; our rested militiamen did their best and we began to feel hope reborn in our hearts, when catastrophe suddenly overtook us.

Everyone was facing the enemy, fighting amid a chorus of hurrahs for old England. All of a sudden, loud cries were raised in the tops of the trees to the rear of our position. Every head turned that way. By the rays of the setting Sun, we were affrighted to see the legion of our enemies bearing down on us, leaping from crown to crown.

The foliage of every tree was swarming with howling and grimacing enemies; the very forest seemed to be alive, marching upon us as in Macbeth, *but we had scarcely time to think. The monkeys, arriving at the last trees, leapt into our ranks, screeching frightfully and whirling their heavy clubs. Minute by minute, further battalions of monkeys leapt upon us from the heights of the eucalyptus and gum-trees, belaboring our troops with irresistible force.*

Campbell's dragoons attempted a charge, but the monkeys, jumping on the horses' rumps, toppled the riders and came at us again with even greater impetuosity.

At that moment, the Farandoulians we had been facing also broke through our lines. I was able to see, in the midst of the heat of battle, a troop of monkeys protected by long ironwood shields advancing in regular formation, while other quadrumanes [36]*–probably members of an elite corps, armed with rifles and commanded by men in bright uniforms–spread out as sharpshooters.*

---

[36] Quadrumanes are those mammals in which the feet are formed rather like hands–including all primates except man. Robida subsequently invents the word bimanes–which will similarly do as well in English as in French–for application to humans, in order to promote the idea that quadrumanes and bimanes are different but equal contingents of primatekind.

Colonel Campbell formed a second front in order to try to face up to all our enemies. We were obviously lost! Suddenly, a strident shout let loose by their leader–whom I recognized to be the terrible Farandoul–cut through the tumult of the battle. At that signal, the fight ceased; a monkey waving a white flag came forward, at the same time as Farandoul moved his horse towards us.

"Soldiers, it's time to stop the bloodshed," he shouted. "You're surrounded. Surrender!"

Colonel Campbell gave the order to cease fire and went to meet him. Covered in blood like a wounded lion, the old warrior was determined to sell his own life dearly, but he wished at least to try to save the lives of what remained of his army.

"Colonel," Farandoul said to him, "continuing the fight will serve no purpose. You are surrounded by 20,000 monkeys, and more reinforcements will reach me tonight. Lay down your arms. I promise to treat you with all due consideration to your bravery."

The old warrior, in tears, decided to capitulate. An agreement was rapidly concluded and the troops, now prisoners of war, surrendered their arms to the monkeys.

Such were the events which will go down in history as the battle and surrender of Cheep Hill.

I am being held prisoner with the staff-officers. Our surgeons are dressing the wounds of both armies. The monkeys, so terrible in battle, now seem very amiable, and full of concern for our wellbeing. I will even say that they seem to me to be rather good chaps.

The most perfect order is maintained in their army. I was able to catch a glimpse of General Farandoul. He is very busy, but he has promised me a brief interview. I will send you all the details and provoke as many indiscretions as I can.

Dick Broken

P.S. I have had a chat with Colonel Mandibul, General Farandoul's chief staff-officer. He has told me the curious details of the composition of the Farandoulian army. The main

134

body of the army is composed of monkeys from Borneo and New Guinea; the elite troops armed with new machine-guns of Farandoul's own design–which explains the sewing-machine sound I mentioned this morning–come from an island where General Farandoul spent his childhood. These monkeys obey their leaders with a discipline that the best European troops would envy. The General is the idol of his army.

A special edition of the *Melbourne Herald* appeared at 8 a.m. on May 17th. The disastrous news imparted by the courageous reporter's remarkable letters threw the entire city into the greatest confusion.

The most distraught of all the citizens of Melbourne was most certainly the scientist Mr. Croknuff. Mounted on a little pony, hired for that purpose, despite his distaste for equitation, he was galloping towards the Governor's general quarters to assure himself of the veracity of the facts. He had no need to question the officers at length to bring himself up to date. A loud fusillade from the advance-posts apprised him of the situation sufficiently. He dug his spurs into the flanks of his steed and turned back towards the Aquarium, bouncing in his saddle.

The environs of the Aquarium had altered considerably since the preceding day. An immense moat, six meters deep and 15 wide, guarded the approach. Hundreds of workmen were occupied in using the earth excavated from the trench to construct a rampart bastioned in the regulation manner. Others were crenellating the walls of the Aquarium. In advance of all these projects, an engineer–a friend of Mr. Croknuff's–had prepared mine-chambers connected by electrical wiring to the Director's office.

Mr. Croknuff went into the grounds. Leaping swiftly from the saddle–which was scarcely difficult, as his feet were almost touching the ground–he advanced upon the laborers.

"Is the moat ready?" he asked.

"Yes sir, it's all ready; the pipes carrying the water are fully functional."

"It's just as well. Give the signal–the enemy's drawing near!"

At a blast from the foreman's whistle, the dam was opened and water–brought directly from the sea by a subterranean canal to serve the Aquarium's needs–poured into the moat, which was soon full. To complete the grounds' defenses, Mr. Croknuff released his famous whale from its tank in the aquarium, along with two little Javanese sharks and a dozen giant octopodes.[37] These redoubtable animals, happy to have more room, were soon swimming in the moat, thus rendering it impossible to cross. Mr. Croknuff was obviously neglecting no opportunity in recruiting his inmates to the defense of the Aquarium.

Mr. Croknuff felt that he was under a greater threat than any other citizen of Melbourne, because he understood that this terrible war had been ignited by him–by his obstinate refusal to surrender Mysora. Mr. Croknuff was utterly determined–victory or death! The Great Aquarium of Melbourne would not capitulate!

What, meanwhile, had become of poor Mysora? The unfortunate girl had not left her moist abode for three months. She, too, was resolute, and nothing–neither pleas nor threats–could make her give way. She had decided that she would rather spend her life in her underwater grotto than ever consent to become Mrs. Croknuff, as the horrid old scientist incessantly pressed her to do,

In three months, Mr. Croknuff had been changed out of all recognition. His heart burned white hot within his breast. A few hairs, favored by this interior climate, had even contrived to reappear upon his cranium. For three months his every waking moment had been consecrated to the tank in which the

---

[37] *Pieuvres* is used here rather than the more familiar *poulpes*, but both words are applied indiscriminately by the French to octopodes and squids; a more detailed reference in the next chapter specifies that one of the creatures in question has eight limbs, so "octopodes" is clearly the preferable translation.

poor girl languished, in company with the whale that was the cause of all her troubles.

Mr. Croknuff spent his days on the platform of the aquarium, trying to soften Mysora's heart. Needless to say, all his arguments were in vain. They were, in any case, in English, and Mysora only understood Malay. The poor girl, with unparalleled constancy, passed her days in walking back and forth across the aquarium in order to give herself a little exercise. By night she retired to her little grotto, wanting to be alone in order to think of her beloved Farandoul without being troubled by curiosity-seekers.

Mr. Croknuff, of course, did not neglect to carry her meals up to the platform of the aquarium. He soon began taking his own in the same place at the same time, but Mysora immediately quit his company whenever he risked repeating his passionate declarations. She had to do that more than once to put an end to such assaults, threatening with expressive gestures to cut the tube that supplied her with breathable air.

Mysora, who expected every day to be saved by Farandoul, understood when she saw Croknuff fortifying the Aquarium that her beloved was coming. Her heart beat faster; the final hour of her ordeal had sounded, and she had to be ready for anything!

At noon on May 17th, Mr. Croknuff went up to the roof of the Aquarium and anxiously followed the vicissitudes of the fervent fighting just outside Melbourne along the Geelong road. Rifle-shots and cannon-fire made the walls of the Aquarium tremble on their foundations; it was obvious that the battle was drawing nearer. Retreating soldiers were beginning to flock back to the streets of Melbourne, their tales of terror spreading through the city. Seeing that the moment of truth was approaching, Mr. Croknuff gave the order to raise the drawbridge and sent his defenders to their posts.

At that moment, some newspaper-sellers appeared, announcing a new edition of the *Melbourne Herald*. Mr. Croknuff called out to one of the criers and asked for a copy. The vendor attached the paper to a piece of string lowered from the rampart, whereupon one of the sharks in the moat leapt out of the water and snapped at him. Fortunately, the poor man fell back in fright, and the greedy monster caught nothing but his bag of papers–which it swallowed, for want of anything better.

On the first page of the paper, with headlines in large letters, were the following communications from the valiant reporter Dick Broken:

Cheep Hill, May 17th, 3 a.m.
General Farandoul.
I chatted with General Farandoul, the terrible leader of the monkeys, for a quarter of an hour. He is still quite young, but his forehead seems to be marked with the seal of genius. By some unknown means, he has become the instructor and commander of an army of monkeys whose devotion to his person is absolute.

His special guard consists of 200 quadrumanes whom he knows very intimately, having apparently spent his childhood with them.

The Farandoulian troops.
At the present time some 40,000 monkeys have disembarked, divided into several brigades commanded by the former mariners of the three-master La Belle Léocadie.
The Enemy's Intentions.
General Farandoul is determined to carry out, with his forces and those he expects: The Conquest of Australia!

The vast project bubbling in his head is the dream of founding an Oceanian Empire in Melbourne; he wishes to bring the simian race–which he calls a race of "imperfect men"–to civilization, bringing it nearer to the human race.

If England does not come immediately to our aid, no one can tell whether Farandoul might not become the Alexander and the Caesar of the fifth continent.

Stand up, men of free Australia, to block the road of conquest!

Cheep Hill, 3:15 a.m.

The Farandoulian troops, harangued by their General, are marching enthusiastically along the road to Melbourne. Colonel Mandibul is in command of the advance guard. Commandant Kirkson has been ordered to take the prisoners of Campbell's corps to Geelong.

I shall try to escape.

Outside Melbourne, 7 a.m.

Thanks to my knowledge of the country I was able to escape from Cheep Hill, and this morning I reached the advance posts of the Australian army, in the midst of the greatest dangers. The battle is joined. The Farandoulians, I regret to say, are gaining ground with every minute that passes, in spite of the heroic bravery of our troops.

Melbourne, 7:25 a.m.

Governor Collingham and his staff have been surprised and routed by an unexpected attack by monkeys falling from the treetops, like that which happened yesterday at Cheep Hill. The army is falling back in disarray towards Melbourne. I am in the thick of the brawl, taking notes for your benefit. We must prepare to fight from house to house, as at Saragossa![38] We must bury ourselves beneath the ruins of Melbourne like the Greeks at Missolonghi![39] To arms!

---

[38] The Spanish city of Saragossa was besieged by the French army in 1808-09, offering unexpectedly heroic resistance after Madrid capitulated to Napoleon in December 1808. The future Duke of Wellington landed at Lisbon in 1809 to begin the campaign which eventually put an end to Napoleon's Empire, so the timing of the siege was highly significant, although Saragossa itself was of no particular military importance.

[39] Missolonghi, where Byron died, suffered a long siege by Ibrahim, the son of Mohammed Ali of Egypt, during the Greek war of liberation, before it fell in 1826.

I will send you the WHOLE story, with TERRIFYING DETAILS of atrocious, heroic and comical episodes, etc, etc, for the afternoon edition.

ANNOUNCE to your readers that a SUPPLEMENT with a literal account of ATROCITIES will appear TOMORROW; I shall make every effort to ensure that I shall be present at every one.

Mr. Croknuff had scarcely finished reading when violent detonations resounded at the end of the avenue. It was an artillery battery attempting to cover the retreat and stop the attackers. There was no longer any hope of that; the fight was on! Thanks to his spectacles, Mr. Croknuff clearly saw a troop of bounding apes fall upon the battery and take possession of it. Standing on his rampart, Mr. Croknuff harangued his men, demanding that they should fight to the last breath, to be buried with him, if it should come to that, beneath the ruins of the Aquarium!

A great hurrah went up in response, and they waited for the attack. Hours went by as innumerable monkeys filed past the end of the avenue and spread out into the city, where the battle still continued in a few places. Then the gunfire dwindled away, eventually ceasing for good at about 4 p.m.

The entire city was in the hands of the Farandoulians, who proceeded to disarm its inhabitants. Only a few patrols of monkeys were visible. As dusk fell, Mr. Croknuff perceived that the posts protecting his Aquarium were the last points at which the English flag still flew.

At daybreak the following morning, the *Melbourne Herald* came out again. A vendor brought one all the way to the Aquarium. It contained the following proclamations:

Residents!
The line attaching Australia to England is broken!
The old name is abolished.
The country will take the name of: FARANDOULIA (THE OCEANIAN EMPIRE).

140

His Majesty Saturnin I, its august founder, will take the title THE MONKEY KING.

Men and monkeys are henceforth equal before the law.

Parliamentary rule is abolished.

The provincial militias are dissolved.

The permanent army will be composed entirely of monkeys.

General Mandibul is appointed governor of Melbourne.

Issued to Melbourne at the general quarters of the Farandoulian armies.

On May 17th,

Saturnin I

Bimanes of Melbourne,

His Majesty Saturnin I, whose heart is overflowing with sentiments of affection for all the subjects of his vast empire, whether they be bimanes or quadrumanes, invites you to be the first to offer to the world the noble example of true fraternity!

Live henceforth in peace with your formerly-disinherited brothers, the noble and generous monkeys who, brought up in the forests from generation to generation, have not been able, as you have, to partake of the banquet of civilization.

Though their manners are as yet unpolished, their hearts remain pure and good; they have forgotten the injuries done to their brothers and are ready to extend the hand of friendship as a sign of reconciliation.

Bimanes of Melbourne, resume the course of your everyday labors in peace, under the protection of the quadrumane armies.

The prosperity of the country will achieve new and greater heights. The united bimanes and quadrumanes will soon astonish the Old World and conquer it with new ideas!

At the Mansion of the Governor of Melbourne,

May 17th,

General Mandibul

Colonel Makako, Monkey Representative of Borneo

Colonel Tapa-Tapa, Monkey Representative of New Guinea

Orders Of The Day:
All bimanes who continue to resist the Farandoulian troops will be brought before a military tribunal.
The bimane Croknuff, Director of the Great Melbourne Aquarium, will lay down his arms before noon if he does not wish to be treated with the full rigor of military law.
Melbourne, May 17th ,
General Mandibul
Colonel Makako
Colonel Tapa-Tapa

VII. The assault on the Great Aquarium.
The horrible wickedness of the bimane Croknuff!
The world devoid of happiness; Mysora is no more.

On reading these proclamations, the bimane Croknuff became green with rage. The Aquarium's downcast keepers seemed disposed to obey the orders of General Mandibul; since all other resistance had ceased, they wanted to know why their Director was so stubbornly determined to fight. A few of them were appointed spokesmen by their comrades, but Mr. Croknuff cut them off.

"Degenerate sons of old England!" he cried. "I won't keep you. Go! Run away! Desert! Abandon the flag of the Motherland! I shall defend it alone, to the death! Tell the invaders that the Great Aquarium of Melbourne will die rather than surrender!"

The employees did not need to be told twice. The drawbridge was lowered in an eye-blink and they all left the enclosure, having disposed of their weapons. Mr. Croknuff, from the top of the rampart, saw them arrive at the first post and observed the felicitations addressed to them by the monkeys by means of hearty handshakes.

From now on, he was alone at his station–alone with Mysora. Australia had but one defender: the heroic Croknuff!

Fortunately, Mr. Croknuff felt that he was well-nigh invulnerable. The approaches to the fortress were garnished with carefully-disposed torpedoes. His moat, defended by the whale, the sharks and the octopodes, was uncrossable. Finally, as a last resort, a mine-chamber charged with 15 kilos of dynamite had been excavated beneath the directorial office. Mr. Croknuff experienced a certain sensual thrill at the thought that if he were blown up, he would be blown up in company with Mysora.

In the afternoon, the monkeys gathered at the end of the avenue. Mr. Croknuff could see, with perfect distinction, Saturnin I giving orders to his brightly-clad staff. Oh, if he only had artillery, what a pleasure it would have been to shower his enemy with grape-shot!

When monkey scouts advanced cautiously to the wall surrounding the grounds, Mr. Croknuff afforded himself the pleasure of exploding one of his torpedoes under their feet. The unfortunate monkeys were hurled into the air, but their commandant–our old friend from *La Belle Léocadie*, Seaman Tournesol–escaped safe and sound, and went to make his report to Farandoul.

Mr. Croknuff having imprudently revealed his batteries, Farandoul postponed his attack.

When night fell, Mr. Croknuff found it inconvenient to have to guard such a considerable expanse of ramparts all by himself. He had to march back and forth all night along the length of his fortifications, rifle in hand, keeping a sharp lookout. When morning approached, he could not stay there. Being unable to see any preparations being made outside for an attack, he lay down on some sandbags. One eye closed, then the other, and he fell into a profound sleep.

He slept very badly! He dreamed that he was the monkeys' prisoner and that Farandoul had him impaled for display in a new Museum of Natural History. Little monkeys came to this Museum to listen to educational lectures on mankind. As

143

the carefully-pinned-up Croknuff served as a subject for the professor's demonstrations, Farandoul and Mysora walked past wearing diving-suits and laughingly pointed him out to their children, who were similarly clad. This horrid spectacle made Mr. Croknuff cry out in alarm and wake up.

Horror! His dream was on the way to realization. The monkeys were surrounding the Aquarium, silently preparing to mount an assault. In advance of the monkeys, men dressed in diving-suits were descending into the moat.

Saturnin I had correctly reckoned that Mr. Croknuff, left alone in his fortress, could not mount a sufficient guard. He had assumed that fatigue would overcome the scientist at the end of the night, and all preparations had been made to profit from this opportunity. In the final hours of darkness, a battalion of monkeys had advanced upon the Aquarium, carrying ladders, wooden beams with which to make bridges, and brushwood to heap up in the moat.

Saturnin, Mandibul and four monkeys, having put on diving-suits, had descended into the moat–repelling the attacks of the Javanese sharks with their air-pistols–in order to fix large beams in place between the two banks. As for the whale, needless to say, it had fled to the far end of the semicircle at the first sight of the diving-suits. It was at the very moment that the monkeys were arriving at the foot of the bastion that Mr. Croknuff awoke. It required 30 seconds of rubbing his eyes and pinching himself to ascertain that he was not still impaled–and that was sufficient time for the monkeys to deploy their ladders.

As they mounted their deliberate assault, giving voice to their war-cry, Mr. Croknuff rediscovered his courage. He seized a ladder and, with a superhuman effort, he pushed it aside, along with all those it carried. The cries were redoubled–the ladder had collided with others as it fell, toppling scores of assailants–but it did not put an end to the escalade. The monkeys, by grace of their natural agility, had nothing to fear from heavy falls; they got up again and resumed their charge with increased vigor.

It was a success. The first line of defense was breached.

Mr. Croknuff, beside himself with rage, howled as he saw that he was on the point of being surrounded by monkeys that were leaping on to the rampart simultaneously from 15 ladders. To perish thus, without vengeance! That single thought gave him the strength of ten, and with a great leap he threw himself backwards into the Aquarium building, whose door he scarcely had time to barricade.

There was only a moment's respite. The second line of defense would be stormed soon enough–but that respite, brief as it was, was sufficient for the enraged Croknuff to put his final plan into operation!

Standing in his directorial office, in the center of the tanks of his aquarium, facing the terrified Mysora, he waited for Farandoul and the monkeys, in order to blow himself up along with them. A single movement of his hand, and 15 kilos of dynamite, bursting forth like a volcano, would rise 1000 feet into the air, along with the wreckage of the Aquarium, its assailants and the last citizen of free Australia.

Outside, the monkeys discussed the situation. Farandoul broke down the door with two blows of a hatchet and came into the building alone. Realizing that the old scientist, in his despair, might commit some act of savagery, he wanted to make one last attempt at conciliation before risking everything to tear Mysora from Mr. Croknuff's grasp. With a single glance, he measured the full extent of the danger. In the horrible rictus disfiguring Croknuff's face, he read the manifest hope of a terrible vengeance and a fatal resolution–and Mysora was there, behind the pane of glass, holding out her trembling hands towards him.

"There's still time!" he cried to the scientist. "Give in, and give me Mysora, and I'll make you Minister of Public Education! All resistance is useless. In a minute, the Aquarium and everyone in it will be in my power, and it will be too late to ask for mercy. Give me Mysora!"

"Come and get her!" Croknuff yelled.

Farandoul realized that only an attack of lightning rapidity could prevent Croknuff from doing any harm. He stepped back to the door and issued an order to his troops. A single voice replied, and the aquarium was invaded in less than a second. Meanwhile, ten monkeys who had been placed at each window were smashing every one–including the walls of the tanks–with single blows of heavy wooden beams. Farandoul and Mandibul launched hatchet-blows at Mysora's aquarium, which no one had dared to breach with a beam.

The entire building made a cracking sound, as if it were about to collapse. A torrent of water gushed from the tanks broken by the beams–and in Croknuff's office, all the inmates of the Aquarium were swarming around the legs of the semi-submerged scientist.

"Hurrah for old England!" Croknuff howled, hurling himself towards his dynamite. "Hurrah! Hurrah! Hurrah!" His lifted arm was about to come down, and his mine was about to do its work, when a hideous creature rose up from the debris of one of the tanks smashed by the monkeys' beams, and fell upon him.

It was his giant octopus–his favorite, before the arrival of the whale–which tore at him with its four pairs of arms and its innumerable suckers!

The octopus held him firmly; he was about to perish in its grip or be drowned in his office.

Mysora was about to escape him...

Mr. Croknuff turned his head towards her. Farandoul having broken the wall of the tank with their hatchet-blows, Mysora had thrown herself into the arms of her triumphant fiancé. Farandoul and Mandibul were dragging her outside...

With a last desperate effort, Croknuff disengaged his arms from the grip of the octopus and triggered the mine-chamber.

A frightful shock shook the ground; a terrible detonation resounded. A jet of flame burst forth like a waterspout. The Aquarium exploded!

Walls, tanks, fish, monkeys–the entire edifice and all those contained within it–were projected violently into the air by the explosion. Their scattered debris strewn across the grounds, forming a circle with a radius of a mile.

Croknuff and his octopus, still locked in their embrace, were seen being lifted aloft amid splinters of wood, at the center of a vortex of fire.

For several minutes, the survivors of this disaster were unable to get their bearings. A cloud of black smoke ascended from the ruins of the Aquarium. The first to speak was an individual who emerged from the moat wearing a blackened diving-suit.

"Help us, *La Belle Léocadie*!" he cried. "There's work to be done here!"

This person was General Mandibul, last seen with Farandoul, who was carrying poor near-dead Mysora, when the mine exploded. Since he had been able to come safe and sound through the fiery furnace, there was still hope for the two young lovers. Mariners and monkeys threw themselves in unison towards the moat.

A hand emerged from the water, then a head, and Farandoul appeared, supporting Mysora's inanimate body. Twenty arms were extended towards him to help him scale the slope with his precious burden.

Farandoul laid Mysora on the ground and anxiously unfastened the young woman's helmet.

This is what had happened:

Profiting from the interval when Croknuff was grappling with his octopus, Farandoul and Mandibul had got through the door with Mysora. The explosion had caught them on the rampart and had precipitated them into the moat while all those who were still inside the building had been blown up with Croknuff. No sooner had they concluded that they were saved, when the sharks and the whale, terrified by the explosion, had passed over them like a cavalry charge, knocking them down. In the confusion, Mysora's air-tube had been severed, and the poor girl had collapsed in Farandoul's arms.

While the survivors collect themselves and take stock of the situation in the disaster area, a silent group now surrounds Farandoul and his fiancée.

Mandibul is standing up, his arms crossed, in the grip of bitter grief. A few monkeys, scorched and blackened, burned in places, exchange sad glances. Farandoul's brothers wring their hands and a few large but furtive tears roll down the tanned cheeks of the former mariners of *La Belle Léocadie*.

Mysora is laid out on the grass, her unbound hair hanging loose about her shoulders, still clad in her diving-suit, her eyes seemingly closed forever! Farandoul has flung his diving helmet away. Kneeling beside the young woman, he searches for the slightest sign of life—one last hope!

Every assistance has been rendered in vain. Alas, Mysora is no more. The horrid Croknuff has not released his prey; his laughing shade may savor at leisure the grief of the unfortunate Farandoul.

O Mysora! Pure soul, enraptured at such a tender age by the enchantments of life, the love of your fiancé, the glorious Saturnin Farandoul, conqueror of Australia, the Alexander of the fifth continent... Your memory, O Mysora, will hover eternally above that distant land, which your chaste face has poeticized. Many tears will be shed in future ages over the tale of your misfortunes; many hearts will beat faster for the sad Mysora. In the same way that strangers with sensitive souls search the undergrowth of the Ile de France for the resting-place of Virginie,[40] so will travelers whose business brings them to

---

[40] *Paul et Virginie* (1788) by Jacques-Henri Bernardin de Saint-Pierre is one of the classic French tragic romances. Having been brought up together on the Ile de France (Mauritius), the eponymous couple are separated when Virginie is sent away to be educated in France. She steadfastly refuses to marry anyone except Paul, although her relatives in France think him far below her social status. The ship which eventu-

Australia turn aside from their routes to make pious pilgrimages to the tomb of Mysora!

But let us pass swiftly over these dolorous facts, lest our souls grow sad and our minds become afflicted by cruel memories.

Let us merely say that, as soon as he was certain of his ill-fortune, Farandoul recovered his strength and courage. His robust spirit resurfaced. He felt that, above all else, he had a duty to his troops and to the security of the conquest for which he had paid so dearly. After giving orders for Mysora's corpse to be carried with great ceremony to the gubernatorial mansion, Farandoul and Mandibul mounted their horses–without bothering to take off their diving-suits–in order to make a rapid review of the encampments of the Farandoulian army.

As trumpets and drums rallied the troops, the monkeys formed ranks and the column set out to march to the Parliament building, where it was based. Soon, no one remained in the smoking ruins of the Aquarium but a sentry charged with preventing bimanes from coming too close.

That day, every Farandoulian position saw the staff of its bimane leaders arrive like a whirlwind. The troops greeted their beloved General with cries and dances of enthusiasm, still unaware of the poignant grief that made Farandoul weep within the helmet of his diving-suit. Overcoming his emotion, Farandoul took every necessary precaution to ensure the well-being and security of his devoted quadrumanes.

Melbourne's barracks being inadequate, Mandibul had thought of billeting the monkeys with the local population, and several regiments were already established in the homes

---

ally carries Virginie back to the Ile de France is wrecked as it approaches the shore; modesty compels her to refuse the help of a lustful sailor and she is drowned. Paul dies of grief shortly afterwards. Robida apparently agrees with those cynical readers who thought the tale a trifle overwrought; Jules Verne, of course, rarely permitted his explorers and scientists any romantic distraction from the serious business of discovery.

of private individuals–but it was necessary to drop the idea, difficulties having cropped up with cantankerous folk who whined about tyranny and fainted away at the sight of the arrival in their homes of a dozen brave monkeys and a couple of quadrumane officers carrying billets for three days lodgings! In order not to offend the feminine part of the population, they contented themselves with occupying public buildings, and Farandoul gave orders for the establishment of a temporary camp in the Melbourne suburbs.

VIII. The organization of the Farandoulian Empire.
Biographies of the principal bimane and quadrumane leaders.
In which the great ideas of Saturnin I
regarding the regeneration of the world in general,
and old Europe in particular, are revealed to the reader.

No resistance had any longer to be feared within the Victoria colony. Before throwing himself into the conquest of the other Australian states, Farandoul judged that it would be sensible to complete the re-organization of the conquered province. He had cleared away its old institutions and was enthusiastic to establish new ones, in keeping with its new situation. A great conference was held in the gubernatorial mansion on the evening after Mysora's funeral.

Ambition was now the sole forceful sustenance of Farandoul's heart. He was determined to establish solid foundations for the empire that his valor was to carve out of the Australian continent. The participants in the conference were General Mandibul, the crew of *La Belle Léocadie*, and–to preserve good diplomatic relations–the leaders of the various monkey army corps.

"Bimanes and quadrumanes," said Farandoul, opening the session, "my dear comrades, I ought to begin by giving you a brief account of the exact situation. Having landed with 40,000 monkeys, we have gained possession of Melbourne in three days. The militias have been disarmed and the inhabitants subjugated; the entire province is in our power.

"Reinforcements will soon arrive; I estimate them at 10,000 monkeys, increasing our forces to 50,000 combatants. That should be sufficient for anything, even to repulse any counter-offensive by the British. But get this firmly into your heads, comrades: it is by discipline alone that we shall be able to found something durable. It is by valor regulated by discipline that we have triumphed; it is by conserving that discipline that we shall ensure the destiny of Farandoulia for ever.

"Today, the bimanes of Australia, crushed and terrified by the suddenness of our victory, still regard us as victorious invaders. These attitudes must be subtly changed, so that they will come to feel that their destiny is linked to ours by a common interest. Tomorrow, under our protection, commerce and industry must begin anew; we must encourage that renaissance with a friendly attitude.

"Our leaders must be vigilant, to ensure that no bimane is molested, and that no disputes arise. Until public services can be organized, food and equipment requisitioned for the army will be paid for in bonds drawn on the future Ministry of Finance. Once again, bimanes and quadrumanes, I insist that the strictest equity be maintained in relations with the local people, and the most exact discipline in every detail of service."

The next day's *Melbourne Herald* acquainted the population with the decisions taken at this conference. At the head of its political section it featured the following decree:

The province of Farandoulia known by the name of the State of Victoria is partitioned into five military divisions.

General Mandibul, governor of Melbourne, takes command of the first.[41]

---

[41] Robida forgets to mention here the rather important fact that Colonel Makako is Mandibul's second-in-command, although he includes Makako in the sequence of biographies that follows. Tapa-Tapa, the other quadrumane co-signatory of Sat-

The bimanes Kirkson, Tournesol, Trabadec, Escoubico, colonels of the Farandoulian army, are named commandants of the second, third, fourth and fifth divisions, with the quadrumanes Lutungo of Java, Ungko of Sumatra, Nasico of Borneo and Wa-Wo-Wa of New Guinea as chiefs of staff.

Saturnin I.

The *Melbourne Herald* followed these decrees with a series of biographical notes on the bimanes and quadrumanes appointed to these high positions. It was, of course, the indefatigable Dick Broken who had obtained all this information, his acquaintance with General Mandibul–begun on the evening of the battle of Cheep Hill–having made him better-known than anyone else to the leaders of the Farandoulian troops.

Here are the notices in question:

Bimane General Mandibul

General Mandibul is the former lieutenant of La Belle Léocadie. *He is a man of 45 years, well-preserved but a little overweight. He has a slightly apoplectic temperament, but has a genuine martial bearing when in uniform. His well-known modesty having forbidden him to give us any biographical details, we shall restrict ourselves to recalling, without mention of anterior campaigns, that he covered himself in glory throughout the conquest, from the first landing of the Farandoulians to the terrible assault on the Great Aquarium, where the last champion of England, the unfortunate and heroic Croknuff, was blown up rather than lower the flag. The appeasement measures taken by the Governor of Melbourne are a certain guarantee of his pure intentions towards us and clear testimony as to his considerable wisdom.*

---

urnin I's initial decrees, is also absent from the list of appointments, although he is similarly included in the biographies–unlike Makako, however, he has no further role to play in the story.

Quadrumane Colonel Makako

Colonel Makako is a monkey from the southern part of Borneo. He is a tall fellow with a very intelligent and animated face. His father, an old patriarch, has led a number of bellicose tribes for many years in their continual wars against the Dayaks. It is rumored that Colonel Makako is very ambitious and some say that his father was not sorry to see him depart with 600 of his most turbulent monkeys. At any rate, he is an authentic feudal overlord, ruling his monkeys with the total authority of a despot.

Quadrumane Colonel Tapa-Tapa

A Sumatran monkey. An amiable and playful character, he has none of the stiffness of his colleague Makako. He has joined the Farandoulian army with a contingent of 800 monkeys, making up part of an entrepreneurial nation that lives on relatively good terms with the bimanes of Sumatra. Tapa-Tapa's compatriots, quitting the interior forests, are gradually coming closer to the towns. Several districts of Siak and Achem [42] are entirely inhabited by them; at Palembang, they have acquired the same rights as the bourgeoisie of the city and live in the same houses as the bimanes, who occupy the ground floors while renting the upper floors to quadrumanes. In sum, Colonel Tapa-Tapa, a simple fellow and a good chap, is entirely in sympathy with us. His monkeys were the first to fraternize with bimanes.

---

[42] Siak and Achem (or Achin), were two of the old Sultanates of Sumatra. Achem, situated in the northern part of the island, became a Dutch dependency in 1873 following a violent conflict. Siak, on the east coast, was similarly gathered into the Dutch fold, although the sultan retained some power until 1946. Palembang, mentioned later in the paragraph, remains an important city in the south of the island to this day.

Bimane Colonel Kirkson

Tall, strong, ruddy-faced, bearded, Anglo-Saxon in origin but absolutely devoted to Saturnin I. Distinguished himself in many battles, notably in the campaign mounted by the mariners of La Belle Léocadie *against the pirates of the Isles of Sunda.*

Quadrumane Colonel Lutungo of Java

A big monkey, five feet four inches in height, with greying fur. He is the chief or sultan of a tribe of large langurs [43] *spread throughout the interior mountains of Java. He has a very grand air about him,* [44] *his features are imprinted with a calm dignity in perfect accordance with his aristocratic manners; one immediately senses, on seeing him for the first time, that one is dealing with a monkey with breeding. His family have reigned in Java for many years over more than a dozen large villages whose inhabitants number 300 or 400. He has furnished the Farandoulian army with a contingent of 350 fighters.*

Bimane Colonel Tournesol

Born June 26th, 18**, in Marseilles, France; was granted entry into the merchant marine with the rank of cabin boy; has served with honor aboard La Belle Léocadie, *notably against the pirates, at least 40 of whom he (to use his own picturesque expression) "de-carcassed." Commanded the monkey advance-guard at Cheep Hill alongside one of His Majesty Saturnin I's brothers; took the English ex-Governor,*

[43] The text has *semnopithéque*; the genus Semnopithecus seems to be identical to the modern genus Presbytis, which consists of the langur monkeys.

[44] *Grand air*, which I have conserved from the original text, usually means "open air" in French; the wordplay is untranslatable.

Sir John Collingham, prisoner during the capture of Melbourne. Short, thin, swarthy, black-bearded, plain-speaking, very pronounced Marseillaise accent.

Colonel Ungko of Sumatra

As calm as his leader is exuberant. Who could believe, on first seeing that tranquil and reflective face, that one is face to face with the leader of the most intrepid escaladers: those monkey acrobats used to living in the highest regions of the forest. His troops are the trapeze-artists of the Farandoulian army; it was they who, passing with the greatest rapidity from tree to tree, executed the outflanking and overhanging maneuvers which baffled the experienced bimane tacticians of England. Colonel Ungko, an innocent in polite society, is transformed in action, becoming the terrible warrior that we know.

Colonel Bimane Trabadec

Thirty-two years old, short and stocky, born in Saint-Malo, France; full of genuine veneration for His Majesty Saturnin I, swearing by none but he and Notre-Dame-d'Auray.[45] As intrepid on the field of battle as he is gentle and simple in private life. Declares himself ready, since His Majesty has spoken of the fusion of races, to marry a she-monkey of good family. Says he will send to Saint-Malo for his documents.

---

[45] Auray is a port on the southern coast of Brittany (Saint-Malo being on the north coast). It was a center of Vendean resistance to the Revolution of 1789; the notorious Breton general Georges Cadoudal–who appointed himself Napoleon's would-be nemesis, involving himself in several assassination plots, including the affair of la machine infernale–was born near Auray and would also have sworn by Notre-Dame-d'Auray. Saturnin Farandoul obviously commanded broader loyalty at this point in his imperial adventure than his august predecessor was ever able to contrive.

Quadrumane Colonel Nasico of Borneo

An exceedingly intelligent quadrumane, remarkable for the amplitude of his forehead and the altogether human length of his nose. A tribal chief, a monkey of good family. According to the Indians, his nation is descended from a company of men driven out of the towns by war, who—turning their backs on the world—must have chosen their wives from a tribe of hospitable monkeys. Nasico is directly descended from the leader of these men; at any rate, power has been in the hands of his family for many years. What seems to confer a certain authenticity on this legend is that the 500 monkeys who have followed Nasico are just as remarkable as he is; their well-developed noses project nobly from faces fully-framed by fine red beards.

Bimane Colonel Escoubico

Spanish by birth, a remarkably ardent man, as indefatigable in war as in pleasure. Makes his troops march to the sound of music. As soon as he entered Melbourne, he requisitioned tambourines and guitars; together with a few monkeys endowed with a talent for harmony he quickly formed a corps of excellent musicians. Proposes to host balls in his residence.

Quadrumane Colonel Wa-Wo-Wa of New Guinea

The best of monkeys. Simple, rustic, honest. Straight by nature, ever amiable, occasionally jovial. Leader of one of the greatest simian nations of Oceania, closely related to the tribe with which H. M. Saturnin I spent his childhood. Wa-Wo-Wa's contingent is also one of the most numerous. This brave leader's monkeys form, so to speak, the line troops of the Farandoulian army. If they are less accomplished in advance-guard attacks and brilliant charges than those of Colonel Ungko, their finest quality is their resilience; at the end of the day, as old soldiers say, they stick to their guns!

Some weeks later, three persons came together in conference with Saturnin I in His Majesty's office in the former

Governor's mansion. These three individuals were General Mandibul, Farandoul's foster-father and the journalist Dick Broken.

"Yes, my friends," Farandoul said, "I see our mission clearly–the mission of Farandoulia, the world's fifth continent,[46] so young and so healthy! To repair the injustices of other continents; to cause the past to be forgotten; to bring back justice and happiness and restore the globe's Golden Age. Never have bimanes had in their hands the elements we have in ours: 50,000 monkeys, so strong and brave; those which arrive every day from all the isles in Oceania; our navy, composed of vessels seized in the ports of the state of Victoria–manned at present by mixed crews, although our monkeys will soon be able to operate them by themselves under the orders of sympathetic bimane officers, whom we shall recruit from every nation.

"With all this, we shall complete the conquest of the Australian provinces that England still holds, and we shall drive the English out of every island in Oceania! The monkeys of Borneo, Sumatra and Java will rise up and join us; then, as a bold move, we shall land..."

"Where's that, Sire?" asked Dick Broken.

"In Bombay!" cried Farandoul. "In India, where the Hindu bimanes and quadrumanes groan under the yoke of perfidious Albion! Remember, Broken, that you are not English; you are Australian–and, henceforth, Farandoulian! As soon as we have driven the English out of India, we shall establish a mixed government there..."

---

[46] The other four must be Europe, Asia, Africa and America; the title of *Voyages très extraordinaires de Saturnin Farandoul dans les 5 ou 6 parties du monde et dans tous les pays connus et même inconnus de M. Jules Verne* presumably includes the formulation "5 or 6" because there was some controversy, even before Ferdinand de Lesseps started work on the Panama Canal (in 1881), as to whether America ought to be regarded as two continents rather than one.

"Bravo, Sire! That's wonderful!" cried Mandibul.

"Wait! Once India is organized, we shall loose several generals and quadrumanes upon Asia, with the mission of opening up Siam, Cochin-China and the Celestial Empire to new ideas; far from considering our task to be over, we shall march upon the isthmus of Suez and thus into..."

"Europe!" said Broken.

"Yes, Europe–old Europe, so proud of its past glories, but where so many so-called civilized peoples maintain permanent armies beneath the scourge of modern times! Europe shall be ours! We shall begin by settling the eternal Eastern Question; Constantinople will be neither Turkish, nor Russian, nor English! At the other end of the Mediterranean, the English yoke will be lifted from Gibraltar... There are monkeys on Gibraltar, unhappy monkeys bent under the knee of the highlander–we shall free them!"

"And France, Sire?" Mandibul said. "I wouldn't be sorry to land one day at Bordeaux and..."

"France! Haven't you understood that I have destined France for a glorious role? We shall make haste to conquer her! I shall make Paris the capital of the world. France, which marches at the head of the flow of modernity, will understand the grandeur of our mission; she will throw herself into our movement with generous ardor! I ask for ten years to complete this great work; in ten years, within pacified Europe, there will be no more frontiers, no lines of demarcation, no permanent bimane armies! Commerce, industry and agriculture will no longer be in want of strong arms; its peoples, no longer having any monarchs or generals with vested interests in war and revolutions, will live in peace under the safeguard of a few regiments of monkeys!"

"I give in, O genius," murmured Dick Broken. "I'm a Farandoulian!"

"You shall be Governor of London!" Farandoul exclaimed. "What do we need, to accomplish all this? Disciplined armies! My good, brave monkeys have only to remain united and disciplined, and the world is ours!"

This single conversation suffices to indicate how the gifts comprising his genius had come together in Saturnin Farandoul. He had it all: grandeur of vision; power of reasoning; boldness of action.

Farandoul set to work courageously, with the devoted Mandibul and Dick Broken–who was completely committed to his cause–as his principal collaborators. We shall not venture to enter into every detail of the marvelous and incomparable adventure which Farandoul set himself to organize; it is for Australian historians to tell the world what those three men did in a few months,

The most serious difficulty, in the early stages, was the state of relations–frosty at least, if not outrightly hostile–manifest between the conquered populations and the conquering monkeys. No relationship was forged between bimanes and quadrumanes; the latter, being good and carefree fellows, were quite ready to fraternize, but bimane haughtiness always kept them at a distance. The only exceptions were a few mining districts on the Ballarat coast and Alberton in Colonel Escoubico's division. At Alberton, the Colonel hosted soirées and balls, seducing everyone with his liveliness and good humor. In his salons, notable bimanes–the women of high society, millionaire farmers and rich arms-dealers–mingled with the quadrumane officers of Wa-Wo-Wa's corps, who had become excellent dancers under the tutelage of the Spaniard Escoubico. At Ballarat, the good relations had had poorer results, the well-received monkeys having been drawn into the miners' drinking-dens, to the great detriment of their natural sobriety.

The Australian press soon began to complicate these difficulties. In the early days, it had kept a prudent silence, limiting itself to recording the decrees of the Farandoulian government without comment. After the first three months of the occupation, however, the papers recovered their courage and launched a petty but lively war of words against the Governor of Melbourne, which never let up. As the monkeys did not read the papers, this could not stir up any trouble in the army, but these scarcely-veiled excitations of hatred and contempt for the government maintained a dangerous agitation among the bimanes.

The council, worried by this development, decided to take drastic action. One morning, the following decree was published:

FARANDOULIAN EMPIRE

The Governor of Melbourne,

Because the entire press, encouraged by impunity, delivers new attacks every day against the paternal government of H. M. Saturnin I;

And because the quadrumanes of the army are attacked daily by the bimane papers, cruel outrages being perpetrated against their dignity without their being able to reply, since they are not yet able to read;

It is decided that:

All the newspapers are suppressed.

Mr. Dick Broken is hereby charged with the creation of an official gazette for the publication of governmental acts.

General Mandibul.

It was high time. The harm that the press had done to the new empire could not be countered right away. The systematic campaign of false news and slyly aggressive articles it had employed, at the instigation of the agents of England, soon bore unfortunate fruit.

The European powers neglected to respond to the letters sent by Saturnin I to notify other sovereigns of his accession to the throne. Monaco alone replied–coldly, it is true, but politely, her geographical situation compelling her to pay the greatest possible respect to a maritime power like Australia. The blackest calumnies were circulating in Europe regarding the new empire and her glorious founders; it was rumored that the monkeys, far from being the armed protectors of a nation of workers and tradesmen, were, to the contrary, abominable tyrants. It was even said that Farandoul was absolutely determined to provide bimane wives for all his soldiers, who were rumored to number 150,000–which would reduce 150,000 unhappy women to live under the yoke of brutal monkeys while their bimane ex-husbands became sad wanderers in the remote depths of the Australian deserts.

There is no need for us to protest against such infamous calumnies. To the contrary, the quadrumane "yoke" was exceedingly light within the Farandoulian nation. Far from seeking to contrive a fusion of the bimane and quadrumane races by mixed marriages, Farandoul stubbornly refused to give the Breton Colonel Trabadec permission to espouse a young and pretty quadrumane, the daughter of Colonel Wa-Wo-Wa. Anyway, it will be enough, to definitively disprove the fanciful rumors that were running through Europe, to say that one of Farandoul's first priorities, after the conquest, had been to bring the families of his warriors to Australia as quickly as the organization of the Farandoulian navy would allow. He had not had time, nor ships enough, to bring in excess of 200,000 quadrumanes of all ages from the distant isles of Oceania immediately, but in the end–thanks to Bora-Bora's fleet, merchant vessels and others seized in the ports–they had arrived. The world was informed of this at once, but the strangest rumors continued to circulate.

Curiously, a few individuals saw in Australia's new situation a colossal opportunity to do business. The biggest matrimonial agency in New York set out to organize an expedition to Australia. Within a month, every newspaper in the United States carried a huge advertisement conceived as follows:

MARRIAGE! MARRIAGE!! MARRIAGE!!!

Notice to spinsters of all ages of an army to marry.

Exceptional opportunity. Magnificent situations offered to ladies. An immense selection of young bachelors, many superior officers among them,

Imminent departure by any possible ship.

Enroll immediately. Send photographs.

The agency quickly assembled a formidable number of hopefuls. The photographs were artfully filed, and the women were notified to be ready to depart at a moment's notice. One morning, at his mansion in Melbourne, Farandoul received a score of stout albums, magnificently bound, containing more than 3000 photographs. At first, he could not imagine why they had been sent, but a letter enlightened him; the agency was offering him wives for the officers of his army, subject to a small fee for each introduction, and announcing the imminent arrival of a first shipment by way of a sample.

Farandoul, infuriated by the indelicacy of the people who engaged in such a business, replied that he would shoot any representative of the agency who set foot in Farandoulia.

He was no less annoyed when, at about the same time, another matrimonial agency–this one French–decided on its own authority to find a wife for him. This French agency had inserted the following notice among the small ads in *Le Figaro*:

RICH MARRIAGE
Good opportunity for princess,
or young person of high nobility.
A monarch to marry.

This advertisement, as one can well imagine, had fervently excited the Saint-Germain district, and a number of likely candidates had been put forward. A dozen examples selected from the collection had been forwarded to Farandoul by telegraph, who had refused them all, at the risk of causing a great many tears to flow. The pure memory of Mysora filled his heart.

Mandibul, to avoid any further annoyance to his friend and sovereign, had a photograph taken of the least naturally-favored of all the monkeys in the army, and sent it secretly to Paris as that of the marriageable monarch. Saint-German shuddered in horror; a few despairing young women took refuge in convents, although one timid spinster of 33 years and 11 months, a descendant of a family that went back at least as far as King Dagobert,[47] refused to withdraw her candidature on a point of principle.

Strict orders were given in Melbourne in anticipation of the arrival of the first shipment from the American agency. When the Yankee ship, carrying 400 spinsters, presented itself at Port Philip, entry to the port was sternly refused and it had to go back to sea incontinently.[48] It was learned some time

---

[47] Dagobert I (c. 600-639) became King of the Franks in 628; he extended the Frankish empire to the Pyrenees, codified their laws and founded the Abbey of St. Denis, who eventually became the patron saint of France. He was thus a King of France long before Charlemagne, let alone the Valois or the Bourbons who had ennobled most of the aristocratic families from whom the suburbanites of Saint-Germain would have claimed descent. The incident of the advertisement may have been suggested to Robida by the career of Orélie-Antoine de Tounens, who set off from France in the late 1850s to claim Auracania and Patagonia for his fatherland. He declared himself King Orélie I in November 1860, having recruited a few native Americans to his cause, but was captured and expatriated by Chilean colonists in 1862. He tried to raise money to "reclaim" his throne, but had to return to South America with no more than a few thousand francs; having run out of cash he returned to France again in 1871 and founded a newspaper, in which he advertised his need for a consort as well as pursuing more elaborate begging tactics. Such pretenders were not uncommon in 19th century France, Napoléon I having deposed many of the former petty kings of Europe and redistributed their thrones to his relatives and cronies. Napoléon III, to whom de Tounens would have had to appeal in the first instance, was neither so powerful nor so casual–and by 1871, following the French humiliation in the Franco-Prussian War, such projects became even more manifestly absurd.

[48] The adverb I have translated as "incontinently" is *incontinent*, whose double meaning in French is more feebly echoed in English. Although English cannot reproduce the full force

afterwards that the representative of the agency, to recover some few of his expenses, had steered towards the isles of Fiji, where he had succeeded in placing his 400 ladies at a discount price with a small tribe of savages afflicted with a superabundance of bachelors.

Thus ended the campaign indiscreetly launched against Farandoulia by the matrimonial agencies.

IX. The Perfidious Schemes of Perfidious Albion.
Lady Arabella Cardigan, a bimane spy,
seduces quadrumane Colonel Makako.
How empires perish!!!

Saturnin Farandoul was able to continue his work in peace. All his time and attention was devoted to the army, which required to be organized and thoroughly trained in order to rise to its task. Farandoul established an immense instruction camp on the shore at Port Philip, overlooking Melbourne Bay. This camp, protected by a line of entrenchments, was connected to a series of constructions which Farandoul had put in place for the bay's defense. The monkeys shifted the earth with considerable ardor and intelligence and became, under Mandibul's direction, excellent military engineers.

At the extremity of the bay, a little fort raised above Rocas Point completed the system of defense.

Farandoul had another object of preoccupation. Alone among all the armies of the world, the quadrumane army had no cavalry! It was a serious oversight, which might have disastrous consequences in certain situations. After serious deliberation, the council decided that it might be wise to utilize kangaroos for this purpose in preference to horses, towards which the monkeys had a certain antipathy. The agility of

---

of Robida's double entendre, it seemed appropriate to retain it rather than use one of the more usual adverbial translations of incontinent, such as "forthwith" or "straight away."

monkeys and kangaroos being in perfect accord, this new experiment ought to yield excellent results.

The camp at Port Philip soon displayed great animation; every morning, under the lofty surveillance of the Generals, the troops were drilled for several hours in the handling of their weapons. The afternoon was given over to the battalion school. Twice a week they played war games. All the regiments moved off, executing collective movements and mounting charges in front of the bimanes of Melbourne, who flocked to see them. Brightly-clad staff-officers mounted on kangaroos ran through the front lines at the gallop carrying orders to the bimane generals. Saturnin I, mounted on horseback at the center of a sparkling general staff, towered over the assembly. The ladies of Melbourne paid particular attention to the hero's five foster-brothers, gathering around them like a guard of honor.

Similar maneuvers were undertaken in the four other military divisions, to maintain the high morale of the troops and give them the necessary instruction.

The example of Colonel Escoubico, the commandant of the town of Alberton, had been followed by other leaders. Brass bands and corps of excellent musicians were formed in every brigade, under the direction of bimane conductors hired at considerable expense. Escoubico's band, organized in the Spanish style, comprised 14 monkeys in the little ivory-topped caps of students, mostly playing guitars, tambourines and castanets. The other musical corps were armed with stout copper instruments which resounded terribly in military marches. Military music was played in the garrisons every afternoon beneath the windows of the commanding general; one could hear all the latest works [49] from Europe brilliantly executed, and equally brilliant pieces born of the musical inspiration of the quadrumanes.

---

[49] *Nouveautés*, here translated as "latest works", also means "fancy goods" in a commercial context, so there is an element of derision in Robida's choice of that word.

Farandoulia had its own maestro, a Javanese langur named Coco, whose character was exceedingly disagreeable by nature, although endowed with qualities of verve and originality unknown among bimane musicians. The maestro had a masterpiece in preparation for Melbourne's Grand Theater: a grand opera *mixte* [50]–which is to say, intended to be played by both bimane and quadrumane artistes. Its title was *The Romeo of the Zoological Gardens.*[51]

The opera's subject, one is given to understand, was the story of a monkey in love with the daughter of the Director of a zoo; this quadrumane Romeo languished in a captivity whose misery the maiden alleviated by her delicate attentions. Love was born in two hearts. The barbarous father having refused his consent, there was a monkey revolt, a ballet, an elopement, a reconciliation with the bimanes and a grand ballet mixte. The most remarkable elements, according to those who first heard them, were a choir of captive monkeys, a song of war and a duo mixte between the daughter of the Director, a bimane artiste, and Romeo, a monkey artiste. Our friend Dick Broken had written the words for this magisterial work, as well as those of a patriotic song mixte, whose couplets were to be sung by bimanes and the refrains by quadrumanes.

To return to our military musicians, who had delighted the bimane population at first, we must confess that after a few months they were playing their concerts to empty houses. The pretty blonde-haired misses had disappeared, doubtless regretfully but probably in obedience to secret orders sent from London.

---

[50] I have left *mixte* in French for the same reason that artistes, which occurs later in the sentence, is conventionally left in French rather than translated into English–i.e., because it is simply not done to talk about opera without adopting a tone of cosmopolitan snobbery.

[51] Robida gives this title in English, although I have taken the liberty of adding the terminal "s" in conformity with conventional English usage.

The sky became overcast; little by little, dark clouds were gathering on the horizon.

Certain indications allowed Farandoul to sense that a storm was about to break over Australian soil. There were vague rumors of an English intervention. The European consuls were showing a certain ill-will, and foreign agents had been reported to be active in the large population centers. A secret campaign by England was making itself felt; perfidious Albion was employing an indirect means of attack typical of her tortuous politics.

It was, above all, the quadrumane army on which the English agents were working–that honest and pure army, which Great Britain did her utmost to corrupt by provoking indiscipline therein and developing within its ranks a taste for the finer things in life.[52] By all means possible, perfidious Albion attempted to tarnish the quadrumanes' virtues and inculcate in them the vices of bimanes. Her weapon of preference was whisky; strong spirits were soon flowing like rivers, and the monkeys were losing the habit of temperance.

Although the Generals kept a careful watch over their troops and dealt severely with the guilty ones, the evil took hold so strongly that discipline was seriously compromised. The quadrumane leaders themselves, in the drawing-rooms that opened to them as if in response to a password, were not always able to refuse the champagne that was offered to them. At the same time, clever spies caused pride and ambition to creep into the hearts of the quadrumane Generals by means of base flatteries and shameful kowtowing to their panache–and, in the end, awakened jealousy in the quadrumanes, directed

---

[52] The French *goût du panache* has a rather elastic meaning, *panache* (literally "plume") sarcastically implying unwarranted arrogance, mild drunkenness and/or delusions of grandeur. I have transcribed the word directly in the following paragraph, although its English usage does not usually carry these sly insinuations, and have rendered the phrase more economically as "taste for finery" later in the chapter.

against Farandoul's bimane companions and Farandoul himself.

The attention of England eventually came to focus on one of the quadrumane leaders: Colonel Makako, General Mandibul's chief of staff–who was, as we have said, a sort of feudal gentleman, infatuated with the nobility and antiquity of his race. Long used to the submissiveness of his family's monkey vassals, he believed that he had the right to give everyone orders, and yielded very reluctantly to the discipline introduced into the army by Farandoul.

The agents of perfidious Albion having quickly discovered the hateful and jealous tendency of his character, Colonel Makako was almost immediately surrounded, flattered and outwitted by them. In the drawing-rooms of Melbourne, the prettiest women in the pay of England watered him with champagne and flattery. They affected to ridicule Saturnin in front of him, to diminish his merits while simultaneously exalting those of "the irresistible Makako." Colonel Makako smiled, and responded to these interested discourses with approving grunts in the rustic and not-very-gracious language of the highland monkeys [53] of Borneo.

In the space of a few months, Colonel Makako had become entirely hostile to Farandoul, and above all to General Mandibul, whose orders he received with anger and ill-will. Like a General prepared for *pronunciamentos*,[54] he was only waiting for an opportunity to raise the flag of rebellion, along with partisans he counted on within the general staff, found

---

[53] The French *montagnard*, here translated as "highland," has a double meaning in French because the term *montagnards* came to be applied to the extremists of the Revolutionary parliament–including the chief perpetrators of the Terror–who occupied the highest-placed seats in the assembly.

[54] In Spain, an authority-figure–almost invariably a military man–who refuses to obey the law, is said to be issuing a *pronunciamento*.

among those who had been corrupted by a taste for finery, hatred for discipline or the abuse of strong liquor.

This is how things stood on one fine morning, after 15 months of occupation, when news spread through Melbourne that an English fleet had been encountered at sea by two Farandoulian ships, only one of which had been able to escape, thanks to the skill of her quadrumane crew. It was true enough, and while the rumor spread through Melbourne, Farandoul gave the final orders for a rapid consolidation of the army.

The English fleet had been sighted off Point Campbell. One of the Farandoulian vessels had escaped, as we have said; the other, whose line of retreat was cut off, had engaged the enemy in violent combat. This heroic ship was the *Young Australia*,[55] a sloop with a dozen cannon, commanded by Captain Jonathan Butterfield, a bimane of American origin recruited to the quadrumane cause.

Five large English frigates, the *Devastation*, the *Warrior*, the *Terror*, the *Devorous* and the *Carnivorous* [56] attacked the little *Young Australia*, deluging her with fire and steel. Jonathan Butterfield, standing fast on his quarterdeck, sailed dead ahead towards the monstrous armor-plated English ships; his courageous crew, comprising only 60 or so monkeys and a few bimane engineers, displayed a heroism worthy of classical antiquity.

The enemy's fireballs having started a fire between the sloop's decks, the quadrumanes fastened her to the *Carnivorous* with grappling-hooks, without deigning to respond to the English signals. The blazing fire made rapid progress, but the

---

[55] The text gives the ship's name in French (*La Jeune Australie*), but as it must have been appropriated locally it seems reasonable to employ an English version.

[56] All these titles are given in English in the text; I have left them unaltered, even though *Devorous* is a very unlikely name for an English naval vessel.

monkeys had already quit the sloop and were playing havoc on the bridge of the *Carnivorous*. When the *Young Australia* finally blew up, carrying a part of the English frigate with her, the last monkeys who had taken refuge in the topsails of the *Carnivorous* were still defending themselves.

Two days after the battle, the English fleet was in sight of Port Philip, and the rapidly-deployed Farandoulian army occupied all the coastal defenses. A state of siege having been declared, a proclamation urged the population to remain calm, the Farandoulian army being sufficient to ensure the security of the province.

Unfortunately, grave symptoms of insubordination had manifested themselves within the army. Some regiments were grumbling, others were demanding additional distributions of liquid rations. Colonel Makako's corps was the most conspicuous of all for its bad attitude and its whining.

General Mandibul, who had remained in Melbourne to maintain order, was astonished by the sloppiness of Makako's service as chief of staff, while Makako visited the drawing-rooms of Melbourne with increasing frequency.

On the evening of the brilliant naval battle of Point Campbell, a grand soirée was given in his honor by an old bimane civil servant; Makako and a few of his officers were received there with a veritable ovation, which enraptured their vanity.

One of those *femmes fatales* for whom historians are, alas, always seeking at the bottom of every great catastrophe, entered the lists in order to tip the balance definitively in favor of England. Lady Arabella Cardigan, an English spy of the most ravishing beauty, made her entrance on the scene. She was newly arrived from Europe with precise ministerial instructions, and her lovely eyes had a devastating effect on the quadrumane general staff, already weakened by the repeated efforts of English agents. Her beauty caused every head to turn as she crossed the room in a regal manner to embrace the host.

Makako was fluttering around the buffet; forewarned by one of his officers, he went back into the large drawing-room at the very moment when Lady Arabella asked to be presented to him.

The patrician beauty of the blonde Englishwoman sparked the enthusiastic admiration of the Colonel like a lightning-bolt. Those huge eyes, that long blonde hair, that tall and slender figure, that aristocratic perfume–everything about her lifted Makako's heart. Appropriately, the orchestra struck up an intoxicating waltz; Makako wrapped his arms around Lady Arabella's body, and drew her into the giddy whirl. They were seen passing through every room, moving in time to the whim of the rhythm and revolving tirelessly in the grip of a delirious music. Makako, transported by his excitement, gripped Lady Arabella's body a little more firmly than was entirely proper, and planted furtive kisses on the one hand that she abandoned to him.

Lady Arabella seemed bent on ensuring that the fervent quadrumane Colonel lost his head completely. Lovingly supported on his arm, she waltzed with him all night. Ten waltzes, 15 waltzes, 30 waltzes were granted to him. The host had given orders to the orchestra, which–without stopping, except to down pints of liquid–rolled out interminable musical fantasies. Long after the other dancers were tired out, their panting partners getting their breath back on the divans, Makako was still waltzing!

The conductor of the orchestra had received reinforcements to replace those of his men who had fallen on the battlefield, but the blonde Englishwoman seemed indefatigable, and the same smile was perpetually fluttering upon her lips.

England's agents were swarming everywhere; observers, more attentive than the quadrumanes, had quickly cottoned on to a number of secret signals–a few furtive glances exchanged in passing between Lady Arabella and certain suspicious individuals. The work of demoralization begun several months earlier was making new and rapid progress.

Some hours after the ball, Makako, irresistibly seduced, presented himself at Lady Arabella Cardigan's house, to lay his devotion and his sword at her feet. The conspirators were there; a conference ensued in which the beautiful eyes of Lady Arabella played a leading role in the action. When they separated, Makako was totally committed to overthrow Saturnin I and usurp his throne, which the inflamed Colonel hoped to share with the blonde lady.

What a dream! Into what rapturous depths had the ambitious quadrumane been plunged! Absolute master of Australia, he would escort her majesty to Europe, of which he had heard such tales–to that England, where Lady Arabella Cardigan had estates and castles. He had to take action; the agents of England had, so to speak, drawn him a plan.

Profiting from the fact that the army was concentrated at Port Philip, it was necessary to work by every possible means, within a few days, to seize the bimane Generals–and, most important of all, Saturnin's five foster-brothers, whose influence was capable of putting an end to the rebellion. That having been accomplished, the irresistible Makako, intoxicated by the honeyed words and languorously veiled eyes of Lady Arabella, believed that he was certain to ward off every danger. He even deluded himself that he might remain, England notwithstanding, master of Australia.

The arrival of Makako at the Port Philip camp was the signal for a renewed outbreak of acts of insubordination. Farandoul and the Generals had done well; they had been able to prevent indiscipline from gradually infecting the best regiments. As England's agents redoubled their efforts, immense quantities of strong liquor were transported to the troops in improvised canteens by bimane ladies, despite Mandibul's stern prohibitions. Although access to the encampments and barracks was rigorously forbidden to bimanes, these ladies succeeded in persuading superior officers to accept a few casks of fine liqueurs, under various pretexts–most frequently as patriotic gifts–on several occasions.

One regiment, which occupied a small redoubt at the end of the line, received in this manner a provision of whisky that it swallowed in haste, in order to make it disappear and avoid any reproaches that Colonel Escoubico might make during his tour of inspection. The result was that within two days the regiment fell dead drunk upon its bastions–and had the Colonel not arrived, the redoubt, deprived of its defenders, could have fallen into English hands. The regiment woke up in the police station, the officers having been cashiered, but this severe treatment did not prevent the same thing happening at another post the following day.

The English fleet, in the open sea, contented itself with tightly blockading Port Philip, without making any direct attempt upon it. This inaction was what caused Farandoul and Mandibul their greatest anxiety. For what was England waiting before commencing hostilities? The increasing demoralization of the quadrumane army was evidently the work of her secret agents; did she wish to attack only when the fatal work would be completed, when the good and loyal regiments of former times would have turned into an undisciplined and unstable rabble?

Alas, the wait was not to be a long one.

Farandoul, kept informed by the reports of his Generals, wanted to react vigorously against the demoralization. To try to recover his old power over the minds of his troops, he summoned the entire army to a grand review on the Port Philip beach, in full view of the English navy. A strict order of the day had to be communicated to the monkeys for the stern repression of all insubordination.

Beneath the bright morning Sun, the immense beach was covered, as far as the eye could see, with magnificent quadrumane regiments. The chiefs of staff, admonished by the bimane Generals, had done their best to re-establish discipline.

The sight was truly magnificent. The infantry occupied the center and the cavalry the flanks, following the order of battle adopted by Farandoul: in advance, the regiments of riflemen; in the second rank of the line, the dark mass of mon-

174

keys armed with Oceanian clubs; on the right flank, the light kangaroo cavalry, lancers and chasseurs; on the left flank, the heavy cavalry, the giant monkeys of Borneo, also mounted on kangaroos but armed with heavy ironwood clubs.

Unfortunately, the English fleet having executed a suspicious maneuver in the open sea, Saturnin I was obliged to remove himself to the little fort at Point Rocas in order to observe it.

The troops under arms put on a good show at first, but towards noon it was necessary to make a distribution of food and refreshments. The quartermaster had orders to convey 300 casks of fresh water–the camp's daily ration, sent from Melbourne that morning–to the field of the maneuvers. The catering corps being entirely won over by Makako, it had already caused Mandibul great concern, but he had trusted in the surveillance of a few solid officers placed at its head. He was still ignorant of grave disturbances that had broken out in Melbourne, of which these brave officers had been the first victims.

On their arrival on the plain where the entire army was roasting under the hot Sun, in consequence of the English fleet's maneuvers, the carriages of the catering corps were greeted by the hurrahs of the thirsty regiments. The distribution was quickly made; every corps had its casks, which were immediately surrounded by soldiers. There was a certain brouhaha while the casks were opened; the quartermaster's fresh water seemed suspect to a few officers, who did their best to prevent the troops from getting to it. The water was clear and limpid, but its odor was definitely too alcoholic.

The monkeys, after having tasted it, refused to obey their leaders. There were a few nasty grimaces at the first mouthful, but a second gulp proved the water to be so extraordinarily pleasant that all discipline was forgotten. They jostled one another to obtain a larger share.

175

The quartermaster's fresh water was kirsch! [57]

The hearts of infantry and cavalry alike were uplifted by joy. Despairing of preventing the distribution, the officers joined in, determined to have their share. Soon, the kirsch had flooded the entire field of maneuver, from one end to the other.

The second part of the infernal plan hatched by the English agents had been put into execution.

At about 2 p.m.–the English navy having ceased its maneuvers–the Generals and their staff left the fort. The trumpets and the drums recalled the soldiers to their posts. The officers ran here, there and everywhere, and the regiments reconstituted themselves, after a fashion, but the entire army was in a visibly emotional state. In place of the former neat and tidy straight lines, irregular zigzags spread out. The cavalry, in particular, stood out by virtue of its awful disarray. Great waves made themselves felt along the battle-front. When those on the right of the first rank began to lurch dazedly, the movement spread from one to another until it reached the far end of the line.

The furious Farandoul set his horse to the gallop. His escort moved off behind him in a whirlwind of dust. The first corps on the right flank was, appropriately enough, Makako's.

At the sight of the Farandoulian general staff, Makako's followers started theatrically. Ear-splitting howls rent the air; the Farandoulian flag was struck, and an immense red banner provided by Lady Arabella was raised in its place. The regi-

---

[57] Kirsch may seem an odd choice, given that it is usually distilled in Germany from black Morello cherries, and is highly unlikely to have been available by the cartload in Melbourne in the 1870s. It is entirely possible that Robida has no other reason for using the name than its flagrant absurdity, but it may be significant that the crushed cherry-stones give kirsch a bitter almond flavour supposed to resemble that of cyanide; Robida might be attempting subtly to emphasize the poisonous nature of the draught.

ments next in line, seized by the contagion of this example, also dispersed; their leaders, won over by Makako, hastened to rally round the general revolt.

That was exactly what was happening! The beautiful army formed up on the beach was no longer anything but a confused mass, from which a storm of incoherent cries emerged. The catering corps continued to provide casks of kirsch, which were immediately opened and drained dry by the ardent throats of the delirious quadrumanes. Their leaders, in the middle of the plain, popped the corks of champagne-bottles sent by England. A few bimane men and women circulated among them, apparently stirring up the hideous rebellion.

A little troop of faithful monkeys had joined the Farandoulian general staff. Their honest figures were colored as much by wrath as profound contempt for the drunken quadrumanes who had sunk to the level of the most degraded bimanes.

Farandoul and his bimane Generals consulted one another; Farandoul's foster-brothers wanted to charge the enemy, but Farandoul opposed that course, in order to try to play for time. After a few minutes hesitation, the little troop took the road to the fort again, leaving the rebels to their shameful orgy.

Nothing remained to Farandoul of his entire army but his bimane Generals, the monkeys of his own isle and a few brave quadrumane leaders who did not want to abandon him, among whom were Ungko and Tapa-Tapa of Sumatra, Wa-Wo-Wa of New Guinea and Nasico of Borneo–400 combatants in all, to hold their own against England and the rebels.

That same evening, one of Dick Broken's orderlies arrived breathless at the fort, having run all the way from Melbourne. A revolution had broken out in the city. The bimane insurrection had triumphed; the quadrumane officials had been obliged to flee–and Dick Broken, barricaded in the Governor's mansion with 200 or 300 monkeys stationed there, was under siege.

Broken claimed that he could hold out against the insurgents for a fortnight, so Farandoul was not too worried about that. The essential thing was to bring the wayward army back to the path of duty. If it persisted in its rebellion, everything was finished; as soon as it became obedient again, the bimane revolution in Melbourne would be promptly stifled.

He had to play for time.

A few monkeys, ashamed of their delinquency, had already come to rally round Farandoul's flag. The rest continued to drink English liquor by day and by night. The provision of food had become the provision of drink; the catering corps no longer transported anything but liquid nourishment.

With no more organization and no more exercises, the disorder surpassed anything of which the imagination could dream. Farandoul was counting on that, to some extent, to regain power. His optimism was understandable; monkeys have lively minds, but bad memories. They are excellent creatures, capable and intelligent, but much too frivolous; it was only by making them repeat the same exercise and actions every day that Farandoul had been able to make anything of them. Now they were on their own, idleness and drunkenness–vices formerly unknown to their race–would make them forget everything they had learned. Farandoul's plan was, therefore, to wait for a week and then to throw himself upon Makako. Once the instigator of the revolt had been punished, and the monkeys returned to the path of duty, they would be able to turn their attention to England. But for that, it was necessary that England made no move either, also waiting for the psychological moment to fall upon the monkeys.

On the evening of the seventh day, Farandoul made his preparations to engage Makako's forces as soon as the Sun rose. The loyal monkeys, who had been drilled every day in the handling of rifles and the firing of cannon, were raring to go. Farandoul's five brothers established them in their positions. As for our hero's foster-father, two days earlier he had undertaken a mission to the rebel camp, where a few brave officers were ready to declare a counter-*pronunciamento*.

The night seemed very long to the monkeys. At 4 a.m., several cannon-shots fired out at sea brought everyone running to the ramparts.

Damnation! England, forewarned of all Farandoul's plans by some undetectable spy, had made their move. During the night, six large transport-ships full of Indian troops were secured in position close to the shore, two kilometers from the fort. Formed up facing the fort were six frigates, four armored corvettes, a few dispatch-vessels and two terrible battleships, each of whose turrets was equipped with 40 steel cannon firing 40-kilo shells. The decks of all these ships were cleared for action. The hour of the ultimate battle had struck!

The rebel camp was in uproar. The monkeys, finally understanding their peril, attempted to organize themselves. Just as Farandoul was wondering whether it might not be too late to get the idea into their heads that they had a common enemy to face, the English fleet opened fire.

The broadsides fired by the corpulent frigates arrived at the fort with a regularity that did credit to their chronometric gunners. The monkeys, with the courage of desperation, set the fort's 20 fire-ports thundering. One heavy marine cannon in particular, operated under Mandibul's orders, worked wonders. One of its shells penetrated the engine-room of the *Carnivorous*, already tested by the battle of Cape Campbell, and did such damage there that the frigate soon seemed ready to sink like a stone.

As for the little fort, its excellent construction permitted it to resist the enemy shells without suffering too much damage. Alongside the beach, the transport-ships went on methodically with the business of disembarkation.

The greatest disorder still reigned within the rebel camp, where a thousand commands clashed with a thousand confused cries. Finally, when the large landing-craft loaded with English, Scottish and Sepoy troops were detached from the transport-ships and were rowed towards the beach, the disorder seemed to reach its peak.

The defenders of the fort stopped firing for a moment to watch what was happening. Deadly fruits of indiscipline and intemperance! The monkeys, still drunk as they awoke, sought in vain to take up their combat positions. Some put their uniforms on backwards, others tried to remind one another of the 12 stages of a charge. Useless effort! Inexpressible confusion! Many, having become wild again, ran on all fours, giving out stupid cries. Warriors of Geelong, Cheep Hill and Melbourne, where art thou?

Makako sought ideas in champagne. O shame! He scratched his forehead and his hindquarters–and all of his staff, by force of their ancient instinct of imitation, promptly set about doing likewise!

Meanwhile, the long-boats reached the shore; the companies they landed fell upon the monkeys who attempted to oppose them there, and drove them back without any difficulty.

The long-boats maintained a continual coming-and-going between the ships and the shore, and 8000 English troops were soon on the ground–8000 brave men burning to avenge the unexpected disasters of the preceding year. Finally, at a signal from the Admiral's frigate, musicians struck up *God Save The Queen* and the English threw themselves forward in two columns to attack the quadrumane positions.

Farandoul and his anxious monkeys waited for Makako's batteries to overwhelm the redcoats and the highlanders, but the cannons remained mute. Profiting from the quadrumanes' hesitation, the English columns scaled the batteries.

The frigates' smoke veiled the battlefield for an instant, but a gust of wind dissipated it. Farandoul went pale. Curses! All his work had come to nothing in the end–the monkeys of Cheep Hill were fleeing instead of fighting!

It was not even a battle; it was a horrible, panic-stricken rout.

Confusion, upheaval, massacre! No more regiments, no more officers, no more soldiers!

The weapons of 40,000 monkeys litter the ground. The cavalry, instead of protecting the retreat, leap from the backs of their kangaroos to climb trees. Fugitives hang in clusters from the branches of eucalyptus and gum-trees, the highlanders chasing them into the forest while the English take possession of their baggage.

Of all Makako's army, only two companies of monkeys have refused to follow the example of their comrades and are holding firm against the English. These brave fellows are aggregated in front of the quartermaster's hut, protected by entrenchments of barrels, some full and some empty. To overcome this last obstacle, the English dispatch an elite regiment. The charge is sounded, the battle-cries burst forth, and the redcoats scale the barricades of casks with a furious impetuosity.

Farandoul and his mariners wait for events to take a dramatic turn–for some act of desperate heroism like that of the bimane grenadiers at Waterloo.

The English, brandishing their bayonets and howling loudly, are at the top of the entrenchment... They hesitate, and pause...

What is happening?

Not a shot is fired, not a monkey budges! The unfortunates are dead drunk! Ordered to guard their provisions, they have not been sober for three days, and are oblivious to everything. The cannonade, the battle, the rout–nothing has been able to penetrate their stupefaction. They are still sleeping like logs and snoring, while the English look down at them, unable to believe their blinking eyes.

It is all over! In a quarter of an hour, an entire army has dissolved, evaporated! The English have taken thousands prisoner; the rest have fled into the wilderness to resume the savage life.

Farandoul and his downcast but furious brothers return to their guns to save some vestige of quadrumane honor by mounting a desperate defense. A hurricane of fire and iron envelops the little fort.

The heroic monkey gunners load and swab angrily–with such ardor that when dusk falls they refuse to leave their guns and continue firing, even after the English fleet has left its moorings and set out for the open sea.

X. How the bimane Generals
imprisoned by the English regained their liberty.
Bora-Bora's treasure.
The lamentable fate of La Belle Léocadie.

On the English side, the joy was unconfined. The colony was reconquered, nothing remaining in quadrumane hands but the little fort and the Governor's mansion defended by Dick Broken.

The day after the landing, Sir Roderick Blakeley,[58] Commander-in-Chief of the English expedition, made his entry into reconquered Melbourne. The city was celebrating, the English flag flying at every window. It was strange to see all the bimanes, finally reassured, pressing around the conquerors and heaping felicitations upon them. The most frightened bimanes were holding their heads high again; every trace of the conquest was disappearing. Already the word "quadrumane" was forbidden, erased from every edifice on which it had been inscribed.

The quadrumane artistes of the Melbourne Opera were shamefully cast out by their bimane colleagues. The perform-

---

[58] On this first appearance the surname is rendered Blackeley, but the more plausible spelling is employed the next time it is used.

ances of Coco's opera were halted, the maestro himself having vanished.[59]

Lastly, as a final ignominy, there was already talk of raising a statue to the man whom more bimanes than ever were calling the heroic Croknuff.

In the afternoon, a long column of prisoners filed between two hedges of bearded highlanders, preceded by a tartan-kilted bagpiper playing merry tunes. Among the prisoners still clad in scraps of their uniforms, Colonel Makako stood out by virtue of his disheartened expression. At the sight of Lady Arabella Cardigan, standing beside Sir Roderick Blakeley, he bellowed lugubriously while lifting his arms in the air.

Lady Arabella leaned towards the General, who smiled while making a sign. The liberated Makako was immediately placed in the hands of the astute Englishwoman.

Let us say at once, so that our readers should be in no doubt as to the fate of the ex-Colonel, that he now became part of Lady Cardigan's household. Lady Arabella, true to her promise, had no wish to separate Makako's destiny from hers. She took him with her to England, to the Cardigan estate, which Makako had deluded himself that he might one day visit as its master.

Unfortunately, Makako is not master there–far from it! At first, he was comfortably lodged in a barred cage in the depths of the great greenhouse of Cardigan Castle, but his submissiveness and misery soon resulted in his being permit-

---

[59] Robida inserts a footnote here, which translates as: "*The rumor abroad in Melbourne at that time was that he had been sold by an English corporal to a famous German musician, who keeps him chained up in a cave and forces him to compose music for his operas, wearing him down by the most undignified treatment.*" Robida presumably belonged to the majority of Frenchmen–whose vociferousness was exceeded only by that of its opposing minority–unimpressed by the works of Richard Wagner.

ted a measure of liberty. Makako is no longer in chains; he vegetates while dreamily indulging his delusions of grandeur and sadly polishing Lord Cardigan's boots. He still sees Lady Arabella from time to time, when she deigns to grant him permission to fulfill the functions of a trusted domestic servant by carrying her letters to her on a silver platter.

Lady Arabella's guests do not always treat him kindly, and Makako's aristocratic heart groans. Despite his unhappiness, the old feudal spirit of the patrician monkey of Borneo still persists. Makako lords it over the servants, and still refuses disdainfully–for lack of time–to enter into communication with a reporter from a great Liberal newspaper, who contacted him in the hope of extracting a few interesting memoirs.

Let us return to Melbourne, where Dick Broken's monkeys were defending themselves desperately.

The solidly-barricaded Governor's mansion resisted repeated English attacks. While supervising the defense, Dick Broken, faithful to his old habits of reportage, sent correspondence from time to time to the *Melbourne Herald*, which had reappeared–but as it simply forwarded his reports to the enemy, he refused all offers of capitulation and responded to the attacks with furious sorties at the head of an elite corps of 50 monkeys.

One of the pavilions at the corner of the Governor's mansion had been taken and retaken 20 times over. For a week, they had fought on the rooftops for possession of the pavilion's cupola. When the English believed that they were definitely in control of it, they installed themselves therein and prepared to move out of it to launch a decisive attack on the rest of the building–but the monkeys swiftly climbed up on the roof and precipitated themselves in an assault on the cupola, dislodging the enemy and replacing the Farandoulian flag, which had only been struck momentarily, at the summit of the monument.

Unfortunately, their food supplies were running out. Dick Broken was careful to say nothing about it in his correspondence, but he was cruelly tormented by fear of starvation.

From the height of their elevated position, the monkeys had been able to watch the long column of their brothers, made captive by the English, filing into the city. Their humiliation had wounded them deeply, but while the cannons of Farandoul's little fort still sounded in the distance, they still clung to a vague hope.

The Point Rocas fort, occupied by Farandoul and his faithful monkeys, still held out–the garrison, when called to surrender, had received the envoys proudly. "So long as we have ammunition to feed to our cannons," Farandoul replied, "we shall swallow the shells of the British lion!"

As everyone knows, though, in addition to its natural bravery, the British lion has a powerful dose of finesse. Instead of continuing a duel of shell bursts with Farandoul, it decided that it would be simpler to let the defenders of Point Rocas exhaust their provisions. A rigorous blockade was established around the little fort, at a respectful distance.

When the English General judged that the right moment had come, he sent new proposals to the Farandoulians, whose courage and constancy he admired. At the same time, he sent the monkeys' former King a letter from Dick Broken, informing him of the want of food and desperate situation of the last of Melbourne's monkeys. Even so, the little fort held out for another week by eking out the last rations of coconuts. The monkeys, who had become transparently thin, still refused to surrender.

In the end, when the impossibility of attempting an escape by sea had been clearly demonstrated, the ultimate decision was taken by a council whose members included both bimanes and quadrumanes.

The Farandoulian flag was lowered, yielding its place to a flag of truce.

The little fort was ready to capitulate!

The conditions were lengthily debated by the Generals. Finally, a treaty was signed for the surrender of the fort and Dick Broken's monkeys. The members of the garrison were granted the honors of war and left with their weapons and baggage. The bimanes were prisoners; as for the quadrumanes, England was charged with their repatriation.

The open mouths of the cannons, silent since the night-watch, seemed to be yawning in despair. As noon sounded, to the sound of fifes and bagpipes, the drawbridge fell and the little fort's garrison filed down the slope towards the English staff-officers.

Farandoul and Mandibul came on horseback at the column's head; behind them marched the bimane Colonels and the hero's five foster-brothers, blackened by gunpowder and covered in glorious scars. Three hundred and fifty brave monkeys of martial aspect, in stained and ragged uniforms, came next, preceded by six monkey drummers playing the funeral march.

It was all over! The following day was the cruel day of separation. The bimane leaders dined with the English General, who acquainted them with the intentions of Her Majesty's government. Farandoul and the ex-mariners of *La Belle Léocadie* would be transported to Europe, far from quadrumane populations that were still profoundly agitated. Because Farandoul had stipulated, as a condition of the fort's surrender, a full pardon for Dick Broken, that individual was set at liberty.

Farandoul arranged with the General that *La Belle Léocadie* should be returned to the monkeys, in order that they might return to their hearths under the guidance of our hero's five brothers. Farandoul's foster-father, despite a thorough search, had not been found among the prisoners–he had disappeared, like so many others, during the rout of Makako's army.

A few hours after *La Belle Léocadie* had put to sea, carrying 100 monkeys, accompanied by an English corvette carrying the rest of the quadrumanes, a long-boat came to take the bimanes to Sandridge to convey them aboard the Admiral's frigate. Saturnin, Mandibul and the bimane ex-Generals having taken their places in the long-boat's stern, the oars fell in response to a blast from the officer's whistle, and the long-boat moved off under their rapid propulsion.

Farandoul could not take his eyes off the shore: that Australian land for whose regeneration he had attempted such great things...

His concentration was broken by a unanimous cry that went up from the long-boat's passengers. A kind of reef had abruptly risen up. An enormous monster with an iron carapace had emerged from the water underneath the long-boat, which now found itself aground on its back, three meters above the waves. Farandoul recognized the *Nautilus*. Good old Captain Nemo had arrived just in time to save him!

The bewildered Englishmen, however, continued mechanically to ply their oars in the empty air, while a great tumult erupted aboard the not-far-distant ships.

The prisoners leapt with a single bound on to the back of the *Nautilus* and ran towards the stern, where the ports were already wide open, inviting them to enter. Before the Englishmen could recover from their surprise, they all found themselves safely ensconced in the belly of the vessel.

In the interior of the *Nautilus*, each one was greeted as an escaped prisoner. The first words of Captain Nemo had been these: "My dear Farandoul, I'm happy to have good news to bring you–the Bora-Bora affair has been successfully concluded."

"I hope that the pirates' banker has been hanged!"

"No, the Sultan of Borneo wanted to appoint him as his Prime Minister; fortunately, the prudent fellow fled with the funds to Sumatra. On his arrival, the Rajah of Sumatra, desirous of ensuring that such a rich foreigner remained in his estates, had him impaled, and confiscated the funds to defray the expenses of that judiciary procedure. I was almost in despair for your credit, when the Sumatran Minister of Justice, unconcerned with regularizing his appointment, thought that the occasion was ripe for beating the retreat, and departed with the cash-box. Now, while I was following the trail of that cash-box in the *Nautilus*, in order to protect your rights, I encountered the ship which the Minister of Justice had chartered for it. I captured it and redeposited the Minister in Sumatra with a receipt for his royal master. And that's how I saved your 54 million coins!"

Ten days after this miraculous escape, the *Nautilus* arrived at the Mysterious Island, and Captain Nemo put Farandoul in possession of his 54 million coins.

Let us rapidly pass over the three months of rest and tranquility that the mariners allowed themselves in the Captain's domains before Farandoul profited from an opportunity to visit the isle of his childhood.

The monkeys taken prisoner by the English had returned to their hearths. His five brothers were there, about to proceed with a reorganization of the island with the aid of the Australian veterans. After a brief sojourn, during which Farandoul carried out a survey of the entire island, in order to ascertain the changes and reforms necessary for the development of civilization, he set out in *La Belle Léocadie* bound for the Mysterious Island.

Soon enough, the 54 million coins made a substantial reinforcement for the arms stowed in the hold of *La Belle Léocadie*. Captain Nemo commissioned Farandoul to carry a mysterious package to Monsieur Jules Verne in Paris, and *La Belle Léocadie* set sail for Le Havre.

Do you know how much work there is to do on such a journey? Our mariners did not have very much free time left over for counting their wealth. Among the 54 million coins, there were many copper ones and not a few that were fake or had been withdrawn from circulation. In the end, the calculations having been rigorously made and checked nine, ten, or 11 times over–as recommended by the wisest professors of arithmetic–Farandoul found that each sailor would have 33,578 francs to set him up. That wasn't at all bad, even for former Generals and Colonels.

They eventually sighted Le Havre; as there was an unexpended balance of 35 francs Farandoul called the sailors together to arrange a share-out.

Alas, all the calculations had been in vain! An ominous splashing set them all shivering. A stream of water soon manifested itself. The cargo of 54 million coins had overstrained the hold; some planks had given way and *La Belle Léocadie* was sinking rapidly.

A lamentable conclusion to such joyful hopes! Bora-Bora must have been laughing in his grave: *La Belle Léocadie* had had its day!

Fortunately, all the mariners could swim. A minute after the poor three-master had finally disappeared, the 17 sailors, with Farandoul and Mandibul at the head, cleft the waves in the direction of the jetty at Le Havre, which was visible in the distance. Having left the ship in order of rank, they came up the stairway to the quay in the same order.

Disdaining the helping hands that were offered to them, they climbed nimbly on to the quay. On arrival there, they all moved as one to lift their arms into the air, the same word on all their lips: "Ruined!"

"No!" Mandibul suddenly exclaimed, patting his pockets. "I still have the 35 francs!"

Farandoul also uttered a cry, in which equal doses of joy and astonishment were mingled. "It's him!"

It was, indeed, him! It was Farandoul's brave foster-father, whom he had recognized as he gazed on the soil of France for the very first time. And in what state did he see him? Wretched, crippled and captive: attached by a chain to a stall set against the parapet of the quay, whose proprietor was selling parrots and exotic curios.

Farandoul leapt upon Mandibul's 35 francs and ran towards the merchant. "How much?" he stammered, in a voice choked with emotion, indicating to the mercantile soul that he meant the tearful quadrumane.

The old gentleman was liberated, and fell weeping into the arms of his adoptive son, all misery and suffering forgotten in that minute of happiness. The poor monkey had had some cruel times to endure. It will be remembered that he was on a mission to Makako's camp when the attack took place; caught up in the rout, he had fallen into the hands of the English, who had sold him in spite of his human rights!

We shall not follow our friends to Paris, which they were able to reach, thanks to advances made by one of Captain Lastic's old fitters. We shall content ourselves with saying that Farandoul religiously carried out his duty to deliver Captain Nemo's letters–which he had, fortunately, saved from the wreck–to the required address.

Firmly determined on another attempt to make his fortune, Farandoul resolved to find his foster-father a place where he would be safe from further vicissitudes. The old gentleman was rather worn out and very feeble. The director of the Botanical Gardens, to whom Farandoul related his anxieties, was moved to tears; he consented to provide shelter for the brave quadrumane's final days, and gave him his own apartment with a little garden.

The separation was cruel, but Farandoul courageously tore himself away from his foster-father and took the road to Le Havre again, with his companions. New projects having gestated in his fertile brain, America would be privileged to see what he might do next!

Eugène Mouton: *The Historioscope*

Paris, March 19th, 1881.
   Dear sir,
   An assiduous reader of the Revue d'infini,[60] *I have followed with as much attention as interest the remarkable work
you have published there on "The Commercial Relationship of
the Assyrians with the Etruscans, with Particular Reference to
the trade in live moray eels* [61] *during the reigns of Kings Evilmerodach and Neriglissor."* [62]

   *It is, indeed, established that numerous and important
commercial connections existed, even before the reigns of
Evilmerodach and Neriglissor, between the empire then
flourishing on the banks of the Euphrates and the autochtho-
nous peoples of Etruria. The Eugubine Tablets* [63] *themselves
contain a passage on this subject which seems to have escaped
your notice, and this passage throws precious daylight on the*

---

[60] *Revue d'infini* [Space Review] deliberately recalls the title
of Camille Flammarion's *Récits de l'infini* [Space Stories], the
book that inspired this story and two other items.

[61] The word Mouton uses, *murènes*, has expanded its taxo-
nomic meaning to refer to the entire family *Muraenidae*, but is
here used more precisely to refer to *Muraena helena*, a Mediterranean fish that was a valuable food-source in Roman
times.

[62] Evilmerodach, the son of Nebuchadnezzar, reigned over
much of Mesopotamia for two years in the 6th century B.C.;
he was succeeded by his brother-in-law Neriglissor, who had a
much longer reign of some 40 years.

[63] The Eugubine Tablets were bronze artifacts discovered in
1444 at the Apennine town of Gubbio, containing an inscription in an Umbrian language.

*hieratic character of the moray eel in Etruscan society. Fur-
thermore, as you very judiciously demonstrate, it was initially
to Evilmerodach, then to Neriglissor (who invariably followed
his brother's plans) that this commerce owed its magnificent
development.*

*Like you, I am of the opinion that it is necessary to place
this period between 260 and 3697 B.C., and that it would be
reckless, or at least hazardous, to formulate a more exact ap-
proximation. Much is already known about the active commerce in live moray eels between the Babylonians and the
Etruscans in the reigns of Evilmerodach and Neriglissor, and
the world of scholarship owes you considerable recognition
for having shed the first light on this important feature of the
obscure history of the Babylonian Empire.*

*Having devoted long years myself to historical studies, I
would be happy to enter into correspondence with you, and it
would give me pleasure to show you, if it would be agreeable
to you, the documents that I possess, relating not only to the
commerce in moray eels between the Assyrians and the Etruscans in the time of Evilmerodach and Neriglissor, but also,
and in a wholesale manner, to all the facts of universal history, without exception.*

*You may find me at home every day, from five o'clock to
three o'clock in the morning; I never go out and almost never
sleep.*

*In the hope that you will shortly take it up, Monsieur, I
beg you to accept my invitation as an expression of the sentiments of high consideration with which I am overflowing.*

> *Your most humble and most obedient servant,*
> *Joseph Durand (of Tarn-et-Garonne)*
> *Member of various scholarly societies*
> *14 Rue des Anglais*

Joseph Durand (of Tarn-et-Garonne)...

What! While my pen is still wet with the floods of ink
that I have distilled from it on the question of the trade in moray eels between two fantastic peoples, in the reigns of unpro-

nounceable kings, it has to find a Joseph Durand (of Tarn-et-Garonne) to steal my question from me!

For it is mine, and mine alone, this question that I have invented! Is there no longer anything new under the Sun, even in history? What will become of the human spirit if science, with its mechanical procedures, succeeds in exhausting that spring to which youth has come for so many centuries to quench its thirst for generous lies and wallow in noble errors?

Joseph Durand (of Tarn-et-Garonne) is a miserable...

On the other hand, I thought, relenting somewhat, when he tells me that he possesses documents relating to the reigns of Evilmerodach and Neriglissor, he seems to be sure of his facts. Then again, perhaps this question of Babylonians eels–a question which, just between us, I have addressed rather lightly–might get me into the Institute! [64]

And that is how, one fine morning last week, I came to present myself at No. 14, Rue des Anglais, where I addressed to the porter words destined to be engraved on my memory as long as I live:

"Monsieur Joseph Durand, if you please?"

In response to this question, the porter looked at me with a singular mixture of surprise and commiseration, as if it seemed to him utterly unexpected.

"You want to see Monsieur Joseph?" he said to me.

"Joseph Durand."

"Joseph Durand?"

"Of Tarn-et-Garonne."

"Of Tarn-et-Garonne? He's certainly here. At the far end of the second courtyard, take the stairs on the left to the fifth floor–the end of the corridor, facing."

I went through the first courtyard. At the end of the second, to the left, I perceived a spiral staircase suspended from the facade of a house, which I shall not describe to you because it was indescribable. Despite the crumbling and dilapi-

---

[64] *L'Institut* (*de France*) is the collective term of the five Academies.

dated state of that gigantic flight, I ventured forth, for better or worse, as lightly as possible. After a prudent and troublesome ascent, I put my foot on the firm boards of the corridor, and I knocked at a door, to which was nailed a card bearing these words:

JOSEPH DURAND
(of Tarn-et-Garonne)
Man of Letters

I heard a sort of sniff or sigh, then the noise of chairs being moved, then the shuffling of stockinged feet. The door opened, offering me the spectacle of "Monsieur Joseph Durand (of Tarn-et-Garonne)."

I say "the spectacle" for that was certainly what it was, and by no means the least peculiar. Imagine a man nearly six feet tall, as thin as a nail, as red as a cockscomb, head forwards, arms akimbo, mouth wide open, eyebrows lifted to form semicircles, offering the most artless and bizarre confusion of bows and other reverential gestures, all at once.

At the summit of his interminable body was a face as gross as a fist, somewhat reminiscent of a red apple that had been lightly baked, so furrowed was it with wrinkles crisscrossing in every direction–except on the forehead, where four or five parallel and evenly-spaced rolls of fat traced the ominous diagram that so often characterizes madness. Two dry and hollow cheeks fluttered like old rags in the breath of Monsieur Durand's words, making it only too obvious that on their converse side, in the interior, there were only toothless gums. As these gums came together they sometimes pinched the lining of the cheeks, producing rifts or pits in their exterior surface: lamentable caricatures of the dimples that laughter, in better times, had hollowed out in the days when the cheeks were less flaccid.

This apparition's coiffure and attire were no less marvelous than his face. Long hair as black as ink, curled into ringlets and glistening with pomade, formed a bunch of grapes around his head, leaving uncovered a bald spot as smooth and yellow as antique ivory. His trousers, whose grey color had once been yellow, were secured about his legs by two pieces of that cotton twine with which one ties bundles of goose-quills; these threads were not even similar, for one was green and the other red. His feet, clad in over-large stockings that had run and whose cords were hanging down, dragged slippers that were threadbare, misshapen and scuffed, disgorging their stuffing in a pitiful manner. Finally, over a chocolate-colored woolen cardigan whose knitting was coming apart in various places, his fantastic costume was capped and completed by a magnificent Bluebeard coat with golden buttons, which superimposed on that mass of threads an effect unprecedented in the history of accouterment: a coat of irreproachable cut, so flamboyantly new that it still bore, attached to the left pocket, a piece of paper on which was inscribed: *M. Durand, 142 francs.*

I am a very cool customer; strange objects, far from frightening me, exert a certain secret charm on me–secret, because that is something that must not be allowed to show, for fear of the disapproval of serious persons. I must confess, however, that this blow staggered me. To leave home on the matter of the moray eel trade in the times of Evilmerodach and Neriglissor, and to fall down before a scholar in pink and green twine, curly hair and a Bluebeard coat, is, you will admit, to cast to the four winds the famous principle that "it is unnecessary to be astonished by anything."

The man before me seemed, moreover, to belong to some extra-human race. Antiquity and absurdity were–how shall I put it?–engraved upon him in the indecipherable characters of a mysterious language. Not one of the letters which toil and the sculptor had chiseled so decisively and skillfully in the features of that bizarrely-ravaged being was recognizable, and I sensed vaguely that some frightful power, entirely disproportionate to the forces of life, must have been exercised upon him.

I am proud to say, however, that this philosophical weakness was short-lived.

What a prodigy! I said to myself. Oh well, he's an eccentric, that's all. Perhaps, if he explains the reasons that persuaded him to adopt such a bizarre appearance, I'll be able to understand that each of the items of his costume has its rationale and that each is the conclusion of some irrefutable syllogism. Have I forgotten my favorite maxim: *Before passing judgment on your brother's actions, acquaint yourself with his heart, his purse and his health*? So many seemingly-inexplicable things can be explained by some distress, poverty or illness that the patient hides with jealous care from the eyes of the world!

Sending my foolish amazement to the Devil in this manner, I resolved to sweep aside with the back of my hand the ridiculous veil presented to me by the external appearance of this unknown person. Having done that, I immediately observed that the unknown man was very polite and very well-brought-up, for the manner in which he welcomed me was no less gracious than the terms employed in his letter.

As I sat down in the armchair that he brought me, therefore, I found myself in that excellent state of benevolent serenity that is the ideal preparation for a conversation on an important subject between two serious men.

Monsieur Durand stood still for a few moments with his head raised and his eyes staring into space. Then, after passing his hand over his forehead, as if to wipe away some vaporous residue that would have obscured his intelligence, he favored me with a bow, accompanied by a vague smile, and adjusted his cravat with a guttural sigh worthy of Saint Joseph. Alternately rubbing the tip of his nose and the base of his chin, he launched into the following discourse:

"I am very grateful to you, Monsieur, for responding so graciously to the invitation of an unknown. In the numerous attempts that I have made to extract humans from their obstinate ignorance or their considered stupidity, I have experienced rejections and frustrations to discourage the most determined perseverance. But nothing will make me desist, and until my dying day, I shall fight with all my might to make truth triumphant. If, after so many vain efforts, I am now addressing myself to you, it is because you are the only one who has dared to tell the truth about history and to denounce truly idiotic inanity. I therefore ask you, Monsieur, to listen to me attentively, and above all patiently, for I should not hide from you that my prolegomena will certainly be long, probably obscure, and perhaps even boring. If you will condescend to follow me with trust and resignation, though, what I shall show you–or, rather, what I shall make you see–will be ample compensation for your trouble. For I shall make you see–*see*, you understand–that which no human eye has ever seen." Then lifting his eyes to heaven with a profound sigh, he added: "And that which, doubtless, no human eye will ever see again, after you!"

The commencement of this exordium had flattered me; the conclusion touched me. I made a gesture of respectful acquiescence, and even deemed it appropriate to reply to the orator's eloquent sigh with the modest sigh of a convinced auditor.

He went on: "But before I say anything else, Monsieur, to establish a sure foundation beneath a relationship which, I hope, will be continuing, it is necessary that I make you aware of my state of mind."

"Your state of mind!" I replied, in a voice somewhat modified by surprise. "Be assured, Monsieur, that I shall receive with the greatest... pleasure any communications with which you desire to favor me on that subject."

"Well, Monsieur, one word will suffice to acquaint you with my state of mind: I am mad."

I started slightly in my chair and, measuring the distance separating me from the door with my eye, I gathered my strength in order to escape with a single bound–simulating, meanwhile, the most gracious smile of incredulity and saying to him: "Oh, Monsieur..."

But he had seen through me. He put his hand on my arm, gave me a stern look, and said: "Am I mistaken? You too! What–does the steadfast mind whose works display such independence hesitate over such a trifle? Whether I am sane or mad, have you not sense enough to judge whether what I have to say is the product of mental alienation or genius? What does it matter if the bottle be cracked, if the wine is good? Fie, Monsieur, are you not ashamed to sort the products of the human mind into the compartments of madness and reason, when they are no more than imaginary categories invented by physicians and philosophers? Leave it to the ingenuity of grocers and confectioners to set things in their cardboard boxes: here are dried figs, there prunes, here sugared almonds, there pralines.

"Do you think that nature cares about such ridiculous classifications? She creates figs, plums and almonds full of life and freshness, and man makes dried fruits and sweetmeats of them, artificial products that have nothing to do with the universal laws of biology. It is the same with ideas: true or false, plausible or mad, they are entirely the work of human genius, and the greatest folly of all is to pretend that distinctions derived from laws exclusively relevant to living things apply to them.

"No, Monsieur, there is nothing in the world but facts on the one side, and ideas on the other. As for rationalizations, classifications and theories, they're nothing but smoke–variously colored smoke, in which, I am convinced, one sees the occasional spark glowing here and there, or even, on feast-days, bright fireworks suddenly erupt. But all of it passes like a cloud, like a flash of lightning; it all fades away, and darkness closes in again on momentarily-dazzled reason.

"Things, on the other hand–*facts*–are what last, what do not change according to the fancy of the hand that touches them or the eye that looks at them. Whether or not it is necessary for you to pass through vertigo and madness to arrive at them, what have you to complain about, if I lead you to facts and things?"

"Monsieur," I said to him, casually settling back into my seat, "you interest me greatly, and I am listening. I have, indeed, often asked myself whether the distinction between reason and madness has as much value as is the general accord attributes to it, and you will lift a great weight from my shoulders if you can prove to me that one can arrive at the truth as directly by unreason as by reason."

"One could not put it better," he told me. "What the vulgar call unreason is to reason in a direction contrary to other men, acting or thinking other than they do. This is the sense in which I am mad, which is why everyone in the house–from the porter who lodges on the ground floor to my housekeeper, who roosts under the roof–takes me for a certified lunatic, to the point of looking suspiciously even at the people who come to see me. You must have..."

"I noticed that! That was why the porter stared at me in such a peculiar way!"

"You see! Isn't that just what I said? But let's get on! Let's leave the stupid to their stupidity, and mind our own business. To begin with, as regards the question of moray eels, here are texts photographed from the Eugubine Tablets, in which I have marked the essential paragraphs. You may take them home to study them at your leisure. I shall soon put before your eyes documents much more explicit and definitive. Before I do that, however, it is necessary that I should acquaint you with the sequence of ideas and endeavors that I had to undertake to acquaint myself with the facts that I want to reveal to you.

"Have you ever had occasion to think about the conditions under which history presents itself to us? For me, ever since my studies began, I have felt a certain unease in the face of these stories of past events, comparable to that which one experiences in looking at certain portraits. One sees a nose, a mouth, eyes, a body, and yet one feels that it does not represent a man; the portrait is nothing but an implausible image, equally lacking in life and truth.

"I have experienced the same thing in confrontation with historic depictions in general, its strength varying in proportion to the nearness of the events to our own time–and in the end, I discovered the reason. In effect, the closer the events are to us, the more the historian's interests become engaged in his interpretation of historical facts–and interpretation is only one step removed from distortion.

"Fundamentally, there are only two kinds of historical method. One consists of accepting facts, subject to the extraction therefrom of conclusions formulated in advance. The other similarly decides to give precedence to preconceived ideas, arranging–inventing, if necessary–facts to justify them. I cannot see anything much to choose between Louis Blanc making the 1789 Revolution begin with John Huss and Père Loriquet describing the reign of Louis XVIII at a time when Napoleon was on the throne, from the point-of-view of verity.[65] The latter method is undoubtedly more candid and more logical than the former, but I have to admit that one is worth

---

[65] Louis Blanc (1811-82) was a socialist statesman and historian who played a key role in the Revolution of 1848, He wrote a history of the aftermath of the July Revolution of 1830 before beginning a definitive history of the 1789 Revolution, whose first two volumes appeared in 1847.

John Huss (1369-1415) was a Bohemian religious reformer burned at the stake for heresy, who became–in the eyes of Blanc and others–a martyr to the cause of social reform.

The accompanying reference to Père Loriquet is to a proposed exercise in alternative history of the kind subsequently undertaken by Louis-Napoléon Geoffroy in *Napoléon et la conquête de la monde, 1812-1832* (1836) and Charles Renouvier in *Uchronie* (1876). The Jesuit writer Jean-Nicolas Loriquet (1767-1845) wrote numerous texts for use in the education of children; his *Histoire de France, A.M.G.D.* (1814; the initials stand for *Ad majorem Dei gloriam*) includes an imaginative rhapsody in which he proposes that all the historical texts used for instructional purposes should be rewritten so as to create a history which, although it failed to materialize, would have provided far better lessons for the young, thus serving the interests of the Society of Jesus far better than actual history ever had.

little more than the other. And when I sought such documents as were recoverable to check the proofs of such and such a fact given credence by people, I saw that every work of history was scarcely more than a copy of preceding works, with a few additional inaccuracies or speculations.

"After living with that dispiriting conviction for some time, I was led to conclude that people would not be able to flatter themselves that they understand history until the day when they would be able to equip themselves with a means of seeing retrospectively, not in stories and tales, but in reality."

"That would indeed," I said, laughing, "be history's ideal. Unfortunately, facts vanish as soon as they are manifest, and they leave no perceptible trace of their passing."

"I don't share your opinion," Monsieur Durand replied. "Facts, in producing themselves, acquire an existence as positive and as indestructible as that of ideas. Like ideas, they take flight across the world, the one soaring unapprehended in space as the other circulates in the memory and traditions of humankind. They never die, any more than ideas do, and they nourish, by means of a continuously accumulated heredity, the treasure of the universal soul. They are somewhere; they are everywhere. Whatever their origin, however far time has carried them away, the universe remains their cage, if you will, and they are not departed from it. And given that I too am within that cage, why can I not reach them?"

"In thought, I will admit—but in experience, in sensation..."

"Yes... I forgive you the objection. It must have a certain force, since it held me up for more than 25 years..."

"What!" I exclaimed. "You have overcome that objection?"

"Yes," he replied, in a firm tone. "After 25 years of meditation and anguish, I have overcome it, thanks to the wave theory of light."

"The wave theory of light?"

"Yes, Monsieur."

"But what connection has that theory with the facts of history?"

"The one that every visible phenomenon has with the eyes that see it; the one established between the table that you are looking at and your intelligence, which perceives the sensation. What is the connection called? Vision."

"But for vision to operate a real object is necessary."

"I tell you that facts are real objects."

"Even past facts?"

"Even past facts. I shall prove it. You know that an illuminated object, touched by light, emits from every point on its surface waves that propagate in a straight line as far as the retina of the eye, producing the sight of the object–isn't that so?"

"I understand that."

"You understand it–good! But have you ever asked yourself what becomes of these waves beyond the point at which your eye perceives their passage? Isn't it true that this perception, particular to you, does not stop them, and that they continue to progress in a straight line, indefinitely?"

"Not indefinitely. If they encounter an opaque body in that line they are intercepted; an eye placed on the other side of the opaque body does not perceive them."

"But if they are not intercepted, how far can they go?"

"As far, evidently, as there is empty space for their propagation."

"So," Monsieur Durand went on, "if every luminous object emits waves that propagate indefinitely in a straight line when they encounter no obstacle, do you not see that everything that exists on Earth, and everything that has happened there, everything that appeared there–if only for a second– since the origin of the world, has emitted images that took flight through the terrestrial atmosphere into interplanetary space? And what becomes of them there? Do they become immobile? Nothing can stop them. Do they become imperceptible? Nothing can diminish them. They are in a medium that is empty, free and neutral. So they are still there, invariably fixed in the order in which they exited from the

in the order in which they exited from the terrestrial atmosphere. For all eternity, unable ever to deviate, they follow the straight line that leads them to infinity: every modification of every object; every movement and action of every living being.

"Lift your eyes to the Heavens, therefore, and if you know how to look, you will see there, projected from space to space and from profundity to profundity, the image of every being and the display of every fact that light has illuminated on the Earth's surface since the beginning of time!"

Monsieur Durand paused, as if to give my attention the time to catch breath. He lowered his eyes momentarily to the ground, then lifted them to look at me interrogatively.

I was considerably disturbed because, despite the manifest absurdity of what I had heard, it had taken me aback; however strong-minded we may be, the infinite always makes our hearts beat faster.

"But if these images," I said, "these projections of things, rise continuously from the surface of the Earth to follow a straight line into space, only the last emission from any given point on the globe can be visible. It must, in consequence, block the view of all those preceding it in the same direction. Thus, I admit that one can see the one, but I believe that it eclipses all the preceding ones."

"You are forgetting," he said, smiling, "two, three, or even four little things: that the Earth turns on its axis; that it oscillates on the same axis, in a rotational movement similar to the swaying of a spinning top; that it describes an ellipse around the Sun; and that the entire solar system moves as a whole in some direction or other. Now, as the Earth turns, changes position and oscillates in space, the result is that each luminous wave that it emits escapes from the atmosphere at a distinct tangent, in the manner of the sparks emitted by a firework, which draw apart as they become more distant. These tangents find enough space, at a very slight distance from the Earth, to diverge without being confused, and the only necessity is to move the point of observation outside the zone within which the waves are still intermingled. It's a simple matter of calculating angles, a trivial detail."

"But when one has admitted that," I said to him, shaking my head, "there still remains another objection, this one insurmountable. If you could go out and place yourself beyond and in front of the point in space which they have reached at the present moment, in order to observe these images, you would be able to see them, because they would find your eyes in their path be reflected by your retina–but here you are behind the space that they occupy. They cannot turn back in their course in order to come and find your eyes."

"That's right," he said, "but you're still forgetting several things. First, it's not absolutely true that we can only see objects placed in front of our eyes. The condition of opposition between the eye and the visible object is therefore not as absolute as you suppose. But even if it were conceded as absolute, if the images chance to find in following their course a screen of some kind to reflect them–that is to say, to send them back to me, is that not turning back in their course?"

"Oh, it would certainly be more convenient to place a screen out there than to go there yourself–and then, indeed, the images would be visible to you. But..."

"There is no but; that is the situation."

"A screen in planetary space!" I cried, in amazement. "A screen in the void!"

"It is not a void; it is a medium of a particular nature, and however subtle you suppose it to be, it has a certain consistency, since it is not nothing. That consistency may vary at such and such a place, under the influence of such and such a cause."

"In any case," I said, "it is a transparent medium, whose precise nature is to transmit light. How can it reflect an image?"

"How? Just as the air reflects them, before our eyes, every day. You are still forgetting mirages–images which, whether on the surface of the Earth or in space, present such complete illusions to the eyes of travelers. How are these images formed, if you please? By a combination of refractions and reflections that heat generates in the layers of the atmosphere. Well, although we are ignorant of the nature and properties of the ether, as we call it, one thing we do know is that the light of the celestial bodies and the heat of the Sun are transmitted through its substance, since they come to us. Why should they not be subject to optical phenomena analogous to the mirages that we observe within our atmosphere?

"This is what you asked for; this is the mirror in which the images of terrestrial objects may be reflected so that they may live again in your eyes!"

"This hypothesis..." I said, a trifle emotionally.

Monsieur Durand got up and, with an imperious gesture, drew my attention to a closed door set behind him.

"You have defended your position well, Monsieur," he told me, "and it is good to see feeble human reason struggle so courageously against truth, like a brave little mouse before a cat. Truth–for this is no mere hypothesis; it is a fact, and you shall see it. Would you care to follow me?"

He opened the door, and we found ourselves in a vast laboratory full of strangely-shaped apparatus. A white-haired workman was laboring there, leaning over a kind of bench; he continued his work as if oblivious to our presence.

"This is my laboratory," Monsieur Durand told me. "It's here, with the aid of this old workman, that I have constructed the instrument without which everything that I have said to you would still be nothing more than a pure dream.

"You see there a Bunsen battery,[66] whose discharge could kill an army of 20,000 men. It's thanks to this apparatus that I've been able to obtain a refractive material of incalculable power.

---

[66] As well as the Bunsen burner, which remained a familiar item of laboratory apparatus throughout the 20th century, the German chemist Robert Bunsen (1811-99) invented the Bunsen battery–though none was ever as powerful as the one M. Durand claims to possess.

"This one is an ozone apparatus, that one a Pictet apparatus for compressing gas.[67]

"After having employed, without success, all known refractive substances, I was eventually led to ask myself whether compressed gases might furnish me with the material I sought. Not having found anything in that direction, I was nearly discouraged, when certain unexplained phenomena turned my attention towards electricity. I set myself on that track ardently.

"It would take too long to explain all my consequent researches, but their result was the discovery that electricity is neither a force, nor a fluid, nor a phenomenon, but a gas, and that this gas, sufficiently compressed under the influence of ozone, may be solidified in a durable form.

"In this state it forms a material a hundred thousand times denser than that of any known substance–and, at the same time, of a transparency infinitely superior to that of the finest flint glass.[68] Now, as refraction is nothing but the deviation of a luminous ray through the molecules of the refractive substance, you will understand that electrozone, as I call it, having an infinite number of molecules, can furnish me within lenses of an almost incalculable power.

"The most perfect apparatus that I have so far constructed enlarged the etheric images by a factor of 25 million, but that is insufficient and I hope eventually to obtain a telescope capable of allowing me to read, for example, the inscription that Leonidas had one of his soldiers trace on the

[67] Raoul Pictet (1842-1929) was a Swiss scientist who was the first to liquefy nitrogen, hydrogen and oxygen with the aid of compression apparatus.

[68] "Flint glass"–given in English by Mouton–is nowadays more usually known as crystal glass. Its distinctive feature is that it contains lead; it has a higher refractive index than ordinary "crown glass" and was, in consequence, often used in the manufacture of 19th-century prisms and lenses.

rocks of Thermopylae.[69] However, that was a long time ago, as you know, and it is a distant prospect.

"Now, Monsieur, prepare yourself for a spectacle such as you have never been able to imagine in your entire life.

"I must, however, warn you that the instrument can only give a direct view, whatever passed during the night or under cover having naturally been unable to produce any external luminous emission. It is the same with everything that took place beyond the bounds of our hemisphere, the luminous rays only being able to propagate within the corresponding part of space."

Climbing a spiral staircase at the back of the laboratory as he spoke these words, he led me up to a balcony under a sort of rotating dome pierced by several openings. There I saw a cylindrical apparatus mounted on cables and wheels, pointed at the sky.

"This," said the inventor, "is the *Historioscope*! It is orientated in the direction of the 15th century; you have only to look through the eyepiece and you will be able to see all of it that you wish."

The miracle was in front of me! As recognizable in the field of the telescope as actors on the stage of a theatre, men of savage aspect–of gigantic stature with bristling beards, animal skins and frightful weapons, mounted on little horses whose manes hung to the ground–were galloping furiously across a plain, where the smoke and flame of fires were visible in the distance. At their head, crossing ruts, rocks, tree-trunks and crumbled walls by leaps and bounds, a kind of giant with a lion's muzzle drew them along, brandishing a colossal sword in one hand and a club bristling with six sharpened iron studs in the other.

---

[69] Leonidas was the King of Sparta who–in company with 300 Spartans and 700 Thespians, all of whom died with him–defended the pass at Thermopylae against Xerxes' vast Persian army in 480 B.C.

"Great God!" I cried, recoiling in fear. "What are those people?"

"Ah," said Monsieur Durand, after having glanced into the telescope, "you've made a good start. You're not clumsy for a debutant. You see there one of the most curious personages of history, at a moment when he is enraged, for it's not a fortnight since he lost one of his eyes in battle–and to bring his fury to overflowing, his friend John Huss is to be burned alive."

"What? That's John Ziska?" [70]

"Himself. What a bestial face, eh? Is he handsome thus? And those Bohemians! Well done! And they call themselves men. Don't tell me that's a human face! What you see there would bite off the head of a baby prematurely delivered from its mother's womb! Yes, it's better than a bullfight."

"It's exciting," I said, gluing my eye to the instrument.

"Follow him, keep following–you'll see!"

I resumed my observations.

"There," said Monsieur Durand, "defending himself on Mount Taurkand... His other eye torn out... His fury redoubles... He clears a passage... Follow him, follow... Another victory... Two, three, four victories... Sigismund makes a treaty with him. John Ziska is Viceroy of Bohemia!"

I kept following. All at once, John Ziska disappeared.

"I no longer see him," I said to Monsieur Durand.

"Keep looking."

"I can see a door panel with some sort of white cross attached to it."

"He's dead. He's been flayed. It's his skin. They're drying it in the Sun to make a drum–because, with this talisman to lead them into battle, the Bohemians believe that they will

---

[70] John Ziska (1360-1424) was a former Teutonic Knight who became the leader of the Hussites and waged war against the Holy Roman Emperor Sigismund, who had Huss burned despite a promise of safe conduct. The conflict is the subject of the epic poem *Ziska* (1846) by Alfred Meissner.

always be victorious. Look there, a little further away, they're knocking over the enemy: the enormous drum that a soldier's beating with his hands, that's him!"

"It's very good, but somewhat brutal," I said. "I've got gooseflesh! Can you show me something less terrible. Hang on–I'd really like to see King Dagobert... Such a popular monarch!" [71]

When Monsieur Durand had turned the telescope fractionally, I perceived a tall, thin man with a slightly sneering attitude, his russet hair hanging down to his shoulders, dressed in an apple-green jerkin and chocolate-colored britches.

"What! That's him? He's entirely as I imagined him; he has a fine boyish air about him."

"Hmm–don't take pride in that. Do you know that without the protection of the canons of St. Denis, the devils would have seized his soul at the moment when he disembarked at Caron? That he had to call the celestial militia very hastily; that there was a terrible battle, the Devils catching him by the arms while the Angels caught him by the feet, and that he was only a whisker away from his soul cooking in perpetuity in the pan where the evil herdsmen of peoples are fried? You haven't seen the gateway of St. Denis, then, where all that is carved in great detail?

"In the first place, in moral terms, he wasn't worth very much; he was an old lecher. He was also very cruel. But he was a good soldier–a good general, even, and an artist–that's

---

[71] Dagobert I (see Note 47) was the subject of a satirical popular song that was composed before the Revolution of 1789 but enjoyed a spectacular increase in popularity after 1814, when it was modified as an attack on Napoleon in the wake of the Russian campaign. It makes scurrilous reference to an incident in which Dagobert allegedly put his trousers on inside out, to which the characters subsequently refer (giving Mouton an opportunity to indulge in some slyly indecent suggestions of his own). Dagobert's chief minister, who eventually became St. Eloi, is also featured in the song.

sacred, of course, it being well-known that artists can do nothing worthwhile if they are forced to bear the chains of morality, which are all right for the bourgeoisie.

"Then again, he has been forgiven because he was an enthusiastic promoter of architecture and the goldsmith's trade."

"Monsieur," I said to M. Durand, "there's something that confuses me... About the costume in the inferior and posterior part of the monarch's clothing. Did our Merovingian Kings have the privilege of lining their britches in the color of chocolate?"

"No. Hozier has established that the lining, in the first dynasty, was sky blue." [72]

"That's odd," I said. "So his britches are the right way round, then?"

"Without doubt."

"Oh well–but the song?"

"The song? Oh! Firstly, like all popular songs, it wasn't made up by ordinary people, whose life doesn't equip them for composition, but by educated men about a thousand years later–the song obviously originates from the end of the 18th century. As for the anecdote, it's true. It's certain–I have even seen it with the aid of the historioscope–that Dagobert did indeed, in a fit of distraction, put his britches on inside out one day.

"He found himself in the chamber of one of the Queen's maids, whom he had visited with a request to sew up a seam; having heard a noise he put his britches back on in a tearing hurry, without noticing that he had got into them the wrong way. On going out, he ran into Saint Eloi, who was going to his workroom, situated at the far end of the courtyard. A few ribald remarks were exchanged–perfectly natural among old

---

[72] Hozier was the surname of a celebrated family of genealogists whose work extended across several generations from the 17th century to the 19th; it is not obvious which one Durand is citing.

friends–but nothing more, and it required all the ingenuity of our historians to make the incident seem important and to present it to the young as the most memorable event in the reign of that perfectly serious prince. Between ourselves, I don't know why the University persists in featuring that bawdy anecdote in the syllabus of its examinations."

While saying this, Monsieur Durand nudged the historioscope's bearing slightly, looked through it and said to me: "Look, Monsieur, if you like artists–here, truly, is one of the most thrilling scenes that the history of art and genius can offer to our admiration. We're in Florence. Benvenuto Cellini is finishing off his Perseus.[73] He had placed the model in an oven that he has carefully constructed with his own hands.

"Look there, to the right of the palace, at this outhouse. Do you see that ruddy smoke rising from the roof, that mouth red with fire into which four or five magnificent young people are throwing wood? Look–the flame grows, shooting like a tongue from the top of the chimney, and through the cracks in the brickwork you can almost see a dark mass that's resistant to the fire. Suddenly, in the middle of that furnace, a hitch develops. The metal isn't melting; the alloy is incomplete. A few more minutes, and the masterpiece, bursting in the mold, will be destroyed! The young men become agitated, lifting their arms to the heavens.

"Then an angry, desperate man can be seen running, his eyes wild and his lips trembling: it's the master, the artist; his glory will perish in the flames! Desperation and enthusiasm give him a glimpse of a means of salvation. He bounds into his house and comes back with his arms full of tinplate, which he hurls into the furnace. He runs back in, comes back out, throwing more in, again and again! A vermilion light reddens the mouth of the oven. The noise ceases. The subservient ma-

---

[73] Benvenuto Cellini (1500-71) was the most celebrated sculptor of his era, and his autobiography became a classic; the account of his casting of the Perseus of the Loggia dei Lanzi is one of the most famous anecdotes therein.

terial dissolves and liquefies under the action of the alloy. It begins to run into the vents of the mold. Benvenuto Cellini and his young assistants embrace one another and give voice to triumphant cries: the Perseus is cast in bronze, and the treasure of art counts one more masterpiece...

"All things considered," Monsieur Durand added, in a soft and slightly sad voice, "that is perhaps the most interesting thing I have to show you in the history of humankind: genius and art elevated to the point of heroism, in creating something eternal and incontrovertibly beautiful. Unless I've missed something, I believe that this is the finest fact in history."

"It's very moving, no doubt," I said, "but it seems to me that one ought to be able to find more important events in history than the founding of a statue..."

"That's obviously possible, because there's so much noise, because certain events have chanced to become more popular than others. The time, the place, and the amount of credit afforded to the first to set them down, make the fortune of one insignificant story, while another more worthy of memory will fall into obscurity. Without going any further, look at Dagobert's trousers: from having once being put on inside out, they became immortal.

"The celebrity of historical facts, like that of men, is a matter of camaraderie, of preservation, and above all of chance. If we think about it seriously, we're forced to admit that we are all, deep down, equally indifferent: what have they to do with the happiness that is the sole and supreme aim of our earthly life? Out of sight, out of mind, my dear Monsieur: the most frightful things, if they happen at a distance, don't really affect us, all the more so if they are ancient. Who ever weeps while reading history? But when we see a great soul, performing a sublime action, brought back to life–when the flame of the ideal, cutting through the vulgar monotony of historical facts, is reanimated for an instant in the night of the past–then the heart might beat faster.

"Since the world became the world, Monsieur, has anything there ever changed, eh? In every time, in every place, every man has always done the same thing, and when they have no one to imitate, they begin to do once more what they have already done, imitating themselves. Events no longer have any variety: it's an eternal repetition."

"And yet," I said, "the different aspects of human societies, of races..."

"That's true. There's one detail that changes: costume. There I'm in agreement with you, but that's all. And that's my philosophy of history. What one calls by that name—which is to say, a series of new facts—doesn't exist, except for costume. As regards wars, massacres, revolutions in decadent empires and progress, they're circus performers which emerge on stage from the wings and go back again, with the same drum-major at their head.

"But there's more. In the theater of human life, men play their roles several times over. Biologically speaking, doesn't nature make new living beings from the bodies of the dead? It's a sad thing to say, but the truth is that everything here, men and things alike, is nothing but second-hand merchandise: if that isn't the case, how can you explain why individuals and races are always reproducing the same stupidities?"

"I can understand that the continual spectacle of such facts has, in the end, made you indifferent," I said. "There is, unfortunately, much truth in what you say. But as well as the history of the remote past, it seems to me that you have a very interesting field of observation at your disposal, relating to things much closer at hand. Can the historioscope not show you the facts of contemporary history equally clearly?"

"Exactly so. It's just a matter of shortening the instrument's range. Would you like to see the Revolution of 1789, the Empire, the Restoration, the Second Empire, the war of 1870, the invasion, the siege of Paris, the Commune?"

"What! I can see people and events again that I've seen disappear!"

"It's up to you–and not just those I've mentioned, but others among whom you've lived more intimately: your friends, your relatives, all those you've loved and are no longer alive."

"No!" I exclaimed, recoiling in fright. "No, excuse me from that spectacle–it would rend my heart! Ah, to see them as specters, forever separated from me by the abyss in which their image floats! Never! Never!"

"I can understand your resistance," he said to me. "For myself, every time the course of my observations happens to bring me the reflection of a friend, someone I loved, I turn away. But wouldn't you like to rediscover the other phases of your own existence?"

"Show me! Show me!" I said, hurling myself upon the instrument.

Monsieur Durand adjusted the telescope.

"Look," he said to me. "Here's the hour of your birth. Turn this button gently and you will see your entire life story unfold before your eyes."

How can I describe the feeling that came over me by degrees as I saw that sequence of scenes pass through the field of the magical instrument, every one of which recalled an extinct joy or an incurable pain? A curiosity more powerful than my anguish chained my eyes to the spectacle. As the episodes succeeded one another, mixed in with the moments of my life, I saw the reappearance of the beloved individuals I had been anxious to see again a short time before–but I saw nothing but shadows. My heart beat like a hammer; emotion gripped me by the throat, I moved my hands as if to seize them and call to them.

And the further my eyes followed the specter of myself, the more I saw it grow pale, bend towards the Earth, stopping from time to time, increasingly less able to bear the burden of life's vicissitudes with every toilsome step. And every one of my sorrows was displayed to my eyes; all the wounds in my heart reopened, one by one, as bloody as they were when first inflicted!

I strove in vain to tear my eyes away. I laughed, I wept, I writhed in despair! "Mercy! Help me!" I cried.

"Ah, that amazes you!" said Monsieur Durand. "You did not imagine that! You thought that your life was yours! See, then, that which happens throughout nature. See, then, with your own eyes, what becomes of all those men, every one of whom believed, in his time, that he was the center of the universe! You can no longer recover them entire; you see their debris passing by, act by act and thought by thought, rolling helplessly along in the torrent of life, which has taken back from them everything that it gave.

"Now, understand this: even as we live, we are already falling apart. Everything that we have been, everything that we have done up to the present moment, has become as distant from us, and as dead to us, as if we had never experienced it. And that is why, when some miracle allow us to evoke the image of our past, the image frightens us as the phantom of a dead man would.

"You can now understand how a past life revived within the eternal monotony of those scenes, alternately harrowing and grotesque, could not but drive me mad–for you see what is happening to the thing that is my body. My decrepitude bears no resemblance to that of other men. I have never known their sorrows or their joys, but like another Atlas–an Atlas who can do no more–I carry on my shoulders the burden of the stupidities and the misfortunes of the entire human race!"

"Even at the price of what I have suffered," I told him, "I don't regret having seen the marvels that you've shown me, and I hope that you'll permit me to come here again."

"As often as you please."

"There's one thing, though," I said, "that leaves a slight uncertainty in the results of your observations. That is that the historioscope only gives you pictures, and that the crowds you see stirring in space with the movements of life are entirely composed of mute individuals. Ah, if only one could hear them!"

"In the present state of my science," Monsieur Durand replied, "we already possess three kinds of apparatus with whose aid we can change sound into light and vice versa. It is therefore possible that, one day, we shall be able to gather from on high the sonorous flood emitted by the voices of the peoples who lived in various epochs of the Earth's past. In the meantime, you know that the photophone already allows us vaguely to receive the sound of gaseous explosions in the Sun's photosphere. I have tried a few experiments with that instrument, and I have begun to obtain some appreciable results on occasion."

He pointed to an apparatus placed on a table. "Here," he said. "Would you like to try it? Apply the receiver to your ear and listen."

I took up the receiver. For a few moments I heard nothing, but little by little it seemed to me that a murmur emerged, similar to that produced by a seashell applied to the ear. I said as much to Monsieur Durand.

"Continue," he told me. "The noise will probably become more distinct. Press the receiver harder."

Indeed, the murmur, gaining amplification by degrees, became a dull and sonorous hum like that of a beehive. The more intently I listened, the more I heard sounds of an infinitesimal acuity penetrating the background noise.

Then Monsieur Durand, lifting his head and extending his arms towards the sky, said: "Do you hear?"

"I hear!" I replied, utterly disconcerted.

"It's the murmur of populations that have passed from the Earth: the distant echo of their speech, their sobs, their sighs, their kisses; the echo of everything that ever vibrated within the human heart, from the first cry of the newly-born to the last breath of the dying. Like the chords of an immense symphony, the murmur comes forth, following these images at a distance in their flight through space and eternity."

Dusk was falling. I felt an urgent need to return home in order to come to terms with the day's emotions. I took my leave of Monsieur Durand.

At the moment of parting, though, I could not help darting one last glance into the historioscope. The instrument was pointed in the last direction to which Monsieur Durand had chanced to turn it. I looked into it.

"What is that shining surface in which the Sun is reflected?" I asked him. "It seems to me to be mirroring tall masses, like monuments. And yet, it's a river! See for yourself!"

"It's the Euphrates–it's Babylon!" Monsieur Durand exclaimed. "Hold on–look there, in the middle of the river. What do you see?"

"What? God forgive me, there are fishermen. They're pulling up their nets... They're opening them... They're taking out large fish!"

Monsieur Durand threw himself at the telescope to look in his turn.

"Fish that resemble enormous eels, with open mouths bristling with triple rows of sharp teeth!"

Transported by emotion, I pushed Monsieur Durand aside and snatched the telescope. I saw the fishermen taking the fish one by one and putting them in large boxes pierced with holes. One packer, with a paintbrush, traced an O at each corner and distributed inscriptions like the *Top*, *Bottom* and *Fragile* of our post offices!

"No more doubt–look!" I said, giving way to Monsieur Durand.

"Well, it's just as I said. These fishermen on the Euphrates are packing moray eels for Etruria. You've seen with your own eyes the first commercial operation trading living moray eels between the Assyrians and the Etruscans, in the time of Evilmerodach and Neriglissor!"

A few days later, I went back to see Monsieur Durand. The porter told me: "He died on the evening when you last came. Two days later, one of his heirs took the body, put it in a hearse, moved all the furniture from upstairs and left."

"For where?"

"He didn't say."

Georges Eekhoud: *Tony Wandel's Heart*

I.

If I can believe the Saturnian Chronicles published after the disappearance of our planet, it was about the year 2250 that human science attained its apogee. Cures for the rabies virus and cholera microbes were known, the result of stubborn research by physiologists. The new anthropology was vertiginously advanced from earlier discoveries. Within institutions like phalansteries,[74] placed under the protection of their originator Charles Darwin, specialists controlled the selection of the human race, while a little-known scholar triumphantly solved one of the most redoubtable unknowns of the universal equation.

It was a surgeon from Flanders, Doctor Van Kipekap, as bold and steadfast as all his countrymen. Incessantly investigating the causes of the phenomena of life, he believed for a long time, with Christopher Wren and Denis,[75] that it was pos-

---

[74] A phalanstery–*phalanstère* in French–was a kind of commune envisaged as the key social unit in the socialist Utopian schemes of Charles Fourier (1772-1837). The word was derived by running together *phalange* (finger-bone) and *monastère*, the former word being used in the sense carried forward by subsequent proponents of the notion of the corporate state. It was actually Charles Darwin's cousin, Francis Galton, rather than the evolutionist himself. who repopularized the idea of "eugenic" selection, which had previously been advocated by Fourier.

[75] In 1657, Christopher Wren (1632-1723), the great English architect, borrow some equipment from William Harvey–who had demonstrated the circulation of the blood some 30 years

sible to substitute for the vitiated blood of a decrepit man that of a child or an adolescent. He took up and extended the experiments begun by Brown-Séquard [76] in past centuries; especially traveling to nations where capital punishment still existed, in order to operate on the condemned. The trials of his predecessors had been carried out on dogs, rabbits, a freshly-amputated arm at most; he was the first to give life to a decapitated head.

One of these resurrections crowned his career as an anatomist. Finding himself in Japan, and learning of the immi-

---

earlier–in order to carry out a pioneering series of experiments in animal blood transfusion. A series of injections of lamb's blood into human patients was carried out in Paris a few years later by the natural philosopher Jean-Baptiste Denis (1625-1704); although the first three patients reported that the treatment had been beneficial, the fourth died. Denis was subsequently sued by the widow, and although the court decided that he was not guilty of negligence, he was ordered to desist from further experiments. Blood transfusions were then outlawed in France until the 1800s, although experimentation was revived in England in the 1790s by Erasmus Darwin (Charles's grandfather).

When Eekhoud wrote "Tony Wandel's Heart" in 1884, there was no similar history of attempted organ transplantation to which he might have referred, although a Dutchman named Job van Meeneren had claimed to have used a bone graft from a dog to repair an injury to a human skull in 1668; a temporary skin graft using skin from a cadaver was allegedly carried out on a burn victim in 1881. The issue of tissue compatibility came into sharper focus in 1901-03, when Karl Landsteiner began the research that led to his categorization of the A/B/O blood groups in 1909.

[76] Charles-Edouard Brown-Séquard (1817-1894) was a French physician and physiologist, one of the creators of opotherapy–better known in English as organotherapy–whose treatments used bodily fluids extracted from various organs.

nent decollation of a rebel soldier, he contrived to subject the mortal remains, following the work of the executioner, to his favorite manipulations. As usual, he waited until the severed head had lost its sensibility, little by little; when the eyelids were closed, the eyes dull and the nostrils immobile, he used a pump to force fresh red blood, free of any clots, into the arteries of the brain. Then, all the invited dignitaries saw the head, formerly inanimate, gradually come back to life, reopen its eyelids and flare its nostrils. The bloodless complexion was reinvigorated, the eyes shone.

As the injection continued, the mouth grimaced, the teeth grated, the eyeballs rolled grievously, teardrops formed. Then, someone having called the murderer by his name, the pupils moved slowly to the side from which the call had come, and the frightfully weak voice of the condemned man asked: "What do you want?"

At that moment, a panic took hold of the breathless and petrified audience. Everyone ran for the door. Even the experimenter's assistant abandoned his side. They knocked over the apparatus, the pump, the receptacles and the head itself–which rolled on the floor, bouncing and howling, trying to nip the legs of the fleeing dignitaries, hampered by their formal attire.

After this scene, three months passed without the doctor pursuing his explorations further.

He took them up again and extended them, armoring his nervous system to proof himself against any surprise, but they no longer succeeded in satisfying him. The phenomenon of resurrection only lasted as long as the continual introduction of blood by means of an artificial and mechanical process.

He tried to recall to life individuals killed by disease and encountered obstacles even more considerable. Often, the new fluid conducted into the cadaver was insufficient to galvanize it. The doctor attributed this failure to the exhaustion or contamination of the organs. It was important that the flowing flesh, the regenerative juice, could reach the channels and reservoirs that required it. The problem came back to the renewal of the essential parts of the body. But which? To replace them all would be wildly fanciful.

Van Kipekap did not hesitate for long. Impulsion being given to the blood as it left the heart, it was this organ that attracted the attention of the doctor. Another consideration, even more serious, dictated his choice. Like Aristotle and Ficinus, he placed the soul in the heart–in contrast to Plato and Descartes, who lodged it in the brain. In his eyes, the heart represented not only the origin and motor of circulation, but the key principle and very source of life. By the substitution of a healthy heart for an exhausted one, he would rejuvenate old men, cure the sick, and realize the fabulous Fountain of Youth that he and his predecessors had expected to obtain by mere blood transfusion.

With this belief, he returned to his experiments in vivisection, in order that his hands might cultivate an indispensable skill and quickness. The extraction of the heart involved an initial large incision made in the breast near to the sixth true rib, then a first section to separate the superior and inferior *vena cava* from the right auricle, a second stroke of the scalpel to detach the heart from the pulmonary artery, a third to disconnect the pulmonary veins and the left auricle, and, finally, a last flick of the wrist to sever the aorta.

When one bears in mind that it was necessary to carry out this extraction in two individuals–to place the healthy heart in place of the contaminated organ, to reattach by means of ligatures the stumps of the veins and arteries to the corresponding junctures in the breast of the individual to be caulked, and to sew up the percardium and the flesh of the thorax–one will understand the innumerable slicings that Van Kipekap carried out on all the beasts in creation, secretly and in seclusion, before experimenting on his own kind.

In the end, he considered his "training" sufficient, and had only to await an opportunity to confront the final test. It came along.

At the hospital in N***, on the Scheldt,[77] where Doctor Van Kipekap had his clinic, he observed one day two neighboring beds occupied by an old invalid and a young injury-victim. Both were dying, with the difference that the former was succumbing to sickness and senility while the other, built to last for a long time, was perishing accidentally.

The innovator had his demonstration.

Having solemnly summoned the most illustrious doctors, his interns and the great men of Flanders, he chloroformed the two patients, carried out point for point the little program so often repeated on innocent stray dogs and congenial rabbits, effectively attaining the substitution of the healthy and intact heart of the man in his prime for the worn-out and degenerate organ of the septuagenarian. The wounded man died, while the invalid awoke following a recuperative slumber, completely transfigured, as vigorous and hearty as a 14-year-old.

Among Van Kipekap's colleagues, some hailed it as an unqualified miracle, others as a fraud or a conspiracy. All of them challenged him to repeat the marvelous experiment. Van Kipekap asked for no more, and succeeded a second time. He operated repeatedly with the same facility. Then the envious bowed down.

Meanwhile, the news of the prodigy spread, dazzling and resounding, to all four corners of the world. Humankind in its entirety glorified this Fleming, who had equipped it with near-immortality.

In truth, the finding only benefited those people rich enough to afford to regain their youth. Such as they would be able to change their hearts as they changed their clothes and their mistresses. With the introduction of a new heart into the

---

[77] There is no Flemish town on the river Scheldt–Eekhoud uses its French name, l'Escaut–whose name begins with the letter N. The formulation is a joke, the reference being to Eekhoud's birthplace, Anvers, or Antwerp, whose name begins with a syllable not dissimilar to that letter's pronunciation.

economy, the other machinery of the human clock was repaired.

It became very difficult to obtain exchangeable organs, because a well-constituted rogue that fate had delivered to a tragic death–and who, having been declared lost, consented to be separated from his irreproachable heart for the benefit of a millionaire mortgaged by old age and excess–did not turn up every day, at the appropriate moment. In normal times, one could only shop around for that desirable article in certain heroic categories: masons fallen from scaffolding, miners surprised by an explosion of fire-damp, railway-passengers crushed by an impact with the buffers, victims of cut-throats, and the same cut-throats in the hour of their expiation.

The heart became the luxury item par excellence, the monopoly of Croesus. Prices soared in proportion to the youth and vigor of the subject. Speculation became involved; the human heart was quoted on the Bourse like any other commodity. Despite the extraordinary prices commanded by that engine, supply invariably fell short of demand. Only war caused a lowering.

The only opportunities for repair extended to the middle classes arose by bombardment. Then, one might witness the most extraordinary of spectacles. Valetudinarians and incurables would drag themselves along in the wake of armies, in breathless anticipation of the following day's butchery, their longevity awaiting the violent suppression of thousands of the able-bodied and spirited. On bloody chessboards where black men were throttled by white, these gentlemen's surgeons and lawyers, lugged around on litters, leaned out over mortally wounded young recruits and conscripts, extending their instruments and pens. From those blond youths who were already dying, the vampires asked nothing more than to sign on the dotted line before witnesses. The surgeon took the place of the minister and the man of law to perforate and butcher each expiring soldier with all expedition. They went in this manner from one body to another, providing a prelude to the mutilations of the rooks and vultures.

Inevitably, abuses occurred and justice armed itself with new laws. In times of peace, many a conscienceless industrialist did not shrink from procuring by crime that which politics was tardy in delivering to him. Assassins supplanted conquerors. The courts investigated abominable affairs of the abduction and murder of children.

Thus, the discovery of Doctor Van Kipekap only profited the tiniest minority of humankind, while worsening the lot of the majority of men in exposing their robustness and their very blood to the ferocious covetousness of the powerful. Serfdom was kept alive under guises as various as ever: prison-seed, hospital-haunts, gallows-birds, cannon-fodder, pleasure-fodder and scalpel-fodder.

II.

At that time, one of the compatriots of Doctor Van Kipekap of N*** on the Scheldt was a poor devil of a paver named Tony Wandel. He was a simple Christian soul in a body worthy of the Homeric era. Married to a blonde pauper, who was his equal in resignation and as beautiful as the legendary burgesses of Anvers and Bruges, the father of three little ones as chubby as Rubens cherubs, he toiled steadfastly six days a week, his piledriver or mallet falling rhythmically and incessantly on the flagstones. He was never idle, except when he had to be; he would have considered it stealing from the four innocent creatures who comprised his paradise on Earth had he wasted a quarter of an hour of the working day or a *sou* of his wages in the pursuit of drunkenness.

Tony Wandel experienced neither envy nor rancor in comparing his lot with that of the aristocrats of N***. He endured the weather as God sent it to him, considering himself unrivalled in that he was able to feed, house and clothe his own.

On Sundays in summer and other holy days, after vespers, the humble family walked lovingly along the river bank.

They inhaled the briny breeze, the fragrance of new-mown hay beneath the dikes, the invigorating perfume of tar. Their eyes would follow the flight of white sails over the greenish carpet of the waves or the corkscrewing smoke of a ferry-boat. Less contemplative, the children would rush up and down the slopes gathering armfuls of selected flowers, while wallowing farm animals and shy horses greeted them with a neigh or a whinny.

As evening approached, after the beneficial walk, they would snuggle together under the vaulted ceiling of an inn at the town gate, pounded by the vibrations of the organ and the dance, and share a *waterzoei*–the Flemish *bouillabaisse*–and slices of bread with white cheese spiced with garlic, all accompanied by a delectable *uitzet*, the beer of beers. They would go home as night fell, contentedly taciturn, the parents carrying their two youngest in their arms.

Thus they labored all their life, while the grey and monotonous weeks went by like a rain-filled sky that Sundays crossed with rainbows. But this humble outcast's felicity suffered an eclipse. One day, the housewife waited much longer than usual for the paver to return for his supper. Anxiously, she ran to his workplace. There she learned from her husband's gang-mates that he had been knocked down while lending a hand–helpful as ever–to decouple a carriage, when the horse, whipped by the impatient driver, took the bit in its teeth and succeeded in starting up the heavy vehicle, one of whose wheels had passed over the paver's legs. She would find the wounded man in the hospital, but–his companions added, shaking their heads–perhaps with two limbs fewer.

Having heard this sad anthem, Nellie hastened to fly off in search of her man. They had exaggerated. The amputation of the paver's limbs would not be necessary, but the poor devil would be crippled for life and would be unable to walk without crutches.

He recovered, but what good was that? No more working for six days, no more walking on the seventh. Little by little they ate through their savings, selling the most elegant of their clothes. Soon, they were heavily in debt, the baker's tally-stick covered in countless notches. Then privation attacked the rosy cheeks of the wife and children.

After that, there was no other recourse left to the paralytic than begging. Every day, leaving the sick woman to look after the little ones, the cripple undertook his painful and humiliating pilgrimage. Tony Wandel, whose muscular arms would still have been able to lift a pick or a mallet with ease, was reduced to extending his hand, at the risk of being taken for an impostor, confused with vagrants and paupers.

Once, when he was backed up against the door of a church, wringing his heart and thinking of his poor angels, telling himself that for love of them he would open his veins and nourish them with his blood, Tony was accosted by a little man in the prime of life. The man had a fresh complexion, thin lips, eyes of different colors, a face framed by salt-and-pepper mutton-chop whiskers, a sly manner and a paunch; he was dressed in black, ornamented and wearing spectacles. In a jerky and metallic voice, this personage subjected the young invalid to a kind of interrogation.

The trusting Tony willingly told the stranger his troubles; although the lad was rather prolix in narrating his adventures, and a chronic lisp stretched the lamentable tale even further, the unknown lent a complacent ear to the hymn of complaint—and, by an approving nod of the head, encouraged the paver to continue.

This mysterious interlocutor was none other than the illustrious Doctor Van Kipekap. While listening to the young chap, the surgeon was staring intently at his new acquaintance. His inquisitive eyes seemed to want to penetrate the outer tegument to analyze the blood and the humors. When the beggar fell silent, the doctor continued his questions.

"And, except for this little misfortune... I beg your pardon, this catastrophe... which has deprived you of the use of your legs, tell me, my dear friend—permit me this familiarity, for your appearance is infinitely agreeable to me—have you ever had any serious illness?"

"I never took to my bed except to make love or to sleep, before this calamity taught me its other functions..." After a pause, the good-hearted fellow added: "At present, I'm in remarkably good health for a useless creature. My stomach aches with an imperious clamor for a nourishment that my arms can no longer earn..."

"Truly, you experience hunger! Adorable young man! A providential encounter! Will you show me your tongue? I'd like to eat it... Will you permit me to take your pulse?... Excellent. And may I put my ear to your chest? There! Perfect! A heart that might beat for a hundred years without missing a pulsation. Sixty-five beats per minute: the normal figure..." He had counted them on his chronometer.

The innocent Tony submitted to this auscultation with all his original deference. The doctor seemed more and more enthusiastic and expansive. He rubbed his hands together. His face became cheerful. He pronounced words that had no significance for the paver in a voluble manner.

"Marvelous constitution!... Solidly build!... Irreproachable well-being! Twenty-three years, and thus beyond the climacteric age! [78] No bile... Blood-supply generous, neither too thick nor too fluid!... Here's one who fits the bill! There are none but the world-weary, malnourished and badly housed, who bring together a similar combination of physiological virtues." Abruptly, he demanded of the cripple: "So, my lad, if I've grasped the moral of your fascinating story, we no longer hold hard to that she-devil life, and we'd quit it without regret, on condition that our entry into the realm of moles would benefit our widow and orphans?"

"Alas, Monsieur, that's exactly what I think. A tragic death is better than a tragic life!"

---

[78] A climacteric is a period in human life when a considerable change in one's state of health is supposedly likely to occur. In the 19th century, such key phases were popularly considered to be multiples of seven and three–i.e. the ages of 21, 42 and 63.

"Well, comrade, what if I took you at your word and asked you to abandon the remainder of your days in exchange for a fortune guaranteed to those you leave behind?"

"I would accept!" the market-trader replied resolutely. "On condition that you show me a Christian door whereby to make my exit from life. Suicide leads to damnation..."

"But a sacrifice like the one you shall consummate to save your family is no longer called a suicide!" said the artful doctor, recalling his casuistry.

"Do you think so, Monsieur? In such a matter, a person of your importance is better able to discern rightness than we mere sheep. Tell me what must be done; I'm your man."

"Marvelous! I was right to come your way, and your character does not give the lie to your physiognomy. Shake my hand! Your widow will gain 500,000 florins before the Sun sets or I'll give away my name."

"My widow! Five hundred thousand florins!" the beggar repeated, as his heart was squeezed by anguish–although hope soon reinflated it.

"Ah, we manage our affairs briskly, my young friend. The bargain set up, the bargain concluded. It will be necessary to do away with you this very day... But before I summarize the details of the transaction for you, and the manner in which we shall fulfill our mutual obligations, would you like to accompany me to a place more suitable for confabulation? Not least because idlers are spying on us, intrigued to see a ragamuffin like you in conversation with the famous Doctor Van Kipekap. We must keep it to ourselves, you understand..."

Luckily, they found themselves in the proximity of a local tavern. Van Kipekap led his placid captive into a room sheltered from eavesdroppers and both of them sat down at a table before a revivifying collation and a delicious flask of dessert wine, which sat in their glasses like liquefied rubies. Then the doctor began to tell his story.

III.

The great man, loyal to his fatherland and a confirmed burgher of N*** on the Scheldt, also counted his among his fellow citizens his principal client, the extremely rich banker Trekkenpluk, a moribund sexagenarian who wanted to recover his health and a new youth at any price, in order to enjoy the fabulous wealth from which death threatened to separate him. For several years, he had been in search of a willing bumpkin who would sell him a sturdy heart, guaranteed faultless by physicians.

Unfortunately, fate had delayed the moment of its acquisition. The number of suicides was diminishing, and suicides skillfully procured at the banker's behest had killed themselves too abruptly, shooting themselves in the heart, not wishing their precious viscera to profit their survivors. As soon as the news reached him that a pauper was on the brink, Van Kipekap, always on the lookout, would dispatch his best bloodhounds to the hovel, but they always arrived too late; the hanged man, who was taken down completely cold, had already danced the last *bourrée*.[79] Assassins were too conscientious in finishing off their victims and maliciously put the scaffold's caterers off the scent. Then, there were the wounded transported to hospital, who presumed to die without forewarning the financier who was animated by the most generous sentiments in respect of them.

As he scoured newspaper obituaries posted by those ingenuous physicians of slaters and plasterers, who verified at their own expense the laws of gravity and falling bodies, the sick man felt the rancor of those capitalists who, consulting a list of successful lottery numbers, perceive that one of theirs is only one figure removed from the winner of the grand prize.

---

[79] A *bourrée* is an Auvergnian dance, whose tune was sometimes played at executions. The word also means a bundle of firewood.

Disgruntled, he proceeded to read the *Accidents, crimes and disasters* notices:

Rue Morgue, this morning, a young (here he pricked up his ears) *manual laborer, a native of the region* (the region! robust and vigorous, then! the reader enticed himself) *18 years of age* (the best age to become useful to an aged millionaire in a heart operation) *being exceedingly drunk* (worthy alcohol! helpful drunkenness!) *fell two stories from the rafters.* (The banker got excited.) *Grievously wounded in the left temple* (ah! ah!) *the unfortunate was carried into a neighboring house* (I shall take your awkward health, rustic adolescent!) *at No. 7, to which our eminent practitioner, Doctor Van Kipekap, happening to be in the vicinity of the accident scene* (what flair the dear doctor has!) *charitably ran in order to extend the assistance of his art to the young proletarian, free of charge.* (Tee hee–that joker Van Kipekap! One knows what your help is worth in cash!) *Unhappily* (what! What does that mean?) *the illustrious physiologist was only able to certify the death* (Help! I'm choking) *of the imprudent yokel.*

The page slipped from the banker's hands as he frothed at the mouth epileptically, howling like a maddened cat. "The imprudent yokel!" he repeated. "Truly, these journalists abuse the art of euphemism. It's thief, blackguard, kidnapper he should be labeled. Eighteen years old! Misfortune! And that Van Kipekap came running to certify the death! Still an eagle, that one! What awaits a society that produces such monstrosities? That's the third scoundrel's heart lost to me!"

To heap misfortune upon misfortune, not the slightest threat of war or revolution was visible on the political horizon. Kings were no longer jealous of one another; the people seemed to have been permanently tamed; anarchists, Fenians and nihilists had been idle since time immemorial. Diplomats wore forced smiles and Prussian captains were going to rust, along with the strategists' compasses. France had given up trying to civilize its neighbors and make them happy in spite of themselves; she did not even attempt the least massacre of the Indo-Chinese or the inhabitants of the Algerian-Tunisian borders.

And old Trekkenpluk was flickering like the flame of a lamp running out of oil; he was at risk of taking his place in the parade filing past Pierrot-la-Mort, just like the lowliest breadwinner. Horrified by the idea of a dénouement whose prognostications were multiplying hour by hour, he clung desperately to existence.

His heirs, distant cousins, imposed themselves upon him in his home in order to fall upon the spoils as soon as he passed on. His flunkeys were not waiting for him to die before robbing him; phenomenal pilfering was the rule in the rich unfortunate's dwelling, and the staff exacted frightful damages in wine and meat. His companions in debauchery, epicureans as egotistical and as hard as he, took great care not to trouble the quietness and animal carelessness of their last days with the pathetic spectacle of this sybarite on his way out.

IV.

While the doctor related these facts to his interlocutor, the dazzled Tony repeated aside the fantastic figure of "500,000 florins!" whose syllables sounded like the clink of gold coins.

The vastness of the offered sum vanquished his hesitation. He imagined an opulent future for his family: his wife lodged in a palace as great as the Beffroi,[80] she and the kids dressed in silk and lace, lying in a feather-bed, the table laid with a eternal Cokaygne,[81] a festival of black puddings that

---

[80] The reference is presumably to the Tour de Beffroi, a famous landmark in Bruges, although the word *beffroi* had previously been used as a generic term for fortified towers.

[81] The land of Cokaygne (whose many other spellings include Cockayne, Cockaigne and, in French, Cocagne and Coquaigne) is featured in an anti-clerical satire about a land of

would not run out until Judgment Day. He saw them drinking from jugs full of delectable uitzet and sadly raising a toast to the salvation, if not the health, of their poor father.

The doctor roused the evangelical lad from his reverie mingling regret and consolation and, as if he had read his mind, proposed a toast to the future orphans and the widow-to-be.

"And now, young man, if you so desire, we shall go to the home of my client, the notable banker Van Trekkenpluk, who is at this moment in time the richest man in Flanders, but also the most pitiful."

"Let's go," said the paver, simply.

An advancement brought them close to the courtyard of the church where the two men had met. Poor cab-horses, heads burrowing deep into their nosebags, were chewing their miserly oats while their coachmen were taking turns to buy rounds of drinks from the counters. Van Kipekap hired a fiacre, helped the cripple up, sat beside him and gave the coachman the name of the Flemish Croesus.

The carriage stopped outside a door with pretentious *mascarons*,[82] that of the Trekkenpluk townhouse. A Hungarian servant opened it to them and led them through hallways and corridors as vast as cathedral naves, stairways of serpentine marble, and suites of rooms hung with Gobelins tapestries, furnished with lacquered cabinets, dressers wrought by silver-smiths charged with fine Chinese porcelain. Persian carpets

---

ease where no one has to work or fulfill any religious duties because food is abundant–the ducks are ready-roasted–and the weather always fine. Its origins are presumably Norman, al-though its best-known representation in England is a 14th-century poem that begins by comparing Cokaygne very fa-vorably with Paradise (which, being controlled by God, still exercises constraints on human desire and behavior).

[82] A *mascaron* is a large design in the form of a mask; they are usually found in pairs.

stifled the noise of the doctor's footsteps and the cripple's crutches.

Passing from landing to landing they encountered clean-shaven and sullen valets with feather-dusters under their arms, with whom the Hungarian exchanged frightful winks. It was the unwonted presence of the pauper that unsettled them, but Doctor Van Kipekap was a powerful man; everyone trembled before his skill, and although the banker's relatives knew about his schemes for the moribund, none would have dared incur the wrath of so prodigious a man by shutting the door on someone in his company.

After a long walk, Tony and his introducer entered the old man's bedroom. They found him stretched out on a chaise longue, enveloped in furs, breathing in a labored fashion. With his yellow skin pasted on his bones, the vitreous expression of his eyes, the inertia of his limbs and the bitter rictus contracting his violet lips, he presented the appearance of a living mummy.

With careful discretion, the doctor brought Trekkenpluk up to date with the morning's events and presented him with his news and precious intelligence.

"An opportunity that will not arise again!" he whispered, leaning over the moribund. "Five hundred thousand florins for him, and the same for me. It's a good bargain!"

The sick man appeared to be reanimated by this last chance of salvation. A flame lit up his hollow eyes, and he inspected Tony from head to toe, with an expression of covetousness so ferocious and so sulphurous [83] that the paver almost ran away.

"I say, doctor," he whispered very softly in his friend's ear, "your client seems devilishly keen to have my life! A nasty-looking villain, with all due respect..."

"But a magnificent payer, on the other hand..."

---

[83] *Safre*, here translated as "sulphurous", can refer various yellow substances, including cobalt oxide and saffron, but the implication here is presumably infernal.

233

"You're right, doctor." And with that, Tony resigned himself to his fate.

No time was lost. Two ready-stamped formal contracts, drawn up long before, were filled in by the two parties. Tony signed with a cross, like the knights of the Middle Ages. Then Van Kipekap supplied the patient with a check for half a million, made out to the impending widow Wandel, payable the same day at the Trekkenpluk Bank.

"May I deliver this *billet doux* to my darling myself?" asked the honest chap, with a trusting smile.

"Did you not understood the terms, my friend? You shall not see your wife again..."

"My God! To die without embracing my irresistible little chickens! But I give in—the sight of them would surely wipe out my resolve. Say, doctor, that you'll put the inheritance into my wife's hand."

"Willingly. Before nightfall, the treasure will be in your home..."

"Thank you, greatest of doctors; I'm sorry for the trouble I've put you to..."

"Not at all, my boy," protested the surgeon, who was insensitive by nature and profession but slightly taken aback by such forbearance and candor. "Now let's get on, for the honorable Mr. Trekkenpluk seems very low today and we can't spend too long chatting..."

On Van Kipekap's orders, and with infinite care, the domestics lifted the old banker—who squealed and moaned all the while—on to a stretcher. They deposited him, more tightly wrapped up than ever, on the floor of a ready-harnessed carriage in the courtyard. The operator and his "subject" got in, with their backs to the coachman.

"Where are we going, doctor?" the young man asked, as two vigorous horses set the carriage in motion.

"Straight ahead! To find a suitable spot, my excellent friend—somewhat isolated, sheltered from any troublesome surprises, where we can properly expedite our little business..." Smiling with encouraging good humor, he clapped Tony on the shoulder in a familiar fashion.

Huddled in front of them, old Trekkenpluk coughed, his face convulsed. Looking at him, the doctor became alarmed and consulted his watch; then he stuck his nose to the window-glass to see how far they had traveled.

An elegant instrument-case and a portable pharmacy had been transported from the surgeon's fiacre to the banker's carriage. Van Kipekap made the moribund take a powerful sleeping-draught, whose effect was immediate.

"He'll not wake up again unless he awakes rejuvenated!" the scholar said, with a certain solemnity.

"In my trade, we call it repairing when we replace the worn-out stones in the road with new ones. The road becomes bad for the old–it's a repair job that we're going to carry out, isn't that so, doctor?" And Tony sang an old workmen's song:

"On, on, honest paver,
"Dig and level the road.
"While the Angelus sounds
"In the distant tower,
"The resonant plink [84]
"Of your falling pick
"Adds amen to the prayer."

Meanwhile, the horses burned up the road.

After an hour of the frenzied journey, they reached the edge of a beech forest. They came to a halt, and the doctor invited Tony Wandel to get down and follow him. They left the road immediately and went into the thickets. Tony carried the heavy instrument-case, in a manner somewhat reminiscent of Jesus carrying his cross.

---

[84] Eekhoud has *plainte argentine* where I have been content with "plink;" I hope the latter can carry the double implication of a metallic sound suggestive of complaint, while wreaking less havoc upon the scansion of what is presumably the author's own composition rather than an authentic laborers' song.

After a hundred paces, Van Kipekap took his companion by the arm again. "How does this seem to you, Tony, my friend? Does the place suit you? An unknown poet would choose no other to exhale a final objurgatory sonnet... ah!"

The place was a sort of clearing. A single magnificent beech towered over the middle of a meadow surrounded by densely packed trees. At its foot the ground was raised. The noble tree [85] cast a great shadow on the grass for several meters around, for the ardent August Sun was unable to transmit its rays through the centuries-old branches.

Tony made no reply to the doctor's question. He understood that the moment had arrived to say his *in manus*.[86] Here or elsewhere, it mattered little to him. With his nose in the air, Van Kipekap noticed a branch extending from the trunk two meters above the ground and almost parallel to it.

"Ha!" the amiable scholar exclaimed. "Here's one that will make an adorable gibbet!"

"As you wish, Mijnheer!" sighed the lad, resigned but slightly melancholy even so. He had not yet attained the age of consistency. The hot bright Sun, the birds fluttering in the foliage above them and the edge of the immutably blue sky reminded him of the happy excursions of yesteryear, along the Scheldt. He sighed deeply, and within his breast the great heart that he would soon give up contracted and expanded convulsively.

Meanwhile, the doctor, confident of the stoical boy's acquiescence, drove half a dozen nails into the trunk of the tree, which would enable the suicide to climb up to the sturdy branch. Then he took from his pocket an elegant cord made of

---

[85] The word Eekhoud uses here is *marmenteau*, which has no simple English equivalent; it emphasizes that the tree in question is preserved as an ornament, forbidden to the woodcutter's axe.

[86] This reference is to a Latin prayer offered up by those about to die; coincidentally, it is given in full in the text of "The Red Triangle" (see Note 123 for a translation).

hemp and silk, as slender as a shoelace but of proven tensile strength, and extended it to his companion with his most engaging smile.

"When you're ready, dear friend, I am at your disposal..."

"Doctor," the lad declared, pale but resolute, "may I ask you one more favor?"

"Speak, my brave boy, but let's be quick–you know that someone's waiting for me..."

"Tell Nellie how much I adore them, that it's for love of them that I'm going and that I didn't want to see them. You'll give them good advice too, won't you, doctor? Because this unexpected fortune might go to their heads..."

"Put your trust in me. I'll take your family in hand. Is that all?"

"God will repay you, doctor! Permit me to embrace you..."

"Gladly, for you're the most determined chap I ever met! No recriminations or sniveling–I like that! We're here, eh? For your convenience and mine, you'd do well to take off your smock."

Tony, always deferential, put himself in his shirtsleeves. The placid fellow threw away his crutches, not without gazing at them with a certain emotion. Then, supported by the doctor, he succeeded in hauling himself up on to the branch, on which he sat himself astride.

Van Kipekap had prepared the noose, whose knot slid smoothly enough to make an English executioner jealous. Tony fixed the cord to the branch and slipped it around his neck.

"Doctor...?" he stammered, at that moment.

"What is it now?" said the other–with a certain impatience, for the moribund in the carriage preoccupied him even more than this excellent proletarian dough.

"Doctor, may God bless you, and my heart serve the old man well..."

"Amen!"

"Wait! One... two... three..." He did not count as far as four; his fingers opened, he lost his balance and pivoted around his seat. His legs lost their grip and he fell, retained four feet above the ground by the cord abruptly tightened by his weight. The cord snapped his neck.

The poor wretch thrashed about atrociously; even his cataleptic legs found their vitality again for that last solo dance.

"The excellent market-trader!" murmured the hard-baked man, confronted by this painful scene. "Let's cut his suffering short and get busy with the other."

With his scalpel between his teeth, taking the same route as the paver with the agility of a squirrel, the doctor rejoined his patient and operated on him in no time at all. Carrying the precious organ, he ran back to the banker, unconscious in his carriage. There, he successfully completed the prodigious work that he had already carried out so often.

The carriage returned at full speed along the road to the house. Hunched over the body of his patient–who was prostrate on the cushions, as limp as a defrocked priest–Van Kipekap continually lifted a silver spatula to his withered lips.

After a few minutes of terrible anxiety, the doctor let loose a loud hurrah. The polished blade became dull. Trekkenpluk was breathing.

V.

When the banker woke up at dawn the following morning, after 17 hours of sound sleep, the old man was no more. Black hair, thick and solidly-anchored, garnished the scalp that had resembled a reef constantly washed by the waves the previous evening. The grooves in his forehead had been filled in and firm flesh had filled out his flaccid cheeks, colored in a most attractive fashion by vivid blood. The hollow and dull eyes were reilluminated in their orbits and the crow's-feet marking their outlines had also disappeared. Instead of a livid and bloodless pout, his lips had recovered the incarnadine of former days, and even his teeth–loose exposed stumps, which he had been on the point on replacing with ivory dentures– were solidly planted in their sockets and impeccably enamelled. This rejuvenation was not confined to the head, but extended to the entire body. It had recovered its stature. The adipose muscles, bundled around the cartilage, stood out as sharply as they had at 20. The thorax bulged. He had recovered the sturdy solidity of adolescence. When he threw himself from the foot of his bed, he scarcely recognized the hearty well-built fellow smiling at him with an insouciant air from the full-length mirror in front of him.

With that, a divine humor possessed him. In a daze, juggling with his shoes, washing himself with childish glee, putting his arms into his trousers and his legs into his sleeves, he nevertheless contrived to get dressed while yodeling, warbling and dancing, without even taking the trouble to summon his manservant. The latter, however, who was snoring in the next room, woke up with a start, extremely intrigued by this *aubade*. As he saw him come running, his mouth in an O, Trekkenpluk struck a new *entrechat* and let out a loud burst of laughter.

"Ha ha! Hee hee! Pom pom! Tra la la! The ineffable head! Why are you looking at me like that, you utter fool? Well?"

The old servant could not believe his bulging eyes. There before him was his master at 30 years of age–the age when Trekkenpluk had first engaged the rascal. But no, the laughing and bizarre Trekkenpluk who had surged forth from who knew where, in the place of the pitiful parishioner of yesterday, was even healthier than any of the Trekkenpluks previously known to Klaes. Never, at any moment in his life, had the rich man's visage been invested with that welcoming and benign expression.

"Well, Klaes, my old servant, I've caught you out, haven't I?" trumpeted the banker. "You've got a peculiar way of waking up a dying men. I'd have been able to cough up my wretched life and let out a death-rattle like a locomotive, while Klaes thought only of coming to wish me bon voyage. Anyway, I've no desire to go, joker that you are! I'm staying with you, and as I hate sullen faces, I'm increasing your wages tenfold. Do you hear, thief? Now run along, you rascal, and butter me ten slices of bread... Yes, ten, not one less. And smarten up my coffee, all right!" [87]

Laughing at the old domestic's stupor, he pranced past him nimbly and excitedly, quit his room and went down the stairs four at a time. His titanic merry laughter and his burbling song, intercut with apocalyptic animal cries, reverberated from landing to landing, filling the dreary corridors and awakening echoes of a pyramidal gaiety that the sumptuous palace had not known for a very long time, if ever.

All the flunkeys were scandalized, but they played their parts in the resurrection philosophically, for they were all well satisfied with the new arrangements that Trekkenpluk made with them. It would have been proclaimed a miracle had not Doctor Van Kipekap long since accustomed Flanders and the world to similarly improbable phenomena.

Trekkenpluk's heirs ground their teeth on finding him as fit as a fiddle and easily capable of sending them all fleeing back to the miserly means on which they had subsisted before their copious pillage. The resuscitated banker, after amusing himself with their discomfiture, took pity on them and endowed them henceforth with pensions with which a king in exile would have been content.

His generosity extended from his family to the vast army of employees slaving away in his offices. Previously he had worked them like slaves, and no commander had ever treated his natives so odiously, but now he rained money down upon these poor helots and awarded splendid pensions to bureaucrats worn out in his service. In place of the peevish, fumbling and implacable overlord whose mere appearance in the office corridors had scared the hungry legion half to death, the re-

---

[87] The final phrase is rendered into English in the original.

heartened paper-pushers, well-ballasted in the gut and the wallet, came to know the ideal boss, a King of Cokaygne, as blooming and enlivening as a Sun.

The petrified soul of yesteryear no longer existed. Along with the heart of humble Tony Wandel, the evil plutocrat incarnated all the virtues of the evangelical paver. The result of this particular transposition of organs had even surpassed the boldest speculations of Van Kipekap himself.

Trekkenpluk's new qualities seemed far more considerable by virtue of being manifest in the midst of a bourgeois oligarchy that was avaricious and materialist, still worshipping the golden calf and a hundred times harder on the poor world than the worst of feudal aristocracies and absolute monarchies. His colleagues in big business, the stockbrokers and financiers, believing that he had gone mad, tried to exploit him and transfer his millions to their own pockets. They soon came to see their error. Generosity had not injured the banker's intelligence; they could not fool him any more easily now than in the past, and their underhand speculations were even turned to the profit of the "pigeon" that they intended to pluck together. He remained doubly superior to them, by his commercial genius and his absolute probity.

But of all the consequences of the two-part operation carried out by Doctor Van Kipekap, the most unexpected and amazing was undoubtedly the banker's marriage to Tony Wandel's widow. This seemingly-extraordinary union was determined by psychic phenomena, which Doctor Van Kipekap did not allow to escape his observation, and which he recorded in *The Mysteries of the Afterlife*, a work collected in *The Saturnian Chronicles* after the demise of the Earth.

VI.

It often happened that the refitted banker thought about Tony Wandel, his gentle and benign savior, but–contrary to what one might suppose–he never experienced any remorse at having sought the generous lad's final drop.[88] He did not consider himself in the least to be the instrument of the paver's horrible end; no, he reported his thoughts of that humble martyr with melancholy sincerity and wept for him as a tenderly-cherished brother, another self torn away from earthly preoccupations by an ineluctable law. He never conceived of Tony's shade as a pitiful and wrathful phantom coming to reproach him for his atrocious bargain, but rather as the sympathetic face of a twin or a double given a spiritual quality, intervening to inspire him in every act of his new life.

The banker submitted with such docility to that influence from beyond the grave that, on the night when Tony Wandel exhorted the solitary dreamer to espouse Nellie, he welcomed this strange injunction as the most rational solution in the world. On the following day, the conformed bachelor instructed Doctor Van Kipekap to go propose this marriage to the paver's widow.

The inconsolable creature rejected the impious proposition with horror, and did not wait for the doctor to finish before showing him the door. The somewhat crestfallen Van Kipekap reported this negative result to his capricious client.

"Nevertheless, it is necessary," sighed the banker. "The other wishes it; he issued the instruction again last night. I must present myself to the eyes of that wounded lioness..."

So Trekkenpluk went to see Nellie. He came unannounced into the room where she was. When he told her his name, she was already staring at him, and the syllables of the

---

[88] I have rendered Eekhoud's improvised portmanteau word *chapechute* as "final drop" rather than translating it literally (as "escapefall"); it is impossible to preserve the alliterative effect.

execrated name were unable to destroy the indescribable sympathy that she had felt for the intruder from the moment of his appearance.

In vain, she summoned to her aid the memory of the horrible bargain that had deprived her of the best of men; the revulsion no longer came. An imperious instinct, more powerful than her reason, stifled her rancor and showed her, in the very executioner of her first husband, the person fated to replace that beloved spouse in her unhinged heart.

What infernal illusion was misleading her? To what aberration had she been delivered? In the caressing inflexions of the voice of the visitor she had long abhorred, though, and in the gaze of those moist and emollient eyes, she found a striking reminder of the dead man for whom she had shed so many tears. The two men were quite different in their stature, features and coloring. Tony was as fair as the banker was dark, and yet they resembled one another in an incontestable fashion. Their features showed no correspondence, but in spite of that, the outline, the expression and the demeanor were identical. The supernatural light brightening their two masks had to be the same. It was as if the soul of the dead man inhabited the body of the present visitor–and that impression on the helpless woman become so pressing and so obsessive that all her hatred for Trekkenpluk melted like a mere prejudice.

At the same moment when he extended his hand to her, she advanced her own. He did not even have to ask her anything; in falling into his arms she accepted. They loved one another as Tony Wandel and Nellie had loved one another. When Nellie had made him a father, he lavished as much affection on his children as those of the paver–but no more.

Now, when Tony's smiling and radiant shade appeared to the banker, he saw it approach the young Wandels as little Trekkenpluks, and embrace them all with an equal and virile tenderness. And before dissipating into vapor with the retinue of ghosts that escorted the grey dusk, the well-wishing phantom finished up by touching his lips languorously to the irreproachable forehead of their mother. And the ecstatic banker found that last caress as natural as the others, feeling no jealousy at all. That became their way of life thereafter. No remorse or bad feeling ever divided the dead man and the living. Had they not, at present, the same heart?

VII.

Trekkenpluk eventually reached 40 years of age for a second time. On the morning of that anniversary, with his conscience at ease and full of the joys of living, he devoted himself cheerfully to his business affairs and silently prayed to Providence that he might be permitted to bring as much happiness to those around him as he enjoyed himself.

An unusual commotion in the street drew him out of this edifying reverie. The passers-by were drawing together, exchanging a few words, then parting at a run–and from one end of the town to the other the sinister rumor was carried: "To the fire!"

The banker did not wait for other news to follow on the heels of the idlers. The fire had started in one of the sinuous back-streets of the plebeian quarter, whose tall buildings sheltered large families of menial workers. One of these hovels was burning like a giant brazier and the foremen had no thought but to stop it spreading to the neighboring buildings. The chain of policemen and the cordon of soldiers respectfully gave passage to the rich burger, who was also invested with the most important civic honors.

Trekkenpluk learned that all the tenants had been able to escape in time except for one woman and two children lodged under the eaves. They were condemned to death, according to the official rescuers; it was impossible to get up to that height.

The flames were roaring in the stairwell and, from one moment to the next, the cracked walls were crumbling. Before long, the first-floor windows had shattered and were darting tongues of flame as red as the doors of a blast-furnace.

The fire, leaving the ground floor, climbed like a conqueror assaulting a hill. Three more staircases and landings and it would reach its victims; three more floors and, an implacable Moloch, it would daze, asphyxiate, lick its lips over and then devour those innocent sacrificial victims.

Trekkenpluk's great heart was squeezed by that thought. Every time a gust of wind drew drifting clouds from the roof, the banker anxiously interrogated the dormer window of the attic in which the unfortunates lived. He urged the firemen, the soldiers and the people on. Around him, strong young men folded their arms nervously, dazed or whining like old women.

Why were they hesitating to conduct themselves like heroes? In their place, Trekkenpluk would not have hesitated for a second. But had he the right to risk his own life? He had a duty not only to his own children but to the paver's widow and orphans. Despairing of awakening a sentiment of valor and duty in these tremblers, he tried at least to ignite their cupidity by promising a fortune to whoever saved one of the wretches— but in vain. No one budged.

The firemen continued phlegmatically to do what was strictly required of them. One of them could be seen, axe in hand and coils of rope on his arms, undermining the walls neighboring the furnace. Jets of water, projected from a distance, evaporated in the Gehenna with a rabid hiss, but the flames, exasperated by this hostile element, immediately reared up as if to defy it. The rhythmic rattle of the pumps was audible, the cracking of the beams, the blare of the signal-horns; the acrid odors seized one by the throat.

"Move back!" an officer commanded.

Trekkenpluk did not hear. He had perceived the silhouette of a blond child at the threatened dormer, waving its chubby arms.

"Please get back, Alderman; it might crumble at any moment!" the officer said to Trekkenpluk.

But the latter was no longer there, having thrown himself on to the soaring ladder.

There is no means of overtaking him. By way of salving consciences, the jets of the pumps are directed in his direction. He has vanished into the opaque swirl. He is lost!

A few seconds of anguish. A miracle! The smoke dissipates. He reappears, carrying a woman on his back and a child under each arm. He is coming back down the middle of the ladder.

At that moment, the sinister cracking sounds are redoubled. The walls are shaking; in the interior, the beams are crumbling; the scourge that sees its prey escaping increases its vehemence tenfold.

Trekkenpluk has only time to throw the children and their mother one by one into the blankets that hundreds of hands are now holding taut at the foot of the ladder. His noble example has enlivened the timorous. The three condemned having been saved, it is his turn to jump to safety.

Too late! The section of wall against which the fire-ladder is leaning collapses with a great noise, sending a fountain of flame and smoke up into the sky like a cluster of fireworks.

Down below, that black inanimate mass emerging from the cinders and the rubble... is Trekkenpluk.

Two firemen have seen him. They manage to reach him, because the collapse of the wall has stifled the flames on that side. To pick him up, to carry him away, takes no more than a second.

A triumphant acclamation salutes him–but, deprived of consciousness, his eyelids closed, the sublime alderman of N*** cannot hear the *vox populi* as he is transported back to his house. He cannot see the tearful mother, who is on her knees as the stretcher passes her by, and who, full of fervent gratitude, kisses the hafts of his litter as if it were bearing the relic of a miracle-working saint.

VIII

"What do you think, doctor?" It is the exceedingly soft voice of Trekkenpluk, laid out on his bed. His body presents the appearance of a single horrible wound, from the soles of his feet to the top of his skull. Van Kipekap, recently arrived, contemplates with a professional eye this rarely encountered case, this superb living burn. From the viewpoint of his doctor, an indefinable smile has illuminated the charred visage of the sick man.

Van Kipekap wrinkles his nose, clears his throat and mumbles: "A new heart transplant might perhaps save you."

"No, no more of that. This time, I expire voluntarily. How much time have I left?"

"Oh, four hours... but, I repeat, before then I might be able to lay my hands on another mortally wounded man, younger and in better condition than you..."

"You know my resolution... don't insist. Besides, what good would the introduction of a new heart do? To supply me with a rascally heart, to resuscitate the original Trekkenpluk or to convert me into a specimen even more unpleasant...? No, I propose something else, impassioned operator that you are. Tell me at once whether my heart–the heart of Tony Wandel– still remains sound."

"As sound, albeit less vigorous, as it was ten years ago."

"Oh well, this 40-year-old heart, guaranteed fault free, will perhaps be the good fortune of one of your clients... especially as I shall abandon it to him gratuitously. Speak, Van Kipekap; don't you know anyone?"

"You don't mean it, my old friend."

"Absolutely. On one condition, however; if I desire that Tony Wandel's heart profit the recipient of your choice, I also demand that my disinterestedness contribute to the well-being of humanity, as was the case in the first instance. Therefore, doctor, you must endow the client who is not only in the most abysmal physical state, but whose gangrenous soul is also in the greatest need of redemption. Do you understand me?"

"So well that I already believe I know the individual in question. What do you think of the academician Foudrapiot?"

At the invocation of the grotesque and venomous metromaniac,[89] the patient forgot his excruciating [90] pain and his abominable martyrdom and could not help bursting into laughter.

"Oh, that will be an excellent joke!" He even attempted to bring his scorched hands together to applaud. "I wonder who the regenerated Foudrapiot will scandalize the most in the Academy–his official concubine, who entertains him like a *Sigisbé*,[91] or the *Jeunesse* [92] who scoff at him and riddle him

---

[89] A metromaniac (Eekhoud's *métromane*), is an obsessive composer of verses. Although recognized by Webster, the word has fallen into disuse in English. The name *Foudrapiot* appears to be compounded out of *fou* (mad) and a derisory diminutive of *drapier* (draper).

[90] *Cuisante*–the word I have translated as "excruciating" carries a double meaning in French that is particularly acute in this instance; it also means "easily cooked."

[91] *Sigisbé* is a French form of the Italian *cicisbeo*, a term popularized in Venetian high society; it refers to a young man who serves as an escort to a noblewoman but is not her lover– although they often served as screen for actual lovers, functioning as alibis rather than chaperones.

[92] *Jeunesse* means "youth" but I have retained the original here because it obviously refers to the contributors to the francophone periodical *La Jeune Belgique*, which was taken over by Max Waller in 1882, soon becoming the central forum of an assertive movement that took aboard the ideas and ideals of the Parisian Decadent movement. It was a key showcase for writers like Maurice Maeterlinck, Georges Rodenbach and–of course–Eekhoud. The sentence in which the reference occurs is a symbolic comment on the ostentatiously respected and impatiently envied status of venerable members of the Académie Française, who had to die before their precious seats became available to younger aspirants.

with epigrams. Doctor, make haste to inform the bewigged pedant... and come back with him presto..."

Two hours later, the transshipment accomplished, Trekkenpluk expired and the septuagenarian rhymer was carried away from his house, plunged in anaesthetic slumber, in possession of the heart of the late and much honored Mijnheer Trekkenpluk, dignitary of N*** on the Scheldt.

IX.

Two days after the death of the banker five young men, artists all, who generally led a Lenten life, were assembled in a tavern in the Rue des Chats at N***, the local eating-place where they dined least frugally. This time, the meal had taken on the proportions of a blow-out, to judge by the number of unsealed and "decorked" bottles strewn confusedly about the table. Each of them, minerva on fire,[93] had been taxing his wits since the soup to sustain a never-ending flow of wit, paradoxes, epigrams, caricatures, etc.

None was chattering as much as the purveyor of this feast, Frank, a painter whose spirited and artistic intransigence made a delightful contrast with his dandy's physique, his languid, vaguely Lamartinian style,[94] his long fine hair, his ex-

---

[93] A minerva was a kind of printing machine named after the Roman goddess of wisdom; Eekhoud, speaking figuratively, obviously has both meanings in mind.

[94] Alphonse Marie Lamartine (1790-1869) was a celebrated French poet–elected to the Academy in 1830–whose work bridged the transition from Classicism to Romanticism. He was also a noted orator and became Minister of Foreign Affairs in the provisional government set up after the Revolution of 1848, when many other French literary men, including Victor Hugo and Eugène Sue, also obtained political offices– with the result that they were all sent into exile after Louis Napoléon's *coup d'état*.

ceptionally vivid blue eyes and his spiritual mouth, a trifle contracted by the pleat of thought–which is generally the pleat of suffering.

Today, he was exultant; he had obviously sold a painting and was eating and drinking, with his hot-headed coterie, the greater part of the price.

He was bragging without pausing for breath, and his harsh, strident voice was as shrill as a horn.

"My faithful friends, my Lords, as we Gauls are... I offer you an enigma: a bare-foot, red-haired, hypocritical, cunning, mellifluous poet, artificial but a very definite third-rater; a Conventioner [95] brandishing a sword of gilded cardboard at the committee-meetings of beer-drinkers, scornful of the decorations obtained by his friends but flaunting in his buttonhole the following day the ribbon awarded him the evening before; an abominable *caloyer*,[96] a critic of Punic faith,[97] anathematizing the endeavors of the young and patrial,[98] having recourse to malign interpolations to injure true poets; an emitter

---

[95] *Conventionnel* was the term used to refer to members of the National Convention established in 1792, which lasted until 1795, although it is here being used in a figurative sense.

[96] Eekhoud has *colir*; although Webster recognises "colire" as an English version of the term he gives it as an alternative form of the allegedly more familiar *caloyer*, which I have therefore used. Webster defines a *caloyer* as an Eastern Orthodox monk; Larousse adds the detail–which is preseumbly what Eekhoud had in mind here–that Chinese *colirs* were entitled to go into people's homes for the purpose of administering public censure.

[97] Punic faith (*foi punique*) is an ironic synonym for treachery.

[98] *Patrial* survives in English–it means "pertaining to the fatherland," so Frank is referring to the fellow countrymen of the object of his spite–but the French word I have translated thus, *patriale*, was already obsolete when Eekhoud used it, thus fitting the general tenor of this florid speech.

of froth,[99] faggoter [100] of cantatas, compiler of farragos, philosopher gaga,[101] dealer in second-hand writings, paper-spoiler
and wholesale butcher. May Apollyon [102] deliver us from the
vile beast!" [103]

Someone scratched at the door of the *cénacle*.[104]

"Come in!" said Frank.

"Pardon this intrusion, gentlemen," the newcomer stammered, bowing. He was a fat man with a round, jovial face and
eyes of different colors, like Eulenspiegel.[105] "I am at your

---

[99] I have translated Eekhoud's *écumeur* literally, as he appears
to intend it, although the French word is very rarely used in
that way; its most familiar usage is in the phrase *écumeur de
mer*, meaning "scourer of the sea"–i.e., a pirate.

[100] Eekhoud's *fagoteur* has an untranslatable double meaning,
its straightforward translation (equivalent to "bundler") being
supplemented by an implication of making a mess or putting
on fancy dress.

[101] Eeekhoud's *gaga* is translatable as "doddering," but leaving it in place probably conserves more of the intended implication, even though it makes the phrase slightly awkward.

[102] Apollyon is the angel of the bottomless pit (Revelation
9:11), best known in England by virtue of his deployment in
John Bunyan's *The Pilgrim's Progress*.

[103] Vile beast is a slightly deflatory literal translation of another of Eekhoud's improvised portmanteau words, *malebête*.

[104] *Cénacle* was the term–borrowed from the conventional
label for the room where the Last Supper took place–that
Charles Nodier adopted for the early meetings of writers central to the Romantic movement; it was subsequently adopted
by similar literary groups.

[105] Thyl Ulenspiegel (1867) by Charles de Coster was an ostentatiously patriotic Belgian transfiguration of the legend of
Tyll Eulenspiegel [Owl-glass], whose life as a prankster–very
loosely based on the 14th-century exploits of a real German
individual–was popularized in a famous collection of tall stories. Its first printed version dates from 1559, although it was

251

service. Twenty-four hours ago I regained my literary virginity. I have sent my resignation to the Academy and *La Jeune Belgique*. I have burned my cantatas and pulped my quinquennial elucubrations. I am thus depalmate.[106] I make honorable amends and swear:

> *"That my leonine verses to bring down venal Art*
> *"Will discover the masculine vigor of Juvenal."* [107]

"Well roared, lion! [108] For an academician, that's not too bad. But who are you, personage a hundred times more enigmatic and abnormal than the enigma I was posing to these gentlemen?"

"I am–or rather was–the answer to the enigma."

"Foudrapiot, then?" the flabbergasted five proclaimed.

"Himself, milords!"

"That's a good one!" cried Frank, who was the first to recover from that entirely natural astonishment. Seized by a fit of nervous gaiety, he flung his champagne in the face of the new member, saying: "*Jaune Belgique* hereby baptizes you

---

probably written in 1483. The text in Kermesses renders the name as Uilenspiegel.

[106] Eekhoud's *dépalmé*, which I have translated literally, refers to *les palmes* [*académiques*]–decorations for services to education.

[107] These lines–*Que mes vers léonins pour tomber l'Art vé[nal]* / *Trouveront la vigeur mâle de Juvenal*–are presumably a quotation, but I have not been able to identify their source.

[108] Eekhoud renders this sentence in English.

Jeune Belgique! [109] Now tell us, I pray you, about the stages of your stupefying conversion." [110]

X.

At this point, the *Saturnian Chronicles* suffer a break of continuity. In all probability, the following documents in the sequence dealing with the avatars of Tony Wandel's heart would have been destroyed in the supreme cataclysm during which the Earth disappeared, along with other important traces of Man's exit from the Cosmos.

We do not know what literary services the rejuvenated and converted Doctor Foudrapiot rendered to his country, but everything leads us to suppose that the old fellow showed as much generosity as an artist as he had formerly shown as a contemptible pedant. Nor is it known how he perished, or who was the fourth possessor of the marvelous organ. What we can guarantee, however, is that it did not disappear with the poet Foudrapiot.

Thus, it emerges from a few pages that escaped destruction that in the 2640s, the heart of the proletarian from N*** on the Scheldt entered into the economy of Tsar Esbrouffripoff.[111]

---

[109] Eekhoud's play on words is probably intended to recall the phrase *rire jaune*, which means constrained laughter, signifying a certain embarrassment on Frank's behalf. In France, unlike England *jaune* (yellow) is not the color associated with cowardice, although it is sometimes associated with treason.

[110] The reference to *les étapes...de conversion*, here translated as "the stages of...conversion" recalls the title of a significant autobiographical work by the French feuilletonist Paul Féval, *Les étapes d'une conversion* (1877).

[111] The first part of the Tsar's surname is obviously derived from *esbrouffer*, meaning to bluff, while the second adds a Russian suffix to a noun derivative of *riper*, meaning to

Abruptly vulgarized,[112] the day after this imprudent acquisition the autocrat made use of his absolute power to proclaim a democratic republic throughout the Russias, and abdicated immediately after issuing this marvelous ukase.

Esbrouffripoff went off to plant cabbages in Siberia ground cleared by several generations of nihilists and manured by their excrement. A fanatical boyar, more Tsarist than the Tsar, ruined by the new regime, sought out the hermitage of the tyrant who had thrown away his throne and stabbed him with a dagger.

The organ, cause of so many perturbations, was not yet tamed, for we find it again, in 2700, back in its country of origin, Flanders, beating beneath the uniform of a General given to gout and grumbling. The ailing veteran, restored to his feet by the influence of this purchase, did not long survive the operation. Commanded by a philanthropic monarch to go forth and civilize a population of so-called savages, he took his role as a legislator seriously and did not massacre the barbarians in question in order to civilize them more rapidly.

One day, the dark-skinned folk, badly advised by traitors, rose in revolt against their benign conqueror. The General refused the pitched battle that the rebels offered him and even forbade his troops to snipe at them. With his arms folded over his breast, he went on his own to confront the mutineers personally. After a few words of appeasement and paternal reproach, he declared himself ready to die beneath their assegais if they judged his death profitable to their country and their

---

scrape, skid or scalp. Eekhoud would not have had the modern Anglo-American "rip off" in mind, but the intended effect is much the same.

[112] Eekhoud's *encanaillé*, here rendered as "vulgarized," usually referred to aristocrats mixing with the lower orders–"going slumming" would be the best translation of the modern employment of the word, although it would be inappropriate to use it here.

race. The savages, disconcerted by this stoicism, surrendered immediately.

This result, which might have been expected to delight the civilizer King, was, on the contrary, very badly received. One of the magnanimous General's officers, sent to the land of his birth to give an account of these events, did his commander some disservice at the Court and represented him not only as a milksop unworthy to command an army but as an ambitious schemer intent on the absolute sovereignty of the colony.

Recalled to Europe, this new Columbus, the excessively peaceful warrior, was court-martialed, convicted of desertion in the face of the enemy and stripped of his arms. His denouncer inherited his rank and his power, to the great delight of the metropolitan militarists. After all, the fat epaulettes and the braid-trimmed kepis said to one another, what good was a commander who did not exterminate several thousand individuals for the greater glory of strategy, tactics and prrr...ogress?

Whether the condemned man make a deal with the recruits, or whether the members of the firing-squad–who were all his friends, his children–trembled as their eyes were obscured by tears, not a single bullet touched his heart... and that obstinate heart survived to protest against triumphant iniquity.

XI.

Doctor Van Kipekap, by applying his discoveries to his own frame, had similarly prolonged his own existence, but without attaining the moral perfection obtained at a single stroke by the banker Trekkenpluk. In possession of his third heart, he was still the same skeptical and materialist scientist, assisting with a sort of wicked joy in the perversion of humanity.

He loved, by means of study and a reasoned choice of organs, to graft a vice to a defect, to magnify a tendency to evil into explosions of crime. A new Wandering Jew, he traveled from continent to continent, comparing subjects with one another, contriving combinations of rogues and unpublished pedants.

However, this diabolical experimenter soon discovered that the differences between the organs became less and less noticeable. They all resembled one another in their baseness. Van Kipekap could transform a miser into a sensualist, a hypocrite into a homicide, a gossip into a slanderer, but he was no longer able to convert one of these "cases" into a fundamentally good person.

Eventually, the doctor acquired the conviction that no greater honesty and human virtue existed than there was in the heart of Tony Wandel, by virtue of its cosmopolitanism and its relationship with all the classes of society in consequence of its peregrinations. He discovered that, in this case at least, the immutable Christian goodness of the element always drew the same triumphant reaction from every body to which it was introduced.

One day, when Van Kipekap found himself in Borneo, he learned that two colonists occupying neighboring plantations had quarreled over the barbaric treatment inflicted by one of them upon his slaves. The other had taken their part. Their master not having listened to reason, their defender had challenged him to a duel.

This quixoticism, to which he was no longer accustomed, made the doctor think. Might I be mistaken?, he asked himself. Might I find, in this new country, a match for Wandel's heart?

Van Kipekap was asked to accompany the adversaries to the battleground. He agreed, but requested to make the acquaintance of the challenger beforehand, thinking: An individual who consents to risk his life on behalf of pariahs is evidently a madman, unless he is the present possessor of Tony's heart! And he ran in double-quick time to the house of the chivalrous colonist.

Van Kipekap was not mistaken. This neo-Batavian [113] was indeed the moral heir of the Flemish proletarian. His name was Kemps de Salardinge.[114] He related how, as a fallen and ruined nobleman who had become a soldier, he had been a member of the firing squad that had executed the General. Knowing that he was ill, given up for dead by his doctors, he had had the sacrilegious idea of appropriating the heart of the condemned man. With the aid of one of his friends, a Jewish surgeon, the operation had been successfully carried out.

While the doctor listened to the story of the enriched and redeemed jonkeer Kemps' adventures, a singular and demanding desire was born in him for the first time. Until now, he thought, this absorbent pocket she-devil has completely metamorphosed the individuals in which she had lodged. But it would be interesting to see whether, set in contact with the blood of Doctor Van Kipekap, she can overcome the strong spirit, impassiveness, cold mathematical reason and willpower that have marked his passage on our planet. If only I might try. It would be a conclusive experiment, at least, and I would be able to observe every phase... Van Kipekap has a stronger constitution than his decrepit brothers. I defy this crazy heart to reduce me to the wishy-washy state of this entire Wandelized series and to make me act in a fashion that reproves my experience and my love of logic!

The more he thought about it, the more he was tempted by this supreme test, and the more obsessive and attractive the idea became.

---

[113] Batavia is an antique name for the Netherlands (also applied to a port in Java, the capital of the Dutch East Indies). Eekhoud's neo-Batave reflects the fact that the Low Countries had been briefly renamed *la République de Batave* [The Republic of Batavia] following their conquest by French Revolutionary forces in 1795.

[114] This surname has the customary uncomplimentary associations, sale meaning dirty and ardent implying fervent enthusiasm.

"Providence!" he cried. "Supreme Being that I deny, do you accept the wager? My soul is the stake. I will believe in you if you can reduce me to the sheep-like role of your Christians. If not, I shall die as I have lived, blaspheming against you!"

At that moment, the doctor wished that his new friend might be the loser of the duel.

Chance granted his wish. During the first engagement, Kemps de Salardinge's breast was punctured by a thrust of the foil. He fell to the floor, blood flooding abundantly from his mouth.

Van Kipekap, having thrown himself forward, anxiously, to examine the wound, realized–but without saying anything, and hiding his satisfaction–that the blade, skirting the lung, had not perforated any essential organ. The wounded man had escaped with his life–but the doctor, to the contrary, exaggerated the gravity of the situation.

"Carry him to my house. Leave me alone with him. None of his family or his friends may come to see him; if that condition is met, I might perhaps save him."

Everyone, having faith in the genius of the illustrious man, submitted to his will and even gave him their effusive blessing.

"You shall have news in eight hours," he told them as he left.

Shut up in his residence again–having no one with him, save for poor Kemps de Salardinge, but a servant who was terrified of him and a pupil whose soul was damned–the doctor carried out his abominable project with all the care, caution, method and calmness that he put into the least of his experiments.

When the time had passed, the wounded man's nearest and dearest presented themselves at the practitioner's house. The latter was atrociously pale, his features drawn, his eyes red, his appearance revealing–perhaps for the first time–some trace of emotion.

Without speaking, he led them to the bed on which the cold body of the noble Kemps de Salardinge lay. The doctor received the family's thanks with embarrassment, and refused any payment. The wound, they said, must have been incurable, since this magician had been unable to save their overgenerous relative. They inherited a fortune and were perfectly ready to forget good old Kemps and Van Kipekap's unusual appearance.

XII.

The swaggering surgeon and positivist atheist lost the bet he had laid with Providence. As soon as he had taken possession of Tony Wandel's heart, he began to cast off his old self. He awoke completely dismantled. He could recall the past but, instead of taking pleasure in his memories, deriving strength from them and discovering a logical connection between past and present, he recoiled in dismay, seized by horror and disgust. His scientific knowledge, his carefully elaborated works and his irrefutable documents all fell apart, broken like waves upon a new and imperious force that had absorbed his being.

He, the eternal laugher, the calculator as certain as an algebraic proof, with sarcasm and negation forever in his mouth, first experienced scruples and then remorse. He even shed tears over the assassination of the wounded man confided to his care, for it was certainly an assassination–a word at which he had previously jeered–that he had committed, and he could no longer silence his conscience with the aid of sophism and casuistry.

That disowned conscience spoke now of implacable justice. No, science did not purify the evil; science did not justify the crime! That was what Tony Wandel's heart contained: the despotic tormentor conscience.

In addition, going against everything antecedent, scornful of himself and his former ideals, there was now a profound pity for humankind in him, while loathing degraded, defiled and diminished machinery, figures and automata. This belated pity was exasperated by the idea that he might not be able, in spite of all his good will, at the cost of heroic effort, to render to his brothers their primordial nobility.

Ah, if he could only dedicate a thousand hearts of this extinct species to that task, perhaps he might avert the end of the world and its inhabitants!

Tony Wandel's widow, the paver's children and the banker's, were dead. The other beautifully-ensouled inheritors of the chosen organ had not had the time to found families in their turn. So the doctor–the last receiver of the treasure–admitted despairingly that which a banker, an artist, a general, a missionary, a colonist and so many other powerful people had only been able to realize under the impulsion of Tony Wandel's heart. He, a simple physician, a man of scholarship and theory, experienced it even more painfully.

He dreamed then of sacrificing himself for the salvation of humankind; he knew the sublime thirst for death–for a redemptive death like that of a second Nazarene...

XIII.

At that time, the Episcopal seat of N*** on the Scheldt was occupied by Cardinal Willebrord Gelof, a fanatical, authoritarian, intolerant prelate clinging obstinately to life. Old and crippled as he was, he still made his lax diocesan flock tremble beneath his crozier.

The time arrived when Gelof demanded from the surgeons a renewal of health and vigor. However, the members of Monsignor's orthodox entourage were aware of the upsets caused in the world for several centuries by Tony Wandel's heart. The chapter of Canons having no desire for the operation to change this prince of the Church Militant into an apostle worthy of the first era of Christianity, the strictest precautions were taken to guarantee the provenance of the organ to be embodied in their master's debilitated frame.

It was of this Cardinal that Doctor Van Kipekap thought.

A priest worthy of Christ might perhaps be able to deliver the last children of Adam from their abject state. It was a matter of deceiving the vigilance of the archbishop's familiars and spies and of providing the moribund prelate with exactly that evangelical heart abhorred by Pharisees and the Rich.

One evening, while wandering meditatively through the streets, he was interrupted by a barricade of heavy paving-stones. A team of artisans was in the process of repairing the road. They had dug a trench and were bent over in a row, hindquarters in the air, bare-armed and open-necked in their shirt-sleeves, tamping and heaving by turns with their rammers and mallets. Laborers moved back and forth, carrying sand and stones in wheelbarrows, running obediently in response to the impatient calls of older men. The ruddy light of several resinous torches, planted at the level of the earthworks, illuminated the bronzed and hairy workmen. Velvet waistcoats, caps, bottles and haversacks were heaped up on either side of the pavement. There were old uncles there, skinny and wrinkled, dry as firewood, beside sinewy adolescents whose shining eyes and vermilion mouths stood out feverishly within dirty faces already grooved by coarse precocious labor. The hour sounded in a church, the bell striking in harmony with the heavy *demoiselles*. [115] The doctor was suddenly reminded of Tony Wandel and his harrowing refrain:

"*On, on, honest paver,*
"*Dig and level the road.*
"*While the Angelus sounds*
"*In the distant tower,*
"*The resonant plink*
"*Of your falling pick*
"*Adds amen to the prayer.*"

---

[115] It is not obvious why the pavers' implements should be nicknamed *demoiselles*, but the reference is probably to the stick-like bodies of damsel-flies rather than to actual maidens.

261

While he contemplated these nocturnal workers, rocked as in a cradle by the suggestive rhythm of their movements, he observed a poor devil in the company whose appearance was more downcast, hungrier and more extreme than the rest. In a sudden flash of inspiration, he saw the realization of his project. He approached the stout workhorses and took the world-weary one aside.

"Would you like to earn a fortune, sleep in a feather-bed, eat and drink as you desire?" he said to him, straightforwardly.

He had to repeat the question, for the other seemed lost.

"Yes? Well, get your coat and follow me."

The paver obeyed, moving like a sleepwalker, and fell into step with the doctor. The others, fully occupied, did not notice his disappearance.

First, Van Kipekap went home and wrote a few letters, which he sealed and left on his desk. They were addressed to his assistants and contained his last will and testament. He opened a drawer and took therefrom a handful of gold, which he slipped into the vendor's calloused hand.

"This is a deposit. In three days you will return here and say that you have come on my behalf. The person who will receive you has orders to pay you 100,000 francs in cash. It's up to you to earn that fortune. I've welcomed you into my home; one good turn deserves another, and I want to return your visit. Off to your hearth..."

The other, still phlegmatic, believing himself to be dreaming standing up, decamped with his extraordinary benefactor. Having passed along the Rue des Va-Nu-Pieds into the Impasse des Roses,[116] they came to a halt before No. 48, a sordid, moldy and unplastered edifice eaten away by parasitic plants.

---

[116] The Rue des Va-Nu-Pieds might be translated as "Vagabond Street;" an *impasse* is a dead end, the roses for which this one is named having the same metaphorical significance that they bear in such English phrases as "a bed of roses" or "coming up roses."

"This is your nesting-place–a few steps from the archbishop's palace? Everything's working out marvelously. Oh, one more question: you're a bachelor or a widower, I hope, without children or a partner?"

"Alone as a plague-victim."

"Let's go up, then."

They went into a somber passage, at the end of which they found a tortuous stairway, a veritable goat-track, to which a greasy cord served as a handrail. The doctor was not put off by the darkness or the nauseating odor. Beneath the roof, the paver pushed open a door; they went into the wretched hovel and the master of the house lit a tallow candle.

The doctor looked around with a satisfied expression; these miserable lodgings seemed infinitely agreeable to him. He consulted his watch.

"Ten o'clock! Good. Now, my brave Tiest Tinkeltang,[117] take off your muddy britches, your patched waistcoat, your greasy cap, your stockings–pardon me, but they're indescribable–and your threadbare slippers. I'll get undressed in my turn; I'll put on your clothes and let you have mine, including the accessories: jewelry, fastenings, watch and chain... That done, you'll leave, and as you are obviously rich, you'll have no trouble finding somewhere to stay. Don't think of coming back here or of telling any living soul about your adventure, and in three days the promised treasure will be yours. Is that understood?"

"Yes, Mijnheer!"

To disguise themselves required only a few seconds.

"And now goodnight, Tiest Tinkeltang; I won't show you out."

Left alone, Van Kipekap prepared with superb firmness of purpose the setting of the drama on which the curtain of his centuries-long life was about to fall. While he went back and

---

[117] Tiest Tinkeltang is presumably a stereotypical pauper in Belgian or Dutch literature or legend, but I have not been able to identify the source of the name.

forth in his final apartment, however, dressed like a starveling, incoherent maudlin phrases, ejaculations of a fantastic verve and wild prayers fell from his lips.

"The forest was more beautiful, my gentle Tony, and the beech-tree from which you swung was a lot better than that filthy joist... the cord is similarly inelegant... but today's hanged man is not worth as much as you, my sublime ancestor..."

Having climbed up on the stool, his head lodged in the hangman's rope, he took a long look through the skylight. Day was breaking, grey and dull, over the billowing rooftops.

"It must be six o'clock in the morning. There's the tenants tumbling down the stairs to go to work. My assistant has orders to wake the Archbishop at this very moment. The operators can be here in a trice... let's get on with it!" He added, with passionate fervor: "May God and Tony Wandel pardon me! And may my heart be useful to Cardinal Willebrord!"

No one said amen, as once had been said beneath the majestic beech-foliage. He sent the stool rolling away with one kick, then struggled and thrashed about, prey to the supreme visions of imminent death.

At the climax of the spasmodic dance, a band of liveried lackeys came into the room, cut the cord and bore the hanged man away to a carriage where the surgeons–colleagues and heirs of the doctor–were waiting.

No one recognized the ragged and grimy hanged man as the opulent, eternal and cheerful Van Kipekap. The Senior Curate, the most suspicious, objected even so that the suicidal paver might be a second Tony Wandel. They laughed at him, and the organ extracted from the still-living hanged man's chest was encased, without further investigation, within the breast of the valetudinary prelate.

When, eight hours later, the fraud was made known, it was too late; the prelate, having the full use of his legs, did not stick around to hear the frightful proof a second time, and found himself much improved by his purchase. He had not waited as long as his predecessors to continue the worthy tradition of Wandelism.

XIV.

Willebrord Gelof began by renouncing purple robes, well-furnished apartments, delicate food and the pleasures of his palace. He sold his horses, his carriages and his gold plate, and gave the proceeds of this liquidation to the hospices. He was seen walking in the streets of the town, wandering in the surrounding countryside, dressed as a simple pastor, giving alms to the poor, exhorting the recalcitrant, proclaiming the religion of Christ.

At first, the Canons and the Senior Curate through that it might be a transient phase, but the generous folly and Christian humility of their superior increased day by day. The incandescence of his clergy became overwhelming when Gelof had the house pulled down, dismissing his parasites and regurgitating the holders of fat stipends and pious sinecures. They still dared not make any overt accusation against him, but while they bided their time, they secretly and slanderously spread abominable rumors about his private life.

Gelof had the clear vision of ancient theologians; the Eddas, the Vedas and the Koran revealed to him the symbolic meaning of the mysteries mocked by new religions, and he found the eternal and unique thread connecting all these incomplete cults to the sole verity. Gelof, disciple of Christ, preached these doctrines publicly. He dared to proclaim that Jesus was the founder of the socialist school and the first republican.

Then, the Pharisees howled and openly challenged his authority. They went to the Pope, denouncing his teaching as a pulpit of pestilence and the treason of Protestantism. They made a show of stepping aside as he passed by, spitting in front of him and drawing away. Gelof heard them murmuring with viperish hisses: "It's blasphemy: we must be rid of it, because it's poisonous!"

He was soon removed from office. The enthronement of his successor at N*** on the Scheldt was attended by much pomp and from that day on he was no longer spared.

In his sermons to the pastoral laborers and to the bandits of the region, the gentle apostle exalted charity above all else. The sophists ordained a punishment of death against anyone who would be so bold as to preach theological virtues.

His heresy was named Wandelism.

Governments and potentates, worked on by ministers of religion, turned an equally evil eye upon this dispossessed Bishop who took the side of the humble and the weak. Nevertheless, Gelof always condemned rebellions and prevented civil war. The Jacquerie [118] summoned him in vain to put himself at its head. After that, the little people, the hungry poor, turned against him. He spoke to them of a future life, of the compensation of their ordeals, of eternal reward. They mocked him, and distrusted him as an accomplice of rich oligarchs, all the more so as preachers of every sort sprang up like vermin from a sewer to exploit the evil passions of these desperate men.

No human authority or philosophy would have been able to hold back that tide. Discord was coming into its own. Populations became profligate in the pursuit of their oppressors, and the liberators of the day before became the persecutors of the day after.

The whole world was soon swimming in blood, and everyone was a victim.

Meanwhile, one man alone remained upright, bringing words of hope and peace, invoking the Gospel and Infinite Love. Barefoot, without pause, he traveled the world, inter-

---

[118] The original Jacquerie was a peasant revolt of 1357-58, although the term eventually became applicable to any popular uprising. The name Jacques is often applied generically to peasants.

posing himself between brothers armed against one another. His soul was anguished by the sight of these universal excesses and he shed tears of blood over all these afflictions, but everywhere he went he was shouted down and execrated. The false priests saw him as a dangerous competitor, the despots as an accomplice of the protests of the crowd, and the populace as a spy, their tyrants' turncoat.

And everyone cried *Noël!* on the day this man, whose Christian virtue none could suspect, and whose generosity none could count up, was arrested in Flanders. They would soon be rid of this nuisance, of this cynical mocker who still dared to acknowledge God and Heaven while the Earth returned to Chaos. He was delivered by common agreement to prosecution by his former Episcopal chapter, who consigned to the stake the placid apostle whom the claws of leopards and tigers had spared in the remotest deserts.

On the day of his execution, advertised well in advance to the four corners of the world, there was a pause in the massacre, so that the torture of the common enemy, to whom the whole human race had put a stop, might be smugly enjoyed in peace.

Myriads of curiosity-seekers flooded from every direction, their swarm spreading out into the fields and the slopes of the hills surrounding the place of execution–and those who would not be able to see his death-throes were hoping that the wind might at least bring them the delicious fragrance of the odor of charred flesh and the sweet music of his heart-rending cries!

At about five o'clock on a winter afternoon, the *cortège*, organized with theatrical precision, conducted him to one of the hills overlooking the town. To reach the summit where the stake was set, higher than the throne of Emperors, the old man had to climb 60 steps. When he appeared, in a white robe, and was attached to the stake, a mighty *hosanna* was raised by the innumerable crowd.

This shout, released by those who could see the sacrificial victim, was propagated for months, echoed from mouth to mouth, into the heartlands of the most obscure countries, beyond the oceans, by the entire human race, immobilized in the same ferocious angst, the same expectant sacrilege.

The flame was put to the pyre. It grew slowly, coquettishly, then rapidly, frenetically.

The martyr looked straight ahead, drowned in dolorous serenity. In the furthest reaches of the landscape, he saw, overwhelming the facing hill, a Babel of extravagant domes, which the setting Sun striped with cinnabar and ochre, and which stood out sharply from the lava-blackened horizon. The priest made out the twin columns of porticoes as high as cathedral spires–and above the principal pylon, in front of a vast succession of terraces extending in stages into the sky, was a white bust of Justice.

And this glorification of the Justice of men, facing the plateau one which the flesh of the last Just Man was being consumed, was a kind of supreme irony, an irreparable defiance hurled at the Creator by that rabble of fallen creatures.

At intervals, livid fulgurations scored the sepulchral firmament. The fire of joy, lit by delirious humanity, projected the shadow of its enormous tongues of flame as far as the distant walls of the Temple, with the magnified silhouette of the patient at its center.

Vaguely at first, that immense and fantastic black silhouette appeared to detach itself from the walls; then, as nebulous as a whirlwind descending into a valley, it passed over the town, overhanging the roofs of the Bourses, the Warehouses, the masts of ships, the chimneys of factories and the dungeons of arsenals like a funeral canopy.

The myriad fascinated eyes, distracted by the execution, were now looking to the side from which that terrifying storm cloud was advancing. The attendants turned their backs on the pyre.

The atmospheric phenomenon, borne by an angry wind, accompanied by the noise of thunder, headed for the plateau of the auto-da-fé. The closer it came, the higher the flames became, revivified as if by the breath of a powerful bellows.

But the storm was taking form. The clouds draped a mantle of darkness about a person of tall stature, with a phosphorescent visage, a vulture's beak, bloodshot eyes and a lipless mouth.

The apparition gained the stake's summit in a single stride. In its hand, it carried a long dagger, which it plunged into the martyr's breast–who was burned to waist-height. When the dagger was withdrawn therefrom, a red bleeding heart was impaled like a fly on its point.

The executioner lowered his arm; the palpitating organ fell off and rolled on the ground. Then the dreadful personage stamped its boot upon the heart of Tony Wandel: the last immaculate heart.

The clamor of the World died down, for the instrument of its hatred was named the Antichrist.

And afterwards, deprived of its last vestige of Goodness, that world had nothing to do but die...

Guy de Maupassant: *Martian Mankind*

I was busy working when my servant announced: "Monsieur, there is a Monsieur asking to speak to Monsieur."

"Show him in."

I perceived a small man, who bowed. He had the appearance of a puny and bespectacled assistant schoolmaster. His clothing was too large, hanging loosely from his thin body at every point.

"I beg your pardon, Monsieur," he stammered. "Forgive me for disturbing you."

"Sit down, Monsieur," I said.

He sat down, and continued: "Mon Dieu, Monsieur, I am deeply troubled by the step that I am about to take, but it is absolutely necessary that I fix upon someone, and there is no one but you, only you... Finally, I have plucked up the courage, but to tell the truth... I no longer dare."

"Then be bold, Monsieur."

"You see, Monsieur, the problem is that as soon as I begin to speak, you will take me for a madman."

"*Mon Dieu*, Monsieur, that depends on what it is you have to say to me."

"Exactly, Monsieur. What I have come to tell you is bizarre. But I beg you to consider the possibility that I am not mad, for the very reason that I admit the strangeness of my story."

"Well then, Monsieur, get on with it."

"No, Monsieur, I am not mad, but I have the distracted appearance of men who are more thoughtful than others and who have gone a little–so little–beyond the limits of the average mind. Just imagine, Monsieur, how few people in this world ever think about anything. Everyone is occupied with his own affairs, his own fortunes, his own pleasures–with his own life, in sum–or with petty and trifling amusements like the theater, painting, music, politics–the greatest nonsense of all–or matters of trade. So who really thinks? Who, exactly? No one! Oh, pardon me... I'm getting carried away! I'll get back to the point.

"It was five years ago that I came here, Monsieur. You don't know me, but I know you very well... I never mingle with the crowds at your beach or your casino. I live on the cliffs. I positively adore the cliffs of Etretat. I know none more beautiful or healthier–I mean healthy in a spiritual sense. There's an excellent pathway between the sky and the sea, a verdant route that runs along the great wall of white rock, which takes you along the rim of the world, the rim of the land, above the Ocean. My best days are those I have spent stretched out on a grassy slope, in broad daylight, a hundred meters above the waves, dreaming. Do you understand what I'm saying?"

"Yes, Monsieur, perfectly."

"Now, would you be kind enough to let me ask you a question?"

"Ask, Monsieur."

"Do you believe that the other planets are inhabited?"

"Certainly I believe it," I replied, without hesitation or any evident surprise.

He got up, moved by vehement joy and seized by a manifest desire to clasp me in his arms, then sat down again. "Oh, what luck!" he exclaimed. "What a blessing! I can breathe! But how could I ever have doubted you? A man would not be intelligent if he did not believe other worlds inhabited. He would have to be a fool, a cretin, an idiot, a brute to suppose that the myriads of the universe shine and spin solely to amuse and astonish that imbecile insect man, to fail to understand that the Earth is nothing but an invisible mote in the dust of worlds... that our entire solar system is naught but a handful of molecules of sidereal life, which will perish soon enough.

271

"Look at the Milky Way, that river of stars, and realize that it is nothing but a smear on the expanse that is infinity. Only think about that for ten minutes and you will understand why we know nothing, we divine nothing, we understand nothing. We know only one place, nothing of anything beyond or outside it, of anywhere else–but we believe and we have faith. Oh! If it were suddenly revealed to us, the secret of the vast extent of extraterrestrial life, how astonished we would be!

"But no... no... it's my turn to be stupid. We don't understand it, because our mentality is crafted to understand none but earthly things. It cannot extend much further; it is limited, like human life, trapped on this little globe that carries us, and it judges everything by that standard. So you see, Monsieur, that the whole world is stupid, narrow-minded, and fully persuaded of the power of our intelligence, which scarcely surpasses that of animal instinct. We do not even have the capacity to perceive our infirmity; we are shaped to know the price of butter and corn, and–at the most–to haggle over the value of a couple of horses, a couple of boats, a couple of ministers or a couple of artists. That's all.

"We are just about fit for tilling the land and clumsily making use of that which lies upon it. Having only just begun to construct working machinery, we are childishly amazed by every discovery that we ought to have made centuries ago, had we been superior beings. We are still surrounded by the unknown, even at the moment when, after thousands of years of intelligent life, electricity has been discovered. Are you and I of the same opinion?"

"Yes, Monsieur," I replied, laughing.

"Very well, then. Well, Monsieur, do you ever pay any attention to Mars?"

"To Mars?"

"Yes, to the planet Mars?"

"No, Monsieur."

"You know nothing at all about it?"

"No, Monsieur."

272

"Will you permit me to tell you a little about it?"

"Yes, Monsieur, with great pleasure."

"You know, presumably, that the worlds of our solar system, our little family, have been formed by the condensation into globes of rings of primal gas, detached one after the other from the solar nebula?"

"Yes, Monsieur."

"It follows from this that the most distant planets are the oldest, and in consequence, must be the most civilized. This was the order of their birth: Uranus, Saturn, Jupiter, Mars, the Earth, Venus, Mercury. Will you admit that these planets must be inhabited, like the Earth?"

"Certainly. Why suppose that the Earth is an exception?"

"Very well. The man of Mars will have a longer history than the man of Earth... but I'm going too quickly. First, I want to prove that Mars is inhabited. Mars presents to us something very similar to the aspect that Earth presents to Martian observers. The oceans there take up less space and are more widely scattered. They are identifiable by their dark hue, because water absorbs light, while the continents reflect it. Geographical modifications of the planetary surface are frequent, thus proving that its life is active. It has seasons like ours, snow at the poles that can be seen to grow and diminish with the passage of time. Its year is very long: 687 terrestrial days, which is 668 Martian days. That breaks down as follows: 191 days of spring, 191 of summer, 149 of autumn and 147 of winter. Fewer clouds are seen there than here; there must, in consequence, be greater extremes of cold and heat."

I interrupted him. "I beg your pardon, Monsieur, but as Mars is much further from the Sun than we are, it seems to me that it must always be colder there."

My bizarre visitor exclaimed very vehemently: "Wrong, Monsieur! Wrong, totally wrong! We ourselves are more distant from the Sun in summer than in winter. It is colder on the summit of Mont Blanc than at its foot. I refer you, moreover, to the mechanical theory of heat of Helmholtz and Schiaparelli. The heat of the Sun is principally dependent upon the quantity of water vapor contained in the atmosphere. This is why: the absorbant capacity of a molecule of aqueous vapor is 16,000 times more than that of a molecule of dry air, so water vapor is our storehouse of heat. Mars, having fewer clouds, must be both much warmer and much colder than the Earth."

"I no longer contest the point."

"Very good. Now, Monsieur, listen to me with the utmost attention, I beg you."

"I am all ears, Monsieur."

"You have heard talk of the famous canals discovered in 1884 by Monsieur Schiaparelli?"

"Very little."

"Is that possible? Well then, in 1884, while Mars was in opposition to us, separated by a distance of no more than four million leagues, Monsieur Schiaparelli, one of the most eminent astronomers of the century and one of the most adept observers, suddenly discovered a large number of straight and broken black lines forming constant geometrical patterns, crossing the continents to link the seas of Mars! Yes, yes, Monsieur: rectilinear canals, geometrical canals, of a similar width throughout their course, constructed by living beings! Yes, Monsieur, the proof that Mars is inhabited, that there is life there, that there is intelligence there, that there is industry there... which can see us. Do you understand? Do you understand?

"Twenty-six months later, at the time of the next opposition, these canals were visible again, Monsieur, even more numerous–and they are gigantic, no less than a hundred kilometers wide."

I smiled as I replied: "A hundred kilometers wide! It must have required strong workers to dig them."

"Oh, Monsieur, what are you trying to say? You do not know, then, that such labor is infinitely easier on Mars than on Earth, since the density of its material constituents is only 69% of ours. The intensity of its gravity is scarcely 37% of ours. A kilogram of water only weighs 370 grams."

He threw these figures at me with such assurance, with the confidence of a businessman who knows the value of a number, that I could not prevent myself from breaking into laughter, and I was tempted to ask him how much sugar and butter weighed on Mars.

He shook his head.

"You are laughing, Monsieur; instead of taking me for a madman, you take me for an imbecile–but the figures I have quoted you are those that you will find in every specialist text-book of astronomy. The diameter is nearly half as much less than ours; its surface area is only 26% of ours; its volume is six and a half times smaller than that of the Earth and the velocity of its two satellites proves that its mass is ten times less. Now, Monsieur, the intensity of gravity depends on the mass and the volume, which is to say on the mass and the distance of the surface from the center, so the indubitable result is that on the planet there is a state of lightness that makes life completely different, regulating mechanical actions in a manner unknown to us, which must lead to a predominance there of winged species.

"Yes, Monsieur, the Ruling Being of Mars has wings. He flies, passing from one continent to another like a spirit, all around his world, although he is unable to move beyond the vestiges of its atmosphere...

"To conclude, Monsieur, can you imagine this planet, covered with plants, trees and animals whose forms we cannot even suspect, and inhabited by great winged beings like our artists' images of angels? Personally, I see them flying over the plains and cities, in the gilded atmosphere that they have there–for although it was believed in former times that the Martian sky is red while ours is blue, it is actually yellow: a beautiful, golden yellow.

"Are you still amazed that such creatures as those could hollow out canals a hundred kilometers wide? The again, just think what science has achieved for us, in a single century... in a hundred years... and remind yourself that the inhabitants of Mars may well be far superior to us..."

He fell abruptly silent, lowered his eyes, then murmured in a very low voice: "Now the time has come that you will take me for a madman... When I tell you that I have glimpsed them myself... The other night. You may or may not know that we are in the season of shooting stars. On the nights of the 18th and 19th, especially, they are seen every year in innumerable quantities; it is probable that we are passing at this very moment through the tail of a comet.

"I was, therefore, sitting on the Mane-Porte, that enormous sheer headland that juts into the sea, watching the rain of little worlds overhead. It's prettier and more entertaining than any artificial fire, Monsieur. All at once, I perceived, directly above me, very close, a luminous transparent globe, surrounded by immense beating wings–at least, I thought I saw wings in the semi-darkness of the night. It was fluttering like a wounded bird, turning on its axis with a loud, peculiar noise, seemingly breathless, dying, lost. It passed in front of me. One might have taken it for a monstrous crystal balloon, full of panic-stricken creatures, scarcely discernible but excited, like the crew of a ship in distress, no longer under control but rolling from wave to wave. And the strange globe, having described an immense curve, came crashing down into the sea some distance away, where I heard it plunge into the depths with a noise like a cannon-shot.

"Everyone for miles around heard that mighty impact, which they took for a thunderbolt. I alone have seen... I have seen... If it had fallen on to the shore beside me, I would have met the inhabitants of Mars.

"Don't say a word, Monsieur. Think it over. Think it over for a long while... Then tell the story, one day, if you wish. Yes, I have seen... I have seen... The first spaceship launched into the infinite by thinking beings... Unless I have merely been present at the death of a shooting star captured by the Earth. For you may not know, Monsieur, that the planets hunt the wandering worlds of space as we pursue vagabonds down here. The light and feeble Earth is only able to intercept the smallest of infinity's passers-by."

He stood up, delirious with excitement, opening his arms wide to describe the march of the stars.

"The comets, Monsieur, which roam the frontiers of the great nebula whose condensates we are; the comets, free and luminous birds, coming towards the Sun from the depths of infinity. They come towards the radiant star, trailing their immense tails of light; they come, accelerating so forcefully in their bewilderment that they are unable to unite with their summoner; after the merest brush with it, they are hurled back into space as rapidly as they fell. But if, in the course of their prodigious journeys, they pass close to a powerful planet, if they feel its attraction and are drawn from their route by its irresistible influence, they return then to their new master, which renders them captive henceforth. Their unlimited parabola is transformed into a closed curve, and it is thus that we can calculate the revisitations of periodic comets. Jupiter has eight slaves, Saturn one, Neptune one also,[119] and its exterior planet one again, plus an army of shooting stars... Then... then, perhaps I only saw the Earth intercept a little wandering world...

"Goodbye, Monsieur, make no reply. Reflect, consider, and tell the whole story one day, if you wish..."

That was all. The lunatic seemed to me less stupid than some mere man of independent means.

---

[119] Although I have left it as it is, this reference to Neptune must be an error. Maupassant must have meant to name Uranus, Neptune–discovered in 1846–being the "exterior planet" mentioned immediately afterwards. (Pluto, downgraded in 2006 to dwarf planet status, was not discovered until 1930.)

Fernand Noat: *The Red Triangle*

The Sun was descending, red in a golden sky. Dark clouds, moderating the splendor of its setting, were so fully reflected in the water that the horizon was not precisely discernible. One might have imagined oneself sailing towards an amethyst temple whose architectural lines were illuminated by the glints and flames of a purple-shaded lamp.

No breeze stirred the vermilion Mediterranean, whose surface was smooth and slick. A gentle lapping at the flanks of the packet-boat testified to its presence, but as no mast disturbed the equilibrium of the fiery horizon, one might have believed it in some well-sheltered port, moored to a quay. Only the slight reverberation of the propeller, like the beating of an artery in a fever, revealed to the impatient passengers that they were indeed making haste towards land, towards France.

The warmth of the evening had brought several officers out on to the poop deck of the *Notre-Dame-de-Salut*.[120] Following the signature of the peace-treaty with the Chinese potentates, the expeditionary force was repatriating part of its general staff.

"Well, gentlemen," said Colonel d'Herbauge, in response to a question. "since the scar I bear on my forehead intrigues you, I shall tell you its history. As it is necessary, however–and it is for this reason that I had to be pressed–for me to go into considerable detail, I wish to say in advance that I have been challenged; if the story bores you or sends you to sleep, you have no one to blame but yourselves."

---

[120] The vessel's name means "Our Lady of Salvation."

There was a general protest, and applause. Cigars were lit, and bluish spirals, slightly inclined toward the stern by the velocity of the ship, rose into the calm air.

The Colonel began his story.

I. The Colonel's Mission

You will all recall, gentlemen, the circumstances in which I was ordered to undertake a special mission by General Bailloud, shortly after the battle of Pao-Ting-Fou.

It was December 22nd, 1900. The General, with only a few companies to command, had fought 2,500 Boxers,[121] putting the major part of their manpower out of commission, capturing four standards and five cannon, and scattering the retreating forces in every direction. All of that was accomplished without our losing a single man! The affair had, therefore, been brilliant and fortunate at the same time, and we were all–officers and soldiers alike–looking forward to enjoying the delights of a well-deserved meal when the General summoned me on the following evening.

"My dear d'Herbauge," he said to me, offering me his hand, "what we did today–all of us together–was no more than half of what needs to be done: the first part, which is to say the easiest. I'm counting on you for the second."

---

[121] The term Boxer, in its Chinese context, arose by misinterpretation of a phrase whose actual meaning was "righteous harmony band" (Europeans mistook the word signifying "band" for one meaning "fists"). It was adopted by a rebel militia, which developed into a secret society that spread through the northern regions of China in 1900, waging guerilla war on Europeans and Christian converts. The uprising culminated in a siege of the legations in Peking, after which it was ruthlessly suppressed.

"General," I replied, in a strained tone, "I am entirely at your disposal, to undertake any mission you deem it appropriate to entrust to me."

His response was an expressive handshake. After a pause, he went on: "We shall winter here. It is necessary, therefore, in anticipation of a severe season in a region where insurrection is universal, to take measures against both the enemies capable of attacking us: the Boxers and the cold. In consequence, while we are constructing comfortable barracks for you, you will go, at the head of two companies of marine infantry, to scour the countryside, in every sense of the word. It's not an expedition that I'm entrusting to you but a succession of bold raids that I want to see you carry out.

"Tomorrow morning you will dash south-east to scatter and further harass those who have escape us; then you will try to discover the reassembly points at which the enemy will try to renew his supplies of weapons and ammunition. You will put everything that you cannot carry off to the torch. You will blow up any fortified earthworks, or pagodas converted into blockhouses. In sum, you will render any counter-offensive improbable, if not impossible.

"Although I don't want to set you a time limit or restrict your initiative, I believe that 20 days should be sufficient, and I hope to see you again here in the first weeks of January."

My program was perfectly clear, therefore. Despite the disappointed expectation of an interval of rest and the unpleasantness of the season that was setting in, I departed, glad of the confidence of my commander and the company of the three officers who would constitute my staff: Captain d'Estival and Lieutenants Vincent and Ménard.

On January 11th, I believed that I had completed my mission. Having covered 300 kilometers, I was bringing back 54 prisoners and 60 mules loaded with ammunition seized from the enemy. Through a discontinuous series of marches and countermarches, skirmishes and surprise attacks, we had cleared the region and chased the rebels far away, despairing of their leaders and their partisans.

Our *marsouins* [122] had burned a great many straw huts, gone through more than 200 boxes of cartridges and got rid of several fortifications by courtesy of dynamite.

With our wages waiting for us, we spoke of nothing but Pao-Ting-Fou. It was an oasis, almost the fatherland! No other winter quarters, no matter what distractions, comforts and feast-days they might offer, seemed more enviable to us than those three months of rest in a bivouac lost in the heart of China.

We dreamed of finding ourselves back among our comrades, of organizing exceedingly friendly and merry gatherings while the winter set in, of enjoying a little of that regimental intimacy which recalls that of the family–and there would also be mail! What joy to find, on our return, those packets of letters that we would untie in haste, those envelopes with multicolored stamps, on which the eye would so quickly recognize the fine handwriting that would make the heart race... The hand of a wife, a sister or a fiancée! And those bundles of newspapers, which one would undertake to read in numerical order, to put oneself back in the picture... And to sleep well and calmly, far from perils and responsibilities, with a roof over our heads, safely sheltered!

All in all, that return would be... but man proposes, and God disposes!

II. The Fugitive

One last effort was required before we turned back; one last reconnaissance remained to be carried out.

The evening before, at dusk, a blood-red light had appeared on the horizon and had not been extinguished until three hours before daylight. The barbarians had probably burned some village; it was important to assure ourselves of

---

[122] The literal meaning of *marsouin* is "porpoise," but it is here being used as a slang term for colonial infantrymen.

the fact. Was it a band fleeing before us, exasperated by failure and fear? Was it, on the other hand, a Boxer counter-offensive, or even regulars summoning new recruits to the fire? In any case, it was one more step in our journey–fortunately, the last. Our return, indeed, was not only desirable but essential. Our men were exhausted; the column was overloaded with captives and new baggage; the cold and rainy weather would soon become very dangerous.

At daybreak, we marched into an empty region devoid of any hut or living soul, through long-abandoned fields upon which native vegetation had already reasserted its rights.

It was about 10:30 a.m.; we were coming into a forest cut through by a path when, all of a sudden, I hear a confused murmur in the rearguard, then cries for help being uttered and answered. I turned around.

Twenty soldiers, having hurled themselves into the woods, were beating the undergrowth. D'Estival followed them, pointing with the tip of his sword at something whose movement I perceived, although I could not see what it was. He urged them on with his sonorous voice: "Be bold, lads! Don't let the fellow escape! That way–there, I tell you!"

And the human pack, dispersed by the pursuit, converged again on the indicated goal... only to hare off again furiously in another direction, put off the scent.

I made a sign. The column came to a halt and d'Estival rejoined me.

"I beg your pardon, Colonel," he said, "but I saw a Chinese in the bushes. Is it a spy following us? Is it some poor devil displaced by the war? I don't know. At any rate, as soon as we caught sight of him he fled into the tall grass. Hold on–I think our *marsouins* have run him down..."

The noise had indeed redoubled: mingled shouts, laughter and gibes were coming closer. Two hearty fellows appeared, dragging by the arms a wretched Chinese of indeterminate age, frightened and breathless. Exhausted by the chase, he was fighting to recover his breath and tremulous in every limb.

I gestured to summon Joseph, my interpreter. Joseph Li was a brave lad, 32 years old, a Christian from Lang-Son, very devoted and intelligent, whom Monsignor Piginier had obtained for me in 1883 during my first campaign in Tonkin. He spoke Chinese fluently, including the majority of the dialects of the southern and central regions of the Middle Kingdom as well as Annamese, and had learned perfect French from our missionaries. This solid instruction and his absolute devotion had allowed him to rise successively from the rank of boy through those of interpreter and secretary to that of worthy adviser... I might almost say friend. He immediately set about interrogating the poor creature, who was prostrate with fear.

Little by little, the unfortunate seemed to recover his strength. He got to his feet. His eyes, black as a startled antelope's, brightened, his tongue loosened, and he began speaking volubly. He was standing up now and seemed to be modulating the words wrung from his heart with respect and compunction. Our soldiers, exchanging reflective glances, cocked their ears at first, then greeted the finale with a volley of laughter.

"Hey, look who's saying his prayers now!"

"Well, my old Celestial," said a mocking Parisian, "you're a rogue. Your neck's itching, so you demonstrate your devotion–but it won't work, you know."

Indeed, the young Chinese, in concluding his chant, had collected himself for an instant, then traced the sign of the cross broadly upon his breast.

The reflections continued:

"He's a Boxer."

"No, he has no uniform. He's a spy."

I had already called for silence, inviting Joseph to speak.

"This man is neither a Boxer nor a spy," the interpreter said, authoritatively. "He's a Christian. For seven months, he was in the service of a missionary, whose name he mangles, but which I presume to be French. He was the sole survivor of the massacre of his village. The Boxers, who had been prowling the neighborhood for several days, fell upon of the village yesterday evening. They killed everyone, burned or looted everything. He offers to guide you to the place where the disaster occurred...The bodies are unburied."

"Are you sure that you're not dealing with a skillful spy? A traitor charged with drawing us into an ambush?"

"I don't think so. He knows his prayers, the responses of the mass; I think he's sincere. Besides"–and here Joseph signified the depths of the woods with a circular glance–"this path that cuts through the undergrowth, these thinned-out tree-trunks and these recently-cut timbers all indicate the proximity of a village. The reddening of the horizon yesterday night corroborates the only point of his story that can be checked: it was a Christian mission that was burning."

"Let's go, then!"

We resumed our march, preceded by the young Chinese. He was flanked to his right and left by acolytes, two *marsouins* who impressed upon him by means of mime that it would be unwise of him to attempt any treason. Revolvers in hand, they gave him to understand that at the first sign of trouble two bullets would immediately be fired at Monsieur. Now impassive behind his sallow mask, however, the reassured Chinese marched with a firm step.

III. The Martyr

Alas, he had told the simple truth. A vast clearing soon opened up before us, inundated with sunlight. Debris was still smoking here and there, the thin plumes of bluish smoke twisting in the north wind. A heap of rubble and calcined beams still indicated the site of the chapel. Flocks of birds spiraled around the anonymous heap of broken walls and mutilated bodies. A few severed heads were still bleeding on their stakes or staining the sands where they had fallen.

This was, however, only a preface to the horrible tableau reserved for us.

Behind a section of wall that we were about to round, the Chinese suddenly came to a halt, his neck twisting. Recoiling, one hand covering his eyes and the other pointing at something, he became stiff and motionless,

A man was attached to a stake fixed in the ground. He was still young. A blond beard matted with blood hung over his breast. A tunic of blue silk, soiled with black clots, was half-torn away, permitting his white European skin to show through. The face, blue with bruises, was horribly contorted. Long bloody threads extended down his cheeks from empty orbits devoid of eyes. Carbonized bones were protruding from the swollen and bloody flesh of the two arms, held outstretched by a horizontal piece of bamboo. The missionary's hands had been burned with torches or spirit-lamps!

Consternation nailed us to the ground. Our 400 men were mute. Like me, they reconstructed the horrible scene; like me, they came to recognize, in that sad and peaceful victim, a son of our race, of our country. That poor human wreck, mutilated and hideous, must have been a beloved, cherished and cared-for child. A woman, having delivered this son into the world from her womb, had nourished him with her substance, wrapped him around with caresses and solicitude, so that one day, on this foreign soil, that innocent flesh might be tortured, that precious life destroyed, an artwork of civilization and salvation smashed!

Leaving the luxury of cities to the satisfied individuals we are, to vulgar mentalities preoccupied with money, ambition, pleasure, this young man of 20 had felt the flame of a distant vocation illuminate within him. He had come to the banks of the Tang-ho as a sacred calling, to teach these brutes the superior ideal of a responsible and immortal soul, to show them restraint and conscience in order that the law of love might shine within them.

The miracle was already accomplished! In these thick skulls, these obtuse souls, debased by centuries of hereditary brutishness, he had–by grace of heaven–lit a spar, awakened a glimmer... pushed back the frontiers of civilization; he had founded a Christian mission. The apostle had secured a future...

And now, in consequence of I don't know what Machiavellian conflict of interests, or German or Italian rapacity, Europe overturns this peaceful land, lusting after pillage and conquest... Dormant paganism wakes, savage and strong. The horizon is aglow with red fires; sinister howling goes up from the surrounding valleys every night. The neophytes and the faithful, beaten down by the rising tide of insurrection, go running to the pastor.

This is the end: the village burned, the flock massacred, and the priest–he above all, the foreigner–saved for last, for the slow and refined tortures, for the savant agonies, for the delirious horrors of the brazier.

Ah! Those flame-spitting torches whose flames are renewed are for him! Oh! Those avid, swelling flames are devouring his bloodied hands–hands accustomed to contact with holy mysteries! His eyes, which have known no other intoxication than the contemplation of the host, and which seek now, veiled by atrocious agony, some corner of heaven in which to discover the crown of martyrdom that is so slow to come! His eyes will not be spared! Night and indescribable suffering invade his orbits and his brain, for see how his eyes have been torn out with sharpened pieces of bamboo!

IV. The Sepulchre

"Colonel," d'Estival said to me in a low voice. "Don't you think, perhaps... The last rites?"

"That's true," I replied, my throat tight. Making an effort to overcome the effect of the distressing spectacle and the painful surroundings, I pulled myself together.

It seemed to me to be a solemn moment. My troops gathered around the tortured man and rendered him the honors due to a brave man. No noble victim ever received a more sympathetic, emotional and religious salute from an officer's sword;

never had arms been surrendered to a conqueror with such spirit.

Meanwhile, a short distance away under the trees, two men silently dug a grave for the martyr. As soon as it was finished, taking infinite care–as if his body were still capable of suffering rudeness–we officers detached the missionary's rigid arms from the cross. With difficulty, we folded what remained of his arms over his breast and laid the corpse out on the grass. It was with twin sentiments of religion and pride that we fashioned a shroud from a tricolor flag; then the four senior Sergeants lowered him into the tomb.

No one had planned a funeral oration, but before the earth was sealed upon him one of us stepped forward and, facing the bamboo cross that our brave *marsouins* had already planted in the ground, recited in a loud voice the immortal and divine prayer that speaks of mercy and proclaims absolution.

V. Posthumous Intelligence

As the last spadeful of sand was scattered on the funereal mound, the young Chinese, whom we had forgotten, sidled up to me, picked up a fallen object and gave it to me, murmuring something unintelligible.

I took the object, directed a mute glance of interrogation at Joseph, and listened.

"It's the priest's prayer-book," my interpreter said. "Quan-Si–that's his name–noticed it and recognized it. As you're the commanding officer, he gave it to you."

It was one of those little books of hours that priests call a diurnal; it was old, worn and dog-eared. The binding was slightly sticky and the pages seemed to be glued together by a brown coating, like that which had clotted the sand.

I suddenly understood, and nearly let the pious relic fall. What was sticking the leaves together and softening the sticky binding was the martyr's blood! Fallen at his feet, the diurnal had received the aspersion of his arteries. I opened it with re-

287

ligious respect, and was not surprised to see written in pencil, on the first blank page, words that brought tears of pity to my eyes:

The Boxers of the Red Triangle are coming, they said. What will become of us tomorrow? In manus tuas, Domine, commendo spiritum meum [123]–*January 8th, 1901.*

I closed the little book again and clasped it carefully. That last prayer and those last drops of blood would go to France to be sent back to his family.

On reflection, something puzzled me. It seemed to me, in fact, that there was a definite duty to which I ought to pay attention, for in a foreign country in a time of war the most trivial details have their importance. The smallest incident can change the complexion of things. I had heard talk of Boxers; the names of many of their sects were known to me, but I had never heard mention of the Boxers of the Red Triangle. Who knew whether, in revealing their existence to me, the missionary might not have rendered me a vital service, even after death? In any case, had not divine justice permitted the blood of that innocent to cry out for vengeance like that of Abel, while pointing me towards Cain?

VI. The Interrogation

Thus, while the men were preparing soup and coffee a short distance away–nature never forgets its dues–I interrogated Quan-Si.

He reacted to the name of the Red Triangle with intense astonishment, then profound terror. He tried to fob me off with stubborn silence, interrupted by a few vague replies, but I wanted to know. I insisted; I threatened...

He lamented: "I shall be marked on the forehead... I shall be delivered to the dragon, which will devour me... For the

---

[123] *"Into thy hands, Lord, I commend my spirit."*

bonzes [124] will know and no one escapes them..." After a pause for reflection, he resumed: "At least, you and the Commander will be like the Father, who listened to everything and repeated nothing?"

Joseph made every effort to convince him. "Calm yourself; you have nothing to fear. We shall leave tomorrow. The Commander will take you with him; you'll be well-guarded. No one will touch a hair on your head while the French are protecting you."

"They will not protect me against the bonzes who arrive by night in large numbers, removing those who are designated and know it. They will not protect me against the dragon that can..."

"You are a Christian," Joseph put in, "and you believe in this dragon?"

"I am a Christian," he replied, vehemently, "but the dragon exists and I believe in it... Everyone believes in it... The poor Father believed in it too, and knew very well that, three or four times a year, they set out on a quest... and bring their dragon two or three young people to devour..."

"But that's the fable of the Greek Minotaur all over again!" said d'Estival, who had drawn nearer.

I gestured to him, telling him not to interrupt.

"Yes, yes," Quan-Si continued, with increasing volubility, "all the bonzes who are charged with providing nourishment to the dragon bear a scarlet triangle on their foreheads. They indicate by that means that they are its acolytes, devoted to its service, destined one day, if ever there is a dearth of victims–and that is not unknown–to sacrifice themselves, to serve as its fodder. According to what our ancestors have told us, the monster's tongue is as hot as fire, as sharp as a lance–and when it is placed on a man, it pierces his forehead in the shape

---

[124] A bonze is a Buddhist monk, originally one from Japan; the word appears to be a variant of *bo*, the name of the sacred tree at Buddh Gaya beneath whose canopy Gautama was supposedly granted heavenly enlightenment.

of a triangle. The monster sucks the blood through that opening or drags the body into its cavern to indulge itself at its leisure..."

"That's enough," I said to Joseph, who was translating one sentence at a time. "It's evidently rank superstition, and it's useless to discuss the subject further. What I want to know now is the nature of the terrain, the geographical location of the pagoda, the number of brigands living there and a description of its surroundings."

I learned that, 20 kilometers to the south-west, this pagoda's roof and turrets were backed by an enormous crag, standing up like a dome in the middle of an enormous clearing. Since the rebellion and the opening of hostilities against the Western barbarians, a number of bonzes, together with 200 or 300 brigands, had been roaming the countryside pillaging, kidnapping and killing the inhabitants. Such was the terror inspired by their somber legend that they were allowed free rein, it being preferable to be robbed, or even killed, than to be taken captive in order to serve much later as fodder for the terrible dragon.

The position was scarcely defended, it seemed. No fortification; no surrounding wall–only a stream, whose course ran into the rocky outcrop, curving as it was diverted around it to protect the three sides of the pagoda, to which access was gained by a bamboo bridge.

I had learned enough, and I sent the poor devil, trembling at his boldness, to share the soldiers' soup.

Joseph led him away.

D'Estival and I walked together for a few minutes more, talking over the next day's plans. We congratulated ourselves on the luck that had informed us of so many useful things, and I showed him the little book that had miraculously escaped the fire and the rapacity of the brigands. Thanks to that note–the missionary's two desperate lines–we would be able to strike at the enemy, terminating our mission brilliantly with a great coup. No one in the entire province would dare to lift his head up for a long time once it was known that the pagoda of the

Red Triangle had been destroyed by the French! We would be able to return to our comrades with our heads held high after such a remarkable feat.

"Captain Vincent!" I shouted to the officer who was presiding over the distribution of the rations. "Come here, so we can discuss a new campaign!"

And we decided that we would leave as soon as possible, once our troops had had a well-deserved rest.

VII. Presentiments

Half an hour later, we were marching in silence through the bamboo forest. The men, rested and restored, seemed to be looking forward to the new conflict. Still distressed by the horrible spectacle to which they had been witnesses, they were glad that they would soon have the opportunity to avenge the Father. We officers advanced more anxiously, saddened by the possibility that one scene of carnage might be followed by another.

D'Estival especially, marching slightly apart and with his head bowed, seemed absorbed in thought. All those who knew him understood what a fine, noble and sensitive nature he had. Tall and slim, from Niort, one of the finest horsemen in the 6th Hussars, when the Chinese Expedition began he had obtained the by-no-means-prodigal favor of being ranked among the officers of the 7th Marine, whose redoublement formed the 16th. Since his disembarkation at Tsin-Tsin, he had not ceased to drive himself forward in a coolly intrepid manner–combined, when the chips were down, with a passion that greatly inspired his men.

On seeing him, fair-haired, rosy-cheeked, well-turned-out and impeccably polite and always attentive, one might have thought him weak, worldly, even effeminate. However, his supple grace and comfortable bearing concealed an uncommon vigor and proven powers of endurance. Similarly, the affability of his character and the extreme good grace with which he defended his opinions were the velvet glove upon the steely fist of a rare energy and the firmness of unbreakable conviction.

This attitude, combined with irreproachable conduct, made him a profoundly respected and well-liked companion. I confess that I had the deepest sympathy for that loyal, firm and gentle nature. I went over to him.

"This morning's discovery upset you, didn't it?" I said to him.

"Not upset, exactly, but saddened," he replied. "Besides, on the eve of an important action–I admit the weakness, if it is one–I'm always a trifle perplexed. Today, I don't know why, the disturbance isn't superficial; it is intimate and profound. A wound is nothing, but death is a possibility, and when that hypothesis presents itself to me, it's always mingled with something more painful than the possibility of an imminent end. I see my native land: all the people I love are present in my imagination, with their particular grace and personal qualities increased tenfold by regret. Perhaps it's an omen... Anything is possible! And that infects my soul with apprehension and anguish...

"I would not say this to anyone who would laugh or be deceived by such sentiments, but to you, Colonel, of whose solid and benevolent friendship I am convinced... To you who has promised me, in the case of a serious incident..."

"My dear d'Estival," I put in, abruptly, "you seem to me to be under some evil influence. Ordinarily so cheerful, you're suffering from black depression today. I've made you a promise, and it's sacred, but I hope I don't have to keep it. We'd do better to leave off. Look at these men marching beside you and behind you: they have faith in us. We're their will, their spirit, their brain. We don't have the right, therefore, to listen to our imagination, nor even our hearts. Duty alone must raise its voice."

"You're right–that's our duty!"

He fell silent, contemplatively.

I respected his mediation... And I no longer heard anything but the noise of the leaves brushing against our clothes and the soft tread of our footsteps on the moist and grassy ground, punctuating the heavy cadence of the march.

VIII. The Pagoda of the Red Triangle

We marched until dusk. A shower had fallen before sunset and droplets of water were dripping from branch to branch, slowly and monotonously, even though the rain had stopped.

The damp and the cold got into us. We felt the sodden linen of our clothing become heavier, and the soil emitted a sepulchral odor. The Moon, which rose amid frayed black clouds, resembled a candle whose light shone in sinister fashion from behind a shade of crêpe.

As we came towards the edge of the forest Quan-si suddenly stopped, crouching down once or twice to obtain a better view through the trees. Then, getting up, he extended a thin finger towards the horizon.

"H'ong-san-Kio!" he said, in a terrified voice.

"The Red Triangle," Joseph translated. "The Pagoda of the Red Triangle!"

I stretched my neck in my turn. By means of the moonlight filtering through the clouds I made out a rocky outcrop, almost square, a sort of cupola, still glistening from the recent rain. At a slight angle to our approach, the pagoda extended its sharply-pitched roofs, like the portal of a basilica.

No noise rose from the grounds; no light shone in the interior; no movement of any animate being indicated the presence of the enemy. There was only the peace and solitude of a winter night. One might have thought oneself in a clearing in a virgin forest had it not been for the irrefutable testimony of the presence of man: the ragged pathway creeping through the trees, and the recently-varnished lacquered ridges of the pagoda, which shone in the moonlight like silver trimmings on an item of ebony furniture.

Without giving any credence to Quan-Si's wild tales, or lending any support to the exaggerated produce of a troubled imagination, it was necessary to be prudent. Although we numbered 300 or 400, while the enemy were no more than 150 strong–perhaps only 80–it was very probable that they were well-armed, and certainly fanatical. The dark legend of that pagoda, handed down from time immemorial, must have been exploited by the bonzes to considerable profit, particularly during times of war. An iron discipline had doubtless been personified in the popular mind, symbolized by the dragon that ate traitors and the weak-willed...

I rejoined d'Estival.

He had regained his cheerful attitude. The strangeness of the place and the adventure, the prospect of some heroic endeavor on the next day, and the atmosphere of astonishment and mystery surrounding the legend we were about to penetrate, had seduced his imagination. The soldier in him had regained the upper hand.

He was also agreeable to my charging him with a mission. I instructed him to work his way around the clearing without breaking cover, and to select a place from which he would be able to keep watch on the enemy and–should the occasion arise–to take them from behind. I entrusted Quan-Si to him, along with Sergeant Mallard, who spoke a little Chinese, and then set about selecting 25 or 30 marksmen to accompany him.

"And above all," I added, "no needless heroics! Exercise prudence! And yet more prudence!"

"Thank you, Colonel," d'Estival said, effusively. "Thank you for your trust and your advice. Don't worry; we'll be very prudent. One doesn't go mad unless it's necessary–tonight, it's a matter of being very careful."

A few minutes later, he had disappeared into the shadow of the foliage. As for us, we camped where we were.

That was a long evening. The damp soil was scarcely conducive to the sleep we needed so badly. The impossibility of lighting a fire, for fear of attracting attention, guaranteed a miserable evening meal. For the same reason, we did not even have the consolation of a cigarette or a pipe to chase away the miasma of the fog that formed under the branches and irritated our throats.

After nibbling something and drinking his ration, everyone found what shelter he could and rolled himself up in his blanket. For myself, having given strict orders to the sentries, I retired to my tent. Joseph shared it with me, stretching out his simple straw mat between my camp-bed and the doorway.

"Do you think we can trust the boy?"

"I think so, Colonel. He's superstitious, but he's sincere."

I threw myself on my bed and was soon asleep.

God knows how long I had been unconscious of the external world when argumentative voices woke me with a start.

"Who goes there?" I exclaimed, instinctively seizing my revolver and standing up abruptly.

"It's Quan-Si, Colonel, who insisted on giving you a message. I told him to stand aside... He doesn't understand discipline, nor the duty owed to a commanding officer. It's not yet six o-clock; I told him to wait. Besides, I don't know what he's done. He came past the sentry cordon creeping through the grass–no one saw him."

"Pass me the message."

By the glimmer of a nightlight, I ran my eyes over the page torn from a notebook on which d'Estival had sent me his first impressions.

Colonel,

I have fulfilled the first part of my mission without attracting the attention of the enemy. I am securely established in the woods, taking cover behind a number of rocks disposed in a semicircle, which are crudely inscribed with geometrical figures and a serpent–probably the dragon. There are also some Chinese characters that are indecipherable, the daylight not being bright enough as yet. The pagoda is not fortified; the stream that surrounds it is no obstacle, one meter or one meter-fifty wide. No one suspects our presence, or yours, for I have seen the Boxers with my own eyes coming to fetch water without a care in the world. If you decide that I should attack first, a reinforcement of 20 men will be necessary, as the garrison seems to me to be well-furnished. If I am only to support your movement, I have as many as I need.

D'Estival

I replied:

Remain where you are. I leave it to you to show yourself at the opportune moment; the least reinforcement at this time would risk our being spotted. We shall attack shortly; you will soon hear our clarion.

D'Herbauge

Quan-si took the reply, crouched down on the ground, and disappeared into the mist, his thin body moving in a reptilian manner.

For a few moments I watched the grass stir, as if in response to the passage of a serpent, then I woke Vincent. Our marsouins received the order to get up silently and to make their preparations. In the absence of coffee, we gave them a healthy ration of tafia rum. I stayed where I was, watching all the young men move forward in the vaporous atmosphere and blueness of the morning. Their complexions tanned by the climate, their drawn features, their hollow cheeks and dull eyes testified to the privations and exhausting quality of the campaign. Nevertheless, they took all these difficulties in their stride, smiling and bantering; they fixed their bayonets and buckled their belts cheerfully.

Was there not a certain poignancy in the way they reminded one another in whispers that they had come so far, through so many hazards, braving so many perils, perhaps to end up in an unmarked grave in the grass of that plain, some kilometers from Tang-ko?

IX. The Attack

The sound of the clarion suddenly burst forth, and then extended vibrantly in the cold morning air.

Having worked our way to the forest's edge, hidden by the trees as we were, keeping to the protective shadow until we were 300 meters from the pagoda, we suddenly hurled ourselves forward.

With the exception of a few expeditions to draw water, our adversaries were asleep. They were, in consequence, abruptly thrown into extreme disorder. They shouted at one another and bumped into one another, searching for their weapons. Some fled in panic towards the pagoda, waving their arms above their heads. Others, who had preceded them, flooded back to the exterior, and the two waves collided, mingled, jostled...

During the few seconds that this confusion lasted, among those billowing heads, my gaze was caught momentarily by something strange. Three or four big fellows, at the heart of the general affray, seemingly self-composed, were organizing the defense, breaking out the stocks of weapons, handing out rifles, hastily posting a number of men at the entrance to the little bridge. Now, all these bonzes—for that is what they were— bore a red triangle with the point downwards on the yellow and oily skin of their shaven heads.

I admit that this apparition, after Quan-Si's description, could not help making a certain impression on me; nevertheless, there was no time to reflect.

Despite the efforts the bonzes made to defend the pagoda, it could not be done.

Scarcely half a dozen shots were fired, badly aimed. The surprise attack had been too sudden, the spirit of our troops too strong. The ditch that served the stream as a bed had not stopped our *marsouins*. Rank after rank they reached it, crossed it with a single bound, then descended like a whirlwind upon the Boxers, while d'Estival, rallying his musketeers, sent the retreating forces back to suffer the blows we rained upon them.

The saber, the bayonet and the revolver were already doing their terrible work, puncturing bellies, caving in torsos, gashing heads and shooting as many as three bullets into the same target. The tide of cork helmets reached the door of the pagoda, only to come back towards us as a determined wave, broken on a rock, returns limply towards the Ocean. A hundred and 20 corpses were scattered about the pavement of the courtyard!

Alas, not all the dead were the enemy's; we had lost a Sergeant. He was there, laid out on the grass: a poor young man with a blond moustache. A bullet had punctured his forehead, and a thin trickle of blood–still bright red–was leaking from the wound, striping the livid and lusterless flesh.

The eyes wide open, the mouth painfully pursed in a rictus of horror and the twisted arms testified to the cerebral disarray wrought by the lead within that organism so vigorous and vibrant hitherto. On the neck, a frightful gaping wound bled. Beside him on the grass was a cutlass and another cadaver–that of his murderer, one of the red-tattooed bonzes, who had killed him with a shot to the head and then calmly knelt down to cut his throat.

I had seen the whole thing happen in the blink of an eye, without being able to save the poor boy. In the heat of the action–he was not far away–I had seen him fall, and his murderer immediately swoop down upon him to complete the sinister operation. With a powerful lunge, I had thrust my saber into him with all my strength. The blade, buried to the hilt beneath the shoulder-blade, had exited from the abdomen after passing through the heart: death had been instantaneous, like a bolt of lightning.

With one foot on the bonze's kidneys, I withdrew my weapon, streaming with blood, and threw it to the ground. With a single kick, I moved the odious wreck of a Chinese to one side and leaned over the body of my soldier, who was quite dead.

He was carried towards the pagoda in the deep silence that follows any great tumult, especially when death, striking unexpectedly, grips the heart of the bravest and seals the lips of the most intoxicated.

X. A Fruitless Search

The pagoda contained four huge rooms, whose sum was adequate to allow me to lodge my entire company. Two spacious halls formed the central body. The first, serving as an antechamber, was empty; the second, a place of prayer, was furnished with the ordinary equipment of a pagoda. To either side, a pavilion opened into the antechamber. They seemed symmetrical and similar, the only difference being that one looked out towards the forest while the other was set against the rock, which thus formed one of its walls.

There was a wide opening in that smooth, vertical grey wall: a dark corridor leading we knew not where. I forbade anyone to go into it, as yet.

Applying the characteristic ingenuity of the French soldier, our *marsouins* were already making camp. Outside, while some were penning the prisoners outside, others were dressing one another's wounds or setting up cooking-pots. Inside, twenty men were preparing the officers' quarters and organizing their mess. They improvised our dining-room with freshly-cut bamboo, boxes of biscuits and the little camp-stools from our tents.

As they sought to place the table outside, the draught of air blowing from the door to the gaping corridor caught my notice and an idea suddenly sprang into my head.

"Stand to attention, you two!" I said to two Sergeants, who were watching their men from a short distance. "When the brigands were retreating towards the pagoda as we attacked, I noticed three devilishly huge bonzes marked with red triangles on their foreheads. What became of them?"

"I beg your pardon, Colonel," said one of the NCOs. "I noticed them too, but there were four, not three."

"You're mistaken," his comrade put in. "The Colonel's not counting the one who shed poor Blandin's blood, and who was impaled by a magnificent saber-thrust. There were three left after that. Now, one is grievously wounded and dying, one other was killed here as he tried to go into that corridor. Damn! It's true–there's one missing. Where has he gone?"

"He must be sought out, brought to me dead or alive!" I said, authoritatively. "I have a particular reason for wanting to know what has become of him. Turn over all the cadavers, look through the prisoners, search the surroundings. I need him."

They saluted, and went out.

Half an hour later, they came back empty-handed. They had found no trace of the last bonze. Several witnesses had seen two of them flee into the pagoda at the final moment. One of them had been killed; I naturally concluded that the other had been unable to get out again and had escaped into the passage, whose twists and turns must be familiar to him.

It was probably just a bolt-hole for use in an emergency: one of those subterranean vaults that are so often to be found in our own county in feudal manors or ancient abbeys–but I hesitated to have him followed and the labyrinth searched. What good would it do? Perhaps the passage was booby-trapped; perhaps a number of the enemy, having escaped with their weapons, were waiting there in ambush. There was no justification for satisfying pointless curiosity.

I had, in any case, resolved to blow up the monument when our troops had rested there for 24 hours. If some of these looters, holed up in some niche, still evaded us, they would receive due punishment for their sins. If, on the other hand, they had fled, would it not be appropriate to show them, and everyone else, the tangible effects of our strength, by making the inescapable power of our vengeance burst forth in a terrifying catastrophe?

I therefore stopped short, placing a guard of four men at the entrance to the underground passage, to be relieved every six hours–in order to prevent anyone from attempting an excursion from that direction.

By the time the dismal work of interring enemies and friends was complete, the daylight was fading. A melancholy dusk fell upon the country, then night enveloped us in its cold, silent and obscure majesty. The sky was veiled by thick cloud, behind which the Moon was invisible.

We retreated into the pavilion, which looked out on to the forest, and which had been converted into the officers' quarters. Between us and the men keeping watch on the suspect entrance, soldiers who were weary–but glad to have a comfortable shelter–extended themselves on their mats and began snoring conscientiously.

Soon, we copied them.

XI. The Murder

We were woken up by a buzzing noise like a swarm of bees, consisting of comings and goings, and the clicking of weapons being picked up. Sitting up on our camp beds, we pricked up our ears at this unusual noise, whose volume was increasing. Spoken words now mixed with curses, imprecations burst forth furiously.

We were soon on our feet.

A Sergeant, who had already rapped on our door, quickly brought us up to date.

During the night, the sentry posted at the entrance to the subterranean passage had disappeared. He had been taken away without any of the four men dozing a few paces away having seen anything of what had happened.

The victim's rifle was on the ground, still loaded. His kepi had rolled across the floor, two meters from the opening. Between the two objects, a bloody stain, as large as two hands, soiled the flagstone and a series of drops of blood, increasingly widely spaced, extended into the corridor, forming a trail. The murderer had carried the body away. On the wall to the right, there was a bloody handprint, like a signature and a challenge.

I considered all these details, my heart constricted. In the lugubrious silence, Quan-Si–who had knelt down beside the red pool, began to intone a monotonous solo lament.

"H'ong-san-Kio!" he repeated over and over. "H'ong-san-Kio!"

The pool of blood did indeed bear a vague resemblance to a triangle, as if a finger had intentionally drawn three points therefrom–but I was preoccupied with other thoughts.

Should we abandon this evil pagoda and deprive my men of the promised repose? Should we appear to flee before some mysterious manifestation? If an enemy were hidden here, should we leave him unpunished, and far more dangerous? My course of action was immediately clear.

"Our unfortunate comrade," I said, in a loud voice, "must have been killed by a cowardly assassin, and killed instantaneously, since he did not make a sound. Otherwise he would have been heard. There is, unfortunately, no hope of finding him alive–but it remains to us to avenge him, and we must exact that vengeance. Tomorrow morning, this lair will be blown up! No stone will rest upon another. I intend that the runaways, on their return, or the local inhabitants, drawn by the explosion, shall find nothing here but a chasm full of debris. I want them to tremble for a long time at the memory of our reprisals.

"On another subject, however, the men who should have been awake beside their comrade, but went to sleep instead, have failed dismally in their duty. Despite their fatigue and the apparent safety of their position, they deserve to be punished. When we arrive at Pao-Ting-Fou, they will spend 15 days in prison, and Corporal Sorin will strip them of their badges tonight...

"Finally, our comrades who were unable to guard an outlet entrusted to their vigilance will be replaced tonight by those who will set you a better example. I, your Colonel, and Captain d'Estival will keep watch on this doorway. That way, at least, I will be sure that my orders will be followed, that we shall have no new murder to deplore, or anything more serious to dread. When the men cannot keep watch on behalf of their officers and comrades, the officers must keep watch on behalf of their men.

"Now, be off!"

This final decision, whose effect on our *marsouins* I had calculated, seemed to them a severe and excruciating, but well-deserved, punishment. Their self-respect was cut to the quick, but their desire to acquit themselves well was excited to the same degree. I sensed around me, in addition to exact and absolute obedience, pledged to total discipline, a sort of atmosphere of sympathetic admiration, in which remorse was mingled with unanimous approval.

For the rest of the day, the men warmed themselves around their bivouac fires, discussing the event. Only a few gangs were working, excavating holes around the gigantic monolith in which the dynamite or melinite would be set. In repose–or, rather, idleness–tragic events take on an even greater intensity. Nothing could be longer than that dismal January day, spent under grey clouds that threatened snow, pricked by an icy north wind that stung our faces.

Finally, evening arrived, redly illuminating curtains of cloud in the direction of the sunset, behind the black arabesques of the roofing, as the sky changed from vermilion to dark green, and then to black.

XII. The Awakening

After dinner, the officers retired. D'Estival remained alone with me, seeking by means of his slightly forced merriment to distract me from the forebodings that he could read in my face.

I admit that, whether by virtue of fatigue or abnormal nervousness, I was not my usual self. His efforts did not succeed in cheering me up. Despite steeling myself against Quan-Si's fantastic tales, I could not avoid finding a strange confirmation of them in recent events. The existence of the pagoda, its situation, the topography of the site, the number of the position's defenders and the bonzes, all marked with the symbolic triangle... Everything was exactly as described, to the last detail. Obviously, there was no man-eating dragon, but the previous night's adventure had been so unexpected and so mysterious that I was still preoccupied, if not obsessed.

Seated on biscuit-boxes with our backs to the wall, a few meters from that black opening splitting the grey wall, we chatted for a long time, occasionally and unintentionally distracted by our private thoughts, which suddenly claimed our attention and broke the thread of the conversation. As the hours advanced, however, we lowered our voices, in the hope that an enemy, reassured by the silence, might dare to present himself. As we were firmly committed to blow the brains out of the first living being that showed itself to us, we had our loaded revolvers in our hands.

From time to time, my comrade put his hand on my arm, thinking that he had heard something, or one of us stopped in mid-sentence... and the silence fell heavily around us. Our ears could hear no sound; our eyes could see nothing living stirring in the depths of the gaping hole. Then the hand was removed from the abruptly seized arm, and the conversation resumed in a lower tone... slower, more lugubrious, lit by a single lantern fixed to the upright of the door.

And yet, it seemed to us that we were not alone!

Was that weak and ill-defined hum, like a dolorous moan, the wind sighing in the roof-beams? Was that vague noise, like the flutter of silken wings, really produced by the bamboo leaves caressing the varnished bricks of the pagoda, impelled by the breeze? Were our possibly-overexcited senses, by making us attentive to a thousand details we would not

ordinarily have perceived, actually deceiving rather than revealing a presence that was real, but invisible?

I have always thought so.

From time to time, we checked our watches, impatiently
waiting for daylight. Then, at about half past midnight, as I put
my chronometer back into my pocket for what might have
been the tenth time, a repetitive but very faint noise sounded
in the subterranean passage. One might have taken it for the
footsteps of a man wearing felt slippers, or walking on a thick
carpet.

The noise stopped suddenly. Then it resumed, but on the
wane, weakening until it died away.

We looked at one another. We could not both have been
duped by an illusion at the same time, victims of suggestion.
Nevertheless, we said not a word, and the silence continued
flowing over us, untroubled by the least susurrus.

XIII. Resolution

At half past one, d'Estival sat up straight.

"Let's go," he said, smiling. "Neither the bonzes nor
their dragon will attack us tonight, but I have a decided desire
to attack them. Like me, you certainly distinguished something a little while ago. Perhaps it was nothing but a scamper-
ing rat or the repercussions of water sweated drop by drop
from the wall–no matter! I don't like these suspect sounds,
these vague anxieties, these mysterious depths, and I intend to
see at close range what they turn up."

As he finished this sentence, he got to his feet, took an
extinct lantern from a corner, opened it, struck a match, and
ignited the wick.

"You won't do anything so foolish!" I said to him.

He stopped in surprise.

"If you forbid me absolutely, Colonel, I'll obey, but I
won't hide it from you that I'll do it with a certain regret. This
is perhaps the only occasion that will ever present itself to me

in this godforsaken country to visit an underworld where un-suspected mysteries might lurk–a whole tartar mythology. [125]
Perhaps an unknown and barbarous cult that must be discov-ered in order that it may be put down. Will you stop me, when we're leaving tomorrow? You'd leave me to regret it forever! Besides which, the covert can't be very extensive or very deep, since the rock–though enormous–is finite, resting on a bed of clay and sand.

"If, on the other hand, I meet your great bonze with the geometric decoration, I promise you that I'll blow his brains out... And if I don't met anyone, I'll come back, unashamed of being empty-handed."

"D'Estival, it's entirely possible that I'll offend you, but I forbid it."

"Listen, Colonel. I don't want to insist–that's not my way–but you have to understand all my reasons. Apart from curiosity, there's another motive involved in my projects, which is impelling me in this instance. This underworld, being very limited, probably has no other opening but this one; it must lead to a sort of cavern destined to receive the cadavers and hide them from the eyes of the ignorant peasantry who believe in the dragon. Now, it's into that oubliette that the corpse of poor Quantin must have been dragged, and it might be that it can still be recovered. That brave lad, as you can't be unaware, has been my orderly for a long time, but there's more: he's my countryman. I know his family. In their eyes, I'm his protector. I intend, therefore, to recover his body, to give it a more worthy grave–and above all, to obtain from it some of those trivial objects that might serve his old parents as

---

[125] I have translated Noat's *mythologie tartare* directly, for want of a better English phrase. The reference is not to the Tartar people but to the kind of tartar that is deposited in wine-casks as a crust or sediment, whose main component is pota-sium tartrate–and thus, metaphorically, to a hypothetical proc-ess of "sedimentation" within oral culture that gives rise to myths, legends and folklore.

sad souvenirs, slightly attenuating the bitterness of their loss: a watch, a pocket-book, a few letters or a mere lock of hair! It seems to me to be a matter of duty, and a sacred duty...

"Then again, the man died at his post, following orders. The enemy to whom we have vowed some dramatic and terrible death–perhaps by the explosion of a bomb–took his revenge on that sentry yesterday morning. His death has spared us. It's only right and just that we should do something for his remains, for his memory–and if, in a short while, I return carrying that unfortunate lad's body on my shoulders, don't you think that we'll have added to the prestige of our education and rank that of humanity and friendship?

"Anyway, how would we look, at daybreak, if no attempt had been made to find out? If, on the contrary, we were able to say to the others: There's nothing frightful in the passage, nothing mysterious in the murder. Yesterday's event was only one of the thousand cruel and everyday incidents of guerilla warfare. We've punished the brigand–that cowardly assassin who struck from behind. We've searched his lair before destroying it. We've taken back from him the corpse of your comrade and the mystery of his underworld. Let Quantin's remains rest in peace in a grave dug by the hands of his friends. His death is avenged...."

I was unsettled. He perceived it, and went on: "Besides, you know how strong I am; I have nothing to fear. All the same, I promise you that I'll call for help at the least disquiet, by firing a revolver shot. While waiting for it to arrive, I'll hold myself together: I'm armed, and not incompetent. What the hell! Two or three adversaries in a corridor don't frighten me any more than they would in broad daylight."

"Go, then," I said to him, "since that's your wish... But be sure to return in 20 minutes at the most. On that, at least, I insist, whatever happens. I insist absolutely, I order it. It's an exact instruction, for whose transgression I shall accept no excuse."

"Don't go on, Colonel," he replied, solemnly. "I promise you... I swear to you... that I'll obey your orders to the letter.

In 20 minutes, I'll be back here–hopefully with the body of my poor orderly. Thank you, from the bottom of my heart."

He shook the hand that I held out to him, inspected the magazine of his revolver by the light of the lantern and disappeared into the narrow passage.

For a little while, I watched the reflected gleam of his lantern dance in the opening and listened to the firm and steady noise of his footsteps... Then all of that gradually died away.

XIV. Remorse and Decision

I had given him permission. Had I done the right thing?

A kind of remorse took hold of me. Was it necessary, after the losses of recent days, to risk adding another? That of a young officer so devoted, so likeable? Just to satisfy a puerile curiosity, in the hypothetical hope of recovering a mortal shell?

I took out my watch. Three minutes had gone by since his departure. I went to the shaft, now dark and silent again. I listened carefully. Nothing!

But if he called for help, who could tell whether the vaults were sufficiently resonant to relay his appeal? Would he be able to call out, in any case? Might not some side-passage open up behind him, from which murderers could spring out after he had passed by, knocking him down and stifling his voice? Or what if some trap threw him into a pit? What if some mephitic gas, retained in some covert of the dark labyrinth, put him to sleep and asphyxiated him? Was it conceivable–every evidence seemed now to point that way–that the bonzes would have left the passage free and wide open with nothing to protect its entrance or its course? Was the avenue, perhaps–certainly–no more than a trap? A trap into which we had easily allowed ourselves to fall?

Six minutes. How slowly the time passed! Still silence.

Most definitely, I had been wrong.

If he had gone to die, struck down by a dagger in the heart–like our sentry, without a jolt or a cry–would I not bear the responsibility, ineradicably, for the rest of my life? And how would I explain this new disappearance to everyone else on the following day? Would not the soldiers I had punished severely for letting themselves go to sleep think that something similar had happened to me? Or, even worse, that I had exposed my subordinate to anger while reserving the safer station for myself? The captain has to be the last man aboard a sinking ship; for him it is a disgrace to survive the loss of his crew.

My anguish became atrocious. I still had not heard anything, and 12 minutes had gone by...

Would I really have the courage to live with my shame, in the event of tragedy? And if, while my conscience was in disarray, faith–upstanding like a rock unmoved by the tempest–forbade even the thought of suicide, why should I not expose myself to the same danger as my companion?

To guard against any eventuality, and as I also had a duty to my two companies, I tore a page out of my diary and I wrote the following words on it:

If Lieutenant Vincent comes to receive my orders tomorrow, at half past five, and finds this room empty, he is absolutely forbidden to search for Captain d'Estival and myself. We will have perished while trying to recover the mortal remains of Private Quantin. As soon as our absence is established, Lieutenant Vincent will assume the command that is rightfully his, prepare for immediate departure, and then light the fuses of the mines, abandoning the bivouac only after having reduced the pagoda to ruins. Then, he will immediately set out, by the shortest possible route, for Pao-Ting-Fou.

I dated and signed that order of the day, and pinned it to the biscuit box with a bayonet.

Then, taking up the lantern, I advanced deliberately into the dark corridor, stopping from time to time to examine its turns and get my bearings. The passage had no forks, and seemed to be sloping upwards.

XV. The Sanctuary

About 20 meters in, some carvings were displayed on the walls. Hesitant at first, crude and sketchy, they became more precise as I advanced, more sharply designed and richer in detail, and the intervals between them diminished by degrees. Soon, all the free space was filled in, covered with arabesques and inscriptions, the former in no style and the latter in no alphabet that I had ever seen before. Eventually, fauna and flora that were new to me displayed their unexpected and infinitely various forms in profusion.

Wonderstruck, I walked through a leafy glade, flourishing amid the grey stone: through an arbor of heraldic branches, whose gnarled trunks issued from the soil in a thousand contortions, springing forth from the wall only to return, pasted to it, embedded within it. They climbed up from the floor to loom over my head, covering it with a strange canopy. Lianas seemed to hang their loops from the ceiling, snaking along it in sinuous lines, twisting into scrolls, enveloping cartouches at the center of which, immutable and endlessly repeated, one symbolic motif recurred: a serpent whose coils framed an inverted triangle.

All at once, quite abruptly, the walls widened out. I had the impression of a void opening in front of me, of empty space, vast and motionless. I raised my eyes.

I stood still, petrified by astonishment and admiration.

How can I describe the indescribable?

Imagine, on exiting from some dark prison, that the dome of St. Peter's suddenly displayed its immense curvature to you, and the grandiose boldness of its architecture–but a dome that was carved out, sculpted to the last motif, like an antique cameo, fashioned like a gigantic concave rose-window with innumerable facets. And all of it resplendent, rippling with fire at the least movement of my lantern.

310

How pitiful the memory of our occidental architecture seemed! In place of the measured proportions and reserved chastities of European art, all the prodigality, all the intoxication, all the folly of the Orient, had thrown own its marvels and treasures in abundance, as if in a fit of madness, upon the walls of that temple. It would have required generations to study the marvels of centuries-old patience set out before my eyes.

What kind of people had devoted themselves to this frightful labor? Had their artists the secret of transmuting matter, to make it obedient to their fantasy? Or could they still exercise the power of suggestion from beyond the grave, to make us subject to such a powerful illusion? What was the lacy drapery that descended so lightly, so vaporously, from the ceiling that one expected to see it take flight like gauze in the least breath of wind? And was this confusion of strange bushes really made of granite, their uniform color notwithstanding, or was it a sector of the jungle transported here and miraculously petrified? Was it with some special enamel, or with fresh blood, that someone had painted those red triangles on that circular plinth...

Obviously, I was in a dome lodged within the shell of the monolith that stood in the middle of the clearing: a stray block left behind on the surface by the last ice age, or some fragment expelled from the Earth's entrails by a plutonic convulsion.

With an obstinacy that had vanquished time, conquering the granite with labor to make the imagination shiver, that rock had been excavated, hollowed out and emptied. Over the centuries, legions of obscure artisans had toiled there, wearing away a little more of the stone every year, expelling a handful of rubble every day, losing any awareness of time or desire for sleep while removed from the Sun that measures life's pleasures.

One could imagine the fatalism of these multitudes, devoid of any horizon or ideal, riveted by attention to detail–but one could also detect the mind that had organized these efforts, pursuing its plan by means of a marvelous synthesis.

Those ribs, of such disconcerting boldness, came together in the keystone of the vault like wicker strands in a
basket-maker's hand; that frieze, whose extension was blurred
by ornaments, forcefully elevated from a golden background
the symbol of the sect, commanding attention. There was a
hidden intentionality in it, to guide the gaze and to steer the
attention into the depths.

I followed that mute compulsion.

I had come out on to a sort of circular balcony whose
ramp, a pure marvel of bronze inlaid with silver, had two ex-
tremities at the same diametrical position. Those bays were the
heads of two staircases which descended in parallel superimposed spirals; they circled between the wall and eight thick
columns, colossal and fantastic, disposed in a circle. They
were eight elephants of extraordinary dimension. As if a terrifying vision had sprung up from beneath, they reared up on
their hind legs, maddened, lifting their curving tusks and
coiled trunks towards the sky. And squashed beneath their
mighty feet, pedestals crushed by their mass, were giant tortoises or improbably-goitered toads.

A vague malaise, like the dread within a dream that pre-
cedes a nightmare, gripped my heart. I tried to react, and to
escape the fascinating impression of these strange tableaux.

XVI. The Monster

In the depths of that colossal well into which my gaze
plunged–for I had heard the resonance of a firm and well-
known tread–I perceived the swinging of a lantern. D'Estival
was there!

He was now cutting across the great cylinder that formed
the base of the circular hall. I saw him approach a triangular
basin rimmed in red marble, placed at the center, lean over
towards the fluid suddenly illuminated by the caress of the
light, then deposit his lantern on a sort of altar set against the
wall. I could not make out anything of the altar, but I could see

the deity that loomed over it–a sort of Buddha with many arms, whose topmost two were extended towards the sky, one holding a triangle, the other a round-headed serpent.

The idol seemed to me to be made of gold; it glowed, yellow and bright, and in its eyes–undoubtedly precious stones–two bluish sparks lit up like the fire of a wrathful gaze.

My companion was examining it curiously when his foot bumped into something long and slender lying on the ground. He turned around abruptly and a furious exclamation, escaping his lips, started a sequence of echoes.

What he picked up, carefully, and held between his arms, was the corpse of our poor sentry! The head, slipping momentarily from the arm supporting it, emerged from the shadows. Horror! His pale forehead displayed the frightful stigma of a triangular bloody wound...

I had just opened my mouth to let d'Estival know that I was there, and that I would help him in his pious task, when the grinding of a rusty hinge made me lift my head again.

Before I was able to make out where the noise came from, the faint sound of a flute became audible. An imperceptible murmur at first, as soft and tremulous as a melody emitted by an instrument of crystal, it grew and became more distinct, louder and louder. The rhythm became more defined, the tempo accelerated and the tone of the refrain was modified by accidentals, before reaching a rapid conclusion in an exaggeratedly shrill note, piercing and prolonged.

I had already perceived what looked like the shadow of a Chinese, seeming immobile against a dimly-lit background. I was not mistaken. A hidden door had opened in the belly of one of the pachyderms facing me.

Lost in the shadow of the immense head, the opening in the vast animal statue must still have been hidden from d'Estival. He raised his head again, interrupted in his task. His eyes sought to pierce the obscurity, but he could not see anything.

From my standpoint, higher up, I could see everything. I had a perfect view of that large shadow: the hands lifted to the level of the mouth; the head slightly inclined to the left; the movement of the body, swaying lightly in response to the cadence of the tune. I wondered what it might mean.

Suddenly, I saw d'Estival turn back to the water in the basin, which was bubbling in the center. He deposited his burden on the ground and swiftly lifted his handkerchief to his nostrils, as if the disturbance of the fluid had released an unbearable odor. At almost the same time, in fact, that odor reached me, exotic and choking. It was something indefinable, like a mélange of nitrous emanations, opium fumes and the kind of incense that catches you by the throat and goes to your head.

The song of the little flute ceased almost immediately. The bonze rummaged in his clothes, took an *oly* [126] from his belt and extended his arm towards d'Estival...

In his fist, something had glinted, sending a brief flash into the obscurity. In the blink of an eye, I understood. Immediately, seizing my revolver, I pointed it at the shadow and fired.

Two shots resounded at the same time, violating the silence, striking up echoes that rolled like thunder. Two bodies fell to the ground at the same time, their cries mingling.

The bonze fell backwards, collapsing into his secret corridor. His feet slid forward slightly at the last moment, hanging now above empty space. D'Estival lay face downwards on the ground. And I, terror-stricken, wanting to fly to the aid of my friend, sensed that odor becoming stronger and stronger, going to my head like an intoxication.

It seemed to me that I had suddenly lost control of myself; that an absolute separation was establish between my consciousness, my will and my body. I tottered. I tried to right

---

[126] Noat has *olyes*, but the only word in Larousse that he could plausibly intend is *oly*, which is a name given by the natives of Madagascar to a kind of fetish, consisting of a small compartmentalized wooden box into whose various sections items supposed to have magical power are inserted.

myself. I wanted to make an effort, to collect my thoughts, which seemed to be running away from me like water though a child's fingers, but I slumped to my knees, my arms dangling over the balustrade, into the void–the void into which my revolver fell, slipping from my inert fingers to rebound unevenly from the irregular surface.

Throughout this bodily collapse, however, my intelligence and my memory remained intact. More than that–curiously enough, my senses seemed to have acquired an extreme acuity, increasing their powers of perception tenfold as they were distanced from action. Although my head was leaning helplessly on my right shoulder, my staring eyes, incapable even of blinking, could now distinguish every last detail of the subterranean sculptures.

I saw, as if I might reach out and touch them, the clothing of the two corpses lying beside one another on the pavement. I could make out every last detail of the bubbling water; I heard its murmur as if it were next to my ear. One might have thought that a fountain was about to burst forth from the depths, breaking through the surface and hurling a jet of water into the atmosphere.

Suddenly, between the oily concentric ripples that were expanding outwards towards the edges of the bowl, a whitish opaline mass surged forth, semi-transparent and gelatinous, like our coastal jellyfish. It was a pyramidal head, at whose apex was a triangular orifice: a sort of three-lipped mouth, whose thick lips were opening and closing with the sound of a moue. On each side, on the ends of short stalks, two gross glaucous eyes glistened, or were eclipsed by blinking eyelids.

That head emerged slowly, rising up on a vertical axis while swaying gently from side to side. Then a body followed: the body of an annular serpent, as white and translucent as the head. A few obscure streaks and sinuous roseate lines, extended in strange spirals within the translucent organism, stood out with much greater clarity than the filthy and uncanny organism itself, which moved restlessly between d'Estival's forgotten lantern and me. I could see the principal parts of its anatomy: a sort of tube following the axis of its body, and some black points, embryonic vertebrae against which its muscles must be braced.

So this was the terrible and mysterious dragon, the fantastic creature for which this superb temple had been carved!

For how many centuries had it been living within this lair? Whence had it come? Into what refuge did it retreat? To what signal was it obedient? Was this a testament to the origin of things, when life, still shapeless and chaotic, diversified into bizarre forms? Was it a giant reptile that had escaped the world's cataclysms, a vestige of so many vanished beings known to us now only by virtue of palaeontological reconstructions?

In that distant land, still virgin to all scientific study, from beneath thick layers of marl, this last representative of an extinct fauna had appeared one day—and the object of horror had immediately been exploited. The atrocious monster had been worshipped. A college of servitors had formed, sworn to murder, or to suicide, for the maintenance of that voiceless, consciousnessless, monstrous existence. Here, obedient to an ever-present and irresistible instinct, humankind, in search of a God since the Edenic Fall, had made do with the monsters of creation rather than suffer that lack.

But the shapeless being, after having reared up, now bent itself back towards the ground, extending its fleshy head across the flagstones, sniffing loudly. Moving alongside Quantin it quivered, following the contours of the corpse, seeking bare flesh; it paused at the hands, then the face, but doubtless recognized there the trace of its passage and drew away. Behind it, a trail of slime stained the dead man's clothing and the sanctuary's pavement.

It soon sniffed out another corpse and reached its face. Its sucker-like mouth fixed in the middle of the forehead like a cupping-glass; it twisted in a spasm of satisfaction, shaking off the water—or, rather, the thick fluid—of the basin.

And then I was witness to the most frightful spectacle of which it is possible to dream.

A sinister cracking noise resounded; it was the mandibles or the jaws of the monster breaking through the skull of my poor friend, to the accompaniment of a plaintive whimper of anguish: the last unconscious appeal that the lips emit at the supreme moment; the last reaction of an organism that death has gripped forever. And the filthy animal gorged itself on blood, sucking in the cerebral matter. Horror! I saw all that substance pass, darkly, into and along the translucent body, following the sinuosities of the digestive tube.

At the end of five minutes or thereabouts, the frightful meal was complete. The body of the monster withdrew, disappearing into the basin; then the head sank, leaving behind a tumult of bubbles cleaving the surface.

On poor d'Estival's forehead, the red triangle displayed its dreadful stigma!

How long did I remain thus: immobile, inert, in an unfamiliar existential state, in an excessive intensity of thought and sense, with haggard eyes, hypnotized by that wound whose obsession was atrocious? I don't know. But it seems to me, even today, that I spent centuries, aging considerably, in that attitude–which probably lasted no more than two or three hours.

Was it a nightmare–one of those terrible dreams that opium can procure, rather than the atrocious reality of actual vision? I cannot be entirely sure, and would rather believe that.

What is certain, however, is that the violent odor that had filled the temple seemed to me to evaporate by slow degrees after the monster's disappearance, and I felt myself recovering my self-possession.

After several failed attempts, I got back to my feet. I braced myself, as weak as a convalescent. Eventually, I was sure of my feet; I waited, standing up, until my strength was somewhat renewed. Then, picking up my lantern, whose flickering flame was about to go out, I went back into the subterranean passage.

At first, a kind of instinct had impelled me to flee, but now I continued resolutely in the same direction; I had fixed my purpose. It was necessary to get help, to retrieve the bodies of our two victims from further violations; it was necessary to destroy the monster.

Already I glimpsed the opening by which I had entered the underworld. I saw it marked out clearly—which indicated to me that day had broken—and I had no more than five or six steps to take in order to reach the room when a sudden terrible tremor shook the ground, and a rumbling sound grew and burst forth, as loud as a thousand thunderclaps.

In the meantime, borne by a terrible gust of wind that seized me from behind and plucked me from my feet, I was hurled like a cannonball across the pagoda.

When I woke up, I was laid out on my camp bed, in the shelter of my little tent. A headache and the pressure of damp bandages informed me that I was wounded.

Standing beside the doorway, Lieutenant Vincent was talking to Joseph. Quan-si, sitting on his heels, was sleeping with one eye open a few yards away.

As I made a movement, everyone turned towards me.

"Don't tire yourself, Colonel," Vincent said. "We'll explain it all to you later. You were stunned by your fall and you have a graze on your forehead, that's all. We'll be leaving in an hour, when the hammock I've had prepared for you is finished. Thus, you shall rest all day and tomorrow you'll be back on your feet. We've been very worried—we thought you were lost... with the others."

"It was pure luck that I found you," Joseph said, to dispel the memory thus evoked, which had caused me to shiver.

"How frightened we were, how grief-stricken and how angry," Vincent went on, "when we found nothing the next day but that piece of paper! I had no option but to obey; I obeyed. I blew up the pagoda at the designated hour. Five minutes afterwards, accompanied by Joseph, I went to inspect the sinister place.

"Instead of the hill and the pagoda, there was a yawning pit, 15 or 16 meters deep, into which the little stream, seeking a new course, was trickling. The rock had been smashed to smithereens, the earth dispersed as dust was settling all around us, darkening the sky like a cloud of ashes.

"We were coming back, with heavy hearts, when I caught sight of a uniform beneath the debris of a roof. I ran towards it; it was you. You were alive, but a beam had brushed your forehead–very lightly–inflicting a graze some three or four centimeters long. It only scratched the epidermis. Here–see for yourself!"

Seizing a little mirror from my open toilet bag, which was on a folding chair, he presented it to me, while Joseph lifted up my bandage.

Surprisingly–by a coincidence that struck me sharply, I confess–the wound was red and triangular.

Quan-si, who had come closer, lifted his arms to the sky on seeing it, then prostrated himself, repeating: "H'ong-san-Kio! H'ong-san-Kio!"

And now, gentlemen, each of you may think what he will–but for myself, I swear to you that every last detail of this story is true; I guarantee it absolutely. I see in it now nothing but a temporary intoxication, a few hallucinatory hours when insensate delirium mingled with reality, accompanied by fortuitous and surprising coincidences. I admit, though, that the memory of that atrocious night never comes back to me without droplets of cold sweat forming on my brow, and my heart stopping its beat for a few seconds.